PASSION'S PROMISE

The draperies of the Lady Madeleine's bed had been pulled closed and the only light was that cast by the leaping flames in the hearth. Wulf turned to secure the bar on the heavy oaken door; when he turned back, she was standing before him.

She clung to him, her heart beating furiously against his chest. Something had frightened her . . . badly.

"What would you have me do?" Wulf asked. He would have promised to catch the moon for her, anything to quiet her.

She buried her face against his chest. "Love me," she cried. The words tore from her throat like a sob.

"I do love you," he said. He cupped her face in his hands and kissed her, a kiss filled with promises.

She pressed deeper into his arms, so that it seemed he could feel the blood coursing through her veins. "Love me," she begged. "Love me tonight, Wulf."

He kissed her again, and soon he was lost to reason, helpless as a leaf upon the wind, compelled by the wild delirium of his passion.

DANA RANSOM'S RED-HOT HEARTFIRES!

ALEXANDRA'S ECSTASY   (2773, $3.75)

Alexandra had known Tucker for all her seventeen years, but all at once she realized her childhood friend was the man capable of tempting her to leave innocence behind!

LIAR'S PROMISE   (2881, $4.25)

Kathryn Mallory's sincere questions about her father's ship to the disreputable Captain Brady Rogan were met with mocking indifference. Then he noticed her trim waist, angelic face and Kathryn won the wrong kind of attention!

LOVE'S GLORIOUS GAMBLE   (2497, $3.75)

Nothing could match the true thrill that coursed through Gloria Daniels when she first spotted the gambler, Sterling Caulder. Experiencing his embrace, feeling his lips against hers would be a risk, but she was willing to chance it all!

WILD, SAVAGE LOVE   (3055, $4.25)

Evangeline, set free from Indians, discovered liberty had its price to pay when her uncle sold her into marriage to Royce Tanner. Dreaming of her return to the people she loved, she vowed never to submit to her husband's caress.

WILD WYOMING LOVE   (3427, $4.25)

Lucille Blessing had no time for the new marshal Sam Zachary. His mocking and arrogant manner grated her nerves, yet she longed to ease the tension she knew he held inside. She knew that if he wanted her, she could never say no!

PAIGE BRANTLEY
CAPTIVE
TO HIS
KISS

ZEBRA BOOKS
KENSINGTON PUBLISHING CORP.

For Heidi, who always believed.

ZEBRA BOOKS

are published by

Kensington Publishing Corp.
475 Park Avenue South
New York, NY 10016

Copyright © 1992 by Paige Brantley

First printing: June, 1992

Printed in the United States of America

Chapter One

Anno Christi 1348

Clutched in the hoary embrace of frost and smoke, the slanted rooftops of Troyes blazed with the first golden rays of Easter morn.

Madeleine de Moncelet threw back the coverlet of her lavishly draped bed and dashed barefoot across the icy stones to gaze from the window of her chamber. Her thin linen bedfrock offered little protection against the keen morning air. A chill shook her slight form as she stood marveling at the beauty of the delicate white tracery, etched, as if by magic, upon the bumped and bubbled surface of the glass. Glass windows were a marvel in themselves, a luxury only the wealthiest could afford. Though the glass was lumpy and the view warped, others made do with oiled skins tacked over window openings, or nothing at all.

"Albertine. Come see," Madeleine called, giving her long dark curls a toss. Her pale oval face was aglow with delight and merriment sparkled from her dark hazel eyes. "Hurry," she urged, for soon the sun would burn away the intricate design.

But the lump beneath the downy coverlet only groaned like a bulky heifer and bore deeper into the bed clothing.

Madeleine, refusing to be ignored, leapt onto the bed. Digging her fingers into the young duenna's ribs with a fury, she tickled the poor girl until she rolled over and lay limp with laughter.

With a shout of "Huzzah," Madeleine snatched away the coverlet. "Arise, lazy Albertine! The kitchen maids are coming for the sheets!" But Madeleine's jesting threats of having her maidservant boiled with the laundry only prompted another obstinate grunt from the chubby young woman with fair frizzled hair.

After much squealing and giggling, Madeleine tumbled the buxom servant girl off the bed and propelled her across the chamber.

"Look, Albertine," she cried, tracing a thin finger over the frosted window. "See, it is a princess astride a lacy white horse."

The duenna, shivering in her rumpled bedfrock, drew closer and peered at the icy collage of interlacing lines. It was a game she and her young mistress often played during the long, damp winters.

"She has a long nose, your princess," Albertine observed.

Madeleine only laughed merrily and pointed to yet another image. "All the better to smell this sweet rose," she said.

Albertine craned her neck, searching the myriad patterns upon the tall, arched window. "Oh, see," she pointed. "Here is her lover."

"But he has no chin," Madeleine giggled. "He is less a beauty than she."

"No matter," Albertine said with a husky laugh, nudging her young mistress. "Do you see where his prick bulges from his hose?"

The observation elicited a high-pitched giggle from Madeleine and sent the color rushing to her cheeks, a condition made all the more noticeable by the milky whiteness of her skin.

"'Tis true," Albertine laughed. "'Tis the size of

6

their tool, not their chin, that makes them worth the bother."

"Albertine, for shame," she tittered, giving her maidservant a look of mock reproach.

"Sweet mistress, how do you suppose men see the fairer sex? Soothly they look last at a maiden's face; 'tis her heaving breasts and rounded backside that interests them more."

Madeleine, who delighted in Albertine's scandalous wit, pranced across the chamber, uninhibited as a wood nymph, and with a wag of her girlish derrière collapsed onto the bed in a fit of giggling.

Albertine, braving the cold, shed her bedfrock and struggled into her rough woolen kirtle. "Why milady," she said, retrieving her hand from a sleeve, "my own little cobbler, who I love with all my heart, has a face like a pork pie, but a prick as long as a donkey's. When we first met—ah, but 'tis a long story."

"Tell me, oh tell me," Madeleine coaxed, settling herself in the bedclothes and ignoring the tolling bells of St. Pierre. The distant bells, whose silence had been observed since Good Friday, now summoned the faithful in a dull, throaty voice.

Albertine also heard the tolling of the solemn iron bells. She shook her ginger-colored locks. "Nay, mistress, if we do not hurry we will be late for Mass and this be the day of our dear Jesu's resurrection."

"I would rather hear your cobbler's tale than Canon Guyot's sermon," Madeleine said, clenching her teeth as she set her bare feet on the stones. By the morning light the hearth held only ashes and the stones of the chamber were cold as a churchyard crypt.

Albertine attended her mistress as she donned her new gown of murrey-colored velvet. The wine-red dress was tightly fitted to the hips then widened and fell in generous folds to brush the ground. The neckline was low-cut, though still modest by the standards of the king's court, and trimmed in ermine, as were the fitted sleeves which buttoned from the wrist to the elbow. Albertine fussed over the folds of the skirt, then bustled about the room prompting her mistress to hurry. "I hear the household gathering for Mass," she admonished. She did not, of course, but said so in hopes of moving her mistress to haste. She may as well have spared her breath.

Madeleine was invariably late for every occasion and this day was to be no different from any other. For Étienne de Moncelet's youngest daughter was accustomed to having her own way. A beautiful child with tousled hair and bold dark eyes so like her father's, she had grown into a willful little termagant as obstinate and sharp-tongued as himself. In a small child such precociousness was charming, but not in a young woman, and her father often had reason to regret his permissiveness.

"They will not leave without us," Madeleine announced, admiring herself in her Venetian mirror of glass backed with silver. She wished they would, for she disliked the long, boring Masses, and worse still, the dire scenes of hell described in most un-Christian detail by Canon Guyot. Looking down, she noticed the buckle of her slipper had come undone. She bent to correct it. When the obstinate buckle slipped from her numbed fingers for the third time, she swore, *"Je renie Dieu!"* At the tender age of sixteen Madeleine was already an abominable swearer. Blasphemy with its sinful charm, the idea of really daring heaven, appealed to Madeleine's rebellious nature. "Hell and eternal damnation," she cursed. "I am weary to tears of arising at dawn only to be bored stiff as a carp by that tedious Guyot. You would think our dear canon visits hell regularly; each week he has some new horror to report."

"Shush, mistress," Albertine pleaded, tugging at Madeleine's curly locks, and none too gently, with a brush fashioned of hog's bristles. "'Tis heresy

8

to speak so."

"According to Canon Guyot, 'tis heresy for one of our gender to speak at all," Madeleine said with a mutinous sidelong glance.

"Men are hateful creatures," Albertine agreed. "They long to hear none but their own voices," she said, expertly braiding her mistress's hair into two thick plaits which fit neatly beneath her coif, a fine samite veil held in place with a circlet of gold.

Clutching a candle in her pudgy hand, Albertine led the way down the steep stone staircase. Colorful rugs from the Orient graced a portion of the hall and tapestries hung from the drab stone walls. The furnishings, even in the château of the Count of Troyes, were few; a massive oaken table, benches, chests, and a brace of huge candles.

A fire roared and crackled in the great hearth and the tarry odor of woodsmoke wafted through the air. Hands cupped before their candles to preserve the flame, Albertine and Madeleine swept down through the cavernous hall, the heels of their slippers clicking upon the stones.

A general state of confusion existed in the hall. The family had gathered before the huge iron-bound doors and servants dashed madly about with cloaks and gloves while dogs romped and barked underfoot.

Margarete and Elenore, Madeleine's twin sisters, resplendent in wachlet-colored velvet, greeted her with peevish glances. Her mother, dressed in a silk gown of pale blue, frowned and scolded Madeleine for her perpertual tardiness. Her father acknowledged her with a brief smile, then returned his attention to her elder brother, Philippe, who was speaking in a low voice on some matter concerning the estates—a question of fines, to which her father nodded in agreement.

Étienne de Moncelet made a commanding figure in his Easter finery. His smoothly handsome features were not overly dissipated by his fondness for wine

9

and food and his dark curly hair was touched with but a hint of silver. Standing beside him, Philippe appeared dwarfed. He was fully two heads shorter than his father and thin as a lathe, looking almost child-like despite his nineteen years.

Seeing that his family was fully assembled, Étienne de Moncelet ushered them out into the brisk Easter morning and into the splendid *charrette* and livery which would carry them the short distance to the walled city of Troyes and the Cathedral of St. Pierre.

Although Étienne de Moncelet was among France's wealthiest nobles, he preferred the bucolic life of his estates and the prosperous, well-ordered tempo of his rich, trade-fair city to that of a court rife with intrigue and scandal. Such had not always been the case, for in his youth the handsome and dashing de Moncelet had been the darling of the court and Paris crowds. But his fierce opposition and inflammatory speeches against the English, Norman though they were, and their presence in France resulted in his being banned from court. The ban, in reality no more than a fit of pique by the king, was of short duration, but never forgotten by de Moncelet; although he pledged his fealty to the king each year, his loyalties lay with a France free of English influence.

The day was bright and blustery and the sky so vividly blue it pained Madeleine's eyes to gaze upon it. Beyond the château's sprawling gardens and red haze of budding trees, the city of Troyes nestled like a jewel on the emerald plain of Champagne. From that distance the fluted spires and far-flung buttresses of the cathedral rose imposingly above the city's towers and huddled roof-tops. It had been Madeleine's grandfather who chose to abandon life within the walls of Troyes, building his château nearby in the pastoral beauty of the countryside, away from the filth and crowded clutter of the city.

*   *   *

Beneath the vaulted dome of the cathedral, tall Gothic windows of stained glass blazed with a rose-hued light and the air was thick with incense. A carved Christ, crucified and crowned with golden thorns, hung suspended in a niche above the altar and statues of melancholy saints lined the walls. From the choir aisles, black-clad brethren raised their voices in a somber harmony as the faithful gathered to hear the word of God.

Madeleine walked beside her brother, looking neither right nor left. Ever since she was a small child, Madeleine had despised the paintings which adorned the walls of the ambulatory. One depicted an angel summoning the rotting corpses of the dead from their graves for the Last Judgment and in another, St. Michael weighed the souls of the dead. There were others, equally gruesome, in which grotesquely misshapen devils tormented sinners. In Madeleine's mind it was this threat of eternal damnation held over the head of the living that was truly evil. Life was a joyous thing and to make it less seemed more a sin than any vice.

Madeleine took little notice of the Mass, less of Canon Guyot in his rich vestment and his black-clad clergy. She found the faces of the faithful and those of their children more interesting by far. Here and there were finely garbed guildsmen and their wives, whose cherub-faced children squirmed and fidgeted; wealthy merchants dressed in velvet and furs; and workers in rough-woven wool clothing. She gazed at their faces, reading them as one might a book, imagining their characters and the lives they led.

Later, when the benediction was given, Madeleine's thoughts were devoted entirely to the *Pâques* feast and the merriment which would follow.

Guests filled the great hall of the château. The

11

many hues of their garments melded into a moving sea of color and the chorus of their voices and laughter raised a joyous symphony. Throngs of servants bore tray after tray laden with food to the banquet table: hams, sausages, black puddings, cheeses, roasts, meat pies, game birds, sweetmeats, and pastries.

Madeleine, warmed by the blazing hearth and the delicious aroma of food, sat beside her sisters: Margarete, tall and plain, who had inherited neither her mother's charm nor her father's handsomeness; and Elenore, with her long, disapproving face and lank brown hair, who was the image of their mother's unmarried aunt, Elzaire, a likeness for which she was often teased.

Madeleine grew quickly bored with her sisters' conversation, which, as always, centered on the available young men who were present. Her sisters were well into their twenties and of an age when most women were at the height of their childbearing years and contentedly pregnant. They, however, despaired of finding suitable husbands. The long cruel war and, more immediately, the disastrous defeat by the English at Crecy several years before had drained away legions of young nobles to perish on the battlefields. There were few acceptable young men to be found in all Champagne and it seemed likely suitable marriages could not be arranged until their father journeyed to Paris and to his estates that year.

Marriage was the farthest thought from Madeleine's mind. She had no wish or need to marry. Her dowried properties would comfortably support her; moreover, she had no desire to be any man's wife. Unlike many women of her day, Madeleine was perfectly capable of managing her own affairs. To her mind, arranged marriages were the most wicked of all. She thought it degrading for a woman to be bartered off like a fattened cow. All told, Madeleine thought a great deal—clearly her father was to blame.

Because he adored her, she had been educated with her brother. But to her father's keen disappointment or perhaps his secret pride, Madeleine had proved to be by far the more intelligent and bold. It was she who had inherited the cleverness, the fiery spirit, and steely resolve of the de Moncelet line. Once, when there were no ears but hers to hear, her father had sadly remarked, "More's the pity you were not born a son." Madeleine, eleven at the time, had for months bemoaned her cruel fate—that of being born female and condemned to live her life at the whim of men and the passing moons.

Madeleine's inquiring gaze wandered over the guests. All around her the drone of conversation ebbed and flowed. She saw her sisters giggling behind their hands; the object of their amusement was a youth with reddish hair. He was dressed in the height of male fashion and wore a parti-colored jupon, a fitted short tunic of red and purple velvet with long sleeves, soft leather boots with pointed toes, and purple hose which were a tight-fitting, often revealing combination of breeches and stockings. Madeleine looked away with a disapproving curl of her lips. Her sisters, she decided, were foolish as geese. But even their absurd conduct could not dampen her merry mood.

The *Pâques* feast rivaled that of the Nativity, and *jongleurs* had been hired for the guests' entertainment. Madeleine watched in rapt wonder as a juggler sent a volley of brightly colored balls into the air. Soon the musicians, dressed in gaily-colored garments with dagged sleeves, entered the hall. They sang tenderly of the bittersweet beauty of love and when the song had ended, another recited a tragic *lai* set to the haunting notes of a flute. The magical images conjured up by the troubadour's words cast a spell over Madeleine and, like one transfixed, she sat dreaming of gallant knights, splendidly attired ladies, and courtly liaisons.

At first she did not hear Albertine's voice. It was only when her maidservant whispered in her ear that she took any notice at all.

"The Lord and Lady wish to speak to you, mistress," Albertine repeated.

"May I stay a moment longer?" Madeleine pleaded, for she longed to hear the last mournful lines.

"Nay, mistress. They await you."

"Why?" Madeleine demanded. She had been enjoying herself and now she was irritated. "I have not acted unseemly, even towards my sisters."

Albertine pressed her lips close to her ear. "Soothly, mistress, I do not know the reason."

Reluctantly, Madeleine threaded her way through the assembled guests, finding the coolness of the dim passageway oddly chilling after the heat of the crowded hall. She went directly to her father's library, where she and Philippe had been tutored under the strict guidance of Brother Michael. It was a close, narrow room with a heavy, iron-banded door and a pair of ornately leaded windows which faced the towers of Troyes. The walls were lined with books from the monasteries of Saint Aignan and Saint Junien de Nouaille and on the massive library table lay the leather-bound accounts of her father's vast estates. In the room's shadowy corners, untidy heaps of parchment and leather rolls cluttered the darkness. Maps and drawings of curious faraway places which had been the source of many of Madeleine's daydreams—the Holy Land, the Orient, the pagan north—filled the room.

Her parents sat in high-backed chairs of the Italian style and warmed themselves before the hearth, for the spring evening was cool. As Madeleine entered, a log broke in half, sending a shower of sparks into the blackness of the chimney.

"Madeleine," her father said fondly, rising from his chair and taking her cool fingers in his. "We will not keep you long from the songs of the trouba-

14

dours," he promised, aware that it was at his insistence that she was called away. "I felt it was full time you knew of our decision."

Alarmed by the hesitant tone of his voice, Madeleine looked from one to the other. Her mother's placid expression and pale eyes betrayed nothing; even her father's normally mobile features were closed and grave. He said, "As you are aware, your sisters have long desired marriages, and, as I am constantly reminded," his gaze shifted uncomfortably to meet his wife's pale eyes, "it is my duty to find suitable husbands for all my daughters." Étienne de Moncelet paused. He knew his youngest daughter's feelings on the subject of arranged marriages and he had no heart for what he had to say. "I first offered Elenore, then Margarete." He paused once more, then went on lamely. "But it is you who was chosen."

Chosen. The word sent Madeleine's mind into a fit. Chosen for marriage? Her face stung with a scalding anger. She felt as if the tears that welled from her eyes might bead up on her burning cheeks and hiss like water on a hot griddle. Her father had all but promised she would not be forced to marry and now he had betrayed her.

The anguished expression on his youngest daughter's face wounded Étienne de Moncelet and he hastened to add, "You have always been closest to my heart, Madeleine. I agreed to your marriage only because Guiles de Luchaire is the finest match in all Champagne. He is a favorite of the court and his barony is a rich one indeed. De Luchaire is youthful as well, vigorous enough to please a young wife."

Madeleine's mother, who until that moment had not spoken a word, advised, "He is a widower with a young child, a babe of less than a year. I thought the child would be a comfort to you."

"No," Madeleine cried, raising her voice above a civil tone. "I do not wish to marry." Turning to her father, who had never denied her anything, she pleaded. "I beg you, Father, do not force me to marry this man or any man not of my own choosing."

Her father's face sagged visibly but he would not give in to her, even with words.

For some time her parents continued to speak to her in calm, mollifying tones. Their words ran through her mind like water; she heard nothing but the angry pounding of her pulse against her temples. When at last she returned to the merriment of the hall, the songs of the troubadours were but cruel noise to her ears.

Chapter Two

In the days and weeks that followed, Madeleine was caught up in the bustle of activity as preparations for her wedding proceeded. Cloth was chosen for her trousseau, she was measured by seamstresses, and fitted again and again. She was given sound, practical advice for managing a household from her mother and the terms of her dowry were laid out and copied by her father's crotchety old clerk, Finistère.

Spring came slowly with its warm winds to coax a multitude of gaily-colored wildflowers from the muddy fields. On a day when plowmen and teams of oxen tilled the soil and songbirds called from the budding trees, Madeleine and Albertine strolled through the sun-splashed afternoon. They walked through the garden, past the stable and the vegetable plots, down along the orchard, and beside the meandering stream. It was a route Madeleine had often ridden on her beloved Minet, the little dappled Spanish mare so named for her dainty gait and cat-like grace. But alas, Madeleine was no longer permitted to ride and so she walked, unhappily. When she had questioned her parents' decision, her mother put her off without an answer, alluding to the dangers of riding. "You could be injured or even killed in a fall from your palfrey," her mother told her in a vague tone. But Madeleine was not to be put off so easily, and asked, "If riding is so dangerous, why then was I permitted to ride in the past?" Isobel de Moncelet bristled at her daughter's sarcasm and, as often happened, sent her to her chamber. There the faithful Albertine, several years older and infinitely wiser in the ways of the world, explained in the coarsest terms that it was to ensure her bridegroom's pleasure. "To keep you tight for his organ. So he knows you to be a virgin, mistress."

Madeleine was aghast. Her parents would do no such thing. But above all, she was puzzled, and asked, "Why is that so important?" Albertine shrugged and replied, "Men set great store by it," and went on to tell her mistress that in Troyes there was an old woman who for a price could make a woman a virgin again and again, and that many sought out her services.

All these thoughts tumbled through Madeleine's mind as she and Albertine strolled past the rows of budding pear trees. A deep and abiding sadness weighed on her heart. She could not imagine herself married; the very thought of it frightened and bewildered her, particularly the intimacy. In her entire life she had never been alone with a man except for her father and brother. And now, because Canon Guyot said a few foolish words over her, she was expected to bed a man she neither knew nor desired and smile politely while he had his way with her.

In frustration she broke a branch from a young pear tree and swished it against her fine linen skirts. Marriage, she thought, was very like being condemned. In one fell swoop she would be denied her freedom and her youth. She felt betrayed by her father and saw her approaching marriage as a sort of slavery, a curse, and certainly no cause for rejoicing. "My heart is sad, Albertine," she confessed.

"Nay, mistress, I will journey to your new home with you. All will be well."

"I do not want a new home," Madeleine said

spitefully, decapitating a daisy with her switch. "I especially do not want a man I have never laid eyes upon. He may be small as a dwarf or fat as a Martinmas hog, or both."

"I have heard he is the flower of manhood; handsome as the very devil and the finest swordsman in all Sézanne."

Madeleine was very tempted to laugh. Instead, she demanded, "Who says this?"

"One of your own kitchen maids," Albertine replied in all seriousness, as if it were infallible as holy scripture.

Madeleine, no longer bothering to conceal her amusement, arched her dark brows. "How is it she knows of such things?"

"Her sister is a servant in the household of Guiles de Luchaire."

"What else do you know of Guiles de Luchaire, dear Albertine?" Madeleine prompted in a voice sweet as a honeyed tart.

"Nothing, mistress. My time is not my own."

"Truly said," Madeleine smiled. "Your time is mine to direct and you will learn all this woman knows and report it to me."

"Our Lord de Moncelet would have me horse-whipped for such gossip."

"No one will horsewhip you, silly Albertine," she said, laughing and playfully swatting her maidservant's rump with the switch. "I may, if you dare disobey me."

Albertine returned the mirthful laugh. "Sweet mistress, you know there is nothing in this world I am fonder of than gossip."

"Not even your little cobbler?" Madeleine teased, for she had badgered Albertine into telling her the story in all its bawdy details. The pair laughed unrestrainedly as they strolled in the warm sunshine.

*   *   *

Late in the afternoon, Albertine loitered in the kitchen as the food was prepared. All the while she kept a watchful eye for Adelicia, the middle-aged maidservant who was the eyes and ears of the lady of the chateau. Adelicia's stealth was legendary and her piercing black eyes all-seeing. Because of her unerring vigilance, many a servant's slothful behavior had been swiftly and severely punished.

In the low-beamed kitchen a feast was being prepared for the Lord of Troyes and the visiting stewards of his estates. The room was humid in the warm spring evening and reeked of ambrosial scents: roasting meats, spices, and the yeasty smell of baking bread.

Albertine blended into the bustling activity and at the first opportunity sought out the kitchen maid with the coil of brown braids and the wart above her eye. She was called Bonne, for she had once been a nursemaid. She labored before the ovens, removing crusty golden loaves of bread with a long-handled wooden paddle. Jolly and broad, Bonne relished gossip as dearly as food.

Seated among her family and her father's stewards at the banquet table, Madeleine was totally immersed in her thoughts.

The air of the great hall was smeared with the odors of grease, smoke, highly spiced foods, and of so many people crowded close. Conversation punctuated by hearty laughter swirled through the room and the background babble of the servants rose and fell, mingling with the sound of dogs quarreling over scraps and the clamor of cooking pots.

Madeleine toyed with her food, unaware of the guests or the groaning feast before her. Only later, when the serving boys brought small bowls of water for the guests to wash their greasy hands, did Madeleine look up to see an awkwardly built boy stumble and spill a bowl of water on her father's clerk, sour old Finistère.

Madeleine let loose an involuntary peal of laughter, for which she received a sharply reproachful look from her mother, causing her to giggle all the more.

Later, in the small solar adjoining her parent's chamber, Madeleine, her mother, and two sisters sat around a huge framework on which a tapestry was being worked. The partially completed tapestry was of her mother's design—a garden scene abloom with whimsical flowers, cherubs, and brightly plumaged birds. It was her mother's most ambitious project, large enough to span the entire wall of the solar, and meant to block the drafts and chill of winter.

Madeleine worked by fits and starts, tugging at her needle and trying to imagine what Albertine had learned of Guiles de Luchaire. Was he truly handsome? Was he gallant, courtly, and kind?

Across the span of the room, three of her mother's women spun wool into thread while by the smoky hearth, Adelicia strummed effortlessly on her lute. The gentle melody flowed through Madeleine's mind. How odd, she thought, that Adelicia, who was homely and thin as a crane, could make such lovely sounds.

Madeleine returned her attention to the yellow bird she was stitching, but only for a moment. The sweet notes of the lute filled the room and soon Madeleine's imagination took full rein, creating one fanciful daydream after another. When at last she felt she would surely die of curiosity, she excused herself and, taking a candle to light the way, went in search of Albertine.

She hurried into the low-beamed kitchen, where bunches of herbs hung drying from the smoke-blackened rafters and a heap of dead game birds lay ready for the plucking. The servants were busily engaged in picking over the remains of food from the table and in the darkened garth, beggars had

21

gathered to compete with dogs and cats and even rats for the offal.

Madeleine did not find Albertine in the kitchen nor in the well house, where two small boys drew pails of water by the haloed light of an oil lamp. They had not seen Albertine, although one thought she may have gone to fetch the night candles. But Albertine was not at the kist where the candles were stored, or anywhere, and Madeleine, fearing her long absence would result in a thorough questioning by her mother, decided to return to the solar.

The route she chose led past the library, where, following the evening meal, her father, Philippe, and the clerk had gathered with the stewards to hear the affairs of the estates. There were disputes to settle, marriages to approve, and the questions of fines and taxes.

The rise and fall of male voices rose above the scampering sound of mice in the darkened passageway. Madeleine crept soundlessly over the worn stones. She did not fear the mice nearly so much as being discovered and forced to give an explanation. Directly ahead of her the library door stood slightly ajar and the smoky oil lamps cast a mellow wash of light into the passageway.

She heard her father's voice, then Philippe's, and afterwards a voice she did not recognize; a steward, she guessed. He spoke in fearful tones of pestilence raging in Marseilles and in the Pope's own city of Avignon. When he had finished there was a flurry of comment. Madeleine heard her father's voice rise above the others. He questioned the man harshly, forcing him to admit his information was second-hand and gained from travelers. Still, the man insisted, he had no reason to doubt their truthfulness, for all told a similar tale. At Lord de Moncelet's request, the man repeated several accounts of travelers wandering through villages where not a single man, woman, or child survived. No sooner had the account ended, when another voice was raised. "Be it truth or lies, 'tis tales like these that have stirred a fear among the peasants. They believe the world will end and speak of witchcraft; it is a dangerous mood, my lord."

The tone of the men's voices alarmed Madeleine more than their words. For a moment she remained, a captive in the thrall of the amber light, then hastened away, silent as a shadow, and returned to the complacent warmth of the solar. Elenore and Margarete took no notice of her return and Adelicia missed not a note. Only Madeleine's mother raised her pale eyes from the tapestry and greeted her daughter with a gentle smile.

Deep in the night, after the household had gone to sleep, Madeleine and Albertine lay together whispering. The April moonlight streamed across the bed in long, smoky shafts and their hushed voices made soft, quick sounds like the rustling of silks.

Albertine clutched a pillow to her bosom and whispered into the darkness. "The kitchen maid says he is handsome enough to melt a maiden's heart, but cruel as well. A devil, who is feared by his servants and all who have met with his black temper."

"What of his wife?" Madeleine asked in an urgent tone. She felt she must know that instant or die of suspense. "Did he love her greatly?"

The ginger color of Albertine's hair was bleached grey in the moonlight. "Nay, mistress. I do not think so. The kitchen maid's own sister was the lady's serving woman, and said her lady was a fair and lovely creature, but meek and much abused by her Lord de Luchaire. She said when her lady grew too cumbersome to service him, he abandoned her for the pleasures of the court and did not return until after she had birthed the child."

"Did she die then of childbirth?"

"Nay, mistress. The kitchen maid says otherwise, but when I pressed her to tell more, she grew silent as a stile. Only would she say that Guiles de Luchaire is the instrument of Satan, and the Virgin's mercy on you, sweet mistress."

Madeleine was too immersed in her own affairs to give any thought to what she had overheard in the passageway that evening. She hardly slept at all; nor did Albertine, as much as she would have liked to, for Madeleine could not stop talking nor asking to hear once more the kitchen maid's every word.

It was days later when Madeleine thought of the steward's words and repeated them to Albertine. But in the sun-speckled garden, fresh from a spring shower, the tale had lost its grotesqueness and had become only a bit of gossip—an event too far removed from their lives to be of any real concern.

Chapter Three

In May, when the bees were thick in the orchard, the courturière arrived from Troyes with Madeleine's trousseau for yet another fitting.

Madeleine and Albertine passed the glorious afternoon in the fragrant shade of the rose arbor. Albertine, lying in the grass, fashioned crownlets of violets while Madeleine read aloud in a bright, clear voice from a book of amusements.

Elenore's arrival was greeted by a look of annoyance from Madeleine and a frown from the frizzy-haired maidservant.

Madeleine dreaded the fittings, which were boring and tedious, and made a face like a martyr as she followed Elenore into the château. Albertine, too, was unhappy. She would now be expected to join the other maids in the household chores and she much preferred sitting beneath the rose arbor to scrubbing garderobes and sweeping floors.

The couturière, with her powdered and rouged face, her two seamstresses, and three assistants awaited Madeleine in the solar. They toiled and fussed for hours over the form-fitting, cream-colored silk gown with its trailing skirt. Tempers flared. The seamstresses snapped angrily at one another and punctured Madeleine with their pins several times. Madeleine was as much to blame as they. She fidgeted unmercifully and screamed louder each time she was pricked. She complained with a whining voice that the heavy silk dress weighed on her like a mill stone. Shortly afterwards, she announced she had developed a headache and when her mother reprimanded her for her unseemly behavior, she pouted.

On the morning Madeleine and Guiles de Luchaire were to exchange their betrothal vows, a serving woman found a dead bird in the hall. Her discovery, which was accompanied by hysterical screams, disrupted the entire household. The kitchen women whispered behind their hands that it was an ill omen and even Adelicia appeared unnerved. But matters were soon set aright by the Lady Isobel, who declared it was naught but idle foolishness and sent the maids scurrying from her wrath.

Outside, the day was blissfully warm and bright with sunshine. Madeleine had dressed in a fine green linen gown topped with a snowy white cotte and an ornate girdle of braided gold. She wore her dark mane of curls loose, covered only with a small veil of transparent silk held in place with a thin circlet of gold. Because the occasion demanded finery she had been permitted to wear her emerald-studded brooch and matching earrings.

Madeleine awaited her father in the brilliant sunshine of the courtyard. Upon catching sight of his daughter, Étienne de Moncelet warmly embraced her. "You are lovely," he exclaimed. "Yes, lovely as an angel. How is it possible I have sired such a beauty?"

Madeleine blushed as she always did in the glow of her father's praise and, smiling into his eyes, assured him her handsomeness had most certainly been inherited from him. "A gift from my father."

"As is that tongue of yours," he laughed, giving her small shoulders a squeeze.

Madeleine's spirits were high as she and her father

rode toward Troyes. The morning sunlight was mellow as butter, birds sang from the meadows, and the soft new grass muffled the drubbing of their horses' hooves. At last she would see Guiles de Luchaire face to face and judge for herself. It was not until she and her father entered the chapter house of the great Cathedral of St. Pierre that the dark thoughts returned to harry her peace of mind.

Sunlight flooded the room through a brace of tall leaded windows, splitting the interior into dazzling shafts of light and shade. The unexpected brilliance all but blinded Madeleine, and for a moment she stood blinking like an owl in the glare.

Guiles de Luchaire, who had arrived earlier and taken a seat opposite the aged Canon, rose swiftly to his feet. He was not so tall as Étienne de Moncelet, but powerfully built. His massive arms and shoulders bulged against his richly quilted tunic of blue lake. He greeted them with a flamboyant courtliness, no doubt fashionable in Parisian circles.

Madeleine caught her father's fleeting expression. He did not approve, she thought, or perhaps he, too, had noticed the odd scent. Still, he smiled and took her cool hand in his and drew her forward, announcing, "Baron de Luchaire, my daughter, Madeleine Marie Angélè de Moncelet."

Madeleine's eyes were drawn not to Guiles de Luchaire's swarthy face beneath the soft felt lithrope, but to the open neck of his tunic and the explosion of coarse black hair which burst from his collar like fur. The sight of it sent an involuntary shiver along her spine, and the thought of how he must look without his clothing leapt into her mind. When at last she raised her eyes, it was only to lose her power of speech to his steady, appraising gaze. Her resolve wavered and she lowered her eyes in an expression of what appeared to be modesty, but was more truthfully dread.

"My Lord de Luchaire," she murmured in a newly found and feeble voice, then curtsied and extended her hand. The scent she had first noticed upon entering the room now threatened to overpower her senses. He was wearing musk, and though many men did, on him the scent took on a queer, oily smell.

Guiles de Luchaire made a low bow and, taking her icy hand captive in his, brushed his lips to her fingertips. "You are a pleasure to behold," he said, and after a pause, "I eagerly await the day when I may content my affection for you." His smile revealed a row of tiny white teeth and the way his thin lips twisted at the corners of his mouth made her flesh crawl.

To Madeleine's great relief Canon Guyot came forward with the marriage contract. Since matters had been decided weeks before, the discussion was brief. Étienne de Moncelet quickly perused the contract one final time, nodding his head in approval.

The date of the wedding was set for September, and Guiles de Luchaire, Baron of Sézanne, consented, promised loyally and in good faith to solemnly betroth himself to Madeleine Marie Angélè de Moncelet, third daughter of the Count of Troyes, and to marry her in the face of the Holy Church within a fortnight following the feast of the Assumption. Madeleine also repeated the vows, and after the documents were signed and sealed, she and her father departed for the château.

Madeleine did not mention Guiles de Luchaire during the ride home, neither did she discuss her future husband with her mother nor give in to the envious taunts of her sisters. But later in her chamber Madeleine spilled out her grieving heart to Albertine.

She told her of the thick-set young man with massive arms and shoulders whose bold features were tainted with an unabashed expression of haughtiness. "I will not marry him," she wailed. "He is lustful and commanding."

"But is he not as handsome as they say, mistress?" Albertine asked, attempting to soothe her.

Madeleine turned on her with rounded eyes. "Oh, Albertine. He is hairy as the carnival man's ape, and he looks wicked and cruel." She fell silent for a moment and then said, "Some may call him handsome. I do not."

A week passed before the day of Madeleine's final fitting. On this occasion she did not squirm or fret, but stood in stony silence devising one irrational scheme after another of how she might yet avoid marriage to Guiles de Luchaire.

Dressed again in a simple frock, Madeleine returned to the garden with Albertine at her elbow. No longer in a humor to enjoy her book, she closed the volume and walked aimlessly through the orchard pouring out her unhappiness.

A short distance away the road to Troyes was crowded by a seemingly endless procession of goods wagons, peddlers, and merchants en route to the market stalls of the city. The first of the annual trade fairs would soon begin, and nowhere in Europe could one find such an array of goods. Shimmering silks were displayed beside gold and silver jewelry, pearls from the depths of the sea, precious spices, lace, and leather goods.

As the bells of Troyes sounded tierce, a cloth merchant arrived at the château in a cart pulled by mules. The merchant was a heavy, bearded man who wore a funny red hat and spoke with an eloquent Genoese accent. He begged for an audience with the Countess of Troyes and sent samples of his rich brocaded cloth with her servingwoman so that the countess might see the cloth's rare qualities. With him were two small black boys dressed in scarlet tunics. The taller of the pair carried a huge green parrot on his shoulder.

Madeleine was intrigued by the bird which squawked and screeched and actually spoke Latin words. Countess Isobel de Moncelet was more interested in the rich texture and vivid colors of the brocades and asked Adelicia's opinion.

The merchant, eager to make a sale to a wealthy noble, explained, "It is from Marseilles, milady, and the last you may see for some long while. For Marseilles is cursed with a pestilence and those of its guilds have all been called to Christ."

The merchant's words, not unlike those of the stewards, fired Madeleine's curiosity. But when she questioned the merchant about the terrible pestilence, her mother put a halt to the conversation by piously remarking, "God in his wisdom punishes those who question his will." The merchant conceded with a smile, but Madeleine's face stung with embarrassment and anger, too, at her mother's blind acceptance. Like a sheep that is led, having neither a mind nor a will of its own. "It is a sickness, Mother," she said with a cutting edge to her voice, "not a condition of the soul."

If Madeleine did not regret her words, she did regret stirring her mother's ire. Placid though she was, once baited she was unrelenting. Madeleine was exiled to her chamber and no one, not even a servant, was permitted to speak to her. Her punishment lasted a full day and a night, for Thursday was the festival of La Fête-Dieu.

"Are you awake, mistress?" Albertine's voice called from the door.

"Yes," Madeleine answered. "Have you brought me a candle?" Her mother knew well her fear of the dark, and as further punishment, had refused her a candle.

Madeleine fumbled in the darkness. Rain thundered overhead, sluicing over the eaves and drilling against the window. Albertine vanished into the pitch blackness of the passageway. A moment later she returned carrying a candle and set it on the carved chest at the foot of Madeleine's bed.

In the eerie glow of the flame, Madeleine hurriedly dressed. Her hands were clumsy in the flickering light, and the rolling crash of thunder seemed inside the very room.

Below in the hall, Madeleine's father and brother prepared to leave on their annual journey to pay fealty to the king in Paris, and afterwards to view the farflung de Moncelet estates. Their journey would be a lengthy one indeed.

Roger Sara, the captain of her father's soldiers, and old Finistère, the clerk, stood wrapped in their capes by the iron-bound doors. Rain dripped from the hems of their long cloaks and puddled at their feet.

Isobel de Moncelet had risen with the laud's bells to bid farewell to her husband and son. She sat at the table brushing crumbs from her bodice. On the table were the remains of their breakfast of cold lamb and fruited tarts. "Why must you leave in such weather?" she complained, pinching a bit of crust between her plump fingers and daintily slipping it into her mouth. "Another day would serve as well."

Étienne de Moncelet rose from his seat, dismissing his wife's concerns with a wave of his hand. The carping tone of her voice grated on his nerves even more than the drumming rain. His gaze fell on Madeleine as she entered the hall. He smiled at her and said, "Well, well, my little rogue. What have you to say for yourself?"

"I wish to beg Madame Ma-Mère's forgiveness," she said in a tone more patronizing than genuinely contrite. Hazarding a glance at her mother, Madeleine saw her round face remained expressionless.

Etienne gave his youngest daughter a brief hug. "She has been punished enough," he announced in a voice meant for his wife'e ears. He tilted Madeleine's chin, chuckling, "It is that tongue of yours, little one; it is as sharp as Sara's blade." He gave her chin a tug and ruffled her dark hair. "You must learn to temper your words with wisdom."

"Her husband will resort to stuffing wool in his ears in a week's time," Philippe teased. He meant no offense—that was obvious from his fond smile. "He may give us twice the dowry to take her back," he laughed, taking his sword and scabbard from a young squire. Hearty male laughter rose above the drilling sound of the rain; even old Finistère was forced to smile.

Madeleine, too, smiled, though the unexpected sight of her grim-faced sisters, Elenore and Margarete, taking their places at the table sent a flush of color rushing to her cheeks. She had not been aware of their presence until that moment.

Madeleine followed her father and brother into the dark, wet courtyard where their company of soldiers waited. Horses and riders moved through the soggy darkness and the clatter of their hooves upon the cobblestones was lost to the drenching downpour.

The rain continued throughout the day, abating then returning in blustery gusts to dampen the celebration of the Blessed Scarament. Isobel de Moncelet, her daughters, and a number of her servants huddled in their cloaks beneath the portico of the Cathedral of St. Pierre. They, like the population of Troyes who lined the city streets ten deep, had come to view the Eucharistic procession.

Canon Guyot, robed in his finest vestments, lead the procession from the cathedral. He was followed by a host of black-clad clergy. Four among them bore the gilded and canopied litter on which the jewel-encrusted Eucharist was displayed in all its glory. Behind them a choir of brethren with tonsured heads sang the praises of the Most Holy, and in their wake the mayor, the magistrates, town clerks, and guildsmen walked from the cathedral with lighted candles that were immediately extinguished by the gusty rain. Once beyond the cathedral's steps, the procession was swelled by the ranks of Champagne's lesser nobles and knights astride their gaily decorated mounts.

François Larousse, the château's seneschal and steward of the Count's holdings in Troyes, rode at the head of the horsemen, his large bald head swathed in a soft purple lithrope with a dagged edge.

The rain came heavier and Madeleine retreated deeper into the hood of her cloak, hardly noticing the procession, vivid despite the gloomy skies, as it wound its way through the streets of the city. Albertine, standing near her mistress's elbow, drew near and said, "Look among the nobes of Sézanne." Madeleine knew it was he, even before Albertine advised, "He rides a huge chestnut draped in lake-colored cloth. He is just as you said," Albertine noted in a whisper. It was true; even the hooded cloak he wore could not conceal his thick-set form and massive shoulders.

As he passed the portico, his gaze sought out Madeleine. She quickly looked away, heart pounding and cheeks aflame.

During the Mass, de Luchaire stood among his kinsmen and gazed openly at her, a bold, penetrating stare which she found both disturbing and somehow vulgar. Only when he directed his eyes toward the altar did she steal a glance at him. His dark hair receded sharply from his forehead, framing his face with a look of obstinacy, arrogance perhaps, which was affirmed by his angular features and swaggering stance. Madeleine averted her eyes, avoiding his glance, unable to decide if it was loathing or fear which made her heart race.

For days afterward Madeleine was strangely silent, lost deep in her thoughts. Only the little Spanish mare, which had been a gift from her father, could bring a smile to her lips.

In the stable, Minet's soft muzzle sought out Madeleine's hand and the shriveled apple. The little mare did not seem to mind that it was last year's apple brought up from the store room's earthen cellar. Minet was a dapple gray—not drab and faded to dirty white as some greys were, but splashed with black as was her mane and her jauntily-carried tail.

One afternoon as Madeleine pressed her face to the soft arch of the mare's neck and cooed to her, she noticed the stableman's tabby cat trot from behind the grain bins with a tiny kitten clenched in her jaws. Up the thick wooden steps she went to the hayloft above.

Madeleine called excitedly to Albertine. The girls were accustomed to the orange cat mewing and brushing against their legs as soon as they entered the stable. They had not seen the tabby for days and wondered what had become of her.

"She has kittens in the loft," Madeleine cried. In only as long as it took the two girls to scramble up the wood slab stairs, they were seated in the sweet-smelling hay admiring the litter of kittens. Three were orange replicas of their mother and two were grey.

It was a joy to hold the little silken bundles of fur, but even that simple pleasure was spoiled for Madeleine by thoughts of her approaching marriage to Guiles de Luchaire. Although she tried to thrust her fears to the back of her consciousness, they returned again and again to harry her peace of mind

34

and now filled her with a grim desperation.

Somehow, she thought, she must free herself from her betrothal vows, but how? Since the festival of La Fête-Dieu she had wracked her brain, devising all manner of ploys. In the end she had rejected all as foolish or impossible. It seemed there was no avenue of escape or appeal left to her, only perhaps prayer. Truthfully Madeleine had never placed much faith in prayer. It was no more than wishing, she thought, and if wishes were jugs of wine, beggars would indeed be happy men. Still, the fat cook swore by the power of prayer, and Brother Michael, who had taught her and Philippe Latin, said with certainty that all prayers were heard. "Be cautious for what you pray," he had once warned them. "It may come to pass."

All these thoughts tumbled through Madeleine's mind as she watched the purring tabby and her family. Suddenly she looked up and asked, "Do you believe in prayer, Albertine?"

The pink-cheeked serving girl released a wriggling kitten into the straw and brushed back a stray strand of ginger-colored hair. "Aye, Mistress," she said with a smile. "Prayers to God and the saints."

"But have your prayers ever been answered?"

"Oh, yes," she assured her mistress, and after a moment's thought, conceded, "Once. I prayed to St. Jean to send me a true lover and he sent my little cobbler."

"St. Jean?" Madeleine questioned, longing to learn more of this patron saint of lovers. In the telling, Albertine whispered that he was more a pagan than Christian saint and once a year on his day fires were lit to honor him. Young couples gathered to dance before the fires and later joined hands and leapt over the smouldering coals.

*   *   *

On Sunday as the cathedral's solemn Mass ended, Madeleine knew what she must do. She found the statue of St. Jean in a niche among the other saints. She gazed at his long, serene face bathed in the rose-hued light, debating what gift she should offer him. After much thought, she twisted her emerald ring from her finger and dropped it into the alms box. She lit a candle, and then another and another, until half a dozen candles blazed, setting the niche aglow with their mellow light. "Hear my prayer, St. Jean," she murmured, and fixing her eyes on those of the painted saint, dropped to her knees and prayed devoutly that she might miraculously be delivered from her marriage to Guiles de Luchaire.

Chapter Four

Silks as bright and fragile as butterfly wings fluttered in the gentle breeze of the market square. Copper pots gleamed in the sunlight; at a canopied stall a fat man wearing a turban displayed leather goods and another, whose skin was as brown as a nut, spread colorful carpets on wooden frames for all to see. The trade fair with its strolling musicians, troops of acrobats, resplendent colors, and exotic sights and smells had always delighted Madeleine, but lately nothing pleased her. She followed listlessly along after her mother and sisters and their serving women. Albertine, who strolled beside her mistress, tried to lift her spirits by pointing out curious sights, but if Madeleine replied at all it was in a dull, disinterested tone.

As the entourage returned through the teeming market to the Grand Rue and the spot where the servants waited with the *charrette,* Madeleine began a conversation with her maidservant. All the day long Madeleine had been sullen and ill-tempered toward Albertine, who least deserved it, and now she attempted to make amends. "Does your little cobbler have his shop here in the market square?"

"Nay, mistress, but it is close by on the rue du Domino, and the shop has a large red and yellow wooden boot above the door."

"He is fortunate to have his own shop," Madeleine said, thinking Albertine and her cobbler would soon approach her father's steward and ask permission to marry. The thought saddened her even more.

"Oh, it is not his shop, mistress, but his elder brother's. He only wishes to have a shop of his own one day."

"Would you leave me then and marry him?" Madeleine asked, feeling suddenly shamed by the selfish sound of her words.

"Nay, mistress," Albertine said quickly, clutching her hand as if to reassure her. "I would never leave you," she promised.

Madeleine gave her a wan smile. "Dear sweet Albertine, do you believe I am so cruel I would bid you stay? Knowing that in your heart you longed to be with your little cobbler?"

Days passed and Madeleine's prayers remained unanswered. At first she was angry with herself for having foolishly placed her trust in prayers, and later mourned for the loss of her emerald ring.

Albertine was the first to notice her mistress's lack of appetite. In two short weeks she had grown thin and pale. Even her newest gowns hung from her slight frame in unbecoming folds.

Isobel de Moncelet was frantic, fearing her daughter's trousseau would no longer fit properly, and commanded the cooks to prepare tempting tarts and rich creamy puddings. Every attempt was made to coax Madeleine to eat, but she steadfastly refused and when she was threatened with having her little Spanish mare sent off to the hacker, she resorted to subterfuge and finally to poking her finger down her throat and bringing the sticky tarts and cloying puddings all back up in the most revolting fashion.

Isobel de Moncelet could do little more than wring her hands. Her rebellious daughter was thin as a broom straw and she would be held accountable when her husband returned. Looking into the mirror, it seemed to Isobel that the number of grey hairs flecking her temples had multiplied ten-fold.

Madeleine's father and brother had not yet returned when the first bann of her marriage was announced on the feast day of St. Jean. As was the custom, Guiles de Luchaire and two of his kinsmen were present in the cathedral. Madeleine suffered through an hour of his bold stares and licentious glances. She was near-panicked by the thought of his hands on her bare flesh and his mouth on hers. How, she despaired, could she be a wife to a man who offended her every sense?

After Canon Guyot had delivered the benediction, Madeleine followed her mother and sisters out into the morning drizzle. She was lost deep in thought as she stepped onto the portico. The scent of musk roused her like a sudden drenching, and she turned with a startled expression to come face to face with Guiles de Luchaire as he stood chatting with her mother and sisters. He bowed gallantly to Madeleine and took her hand, a hand she had not offered, and gazing into her eyes as if he meant to devour her, raised the cool hand to his lips. But before he could consummate the act, Madeleine twisted her fingers from his grasp and without a parting word, hurried to the waiting *charrette.*

In the ancient walled city of Troyes, life went on in peaceful prosperity. By day the market stalls bustled with tradesmen and by night the taverns were filled to overflowing. In the narrow, cluttered streets of the city women gossiped at the wells, the shouts of children filled the air, and cattle were driven daily through the streets to pastures beyond the walls.

The spring rains had given way to a delightful summer and in the nearby Château de Troyes, the wife and daughters of the Count de Moncelet had little more to concern themselves with than the pleasant task of enjoying the warm, sun-filled days.

Elenore and Margarete waited impatiently for their father's return. Each longed for a marriage contract, a handsome young husband, and a household of their own to manage. They spoke of little else, and spent long hours in the shaded cloister of the garden with their needlework gabbling over their future husbands and households.

Occasionally Madeleine entered into their conversation, but her sisters, who were much older, considered Madeleine a mere child and did not always bother to conceal their resentment of her approaching marriage to Guiles de Luchaire. He was a far better match than they could hope to obtain. He was wealthy, a favorite of the court, and his prowess on the tournament field and in the bedrooms of the Parisian court were the source of many a rumor.

"I hear he has at least three mistresses," Elenore said peevishly, snipping a thread from her needlework and choosing a darker shade from her basket.

"They say he neglected his poor wife," Margarete added for good measure. "He was in Paris when she gave birth and only returned for her funeral."

Madeleine flushed with anger and rose to defend him, or perhaps it was herself she defended. It wounded her to think her sisters would be so petty, that it pleased them to make her miserable, and only because she had been chosen over them—a situation she would have gladly reversed if only she were able.

Consequently, Madeleine spent her time with Albertine. Like most peasants, Albertine could neither read nor write but she was wise in her way, able to amuse her young mistress with her observations of life and send her into gales of laughter with her risqué tales. Despite Madeleine's unhappiness there were times when, if only for a few brief moments, she was again merry and carefree.

In July, the glorious summer sun became cruelly hot. At noon the market stalls of Troyes were deserted. Merchants retreated into their bedrooms or to taverns where wine and ale were served and there they remained for the better part of the scorching afternoon. Elenore and Margarete no longer went into the garden where the browned grass languished beneath a brassy sky and the heat penetrated even the deepest shadows of the shade trees.

Aside from the daily Mass read in the château's chapel by Father Beniot, Finistère's assistant, and an hour spent with her mother and Adelicia in which she was expected to improve her social graces and acquire a deeper understanding of household management, Madeleine's time was her own. More often than not, Madeleine found an excuse to avoid both chores. She would brave the heat and walk in the woods near the château's gardens with Albertine or watch the peasants at work in the fields. On lazy afternoons they sometimes passed the hours fishing in the mill pond, where they tossed bread left from their lunch to the geese and laughed at their antics.

Slowly, Madeleine became resigned to the futility of prayer and to her eventual fate as the Lady de Luchaire. The fact that her sisters and apparently many women at court longed to be in her place made her wonder if she had judged Guiles de Luchaire unfairly. Was he truly the lustful beast they said? In her heart, Madeleine suspected he was. But why, then, were these same women rabid with envy? It was as illogical as giving an emerald ring to a wooden saint, a folly which irritated Madeleine more each time she thought of it.

*   *   *

One sticky, breathless evening when the heat of the day lingered long past the matins bells and a little sliver of moon rose above the fields, a young squire in the service of Madeleine's father arrived bearing a letter. The Lady Isobel dismissed the boy and quickly opened the folded and sealed parchment.

"What does he say, Madame-Ma-Mère?" Madeleine asked, as she dodged behind her mother and raised herself on her tiptoes to see over her shoulder.

Elenore and Margarete quickly set aside their needlework and crowded close, plying their mother with questions until she silenced them all with a disapproving frown. Only after she had first read the letter herself did she then read it aloud. The letter began with the usual salutations followed by her father's announced intentions to arrive within the week. He predicted Elenore and Margarete would be especially pleased with the news he brought, and he asked after his 'dear little one', Madeleine. He promised gifts for all and went on to say Philippe had ridden in a tournament at court and won his spurs. He also intimated that while in Provins, Philippe had become enamored of their host's daughter, and since that day hardly an hour elapsed without his mentioning her name.

News of the master's return threw the entire household into a fit of chaotic activity. The hall and solars were swept and the heavy eastern rugs, which added color and warmth to the stone floors in many rooms, were laboriously carried into the kitchen garth by several household varlets and beaten with poles. The resulting fog of dust drifted into the kitchen and a noisy imbroglio erupted between the screeching cook and the young rug beaters. Elenore and Margarete harried their maids, calling for one gown then another to be lifted from their trunks, shaken out, and inspected for moth holes and broken seams.

The frenetic bustle of activity left Madeleine feeling weary and a little sad. Although she would be pleased to see her father and brother safely home, each passing day brought her nearer to the morning she must marry Guiles de Luchaire. Twice she had managed to slip away and ride Minet, but the cherished hours quickly passed and once again she was confronted with decisions over her trousseau and the harsh realities of her approaching marriage.

On the feast day of St. Paul, a pale metallic sun wandered through the morning mist and the dusty road before the château wavered flat and white in the glare. As the bells of Troyes sounded tierce, a kitchen maid drawing water from the well house saw a monk in tattered robes enter the garth. He was thin as a lathe and his gaunt features were etched with dirt. He asked the maid for water and if he might have a scrap of food.

She set her pail before him and from the kitchen brought a fresh baked loaf of barley bread. The monk thanked her with a snagged smile and, squatting barefooted in the dust, bolted down the bread like a starving dog. The kitchen maid feared he would choke, for watching him devour the bread felt near to choking herself and hastened to offer him the pail of water, entreating him, "Drink."

He gave her a queer smile and took a sip as if to please her, then asked, "Whose lands are these?"

"The Lord de Moncelet's," she said, and afterward felt she had done wrong to say. The familiar scents of the kitchen hung in the garth, but all else seemed strange; the heat, the hazy sunlight, and the monk's glinting bead-black eyes.

He consumed the last scrap of bread, cramming it into his mouth with his fingers. The gaping, toothless mouth appeared bright and pink as sass for

43

his layer of dirt, and when he had stuffed the last crumb into his lips, he licked his fingers and said, "God's mercy upon his soul and those of his house, for the plague that slew Avignon is at my heels. King Death is coming, gathering souls as a reaper gathers sheaves. These eyes have seen his face, and I have felt his hot breath on my neck." He ranted on, a tale so hideous that the frail wisp of a woman threw her hands over her ears and fled screaming into the kitchen. When at last some reason was coaxed from the trembling maid, several male servants went to question the monk but found no sign of him, not in the garth, nor on the road beyond.

The Lord de Moncelet's joyous return was marked by feasting and merriment, and the pall of dread cast by the raving monk's words was all but forgotten.

Elenore and Margarete learned the names of their future husbands and something of the households they would manage. There were amusing incidents to share and gossip brought from the king's court in Paris and the estates. The greatest surprise was Philippe's announcement that he had chosen a bride, and all that remained to be completed were the negotiations concerning the dowry.

Madeleine was pleased for her brother's sake. He was obviously in love. The change in him was remarkable and though Madeleine attempted to conceal her amusement, she could not. He had gone away a boy and returned a man; everything about him was different. Madeleine plied her brother with questions about his future wife, so much that he became quite exasperated.

Étienne de Moncelet had brought gifts for his wife and daughters, but for his youngest daughter, Madeleine, he had brought something very special: a small chest of finely carved camphor wood set with inlays of gold and ivory. The chest, in itself, was a fine gift and Madeleine graciously thanked her father. "You have not yet opened it," he told her, his dark eyes fairly brimming with anticipation.

Madeleine smoothed her fingers over the delicate carvings, then gently lifted the lid of the fragrant wooden chest. What she saw dazzled her eyes and rounded her rouged lips to form the word, "Oh!" The glimmer of gold and glitter of jewels all but took away her breath. Madeleine examined each piece of jewelry, finding one more beautiful than the other; chains of braided gold, jeweled brooches, rings, and dainty bracelets set with pearls and carnelians.

Madeleine stammered out her gratitude, hardly able to find words fine enough for such a gift. "Had I given you gold coin," her father explained, "your husband could rightfully lay claim to the sum, but these are yours, my daughter, to wear or use as you deem fit. My heart is easier now, knowing that you are provided for and well pleased."

The harvest which was about to begin promised to be bountiful, far superior to the lean ones of the past few years. There would be food aplenty for man and beast alike on the estates held by Étienne de Moncelet.

There was little to trouble the Count of Troyes that summer of his forty-eighth year. His accounts stood settled. His quarrel with the old king was behind him, his estates prospered, the trade fair grew richer with every season, and soon his children would all be safely married. The future seemed fair indeed.

But hardly had the dust from his goods wagons settled when a squire rode into the château's bailey. He was no more than a boy and came to the solar stiff-legged and limping from long hours in the saddle. He had ridden from Bardane, the lands held under the stewardship of Jean Suchet, without food, water, or rest to deliver his lord's message. Although the boy's features were caked with dust and his lank brown hair hung in cords, no amount of grime could conceal the grim set of his mouth nor the agitated tone of his voice.

De Moncelet quickly unfolded the letter and read Suchet's rambling account of finding the corpse of a missing shepherd and his flock of several hundred sheep rotting in the summer's heat. The estate's miller and his family had also died and there was ugly talk of witchcraft among the peasants; many had fled.

Étienne de Moncelet called Roger Sara from his duties in Troyes, where he and his troops kept order, and later that afternoon de Moncelet, Roger Sara, the young squire, and two dozen soldiers rode off toward Bardane.

Philippe watched until they were out of sight. Earlier he had pleaded with his father to allow him to ride along, arguing that their combined presence would calm the peasants' fears. But Étienne, fearing for the safety of his only son, forbade it.

Philippe insisted, pointing out that the land surrounding Bardane was marshy and known for fevers, but his father refused to listen. "You treat me as if I were a child," Philippe angrily accused, striding after his father.

"Do you challenge my authority?" Étienne demanded.

"No, Father, it is your wisdom I challenge. These lands will one day pass into my hands and it is vital that the peasants accept me and learn to place their trust in my judgment."

Étienne thrust his hands into his riding gloves. "All that is true enough," he agreed, "but this day your place is here with your mother and sisters. I do not know what lawlessness I shall find in Bardane."

Philippe made an impatient grimace. "It is naught but marsh fever and the work of simple minds. Your steward said as much in his letter." Philippe hastened to keep abreast of his father.

"It was not marsh fever which blackened the flesh of the shepherd and the miller's family."

"Witchcraft, then," Philippe said with a touch of sarcasm. But before he could speak again, his father turned on him with a stormy look. "I have made my wishes known and you will abide by them." And with those words, he mounted his horse and cantered across the courtyard where the soldiers awaited him.

Late in the day when the lengthening rays of the sun cast enormous shadows, Madeleine walked among the rows of carrot fern and spiky blue-green onions. All her thoughts were directed toward a single aim: choosing the largest and sweetest carrot. Up and down the rows she paced until she chose what was surely the most succulent carrot in the patch. How wonderfully earthy it smelled; grit clung to its bright cylindrical form, and the fern, crushed by her grip, emitted a spicy, fennel-like fragrance. In the stable, she spoke to the old stableman, Onfroi, as she fed the carrot to her dappled mare. Together she and Onfroi talked and watched the half-grown kittens tumble in the straw.

Onfroi was fond of talking. Often he knew more gossip than the kitchen women. He told his mistress of the young squire's coming and of the lord's hurried departure. Madeleine was surprised. She knew nothing of her father's leaving. "Some trouble in Bardane," the old man replied, adding, "The young squire said sheep were killed and spoke of witchcraft." But when Madeleine directed more pointed questions toward the old man, he shook his grey head. "No one tells me anything, mistress. I only know what I hear." Onfroi returned to laying fresh litter in the stalls, and several times Madeleine heard him humming to himself as he shuffled about the stable.

Madeleine remained in Minet's stall, stroking the little mare's neck and scratching her ears. It was nothing, she thought, and was certain she would hear the whole story that evening in the hall.

It was twilight when Madeleine walked from the stable. In the half light she noticed her brother by the stream below the stable, aimlessly pitching stones into the water. The vesper bells were ringing as she went and stood beside him. He was cross with her and complained bitterly over his father's reluctance to share any responsibilities with him. Madeleine was sympathetic, but when he told her the particulars of the incident, she took her father's part against him. "He fears for your safety," she told her brother in a gently scolding voice. Philippe gave his sister a sour look and mumbled something she could not quite make out, then stalked away.

Madeleine did not understand her brother any longer. Once, she and Philippe had shared their greatest secrets. They would play together and talk for hours. Then suddenly Philippe had grown taller, his voice deeper, and afterwards considered her a silly fool. Indeed, lately he considered everyone but himself to be a silly fool.

In the morning, Philippe behaved obnoxiously toward everyone and later amused himself by running his hounds. He returned with the dogs bounding before his horse and the battered remains of a fox slung across his saddle bow. In the courtyard the tawny-colored hounds milled around his horse's legs, barking noisily. Madeleine came out and stood on the château's steps and frowned into the sunlight.

Philippe, whose face was full flushed from the heat of the day and the excitement of the chase, turned his horse and, raising a gloved hand, saluted his sister. "I've bested Reynard," he called with a laugh.

Madeleine thought it cruel and told her brother as much, but he only laughed and reminded her, "'Tis one less to rob your precious geese."

Madeleine knew it was true. The foxes robbed the nests and carried off the goslings. She did not say another word. She pressed her lips together exactly as her father did when something displeased him and went inside.

On the morrow, the couturière, whose fat powdered face reminded Madeleine of a sugared pastry, arrived with her seamstresses to measure and fit Elenore and Margarete for their trousseaus.

Madeleine met her unexpectedly as she entered the solar and greeted her politely. The woman reeked of perfume, a heady rose scent with spicy undertones identical to the fragrance Madeleine had recently purchased to perfume her trousseau. The scent was spoiled for her now. Whenever she wore it she would be reminded of the dough-faced couturière.

With so many women underfoot, Philippe rode off toward Troyes and did not return until the following day. Madeleine did not bother to ask where he had been, but their mother did, and Philippe artfully lied. All during the evening meal Philippe acted strangely disturbed. Madeleine knew it was not the lie he had told his mother, for he did that regularly. When she saw him alone she asked what was troubling him, but he would not answer her directly and walked away.

Madeleine chose not to spend the evening in the solar with her mother and sisters. She was bored with her sisters' endless chatter of trousseaus, households, and of children not yet conceived. She preferred sitting in her chamber, where at least it was quiet and she and Albertine could discuss their own interests. They played several games of draughts. It was late when they extinguished their candles and went to bed.

Madeleine was the last to visit the garderobe at the end of the darkened passageway. Of the many rooms

49

in that wing of the château, Elenore and Margarete's large room was opposite Madeleine's, and Philippe's the last before the steep, curving staircase. No light showed beneath the doors and all was silent.

A commotion outside their door roused Madeleine and Albertine. They groped for their clothing, colliding in the pitch blackness. In only a matter of moments they donned what garments they could locate and dashed to the door. The passageway was empty, but as they neared the stairs, the sounds of voices and cries echoed from the hall below.

Madeleine raced down the steep stairs at a breakneck pace, arms outstretched and hands braced against the walls to keep from falling. The darkened hall was filled with servants and soldiers and a confusion of voices.

At the foot of the stairs, Elenore and Margarete brushed past Madeleine with stricken faces. For an instant, Madeleine saw Philippe by the doors. His face in the flickering candlelight appeared mask-like and white as his shirt. At first she did not see her mother, but as the crowd parted before the doors, she caught a glimpse of her. A young squire carrying a lamp followed close on her heels, and in the unsteady lamplight Madeleine saw her father carried into the hall, supported on either side by a soldier. With each retching breath, a drool of frothy blood bubbled from her father's blackened lips and the breast of his jupon and the shirt beneath were soaked with blood.

Madeleine gasped as if all the air had suddenly gone from her lungs and with a mute cry ran sobbing after her father, attempting to grasp his hand as the soldiers carried him through the hall and into the solar.

At the door to her parents' chamber, her mother blocked the way, refusing to allow her in. Madeleine pleaded and begged to see her father, but to no avail. For hours she waited bravely by the door, hoping against hope. Adelicia came and went, and later the physician came again. At dawn when Canon Guyot, who had been summoned from Troyes, entered the room to administer the last rites, Madeleine knew there was no hope. She sat down on the floor before her parents' chamber and sobbed.

"Plague!" The word fluttered from the lips of the count's own physician. *Plague*. It was a word as ugly as a bat, and like a creature dazzled by the light, winged a haphazard path through the château spreading terror among servant and soldier alike.

Even as the family gathered in the chapel to pray for the soul of Étienne de Moncelet, their servants began to slip away, and before word of Roger Sara's death reached the ears of the new lord and heir, his men at arms deserted by twos and threes, melting into the pre-dawn darkness.

Canon Guyot advised against a Funeral Mass sung at St. Pierre's, but Isobel de Moncelet, normally a placid woman, made a frightful scene. Even her late husband's physician could not dissuade her. "I beg you, milady, do not enter Troyes for it is the kingdom of death."

Canon Guyot, wringing his thin hands, pleaded, "The death bell rings morning, noon, and night, milady. Think to the lives of your family." Such pleas fell on deaf ears; Isobel de Moncelet would have no less than her husband's due.

The humid night gave way to an oppressively hot morning. In the courtyard a *charrette* was draped with black cloth and made ready to bear the body of the Count of Troyes on its final journey.

A finely polished coffin was brought from Troyes. The few remaining household servants congregated in the hall to watch the coffin be carried into the château. Madeleine viewed the scene with red-rimmed eyes. She had not been permitted to go to her father's side as he lay dying, and now her grief was ten-fold.

Moments later, a startled chorus of cries escaped the lips of the onlookers as the man supporting the foot of the coffin collapsed and the lacquered box slid backwards, striking the stones of the hall with a resounding clatter. A man from among the household servants took the fallen man's place and the coffin was slowly maneuvered through the solar.

Étienne de Moncelet's blackened body was wrapped in a length of finest linen and laid in his coffin. Elenore and Margarete stood by morosely, clutching hands. They grieved for themselves and the husbands they had lost. Their marriages would be delayed, perhaps forever, by the plague and the cruel hand of fate. Madeleine clung to the door frame of her parents' chamber, watching with glazed eyes, unable to reconcile herself to her father's death. Philippe sat beneath the windows of the solar, staring at the floor.

After seeing her husband closed in his coffin, Isobel de Moncelet, not knowing where else to turn, sought solace in the château's chapel. Her serving woman, Adelicia, accompanied her and, after a time, Madeleine followed.

Even in the heat of the day it was cold in the dreary little chapel and Madeleine, mindlessly reciting her prayers, lost all sense of time. The tolling bells jarred her from her trance. She looked up to see Elenore and Margarete enter the chapel and, a moment later, Philippe.

After making his obeisance, Philippe came to the altar and, raising his hand to trace the sign of the cross upon his forehead, collapsed against the altar rail. At first it was thought the heat of the day, his grief, and too little sleep had felled him, but it was something much more sinister.

He was carried to the château, and for the next

52

three days Isobel de Moncelet refused to leave her son's side. Madeleine was again shut from the room but kept a vigil just beyond her brother's door, praying aloud until her voice failed her and sleep stilled her lips.

The body of Étienne de Moncelet was temporarily interred in the crypt beneath the château's chapel, and all prayed to God Most Holy that his only son would not soon join him.

Before dawn of the fourth day, Philippe died. Not an hour later, Adelicia discovered Elenore and Margarete ill with a high fever. Madeleine's mother and Adelicia shut her from the room just as they had with her father and Philippe and so she prayed with old Finistère, her father's clerk-priest. Late the second night her sisters died within moments of each other. As Elenore and Margarete lay dying, the count's physician also fell ill. He spoke with rambling words of seeking a cure in Paris and fled north with his servants. Madeleine saw him carried from the château. He appeared already dead.

Adelicia took ill soon afterwards and Isobel de Moncelet untiringly nursed her dear lady-in-waiting. Adelicia, who was in truth a less fortunate relative of the Lady de Moncelet, had come to the château as a young woman for training. Because she was ungainly and without a dowry she had remained unmarried, content to live in the shadow of her kinswoman, share her joys, her family, and her great house. The fever consumed Adelicia's frail body as greedily as flames devour parchment.

Isobel de Moncelet and old Finistère took ill a day later. No one remained to forbid Madeleine to nurse her mother and the old clerk. She and Albertine labored for days without sleep, but in vain.

As Finistère breathed his last, the cook wailed that there would be no one to administer the last rites to the Lady Isobel. In a rage, Madeleine brought the flat of her hand across the fat woman's face, silencing her. "My mother will live," Madeleine screeched, "and she will have no need of a priest!" But that evening as the first stars appeared, the Countess de Moncelet slipped from life. It seemed to Albertine that Madeleine, as well, no longer belonged to the world of the living.

With her own hands, Madeleine helped to inter her family's bodies in the crypt beneath the chapel's altar. There were few to help. The only remaining servants were Albertine, the fat cook, and Onfroi, the old stableman. Together they said the prayers, but when it was done, Madeleine refused to leave the chapel. Albertine attempted to reason with her mistress, and wheedled and bullied her but to no avail. She would not leave her vigil before the altar. In the end Albertine had no choice but to remain at her young mistress's side.

Madeleine prayed night and day, refusing to eat and seldom allowing herself to be coaxed into taking a sip of water. Crazed by grief and exhaustion, her monstrous guilt became too great a burden to bear. She twisted her thoughts until she believed that her impure prayers, tainted by her wicked pride and selfishness, had delivered her from Guiles de Luchair, but at the cost of all those she held dear.

Chapter Five

In Reims, black flags fluttered from the steeples of the bishop's cathedral to serve as warning to travelers that the plague had come.

Heribert, Bishop of Champagne, watched from the tower of his residence as every day bodies of the dead were borne to the cathedral. Daily the numbers increased. Morning, evening, and night the passing bells tolled until the whole population of Reims was filled with terror.

Death took priests and laity alike, men and women, young and old. As in other places the mortality became so great it was impossible to bury the dead.

Heribert prudently refused to set foot out of his residence. Neither were his college of novices, which numbered well over a hundred souls, nor his clerics permitted to venture forth, but rather shut themselves off from the world and prayed daily for the deliverance of their city and the souls of the departed.

For the moment, King Death held sway in France, but Heribert knew very well that all in this world was but temporary, and when he was not at prayer, he poured over his accounts. Death meant no end to taxes and dues, and Heribert directed his clerics to apply the tally of deaths per day in Reims to what he may expect on his estates, taking into consideration his physician's belief that rural areas would not be so hard-stricken. Without a doubt, Heribert's coffers would suffer, but forewarned, he would be armed with the knowledge of what must be done long before others had recovered from the blow.

As the day faded into a dusty haze, the light from the massive arched windows of the bishop's office grew deceptively dim. Heribert whose shoulders were hunched over the leather-bound accounts of Charmy and the lands to the southwest, came upon a line he could not quite decipher. "What is this, Dubic?" he questioned in a sharp tone.

The senior cleric, a heavy choleric man with frost-white hair, hastened to the bishop's side and straining his weary eyes for enlightenment saw his own hand had made the entry. "The lands ceded to Cardinal Gaspard, Your Grace."

Heribert made only a curt one-word reply, more of a growl. "Gaspard." The mere mention of the man's name grated upon his sensibilities like a steel blade drawn across a stone. For some years a grievous animosity had existed between the then Bishop of Clemancy, Aucussin Gaspard, the son of a minor Burgundian noble, and Heribert de Moncelet, Bishop of Champagne and second son of Thierry de Moncelet, Count of Troyes. At its crux was a territorial dispute over the villages and lands of Viezon. Both had laid claim to the rich farmlands, and in years past had fought many skirmishes and one pitched battle, all indecisive, to determine to whom the vassals of Viezon would pay taxes, dues, and fines.

However, it was the coveted seat of cardinal which truly set one tooth and nail against the other. Gaspard, because of his favor in Avignon and his ties to the Norman lords, had emerged victorious on both accounts while Heribert, who was left to sulk in Reims, waited patiently as a spider to exact his revenge. In a France divided by war and political foment, where rumors circulated that the aging Philip of France, whose two sons had little support among the nobels and clergy, had been approached by the papacy to accept the English King Edward as his heir and thus insure peace, Heribert reasoned he had not long to wait. For even if Philip were foolish enough to accept Edward as heir, France's powerful nobles would never bow to an English king despite his Capetian ancestry. Even Philip's eldest son's right to the throne was contested, for among the powerful nobles there were already several claimants who would wrest the throne from John.

The disastrous war had compounded France's ills. Quite simply, it was Edward the English King's claim to the French throne, through his Capetian ancestors, and English claims on French territory which had begun the war. The resounding French defeat several years before and the fall of Calais had done little to settle the dispute. Indeed, it had left France even more dangerously divided. A truce had been negotiated, but Heribert knew with a certainty that so long as the English laid claim to French soil and the throne of France was contested there would be strife.

A cleric, weary from long hours in the saddle, arrived in Reims late one hazy July evening as the vesper bells sounded. The cleric, a pale young man with a receding chin, presented a letter to the bishop. Written in the wavering hand of Canon Guyot, the letter extended the canon's heartfelt condolences to His Grace on the deaths of his beloved brother, Étienne de Moncelet, his dear sister in marriage, and his loving nieces and nephew. In an unsteady hand the canon had written:

> God for the sins of men has levied a terrible punishment upon the world. Such is the cruelty

of heaven that the saintly and faithful who serve God with humility have also been carried off by the hand of death. May your dear brother and his family rest in peace with Christ as we piously believe.

Heribert stooped slightly, angling the parchment so that the light from the candles fell upon the script. A feeling such as he had never known before, one of wild exhilaration, surged through his veins. Only his long years of discipline enabled him to hold in check his exultant joy. With his brother's vast estates added to his own, he would become the wealthiest and most powerful bishop in all of France. Avignon would come pleading to him for favors and the King of France would remain on his throne only so long as he had the blessing of the Bishop of Champagne.

In his haste to claim his inheritance, Heribert gave no thought to the awful toll death had levied upon Reims. He concerned himself only with his beloved novices who labored for the glory of God and Holy Mother Church. Neither did he trouble his thoughts over his men at arms, other than to know he had a certain number of soldiers. When their numbers were depleted, he merely purchased others. After all, soldiers were meant for killing and dying. Within the year he had replenished his dwindling forces by purchasing a troop of one hundred and fifty men at arms from the estate of a Lombard nobleman. A soldier could be bought for the price of a mediocre horse. All told it was a modest sum and of little consequence to a man as wealthy as the Bishop of Champagne.

It was Heribert's trusted cleric, Dubuc, who informed him that his mercenaries numbered only one hundred and twenty.

"That is not possible," Heribert scowled. "I have paid and paid dearly for one hundred and fifty. What has become of them?"

"They have perished, Your Grace."

"No," Heribert's voice rose sharply. "I do not believe it."

Dubuc was insistent. "It is God's truth, Your Grace. They have died of the sickness." His voice was as strident as that of a nagging woman. "And I have no assurance that on the morrow their numbers will not be fewer still." Dubuc went on to say he considered it ill advised to face the dangers of travel with such a paltry force. He himself could not have been lured from the sanctuary of the bishop's residence by the promise of a seat in heaven.

Heribert waved aside Dubuc's trepidations. No, he was not to be denied. His time had come and neither pestilence nor death must delay him. *"Carpe diem,"* he reminded his cleric. "For the day comes but once."

It was a dying city Heribert, Bishop of Champagne, abandoned in the tumultuous wake of his horsemen and goods wagons. The route he had chosen circumvented much of the city. Even so, the grim face of pestilence lay in wait at every turn. So heavy was the stench of death that it lay upon a man's tongue like a foul taste. Time and again they encountered the *gavotti*, peasants of the basest class, who cared not for heaven or hell and who, for a silver coin or more often whatever they could steal, collected the dead from doorways and garrets. They pushed carts laden with corpses through the streets, bellowing, "Drag out your dead!", and only grudgingly did they give way to the holy procession.

The bishop and his retinue journeyed ever southward. Day after day they came upon deserted villages where those who had not perished had fled, leaving behind all their worldly goods. Doors stood open and cattle wandered aimlessly through garden plots, eating their fill.

At the Abbey of Bon Enfants, where sixty-two

Dominican brethren had dwelled, only a single monk survived. And he, so long in the company of death, came timidly out into the blazing sunlight, blinking and babbling like one seized with lunacy. "Holiness," he wailed, "I do not know how to tell of the cruelty and pitiless sights I have witnessed." Tears streamed down his heavily jowled face and his eyes appeared fixed in their sockets. He could hardly speak for sobbing and he told how he had buried the last of his brethren and now awaited the end of the world.

Before continuing on his journey, Heribert blessed the graves of the brethren and offered up a Mass for their souls. These simple acts of faith seemed to comfort the grieving monk and allay his fears of doomsday.

With the Abbey of Bon Enfants behind them, the countryside became one of gently rolling hills and deep thickets, perfect cover for thieves and all manner of lawless men. Fearful of what the roadside thickets might conceal, Heribert sent for the captain of his guard. "Send a small force of men before us," he commanded, "to guard against an ambush."

It was done. Half a dozen soldiers set out before the procession to scour either side of the roadway. Among them were a Saxon and a Moor. The Saxon was a tall youth with a thatch of barley-colored hair. He was called Wulf and in his twenty-three years he had seen much of death and dying. He and the Moor moved away from the main body of the procession at a trot, reining their horses into the undergrowth that verged upon the rutted roadway. The Saxon chose the left, the Moor the right.

Ahead, the land fell away abruptly, down into a deep shadowy glade. From the tail of his vision, the Moor caught a glimpse of the barley-colored hair and bay horse as the Saxon vanished into the thicket.

Entering the cool wood, Wulf ducked to avoid the limb of a low-branching tree. A sudden chill stood the hair of his neck on end and his every sense strained at his surroundings. Flashes of green, light, and shadow jerked past his eyes as the bay crashed through the close set young trees. The horse made an appalling amount of noise and he knew only too well that if anyone lay in wait they would have had ample warning of his approach.

Deeper into the thicket the ground became marshy and the sweet moistness enveloped him. He heard the buzzing of insects and his nostrils caught the keen musk of earth and leaves and something else. A faint pungent odor, at once unrecognizable yet strangely familiar. As he raised his arm to shield his face from yet another clump of leaves, he heard the Moor call out, "All's well," and he replied in turn, "All's well."

Where the trees thinned, a lush carpet of lichens covered the earth. In places, water stood on the spongy ground, sucking at the bay's hooves and forcing the animal to alter its gait.

The odor grew more pungent with every stride—stinking, sick, and sweet. He came upon it suddenly and, believing it to be a fallen tree, broken and furry with mold, rotting into sweet decay upon the marshy earth, gave his horse its head and let it choose the path over the swampy ground. In another stride he was upon it.

What he saw was not a broken tree but a pair of putrefying corpses, and the thick velvet-like fur, not mold, but a swarm of flies that rose up like a cloud to attack him. He flailed his arms at the biting, buzzing swarm and set his heels into the bay's ribs. With a snort the panicked animal flattened its ears and lunged forward, taking him into a grove of young oaks where branches lashed at his face and arms, nearly unseating him. The horse blundered on a short distance, bolting up a rise before Wulf could check its headlong flight.

He sawed at the reins, pivoting the animal in a tight circle. The bay lurched to a halt, tossing its head and snorting. He laid a steadying hand on the horse's quivering neck and turned his stinging face toward the corpses. He saw them now, saw them for what they were. Two men, most likely peasants, brothers perhaps or friends, who had fled the sickness only to fall ill and die in the cool shade of the trees. There were worse places to die, he thought, and blotting his bloodied lip with the back of his hand, heard the Moor call out, "All's well." Wulf turned the bay, urging it forward with his heels, and replied, "All's well."

Chapter Six

The days stretched into weeks and, as if it were the pronounced judgment of some evil god, a drought descended upon Champagne. For days the sun baked down from a copper-colored sky. Not a breath of air stirred the stifling heat or rustled the withered leaves. Heribert, Bishop of Champagne, his heavily laden goods wagons, and his horsemen plodded southward. The hooves of their weary horses drove a choking fog of dust into the still air, clouding their vision and swirling over them like a curse.

Death was everywhere, lurking in the heat of the midday sun, in the twilight haze of evening, and in the dark of night. Madeleine's life became an endless string of anguished days and nights filled with grief and hellish guilt. Had her unpure prayers brought down perdition upon the heads of those she loved?

Night and day she prayed in the chapel, ignoring Albertine's pleas to eat, to drink. "It was my prayers that brought the sickness," Madeleine wailed. "A punishment for my selfishness and wicked pride. Oh, Albertine, I wish to God I had not been so evil."

"Nay, mistress," Albertine argued, repeating the words of the lord's physician. "He said it came from the east, mayhap carried on the winds. You see, it was not your prayers at all."

But Madeleine would not be consoled, neither would she leave the chapel, where the stone walls sweated and the still air was ripe with the stench of mold and the noisome decay rising from the crypt below.

The sound of a horse's hooves on the cobbled stones of the courtyard and shouts of, "Hullo! Hullo!" roused Albertine from a fitful sleep. At a glance, she saw her mistress slumped against the altar rail, fast asleep. She did not wake her, but crept to the door. Unaccustomed to the light of day, Albertine squinted into the glare. Through the haze, she saw a villein astride a leggy, roan-colored horse.

The villein, sighting her, another living soul, cantered toward the chapel door, calling, "Who among the house of de Moncelet lives?"

"My mistress lives," Albertine called back. "Who has sent you?"

"My Lord de Luchaire to bring word to his betrothed, Madeleine, a daughter of the house."

Albertine winced as if she had been struck a blow. Saints had perished, she thought angrily, but Guiles de Luchaire lived.

"Go away," she shouted, and throwing her full weight against the chapel door slammed it shut.

The sound of the door jolted Madeleine into awareness. She stumbled to her feet, dazed with sleep. "Who asks for me?"

"Guiles de Luchaire," Albertine replied, reluctant to say his name.

"He is dead," Madeleine insisted. Had she not bought his death with the lives of all she loved, her wicked prayers and emerald ring? "He is dead," she repeated.

"Nay, mistress, it is his villein who asks after you."

Madeleine threw off Albertine's protective arms and tore from the chapel like one possessed. "Wait!" she shouted after the retreating horseman. "Who has

64

sent you?"

The villein wheeled his horse round. "My Lord de Luchaire," his voice came back. He judged the young woman on the chapel steps to be the lady Madeleine. She was dark-headed and sunlight flashed from the rings on her hands and her clothing, though filthy, was that of a noble.

"Guiles de Luchaire?" she called.

"Yes, milady," the villein reported, trotting the roan back across the courtyard.

"You have seen him?" Madeleine shouted, incredulous.

"Yes, milady, this very day."

"No!" she screeched. It could not be true, it could not be.

Though he found her strangeness confusing, the villein said, "Do not despair, milady. My Lord de Luchaire will come to your side with all haste."

"No!" Madeleine howled, charging down the chapel steps like an enraged animal. "Tell him he is not welcome here. Tell him I will see him in hell!" Her furious eyes searched the ground before her feet. In an instant, she dropped to her haunches, clutching and grasping loose stones to hurl at him.

Rocks sailed through the air, bouncing onto the cobbled courtyard. The villein raised his arm before him, ducking the barrage, but the horse beneath him shied and lunged sideways. He clawed wildly at the reins and, turning the animal, galloped from the courtyard, shouting over his shoulder that she was a madwoman and other words she did not hear.

Her whole being shook with fury. She was deaf and dumb to everything but the frenzied release of lobbing stones after the retreating horseman. She crouched there in the dust, sobbing out her rage and flinging stones until he was out of sight.

As evening closed, the walled city of Troyes was

sighted by the bishop's guards. Heribert disliked riding at night, but with his goal so close at hand pressed onward.

A full moon climbed serenely through a mottled sky as the procession entered the city. In the quicksilver moonlight, shadows fled among the darkened houses and down the narrow, airless streets. No human sound broke the unearthly silence. Only the gritty dust stirred by their passage and the stench of death rose up to greet them.

In the Ruelle des Chats, the dead still lay in open doorways. They saw their grotesque forms even in the blackness of the street, where the corbelled upper stories of the houses loomed irregularly and in places blotted out the sky.

Even on the Grand Rue corpses of the dead were to be found, and the buildings set one against another gave a sense of closing in upon the street.

Dubuc, who rode beside his bishop, raised his eyes to heaven and crossed himself, declaring in an awed voice, "It is the city of the dead."

The young priest, de Grailly, riding to his bishop's left, turned in his saddle and fixed his white-rimmed eyes upon the elderly cleric. "Surely, not all have perished?" he asked, looking then to his bishop for confirmation.

Heribert de Moncelet looked neither left nor right, for though he would be loath to admit it, he too had fallen under the eerie spell of the vacant blackness and flittering moonlight. In his stoutest voice, Heribert ordered that a holy chant be raised by his retinue "so that all Troyes may know of my coming, be they living or dead." And with a motion of his gloved hand, he hastened de Grailly to carry his order.

One by one the bishop's novices, clerics, and troops raised their voices in a Latin chant and like a magic charm the surging sound drew the populace from the darkness. Candles flickered in the night and those who had lived so long with the fear of death rejoiced, mobbing the streets to view the glorious sight. Some cried out, "Alleluia!" while others wept with joy, for the emissary of Christ on earth had come to drive the evil pestilence from their midst.

Before the doors of the Cathedral of St. Pierre, Heribert blessed the faithful who had flocked after his procession. He wasted no time in installing his priests in the deserted cathedral, and at the empty provost's hall, he set his soldiers in command.

Troyes was his; there remained only to claim his brother's château. As the first light of dawn streaked the eastern sky, Heribert rode out from Troyes, secure amid his beloved novices, clerics, and a troop of fifty of his mercenary soldiers.

Only the fat cook moved about the kitchen of the château. After she had shooed the cats from the bins, she stirred several handfuls of barley into a pot of bubbling water. She ran a ladle through the mixture several times; woolly clots of steam rose from the pot. She yawned sleepily, then went to fetch a honeycomb from the larder. As she returned with the sticky comb, she saw Onfroi hobbling on his stiff leg through the kitchen garth. She had never seen the old stableman move so quickly; the curious sight stopped her in her tracks.

In the solar, Madeleine labored over her mother's huge embroidery frame. The news of Guiles de Luchaire's survival had enabled Albertine to lure her from the chapel. But no sooner had she returned to the château, than Madeleine became obsessed with completing her mother's unfinished tapestry and worked over it without rest.

Albertine worked beside her mistress. She was not fond of working embroidery, but did so in a spirit of thanksgiving, so grateful for her mistress's renewed interest in life that she would have gladly taken on any chore.

The cook's shrill voice reached the solar long before Onfroi. The old man stumped beneath the door arch, shouting, "Milady, there are horsemen on the road before the château! So many, I could not count them." The fat cook, red-faced and breathless with exertion, waddled after him. "I can make no sense of what he says," she carped.

A sudden look passed between Madeleine and Albertine. Both minds shared a single thought: Guiles de Luchaire had come to take possession of the château. Albertine sprang from her seat and ran into the hall. Hoisting herself into the embrasure of the window, she peered through the wavy glass. Madeleine followed at her heels, straining to see. "Is it he?" she questioned. A bitter mingling of anger and fear welled up in her chest and threatened to smother her. "Tell me," she cried, "is it he?"

"Soothly, I cannot tell, mistress." Albertine had seen only soldiers, proof enough for her. "They mean you harm, I am certain of it," she said, taking her mistress's arm and entreating her to hide herself in the woods while there was still time. But Madeleine pulled herself up into the window to see.

The cook, who was too fat for such a feat, waddled to the doors and opened them. Her jaw dropped and, with a gasp, she drew back and solemnly made the sign of the cross upon her broad bosom. "It is a holy procession," she exclaimed, "led by a bishop of Christ."

The old stableman crowded in beside her to see and, with a snaggled smile, turned and said, "God has heard our prayers, milady. All will be made right."

Albertine grabbed Madeleine's arm and pulled her from the embrasure. In such times she trusted not in any man, be he bishop or brigand. "Nay, mistress," she cried, "Come while there is yet time to hide."

Madeleine shook her head, wrenching her arm from Albertine's sweaty grasp. "If it is truly a bishop," she said, "he is my father's brother. Oh, Albertine," she said and laughed. "Do you not see? We are safe now!"

Though Albertine pleaded and tried to hold her mistress back, Madeleine, whose senses were too dulled by grief and exhaustion to know fear, slipped from her hands and hurried into the dusty courtyard to greet the riders.

The air of the courtyard was thick with the overpowering odor of sweat, horses, and leather. The milling horsemen jammed the courtyard, rough-bumping and jostling, and raising a haze of dust.

Heedless of the danger, Madeleine set her gaze upon the jewel-encrusted mitre bobbing above the crush of riders and walked towards it. Time and again, horses slid before her, tossing and side-stepping from her path. A coarse tail raked across her face and harsh male shouts assailed her ears. Powerful flanks and dashing hooves blurred before her eyes until the colors of the horses melded together in a great writhing mass, parting and closing before her. Still, the mitred hat floated above the moving sea of horsemen, appearing disembodied like an object in a dream and just beyond her reach.

At first she did not realize what had happened, only that the very breath of life had been knocked from her. She rose above the bitter-tasting dust in a dizzy faint, a walker on air. Strong arms held her fast and a male voice commanded, "Raise your legs, pretty lamb." The dialect he spoke was neither *langue d' o-ïl*, nor Saxon or even Lombard, but a coarse mingling. Yet she understood, instinctively, when he boldly grabbed her leg beneath her skirts and swung her astride the curvetting horse.

He pulled her hard against him and, laughing into her ear, said, "You do that well. It would break my heart to see you trampled." The rough stubble of his jaw scourged her face and when she twisted to swat at him, he kissed her. It was no more than a graze, for foolishness, the way young men do. His lips brushed past hers and he laughed.

He seemed to have more hands than normal men, and as quickly as she wrestled one away, another clasped her in some other private place. Madeleine's face burned with outrage and her bright, scolding voice soon made them the object of the surrounding horsemen's crude jests and riotous laughter.

The noisy alcercation brought a square block of a man, astride a dark horse, a captain of the guards by his mail jerkin, from the ranks of the horsemen. "Christ's blood," the captain swore loudly. "What foolishness is this?"

Wulf clamped a large hand over the wriggling girls' mouth, effectively silencing her. She was no sweeter-smelling than the men he had ridden with for weeks, but at least she smelled female, and the feel of her soft flesh in his hands was like an aphrodisiac. "I pulled her from among the horses," he said honestly. He saw no harm in what he had done to save a serving wench, and reining in his sidling horse, faced the captain with a grin.

Several nearby horsemen spoke up, attesting to the truth of his words. "She walked before my horse and I nearly ran her down," one offered in his defense. The captain looked back to the Saxon and the squirming girl, but as he was about to pass judgment, the girl thrashed free.

Madeleine threw herself against her rescuer, screaming at the top of her lungs. "Filthy dog! Take your hands from me! I am Madeleine de Moncelet, daughter of the Count of Troyes!" She could not have accomplished more had she been Medusa and

70

turned them all to stone; the effect was much the same. Her rescuer released his grip, though her breast still stung from his grasp, and the captain of the guards blanched grey and lifeless as his mail.

From this new perspective, Wulf noticed her hands were covered with rings and the clothing she wore, though filthy and thoroughly rumpled from their tussle, was of fine material, not the clothing of a servant girl.

As if Madeleine had willed it, the mitred hat came to her. Wulf's discomfiture was such that he quickly dismounted and lifted the lady Madeleine to the ground, handling her as if she was made of glass. Even at that she fought him. She shoved at his hands, stumbling to gain her feet. A flush of heat rose from her bodice, inflaming her cheeks. She would have satisfied her fury with yet another angry outburst had the blue eyes, brimming with eager boyish impudence, not ambushed her thoughts and left her suddenly mute and bewildered. With a toss of curls, she turned to the long, narrow face beneath the jeweled mitre and addressed him as *Uncle*.

Heribert, Bishop of Champagne, stared in startled silence at the slip of a girl in a soiled gown. A sheen of moisture shone on her youthful face and her dark hair fell about her shoulders in disarray. No phantom she, risen from an uneasy grave, but Madeleine, his brother's youngest child and heir. He cursed her name beneath his breath and shouted for a soldier to hold his horse so he might dismount. By the time he set his velvet boots upon the cobbled stones of the courtyard, he had regained a measure of composure. He screwed a smile upon his long face and, embracing his niece, declared, "God in his infinite mercy has spared you, my child. Thanks be to God."

Madeleine withered from the suffocating embrace. His silken robes clung to her damp flesh like spider's

71

webs and he reeked of myrrh and long-dried sweat, and when he planted a kiss upon her forehead, his fetid breath was hot as frumenty.

All day long Madeleine watched the bishop's soldiers make their camps in the fields beyond the château. Coveys of birds winged skyward, flushed by the onslaught of men and horses. The birds wheeled in great circles, coming to ground only a short distance away, where they might still feast on the ripened seed heads. There were no cattle in the fields—all had wandered off or been stolen and butchered. The reapers who had manned the scythes were gone as well. Those who did not lie rotting in their huts had fled, leaving behind all their possessions and in some cases even their families.

For the first time in weeks, Madeleine gazed into her Venetian mirror. She was shocked by her appearance. Her clothing was rumpled and stained and the hem of her skirt hung in rags. She glanced then to Albertine, who neither looked nor smelled any better, and declared, "We are filthy as beggars."

The pair toiled half the day carrying pails of water from the garderobe, dipped bowl by bowl from the wooden barrel which held water for bathing. They doused the stale water with perfume, washed, and afterward donned clean clothing. As a rule Madeleine wore simple clothing and though the material was finer, the cut was little different from the plain country frocks worn by Albertine.

In the hall that evening there was precious little for supper. Heribert, sitting at the head of the table, blessed the food—a watery stew made of stringy meat in which slices of turnips and carrots floated. Barley bread and rancid-smelling cheese completed the fare, along with the château's own stout wine. The youthful novices greedily devoured the food, but

Madeleine sniffed at the stew and rank cheese and ate only barley bread and sipped at her wine.

Just at evening, Madeleine and Albertine walked out in the garden. Crickets sounded in the deep grass and on the opposite bank of the stream, which flowed in a lazy arc beyond the stable, the soldier's campfires glowed in the dying light. Madeleine returned to the solar to find her mother's huge embroidery frame had been disassembled and the tapestry folded away. Her protests roused only a disinterested shrug from the novices and so she retired to her chamber, planning to speak with her uncle in the morning.

Albertine plaited and arranged her mistress's long dark hair and, after a time, Madeleine proposed a game of draughts. She and Albertine were thus involved when a young novice with a wavering voice and fluttering eyelids came to the chamber door. It seemed a painful chore for the boy to speak, but finally he managed to explain that he had been sent by His Grace to fetch her. Madeleine remembered him from the hall—the fat boy who had stared at her with the patience of a cow all during the meal.

She followed him to the library where a brace of candles burned and her uncle and his clerics sat before the open ledgers of the estates. Heribert asked her endless questions concerning the lands and stewards, twisting her words and confusing her thoughts so that she completely forgot about the tapestry.

Before their unexpected meeting in the courtyard, Madeleine had not seen her uncle since she was a child of nine. The occasion had been her uncle's appointment as bishop and she recalled the great ceremony in the Cathedral of St. Pierre, though what remained freshest in her memory was the violent argument she had overheard between her father and his younger brother, Heribert. She no longer remembered the subject of the disagreement—only the angry, hate-filled words that had passed between them.

With his knowledge of law, his brother's records, and what he had gleaned from his niece, Heribert set his mind to salvaging what he might, for he was not a man to accept defeat easily. Candles burned late into the night as he and his advisers conferred.

Upon arising on the morrow, Heribert's first act was to compose a letter to Roland du Boulay, Duke of Burgundy, proposing a marriage between the duke and his niece, Madeleine de Moncelet. Her sizable dowry was listed, as well as Heribert's assurances as to her loveliness, her youth, and robust good health. The duke's immediate need of an heir was also mentioned as were other considerations. In summation, for the contract hinged upon this point, Heribert made known his earnest desire to hold title to the lands of Viezon as well as all taxes, fees, and fines. With the message dispatched, Heribert embarked on the task of setting his brother's estate in order.

Following a breakfast of boiled barley sweetened with honeycomb and cider to drink, Madeleine went to the stable intending to ride out on her Spanish mare. A churlish guard with a greasy beard halted her at the stable door. He crudely informed her that she was forbidden to leave the grounds and escorted her and Albertine back to the garth.

Madeleine stalked into the garden, spewing out her frustrations to Albertine. Butterflies fluttered before them as they walked along the fragrant paths, fitfully picking bouquets of cicely, clove pinks, and ragged ladies. "He has entrenched himself in my father's house and now he has made me a prisoner," Madeleine spat out hatefully, adding yet another grievance to her list.

Madeleine had no sooner entered her chamber and removed her straw hat when she heard loud voices rising from the courtyard. She laid her bouquet upon the unmade bed and rushed to the window. It was possible to see the courtyard directly below, but only if she leaned precariously over the embrasure and hung her head out the window.

Albertine followed her mistress's lead. "What is it?" she asked, flinging herself into the window beside Madeleine. Her floppy straw hat banged against Madeleine's ear and the bouquet of flowers she clutched bobbed before their faces.

"Guiles de Luchaire," Madeleine breathed, pushing the flowers aside and riveting her eyes on the scene unfolding in the courtyard where Guiles de Luchaire stood with his hands on his hips and his feet planted widely apart. At his back were a dozen armed and mounted villeins.

Burning with curiosity, Madeleine stretched a bit farther out the window. Only then could she see clear of the château's ornate facade and watch her uncle, flanked by a number of his guards and priests, standing atop the château's steps. De Luchaire and her uncle were quareeling, which was obvious from their stance and the menacing sound of their voices.

Albertine nudged closer, whispering, "He is nearly bald on top," and pointed out the thinness of de Luchaire's dark hair. He was bareheaded in the sunlight, and as she was directly above she saw only the top of his head.

"Shhh," Madeleine hushed her, straining her ears to hear what was being said above the restless sounds of the horses and the clanking of mail and weapons. In an instant it was ended. Guiles de Luchaire was again astride his large, tawny-colored horse. It reared, pawing the air with its hooves and, while Madeleine watched open-mouthed, Guiles de Luchaire raised his clenched fist and shook it at her uncle. A bishop of the church!

At that moment, Albertine teetered and lost her balance. She gave a frightened yelp, dropped her bouquet, and clawed wildly at the stones of the embrasure. Madeleine seized her firmly by the waist, but the armload of flowers fluttered down upon Guiles de Luchaire and his villeins. All eyes focused on the window. Madeleine ducked inside, her face ablaze with mortification, and dragged Albertine after her. "You clumsy goose," she swore. She was furious.

"Mistress, I nearly fell. Oh, sweet Jesu, I would be dead."

"I almost wish you were," Madeleine said spitefully. "The hairy beast will think I care for him, and all because of you." With a black look, she leapt to her feet and flounced upon the bed in a fit of pique. It was late in the afternoon before Madeleine spoke to Albertine again, and eventually apologized for her ill temper.

The flower incident was touched upon briefly over supper in the hall, but it was secondary to the religious discussion and Heribert was satisfied that it was the actions of a gawkish serving girl. He intended to replace her as soon as matters were settled.

When Madeleine inquired as to the subject of his and Baron de Luchaire's converstion in the courtyard, Heribert silenced her with an impatient glance.

Madeleine had not long to wonder. The cook heard from Onfroi, and Albertine from the cook, and before Madeleine slept that night, she knew her uncle had set aside her marriage contract. She slept well that night.

By the third day, the interior of the château had taken on the appearance of a monastery. Religious symbols adorned the walls and everywhere Madeleine looked the furnishings had been altered or rearranged. Rumors circulated that the bishop's guards snatched wandering peasants from the roads and city streets and forced them to work in the fields. It was also said that many of the servants, newly brought into the château, were the tenants of other lords. It seemed His Grace came by cattle in a similar fashion, for Madeleine had witnessed his guards driving herds of cows, pigs, and sheep past the château. Although she disliked her uncle's methods and mistrusted his motives, he had spared her from marriage to Guiles de Luchaire and for that alone she felt obliged to forgive him a multitude of sins.

Chapter Seven

A week passed. The winds shifted to the west, bringing brindled skies and soft slow rains which colored the days mouse grey and drifted across the thirsty fields of Champagne like a mist.

In the adjoining barony of Sézanne, Guiles de Luchaire and his clerics labored over a draft of a letter entreating his royal majesty, Philip of France, to intervene in Avignon over the matter of the annulment of his marriage contract to Madeleine de Moncelet. Added to this were his further demands that Heribert, Bishop of Champagne, be brought to task for his flagrant violations of the laws of God and the kingdom. The clerics had also begun the long and tedious process of launching a formal complaint to the Pope in Avignon, but lacking the support of a bishop or cardinal, the legal process within the church could conceivably take a year or more.

The more learned of the clerics, the priest, Constanzo, advised his seething young lord not to expect a swift reply. "His majesty, the King, is old and frail and our Holy Clement is a most cautious Pope."

Guiles de Luchaire gave no hint he had heard the priest's words. He stood before the windows of his keep and frowned across the soggy fields. In the fading light the outline of his powerful shoulders was only hinted at and his furrowed brow was eclipsed by shadows. After a moment, he turned and said, "Rest assured, Constanzo, I will have what is mine, even if I must spill a bishop's blood to gain it."

A young boy carrying a lute and dressed in silks of scarlet kermes and white came to the door of the keep. He hung in the darkness a moment, then made a move to go. "Come here, Hugh, and play for me," de Luchaire bade the boy. He smiled at him and, turning to the clerics, dismissed them. "Constanzo," he said suddenly, calling to the priest as he went through the door arch. "See that my letter goes with godspeed."

To the left of the kitchen garth, where a brace of current bushes grew thick and dense nourished by the garderoom drainage, stood the château's armory and barracks. Both were constructed of the same iron-grey stone as the Château de Troyes, but were squat and squarely built. They shared none of the grace of the grand château and crouched in a formidable line atop a rise overlooking the Troyes road.

With the soldiers of the provost so close at hand, there had been no need to keep a large force within the château's walls. The barracks were small, accommodating scarcely twenty men and those few only under cramped conditions.

Wulf preferred to camp in the meadow where the majority of the bishop's guard made their quarters in tents. He, the Moor called Harun, and the Lombard, Agnolo by name, had served together in Bergamo and now shared a battered tent. It was comfortable enough in fair weather, but with the advent of the rains, the floor became a quagmire.

Harun had taken to sleeping in the crotch of a tree a short distance away in a little copse where the horses were tethered at night. The Lombard, Agnolo, had been raised by a Tuscan pig herder and remained in the tent. But Wulf, like Harun, could not tolerate sleeping in the mud. He had bribed the old stableman, Onfroi, into letting him keep his horse in the stable and by night was sleeping in its stall. It was costing him his silver coins, but at least he could sleep in comfort and his horse was not forced to stand in the wetness day and night until its hooves rotted.

The handsome dark bay was worth the price of ten leigemen like himself and had come with him from Lombardy—a gift presented to him by a Lombard Prince whose colors he carried to victory in a tournament. It was given by a man who possessed a hundred such horses and with little more thought than if it had been a coin tossed to a beggar. Wulf had named him Loki, after the dark god of mischief, though unlike his namesake the bay was obedient and remarkably even-tempered. Wulf had few other possessions: a saddle, a dagger, and a knight's sword . . . finely honed and double-edged with an intricate handguard, which was worked in silver and marked with runes. It was the sword his lord, Hasso, had touched to his shoulder as he lay dying. Of late the recollection had not much troubled him, but there were times when it haunted his thoughts and the memories returned like carrion birds to pick at his consciousness. He knew in his heart that had either son still held a spark of life, Hasso would not have squandered his last breaths on a bastard. He could see him still, lying propped against a tree, a great gaping hole in his chest. He was broken inside and slowly bleeding to death, yet refusing to die with the thought of a stranger holding Rügen. Wulf settled deeper into the straw of the stall. All of life was a cruel jest, he thought, and after a moment closed his eyes.

Heribert had relented on the issue of the tapestry and allowed Madeleine to have the servants erect the huge framework in the room once occupied by her late sisters. She and Albertine often went there to work. Perhaps one third of the great tapestry was completed. Madeleine bemoaned its size, doubting she would ever finish it even if she attained the age of Methuselah.

Though vaguely discontented, Madeleine did not find her life unbearable, at least not until the following morning when she was summoned to the library.

Heribert sat in her father's Italian chair. He greeted her and said, "Since you are my niece and now my ward, dear Madeleine, I feel it is my familial duty to guide you along the most advantageous path. The tragic death of my brother and his family members has left you sole heiress to his city of Troyes and his estates. In fact, my dear, you now possess a fabulously rich dowry—much too rich to be lavished on a foppish baron. You do, of course, agree, do you not?"

Madeleine could not have agreed more and replied, "My betrothal to the Baron of Sezanne was not of my choosing."

"Then you would have no objections to my setting aside your marriage contract due, shall we say, to the tragic circumstances of the past few months."

Madeleine looked at him with a perplexed expression. From all she had heard, he had already done so, but she answered, "None, Your Grace."

"Excellent," Heribert said, rising from the chair and clasping his hands together as he slowly circled the room. "My child," he began, "I do not wish to raise your hopes too high, but the possibility exists that you may one day be the Queen of France. I have in mind for you an alliance with Roland du Boulay, the Duke of Burgundy. He is a champion for the cause of a France free of English rule and as a Valois he had a legitimate claim toward the throne."

Madeleine interrupted him. She could remain silent no longer. "I do not wish to be the Queen of

81

France. Neither do I wish to marry this Valois duke. I wish ony to be left in peace.'' She saw her uncle's features harden and hastened to say, "Surely we can come to terms. I need only a small estate for myself— a manor house would do. Send me away to Bardane or Vemy. I will not trouble you. You may have the rest; I will give it all to you. I want only to live my life as I choose.''

For all her passionate entreaties, Heribert's response was but a single ironic snort. "Life is indeed cruel," he mused. There was nothing on earth he desired more than the power and influence that his brother's estates would afford him, except perhaps the papal crown. "Here, you wish to make me a present of the richest estates in all France and I cannot accept," he remarked with a twisted smile. "How truly unfortunate for us both." He returned to the chair and sat down heavily. "By law, I may come to your inheritance only by your marriage or your death." He raised his eyes to Madeleine and said, "So you see, you have no choice. You may go now."

Madeleine stumbled to her feet. "I will not marry him," she cried, "I will not," and clenching her small hands at her side turned and fled the chamber.

From that day forward, Madeleine did all in her power to thwart her uncle's wishes. A week later, she learned by way of the kitchen that Falkes Delouvrier, a knight once dismissed by her father for the inhuman treatment of his peasants, murder in fact, had been chosen by His Grace to be Provost of Troyes. It was damnable and she vowed to speak out against it.

In the hall, the stale air reeked of grease and humanity. Not one place at the immense table stood empty. Heribert, Bishop of Champagne's chosen topic was *Faith*, and all dutifully listened to his preamble and the words of St. Paul.

"Faith," Heribert announced in his fine baritone, "is the substance of things to be hoped for, the evidence of things that appear not . . ." while from the kitchen a shuffling line of servants and pages circled the table, arms laden with platters of spitted hares, venison, black puddings, stewed fruits, and loaves of crusty bread, fragrant with the scent of yeast.

Madeleine's icy countenance and the fact she took little of what was offered was in no way unusual and gave no hint of the fury brewing within her heart. She was determined to be heard on the matter of Falkes Delouvrier, though she did not know exactly how to broach the subject.

As he spoke, Heribert's gaze swept over the lengthy table, past the solemn faces of his novices to where his brother's daughter, Madeleine, sat with her ginger-headed maidservant. Plainly, the two young women, most noticeably his niece with her décolletage, dark curls, and dramatic side-long glances, were a distraction of the basest sort. Still, life was filled with temptations and Heribert was of the opinion his novices should learn chastity just as they had learned faith . . . with testing. "By faith," he continued, "We understand that the world was framed by the word of God; that from the invisible, visible things might be fashioned. Without faith it is impossible to please God. For he that cometh to God must believe that He is; and is a rewarder to them that seek Him."

The novice to Madeleine's right sucked noisily at a hare's leg bone, another spat a pad of gristle onto his plate, and the boy opposite her stuffed his jaws with bread and black pudding. The sight of the gristle glistening with spittle and the cloying smell of the pudding nudged the last prop from beneath Madeleine's reserve. "What is the reward for murder, Uncle?" she asked, raising her voice defiantly and fixing the long face in the center of her vision.

Taken aback, Heribert had no chance to respond

before Madeleine pressed her attack by suggesting in venomous tone, "Could it be the coveted post of Provost of Troyes?"

The line of his jaw tightened. With a look akin to malice, he molded his features into a facsimile of his former calm composure, hooked a smile upon his thin lips, and said, "In the spirit of Christian forgiveness and because you are my brother's child, I will this once overlook your blasphemous outburst, Madeleine."

"You dare accuse me of blasphemy, Uncle?" Madeleine shouted. Her eyes sparked in the candle-light. "It is known by all that Falkes Delouvrier was a cruel and brutal master to his serfs and that he beat to death a serving girl because she refused to endure his lewd demands. Had he not escaped my father's justice, he would have long ago hung from the pillory by his foul neck. It is he and his crimes that are a blasphemy," she ranted, her voice rising shrilly. "I demand you dismiss him and have justice done!"

Heribert took a deep breath and, in an aside directed at his protégé, said "The moon grows full." He then directed his eyes down the table and summoning a loud voice, announced, "Falkes Delouvrier has confessed his sins."

"And is therefore nearly innocent?" Madeleine sneered mockingly.

"You, my dear niece, would be far wiser to demand less and be silent in the face of my authority." And in a patronizing tone, meant to humble her, he admonished, "I advise you to engage your energies in prayer and seek absolution for your gender's mis-guided and weak nature."

His smug words and crooked smile sent Madeleine to her feet in a fury of rebellion, her entire being ablaze with anger. "The weakness of my gender can in no way compare to the weakness of your soul. You, who care for nothing other than what your greedy hands can grasp; not honor, not justice . . ."

Albertine cowered amid the verbal barrage; indeed, all eyes in the hall were on them. She sat braced and white-faced with lips parted in disbelief. Her fear-widened eyes leapt helplessly from one to the other. At last she clutched at her mistress's thin arm and, with imploring eyes, begged her to be silent.

Heribert, roused from his seat, bellowed back, "Silence, do you hear?" A sudden gesture of his jeweled hand sent de Grailley rushing from his place, striding quickly down the table's length. As he passed the hearth, he snapped his fingers before a pair of idle servingwomen and beckoned them to follow.

"I will not be silent," Madeleine screeched. "Injustice screams for equity, crime for punishment. I will tell all with ears to hear of your unholiness!"

Albertine saw them coming and shook Madeleine's arm, "Shush, mistress, I beg you. Oh dear Jesu," she pleaded, but to no avail.

Madeleine ignored her tearful entreaties. "Unholy bishop who keeps faith with a murderer!" she screamed, flailing her arms in an attempt to fend off the priest de Grailley's sweaty hands and the flabby arms of the servingwomen who came at her all at once.

"Silence!" Heribert boomed. His mighty voice reverberated from the very timbers of the hall. "Like all your sex, you have an evil tongue. Do not think your blasphemy will go unpunished!"

Madeleine balked and scuffled. "Tyrant! Despiser of women!" she screamed at the top of her lungs as she was dragged into the passageway amid the smoke and clatter from the kitchen. "Punish me—it will not lessen your sins," she shouted and, fighting free momentarily turned to scream one last insult at her uncle. "God will not forgive you, nay, not even St. Paul!"

After a moment, the discordant screeches faded. Heribert settled again in his place, cleared his throat, and took up his second topic, charity. He said, in the words of St. Paul, "If I speak with the tongues of men and of angels and have not charity, I am become as sounding brass or a tinkling cymbal. And if I should have prophecy and should know all mysteries and all knowledge, and if I should have all faith, so that I could remove mountains, and have not charity, I am nothing. We see now through a glass dark in manner; but then face to face. Now I know in part; but then I shall know even as I am known."

Madeleine's tirade resulted in her being exiled to her chamber for a week. Her imprisonment did little to improve her temper. Shortly after her sentence was lifted, she again spoke out, this time goading her uncle to violence. It was the occasion of signing her marriage contract to Roland du Boulay, Duke of Burgundy. Madeleine refused to sign and, hardening her jaw in the mold of her father's, said, "I cannot prevent you from forging my signature upon this contract, but I will never marry your Valois duke."

Heribert took a deep breath, drawing upon his last reserves of patience. "It is for your own ultimate good and for the good of France."

Madeleine cut short his words. "We both know who will profit most: His Grace, the Bishop of Champagne!"

"Enough!" he shouted. "You are of my own blood, Madeleine, and for that reason alone I have been lenient with you. Do not force me to take harsher measures."

Madeleine's eyes blazed. "Oh, I am virtually a prisoner in my own home," she lashed out. "What harsher measures might you take? A grave!" She saw only the flash of his ruby ring. The blow from his open hand knocked her backward several steps. She gasped, cradling her aching cheek in her hand. Her eyes filled with tears, she would rather have been burned as a witch than give him the satisfaction of seeing her cry.

Heribert bellowed for Madeleine's maidservant. His harsh shout struck Albertine like a whip. Poised at the door, she had heard every word and her anger was such that when she entered the room her plump face appeared hard and white as a folded fist.

"Take your mistress to her chamber," Heribert commanded, turning his back to them.

Blinded by tears, Madeleine rushed from the room. Albertine hurried after her, guiding her up the snail curl of steps. "He is naught but a vile toad," Albertine breathed. "I fear for your safety, mistress."

For days, Madeleine said nothing. She passed her time in speculative silence, laboring over her mother's huge tapestry.

In his daily prayer, Heribert asked for strength and guidance from above. He saw his niece's new-found demureness as a sign and thanked the Lord God for his intercession.

The heat of the late-summer day made working over the tapestry a chore. So close was the air of the room that Madeleine's and Albertine's perspiring arms were rubbed raw by the rough backing of the cloth they worked.

All afternoon, Madeleine had watched the clouds billow and stack into high pyramids, but it was the changing light which drew her down the steep stone steps and into the kitchen garth, where the sky and all below were tinted a menacing shade of yellow. In the distance, dark clouds boiled over, spilling flashes of lightning. A breeze, cold as a sudden draft, touched her face and lifted her damp hair. A storm, she thought, her emotions rising to race with the wild tumult of clouds. The very air seemed charged with the fury of the approaching storm.

At the sound of footsteps behind her, Madeleine

turned to see Albertine. She came from the kitchen and stood before the garth wall where the ivy clung to the stones and the lilac bush straggled onto the well house roof. "A storm is coming," she said, raising her plump face to the mix of clouds and forked lightning. Presently, she looked away and said, "Come inside, mistress," and crossed the garth to where Madeleine stood.

"I want to watch the storm," Madeleine replied obstinately. A flash of lightning split the clouds, followed by a low growl of thunder.

"Nay, mistress. I was sent to fetch you. His Grace fears for your safety."

Madeleine stiffened at the mention of her uncle's name. "Tell His Grace I do not wish to come inside."

"Please, mistress," Albertine implored, taking her by the arm and whispering, "He will send one of his guards if you do not obey."

Madeleine stubbornly delayed a moment longer. "May God damn him and his guards," she said, her eyes flashing past Albertine to the high arched windows of the library where her uncle's gaunt form was outlined in the lurid ocher light.

Madeleine climbed the stairs and attacked her needlework with a passion. She muttered that the light was gone and in the same breath raved, "I would sew the night long were it a shroud for His Grace and might hasten his end."

Albertine sent her a warning glance. "There are ears and eyes we do not see," she murmured.

"I would gladly say as much to his scheming face," Madeleine said, and loud enough that all might hear; the serving boy walking past the door and the women who wielded brooms in the passageway, driving dust balls before them.

Thunder crashed and rolled above their heads, jarring the very stones of the walls. In a fit of anger, Madeleine carelessly stabbed a needle into her finger and drew blood. Albertine, knowing well her mistress's temper, cringed.

Madeleine stuck her wounded finger in her mouth and sucked on it, tasting her own blood and hating her uncle for all he was. After a long moment, she removed her finger and examined it. "I will take holy vows," she said in a voice so quiet that Albertine stared at her. "Vows, mistress?" she asked, uncertain if she should be amused or solemn.

"I do not jest," Madeleine said, fixing her eyes upon her serving girl's fleshy face. "I would much prefer the cloistered life to the one to which my uncle has condemned me. Nay, I would prefer death. Do not look at me so, Albertine. I mean to live my life as I choose . . . or die! I will not relent. Say you will help me?"

"Soothly, mistress, I will do your bidding, but I fear for your life if you are discovered."

"It is for *your* life I am concerned. You must swear to leave the château that very night. Will your little cobbler take you into his house?"

"I know not if he is among the living or dead, and it is not his house, but his elder brother's. Albertine saw the look of deep concern as her mistress's dark brows drew into a frown. "Do not fear for my welfare," she insisted. "There are many men who could find use for a strong healthy woman, men being as they are," she added with a short laugh.

Madeleine's days of silence had been put to good use. She had laid her plans with care and, with Albertine's help, she would soon be beyond her uncle's grasp. Albertine secreted an outfit of Philippe's clothing from his room, and assisted her mistress in designing and sewing a band of padding in which to conceal her jewelry as well as serve to bind her small breasts. Madeleine found the garment awkward at first, but the effect was perfect: flattening and padding her chest and thickening her waist in order to attain a male figure. The jewelry was of paramount importance, for it was the means by which she would buy her way into the priory. Once it was sewn into the chest padding, it was completely undetectable.

Albertine had agreed to crop her mistress's long hair, although she thought it a sin to do so. The deed would have to be accomplished by candlelight moments before their escape. She had also agreed to carry the dark curls away with her, dropping them a few strands at a time as she made her way through the forest.

Troyes was also Madeleine's eventual destination. The priory of Notre-Dame-En-l'Isle which was beyond the old city. In order to confound their pursuers, Madeleine had decided that she and Albertine must not leave the château together and that they must travel by different routes.

The conspiracy took on a hilarious note when Madeleine, realizing much of her preparation would have to be accomplished by the light of a single candle, practiced donning her disguise one last time.

Albertine lay across the bed, supporting her face in her chubby hands. Something, she thought, was missing. All at once, a look of pure enlightenment flashed across her features. She scrambled from the bed, ducked into the passageway, and darted off before Madeleine could question her.

The maidservant returned with a down-filled pillow and a mysterious smile on her lips. She nudged the door to with her curvaceous hips and, leaning back against it, giggled uncontrollably as she pulled what appeared to be an endless strip of linen from between her breasts. "The seamstress is dull as a rusty knife," she tittered, referring to her plunder of the linen kisk. "I might have been a fly, for all the notice she paid me."

Because of its absorbency, the linen was used by the seamstress and every other woman of the château to catch their monthly flux. Though the linen strips were washed and used again and again, washing was not a gentle process and large amounts of linen were stored away.

Madeleine made a perplexed face, looking first to the pillow, then to the ever-lengthening coil of linen lying upon the floor, and finally to Albertine's plump, mischievous face. She did not understand.

"A prick!" the ginger-headed maidservant said with a wink and a mirthful little laugh. "Why every Jacques and Jean has one between his legs, and proud as pie of it."

Madeleine burst into giggles. She had not given such realism a thought. The pair went to work, carpriciously cutting and sewing. One was immense, another the size of a noodle. When at last Albertine held up the ludicrous fruit of their labor and declared with much fanfare that they had fashioned every maiden's dream, Madeleine could not speak for laughing.

Amid a blizzard of downy grey feathers, they stuffed the cloth manhood, then wound it with linen strips.

"See, here is its head," Albertine giggled, adding an extra round of linen. Madeleine, who could hardly breathe for her aching sides nor see for the tears glistening in her eyes, squealed out as if for mercy, "Oh Albertine!"

"'Tis true, mistress, they all have little red faces," she mimicked, "and will spit at you if you tease them."

Madeleine cramped with laughter and collapsed in a fit of giggling, flopping into the feathers and sending them fluttering into the air like leaves in a windstorm.

The hilarity did not end with Albertine's ingenious method for binding the invention to Madeleine, for it was funnier still when they attempted, on hands and knees, to chase, corner, and capture every downy feather that skittered across the stones and took flight.

91

It occurred to Madeleine one day that they should reconnoiter their escape route. "What if we cannot find our way in the darkness, or we are seen by the guards?" she argued. Albertine thought it sheer madness but, as always, agreed. Several times they slipped from their chamber in the dead of night, fumbling through the utter darkness of the château, and once ventured as far as the stable doors.

On the day they planned to make good their escape, Madeleine was summoned to the library by her uncle. With him was a thick-set priest, whom he introduced as Father Evarrard. The priest had lank mouse-colored hair and a wide gap between his front teeth, which caused him to speak with a lisp. He was in the service of the Duke du Boulay and looked Madeleine up and down as if he were choosing a brood mare. He stared at her and asked impertinent questions and Madeleine answered him in kind until Heribert, made visibly uncomfortable by the exchange, summarily dismissed her to her chamber.

Chapter Eight

A full moon hung above the château's towers as Wulf's duty watch ended. He was accustomed to standing guard during the day and had nodded off several times, only to awaken with a jolt. He remained on the battlements for a short time, engaged in a conversation with Jehan, the fat youth from Anjou, whose watch followed his. The youth was considering the purchase of a dagger from a craftsman in the city and, after describing the weapon in detail, asked Wulf's opinion of its worth.

In the close darkness between the buildings, Wulf walked the familiar hard-packed path past the currant bushes and along the stone wall which marked the boundary of the kitchen garth. He made for the stable in an unhurried gait. Past the well house, the ground fell away in a gentle slope toward the stream; nearly dry that time of year, it pooled and shone like silver in the moonlight. In the pale gauzy light every feature of the landscape took on a gilded luster. His gaze roved to the massive maple hedges of the château's garden, which cast fantastic shadows in the bright moonlight, and beyond to where the black-stained outline of the woods rose against the clear night sky. As the view came fully within his field of vision, Wulf's eyes detected a movement at the forest's edge. He halted and drew his eyes back across the scene, uncertain.

Had it been a trick of the moonlight, or a shadow cast by the trees? It was a figure, he decided, though he glimpsed it fully for only an instant. Whether a man or a woman he could not tell. He watched as the form moved stealthily into the blackness beneath the trees and vanished. He stood there for a moment in the mocking moonlight, then walked on toward the stable, debating what action to take. Should he forget what he had seen, curl up in Loki's stall, and fall asleep? Or satisfy his growing curiosity? He chose the latter.

In only a few moments, he had thrown a saddle on his horse and ridden to the spot where the mysterious figure vanished into the forest. He dismounted as a riderless horse made far less noise, and, moving cautiously, led his mount for some distance. After an hour or so he was nearly satisfied that he had lost the object of his search, when from the outer perimeter of his vision he caught sight of something moving through a thicket. In the darkness of the trees, he was too far away to make out what was thrashing through the brushy glade—a deer perhaps. It seemed to be heading south and east toward the city of Troyes.

Rather than close in from the rear and risk blundering upon it in the darkness, Wulf moved off on a parallel course, keeping to the higher ground. His position put him up wind of his quarry; he reasoned if it was an animal, his scent would flush it from cover, thus ending the mystery. For the next hour, he caught occasional glimpses of it. After a time, he was certain it was indeed human, and, judging from its movements, a woman. It was still too dark for his eyes to confirm his suspicions.

The sky streaked with light and slowly the images sharpened and became more defined. He saw it was a woman, and she carried a large parcel on her back. As

94

the light in the eastern sky intensified, her hair took on a reddish, ginger color, and he recognized her as the maidservant of the Lady Madeleine. Were her belongings in the parcel? It was large enough. And why had she left the château? Dismissed by His Grace? A possibility.

Wulf followed her to Troyes. Inside the Paris gate, the city was already awake. Carts and cattle lumbered through the streets, women and children drew water from the wells, and guildsmen opened their shops. At last Wulf hoisted his exhausted body into the saddle. He was careful not to follow too closely, though a number of horsemen moved along the streets. Eventually she led him to a cobbler's shop on the rue du Domino, where an old woman admitted her through an alleyway door.

Had she been dismissed? If so, he had wasted a night's sleep. If, on the other hand, she had fled, there would be a reward; and he knew where to find her.

Wulf waited nearby for several hours, lounging beneath the shade of a large chestnut tree which marked the yard of a livery. When the serving girl did not reappear, he led his horse from the shade, mounted, and returned to the château.

He approached at a leisurely trot. From as far as the road, he could see something was amiss. A great number of soldiers, novices, and household servants milled over the grounds, shouting back and forth and dashing off in a frenzy of confusion.

A guard, one that Wulf knew only by sight, halted him in the courtyard and told him to report to the armory. "What has happened?" Wulf asked, observing the frantic activity.

"The Lady Madeleine is missing," the guard replied. "Run off with her serving girl. There is a reward," he advised, before turning away to answer the call of another guard.

At the armory Wulf learned the reward was indeed

a handsome one—twenty livres; hardly enough to buy his freedom, but definitely worthwhile. As anxious as he was to return to Troyes, he was obliged to wait for the captain. Like the others who had stood guard duty during the night, Wulf was closely questioned. The captain also cautioned him not to speak openly of the lady Madeleine's disappearance lest word of it reach Sezanne and the ears of Baron de Luchaire. Wulf did not mention his late night game of fox and geese, or that he knew where the runaway serving girl had come to roost, but hastened to the stable to feed and water his horse.

He led his horse into the stable yard where the flies were thick and the heaps of manure steamed in the midday heat. At the trough, he let the bay drink then walked it to its stall and unsaddled it. In the rear of the stable, old Onfroi, with his fringe of stringy white hair and grizzled beard, was forking down straw and muttering to himself. Wulf paid him no mind, and taking handfuls of straw, rubbed down the bay's sleek hide. He had just finished with the horse's hindquarters when the old man came and stood before the stall. "A horse is missing," he grumbled. "The captain tells me I am naught but a stupid lout who is unable to cypher, and that may well be true," he said with a shrug. "But a horse is missing all the same, and he is the greater fool."

"The captain is thick as a stone," Wulf said in agreement, dipping a pail in the grain bin. The bay followed his every movement with large expressive eyes and, when he returned with the pailful of sweet-smelling grain, reached out its muzzle. Wulf pushed the large head away, emptying the pail into the feed box. "Which horse is missing?" he asked the old man, setting down the pail and laying an arm over the bay's withers as it contentedly ground down the grain.

"A red mare," the old man said, honesty etched in

every line of his weathered face. "She belonged to my lord's son. There is a white stripe on her forehead and she has a split hoof. This hoof," he indicated, pointing to his own arthritic foot, for he knew not right from left. "It is healed, but can be seen by any man not blind."

"Did your lady take the horse?"

"Na, na. She would have taken her own mare, and the mare be there, still be waiting for her."

"The lady's serving girl has run off," Wulf said, certain the old man knew as much. "She may have taken the horse," he suggested, angling to learn more.

"No," the old man grunted and hobbled away, muttering, "but a horse is missing."

While the bay swished flies and ground noisily at the grain, Wulf lifted the dampened rug from beneath his saddle. Seeing the old man was nowhere about, he entered the room where the saddles and harness hung from the walls and exchanged the rug for a dry one—a fine, thick saddle rug of wool. He laid it on the bay's back, admiring its quality and denseness. Loki turned his head inquisitively, pricking his ears forward. "What do you think of this?" Wulf asked with a smile. "Do you think I have made a wise trade, unh?" The bay snorted softly and turned to root in the empty feed box.

Wulf was eager to return to Troyes and soon he and the bay cantered from the stable yard. At the château's gate, he was forced to rein in his prancing horse abruptly and give way to a party of four on horseback: the bishop's newly-appointed canon, two priests, and a middle-aged woman, who rode side-saddle upon a small black palfrey. Wulf gave them a look of passing interest and, no sooner than their horses had cleared the gate, gave Loki a nudge with his heels and headed toward the spires of the walled city.

He returned to the cobbler's shop. At first he watched from the yard of the livery, noting the comings and goings of customers. Several hours passed uneventfully before he decided to enter the shop and confront the former maidservant.

With its shutter set back from the huge window openings, the shop was one with the heat and dust of the street. He saw no activity within, and inside he found the shop deserted. An assortment of boots and slippers in various stages of repair lay on one long, narrow table, while another held shoes half-made upon lathes. A variety of wooden-handled knives and leather punches lay scattered about amid stacks of brilliantly-dyed hides. He was instantly aware of the pungent, earthy tang of leather, and of . . . food, an odor he at once identified as fried sausage.

His nose did not mislead him. In a back room he found the family seated at a rough slab table. A sickly-looking young man seated at the table's head made a motion to rise, but the ginger-headed maidservant was quicker, and with a hand upon his arm bid him stay.

To Albertine, the lean soldier standing in the door arch looked not at all like a customer seeking service. She guessed his mission by his manner and his searching eyes, and knowing full well her own guilt made a pretense of ignorance—one she hoped might pass for innocence. In a steady voice, she said, "As you can see, sire, we are taking our bread. Surely your need is not so urgent that you cannot wait until we finish our meal."

Wulf's eyes roved over the room and the hallway beyond. He came and stood before the table. "I have not come for a pair of boots," was his terse reply. He brought his gaze to bear on the maidservant's plump face and in a tone more brutally blunt then menacing, demanded, "Where is your mistress?" He was convinced she was there, and if not, close by.

"Where have you hidden her?"

The old woman and the three ragged children stared at the table top, blank-faced; their features were marked with fear. But the young cobbler, who yet bore the faded purple blotches of the sickness, spoke up in a weak and quavering voice. "All of my house that have not been called to Christ sit here before you." The few words seemed to exhaust him; his breath came in rapid, shallow gasps and his calloused hands lay on the table. It seemed too great an effort for him to lift them.

"This woman is not of your house," Wulf pointed out in his abrupt manner, "but a maidservant bound to the house of de Moncelet, one who has wrongly fled."

Albertine leapt to her feet. "That is not true, sire," she said, her face flushed with emotion. "I have my mistress's approval and good graces. I need no other's permission!" She crossed the room with quick steps to a heavy, iron-strapped buffet. From among the wooden trenchers and cups, she took a parchment and offered it to the soldier.

Wulf unfurled the paper and angled it in the dim light. It was as she said, a writ of manumission scribed in Latin and signed with a flourish by Madeleine Marie Angélè de Moncelet, Comtesse de Troyes. He carefully rerolled the parchment and handed it back to the maidservant, confident that neither she nor her cobbler knew one curved line from another and could not possibly have been the author. "Where is your mistress?" he demanded, becoming impatient.

"At the château de Troyes," Albertine replied at once with raised brows and an air of innocence.

"A lie," Wulf told her. "You have hidden her here or close by."

While the food on her trencher grew cold and tasteless, Albertine repeatedly denied any knowledge of her mistress's whereabouts.

Wulf was unconvinced. He searched the house with the thoroughness of a ferret in a rabbit warren, prying into every nook and corner from the dirt cellar to the solar and the store room rafters. He found nothing.

Chapter Nine

In the darkness, Madeleine's sense of direction had become confused. She wandered for hours along the city's massive walls. Only when dawn painted the eastern sky with pastel pinks, blues, and yellows did Madeleine realize her error. Far to her left, the bleak silhouette of the viscount's tower and the pointed spires of the church of St. Jean-au-Marche rose above the rough-cut limestone walls.

She had come too far and with near-fatal results. In the queer half-light she saw the charred remains of a wooden bridge which had once spanned the Moline canal. After the first few lengths, the bridge ended abruptly in mid-air. Below was the canal, where she would have surely plunged and drowned had it not been for the good sense of her brother's horse. The animal had balked in the dark, refusing to set foot on the wooden planking.

As the darkness retreated, Madeleine saw several corpses had come to rest along the canal's bank, and beyond, in the narrow strip of land which lay between the city's wall and the confluence of the Moline and Meldoucon Canals, bodies of plague victims had been heaped in grotesque mounds. Obviously there had been an unsuccessful attempt to burn the bodies, hence the damage to the bridge. It was a hideous scene, doubly so when the breeze shifted and the sickening stench threatened to overcome Madeleine's senses.

She turned her horse, retracing the way she had come. She was certain she had overlooked the Croncels Gate in the dark. The stench borne on the breeze followed her. Twice she was forced to dismount and empty her churning stomach. Her greatest fear was that she would find the priory vacant, or worse still, its inhabitants all dead where they had fallen. She urged her horse on, willing herself not to give in to her heaving stomach or the terror her thoughts held concerning the priory, for to whom could she then turn?

It was the Tanner's Gate she found and, rather than risk searching further, entered. The noisome odor of the tanner's quarter was equally foul, but she was some comforted by the fact it was the offal of animals, not humans.

Keeping to her right, she made her way along the warren of little streets which surrounded the Rue de La Grande—Tannerie. The sight of so many people abroad in the streets left Madeleine doubting her senses. Though many had died, life went on as always. Peddlers, butchers, and tanners went about their business as if nothing was amiss. Sleepy maidservants and housewives drew water from the wells and children shouted to one another in play. Chickens fled and honking geese flapped before the hooves of her horse and in the vacant doorways and alleys, dogs and cats lurked in the shadows and foraged for food among the rats and pigeons.

Madeleine noticed a group of boys loitering before one of the post-and-beam houses which crowded cheek by jowl and jutted onto the narrow street. The boys rough-wrestled one another and shouted lewd remarks at passersby. Madeleine paid them no heed until one took out at a run, motioning the others after him. The taller of the boys lunged at her horse, grabbing the reins before she could turn the animal,

102

put her heels to its flanks, and make good her escape.

Madeleine had no whip. If she had, she would have laid it aside his pockmarked face; instead she landed a blow on his shoulder with her soft leather boot and commanded him to unhand the reins.

The pockmarked boy, now joined by several others, only laughed and called out to a large man with a florid face and a long knotted nose. He addressed the immense but badly misshapen man as "Bresse," and called, "I have found you a *jongleur* for tonight's performance." The big man roared with laughter and bade the boys, "Bring the little lad along."

They pulled Madeleine from the horse's back. She fought like a cornered rat, kicking, biting and gouging, but she was no match for the boys—the youngest was as tall as she. Mauled, though uninjured, she was bundled into the post-and-beam house and dumped unceremoniously onto the filthy floor. But not before she had sunk her teeth deeply into the pockmarked boy's right hand.

Stinging from indignation and rough handling, Madeleine scrambled to her feet, swearing loudly amid a gale of crude laughter.

"Where did you steal the horse, boy?" the big man demanded.

"I did not steal it," Madeleine shouted, shuddering at the falsetto sound of her own voice. She lowered it at once, modulating the tone as best she could. "It is my brother's horse."

Bresse laughed. "It looks like a horse which was recently stolen from me."

"Aye," the boys chorused loudly.

"My brother will crush your empty skulls," Madeleine threatened with convincing male bravado—convincing to all but herself; she was terrified. The pockmarked boy moved menacingly close and cuffed her ear with his uninjured hand. "Watch your tongue, horse thief!" His other, the one she had bitten, was bleeding freely and held tight against his side.

"If it was my horse," one of the younger boys said, "no little piss of a brother would bounce his ass on its back."

"Aye," another agreed.

"I wager your brother is dead," Bresse conjectured. He grinned, adding a third and fourth chin to his fat face and broadening the width of his knotted nose. "How would you like to be an actor, boy?"

For a long moment Madeleine stared at him, speechless. A door creaked open at the far end of the room and a frowzy-looking woman with unkempt hair and rumpled clothing wandered in and stood with her hands on her ample hips. Madeleine ignored her. "I would not," she replied and, swearing mightily, referred to the lot of them as whoremonger's sons. "I am in search of my sister, my only living relative, who serves Christ in the priory of Notre-Dame-en-l'Isle."

"Then you may well be alone in the world, my boy," Bresse said, though not unkindly despite the curses which had been flung at him. Buffing his fat nose with a forefinger, he went on, "I am told that all who lived within the old city have died of the sickness. The gates are sealed by the bishop's orders and only those given permission by the provost may enter."

"Soldiers stand guard," the boy with the bad skin said, adding, "Not a day passes without a suspected looter behing hung from the gibbet before the Provost's Hall." Aye," the youngest of the boys said in a mocking voice. "They hang horse thieves as well as pinch purses."

"It is true," Bresse said with a crafty smile. "You are fortunate we found you. In time, we will be traveling south, but for now I can use a boy of your size."

Madeleine gazed around the low-ceilinged room;

even in the dim light she could see the walls were lined with loot. The realization left her weak-kneed and with a sinking feeling in the pit of her stomach. Knowing what she did, they would not allow her to leave; she would be one of them or dead.

The frowzy woman, who now leaned languidly against the door arch, asked, "Can you sing, boy?"

Madeleine took a step backward, clenching her small hands into fists and fighting back the tears which threatened to spill down her cheeks. "I have sung in church," she finally managed.

The woman crossed the room with swaying hips, gave the large man a shove, and, pushing past him with a sly smile, placed her chubby arms around Madeleine. "You have frightened the boy," she accused, drawing Madeleine's face to rest against her broad bosom. "He is only a slip of a thing," she said, and turning to Madeleine, asked, "What is your name?"

"Alain," Madeleine croaked. She could think of no other at the moment.

"How old are you, little one?" she asked, tweaking Madeleine's cheek.

"Fourteen," Madeleine answered, wondering desperately if that was too old to account for her soprano tone.

Bresse's voice exploded like a crash of thunder. "By St. Aventin's sanctified ass," he swore. "What ails you, boy? Someone must have taken a knife to your sac." His comments were seconded by uproarious laughter from the other boys and still more crude remarks.

"Stop it! The lot of you." the woman shouted angrily and, taking Madeleine's face in her hands, tilted it upward, remarking, "He is the prettiest boy ever I laid eyes on; he is worth his weight in gold, this one." The boys made faces and groaned. "Mayhap he is Adonis," Bresse scoffed, adding, "but at least he is the right size to play the part of a girl." He then addressed the frowzy-looking woman as Marie and directed her to keep watch on the boy until he returned.

Madeleine was hoping to be left alone with the pudgy woman, imagining she could easily escape from her, but to her dismay, the pockmarked boy remained behind as well. He followed them into the kitchen and sullenly flopped down on a bench near the door.

Marie filled a tankard with ale and sat it before Madeleine. She dipped one for herself and one for the boy. Then from a wooden box she took a long narrow loaf and pulled it into chunks. Madeleine was reluctant to eat, but too hungry to refuse. While Marie sat opposite her and talked, the boy with the pimpled face took up a lute and plunked at it.

According to the plump, slovenly Marie, Bresse was a famous *jongleur* and had performed before the king in Paris. She listed his many talents, although thievery was not among them. An oversight, Madeleine decided, for from all apperances he was a virtual prince of thieves.

When Madeleine had finished the bread and downed most of the ale, Marie said, "Let me look at you in the light." She towed Madeleine before a large uncovered window opening and peered at her eyes. She pulled back her lips and counted her teeth, checked for bumps on her head, and examined the shape of her ears.

Madeleine did not protest Marie's strange inventory too loudly, for her manner was casual as a physician's. But when she ran her hands over the globes and orbs of her body, Madeleine wriggled and jiggled away. Fortunately, for Marie's pudgy fingers were about to close on Madeleine's masculinity—the wad of material she had bound to her mons.

"Owee!" Marie laughed. "You have a big staff for such a little pup." Madeleine blushed to the roots of her hair. Marie laughed even harder and hugged

Madeleine until she was breathless. "You are a sweet one," Marie exclaimed, "and so innocent. Listen, my little Alain," she began in a hushed voice, "Bresse can do you a great service." She then proceeded to ask one question after another until Madeleine's mind reeled from the interrogation and she was uncertain which lies she had told and which she had left unsaid. "You can be the page of a fine knight," Marie promised, "if you do as you are told. Or find yourself a guildsman who will apprentice you. Most of all Bresse's boys go on to find lucrative trades."

Madeleine was skeptical. "Why then does he remain here?" she asked, motioning with her head toward the pockmarked boy. He was still plunking at the lute and seemed to take no notice of their conversation. "He is not as pretty as you," Marie cooed. Madeleine did not fully understand, but her tone implied something unsavory.

Marie insisted she learn a song and, with the boy accompanying her on the lute and Marie coaching, Madeleine sang out in a faltering voice which grew more confident with practice.

Marie said it would impress Bresse. It was a song from the play they would perform that very night in the Red Rose Tavern. Between songs Madeleine learned the young boy who had played the part before her had gone on to become the personal servant of a Genoese merchant.

Marie also said the play they would perform that night was about Adam and Eve and how they came to be cast out of paradise. "You will play the part of Eve," Marie told Madeleine, mentioning that the pockmarked boy, who was called Click, would play the part of Adam.

When Bresse returned, it was with a gang of fifteen or twenty youths. He and the boys—some looked to be seventeen or eighteen and were the size of grown men—went directly to the solar above. From the sound of their voices, they were having a serious

107

discussion, and several times Madeleine heard the names of streets and then something she could not quite make out concerning the provost's guards. Later the boys left, a few at a time. Only the three who had helped Click pull her from the horse remained.

The afternoon was spent in rehearsal. Bresse's fat face glistened with sweat as he delivered his lines. He played the part of the devil and directed the other actors as well. Bresse was clearly pleased with Madeleine's performance. Afterwards, he cuffed her shoulder playfully, a blow which nearly knocked her off her feet, and exclaimed, "Said like a true *jongleur*." As he strode past Marie, he said in an aside, "The voice could be sweeter, but by St. Nizier's festered prick, he is the best damn Eve we ever had."

"I told you as much," Marie said with a confident smile.

Later, when Madeleine found the courage to ask about her horse, Bresse told her the horse was payment for the acting lessons. Madeleine boiled with anger, but was afraid to pursue the matter any further. Truthfully, she no longer had need of the horse. The priory was within walking distance, if only she could escape from Bresse and his troop.

When the time came to don their costumes, Madeleine was nervous enough to swoon. Much to her relief, all were too intent on dressing themselves to pay any notice to her. First she struggled into a tight-fitting linen garment which covered her torso, except, she discovered to her profound embarrassment, for the cheeks of her derrière. On the front of the pink linen garment was a cluster of fig leaves, fashioned of stiffened linen, and two red dots of dye meant for nipples. Over this she wore a white gown and mantle. There was also a wreath of paper flowers which she hurriedly slapped atop her head.

Click laughed at the sight of her and, in the manner of an elder brother, straightened the wreath. Afterwards, Madeleine noticed his hand still bore the inflamed imprint of her teeth and she mumbled an awkward apology. Click shrugged it off, replying that he would have done the same, and to prove there were no hard feelings gave Madeleine's shoulder a comradely shake.

Marie, dressed as an angel of the Lord, steered Madeleine to a bench and painted her face with rouge and kohl.

After much shouting and cursing, the *jongleurs* loaded their wagon and set out from the tanner's district. Marie began a song as they jounced along and the others soon took up the refrain. Madeleine, seated beside Click, silently gaped at the passing panorama of the city. After a while Click noticed that she was silent and elbowed her. "Sing," he said, threatening to box her ears. She did so, half-heartedly. People came from their houses to stare and a horde of children ran skipping and dancing beside the wagon. The *jongleurs* waved heartily to the citizens of Troyes, beckoning them to follow, while Madeleine, stiff with shame, sank down behind a painted wooden tree in an effort to conceal herself. There was no need, for even her own mother would not have recognized her beneath the layers of paint.

In all her young life, Madeleine had never glimpsed the Troyes that lay beyond the Grand Rue, the market stalls, and the cathedral. She had never seen the narrow streets filled with filth and foul smells where poverty and cruelties abounded. How, she wondered, had she been so blind?

The Red Rose Tavern was housed in a three-story post-and-beam building set back in a drab square off the Grand Rue. The interior was smoke-filled and dim, the only light cast by oil lamps and torches. Even at that early hour the tavern was packed with an assortment of foreign merchants, nobles, guildsmen, and soldiers. Some ate, others drank and tried their luck at gambling; prostitutes drifted through their midst and lean, scruffy men with leaner eyes—cutpurses, Madeleine imagined—loitered before the tavern's door.

Several times Madeleine considered slipping away in the confusion of unloading the wagon and setting up the stage props, but Click was always nearby; Bresse, omnipresent, strode back and forth shouting orders to carry this and that. By the time the stage was set, Madeleine was exhausted and perspiring mightily.

A hush descended over the crowd as one of the young *jongleurs* stepped onto the platform and announced to all in a remarkably loud voice, *"Le Mystère d' Adam."* With those words as a cue, Marie, by way of ropes, hauled the curtain back to reveal paradise.

The stage had been strewn with waxed paper flowers and greenery painted on a linen backdrop. The wooden tree stood to one side and red-painted paper apples dangled from its limbs.

Bresse stepped forward in flowing golden robes and with a dramatic flourish of his arms introduced himself as God. Click wore a red tunic and Madeleine a white gown and mantle; they appeared before him as Adam and Eve. Click molded his pockmarked face into a calm visage and Madeleine, as she was instructed, set her features in a more modest air.

The boy *jongleur* took the stage once more and read: "In the beginning God created heaven and earth, and created man in his own image and after his likeness." Marie stepped forward and led them all in a little song. When it had ended, the boy raised his voice again, saying, "And the Lord God formed man of the dust of the ground, and breathed into his nostrils the breath of life, and man became a living soul."

The dialogue began when Bresse boomed out instructions in a godly voice and led Adam and Eve into paradise, where he pointed out the forbidden fruit. He then retreated to the church, a flimsy wooden facade, leaving Adam and Eve to walk about paradise wearing delighted expressions.

As Click and Madeleine crossed and recrossed the stage for the third time, and their faces were indeed beginning to ache from their delighted expressions, two young *jongleurs* dressed as demons leapt from behind the curtains. They wore masks fashioned with grotesque features and tantalizingly pointed out the forbidden fruit to Adam and Eve.

Bresse, concealed by the curtains, stripped off his golden robes and reappeared as the devil. Sidling up to Adam, he tempted him to pick the forbidden fruit. But Adam remained firm. With a downcast countenance, the devil retreated to the opposite side of the stage where another flimsy facade denoted the doors of hell, a position from which he then called the two demons to him and held a secret council.

The whispered conference ended with Bresse, who was dressed convincingly in horns and a spiked tail, sallying forth among the audience and stirring a noisy reaction. After he had raised a chorus of shouting, he returned to the stage and addressed Eve. With a smiling face and flattering air, he told her she was far more intelligent than Adam.

It was Madeleine's cue to speak and though she felt numb to her toes, she managed to reply in a shrill voice, "Adam is a little hard."

"Though he be harder than hell," the devil promised, "he shall be made soft." And in an oily voice, the devil praised Eve's beauty, saying, "You are a gentle and tender thing, fresh as a rose, white as crystal. You are too tender and he is too hard, but nevertheless you are wiser and more courageous."

Madeleine made a show of resistance, and Bresse departed, his spiked tail bouncing along behind him.

Click, who had been watching mistrustfully, approached and berated her for listening.

This was the cue for Marie to rise up at the trunk of the forbidden tree with a puppet, fashioned in the form of a serpent, on her arm.

As they had rehearsed, Madeleine cocked her head to the serpent's mouth, then plucked a paper apple and offered it to Click. He took the apple, distorting his mouth as he made a pantomime of eating it, then with a doomed expression, realized his sin and fell to his knees.

The curtain swept closed. Madeleine and Click threw off their outer costumes to reveal those pinned with fig leaves, and when the curtain opened they began their lament.

Bresse strode onto the stage costumed as God while Madeleine and Click scurried across the stage and crouched in shame. When God commanded them to rise, they groveled and wept and confessed their sin. Adam blamed his error on Eve and she on the serpent. But God refused to listen, and in a terrible voice pronounced his curse on them and the evil serpent and drove them all from paradise.

Marie, after struggling into a pair of wings, returned dressed as an angel of God and barred the gates to paradise with a shining sword. On the other side of the stage, Click and Madeleine, wearing expressions of drudgery, took up a hoe and spade. Stooping and bending, they made a show of tilling the earth and planting seeds. Afterwards, they slumped down to rest and gazed at paradise lost, weeping mournfully.

While they were thus occupied, Bresse, again as the devil, crept in and sprinkled the stage with thorns and thistles the size of a man's fist and fashioned of waxed brown paper. As Bresse slipped behind the doors to hell, Click and Madeleine spied the thorns and thistles. They leapt up, smitten with grief, then threw themselves on the ground, beating their breasts. Once more Adam berated Eve. No sooner than Click had delivered the final line, Bresse entered wagging his spiked tail and accompanied by his two demons, who carried iron chains and fetters.

Click and Madeleine resisted, unintentionally knocking one of the demon's masks askew. But the demons succeeded in placing chains on their necks and leading them off towards hell where Marie, hidden behind the doors, waved an oil lamp, producing suffocating puffs of smoke. Click and Madeleine were then shoved, coughing and sneezing, through the doors of hell while the devil and his demons danced gleefully across the stage, clashing pots and kettles and making a deafening din.

That seemed to be the audience's favorite part of the play and the sound of their cheers and hooting reverberated through the huge room. It was the moment Bresse chose to gather his *jongleurs* and, all joining hands, they took a final bow.

As the stage props were being dismantled, Madeleine noticed that Bresse had vanished. But Click had not, and he was never more than two steps away.

Marie oversaw the packing of the wagon. Madeleine lifted, carried, and tugged. Nothing seemed to fit as it had before and Madeleine was puzzled by the lack of space in the wagon. The props which had previously fit with room to spare were now stacked precariously high. There was hardly a place for any of the *jongleurs*—little more than a hand or foothold.

Wulf leaned against the wall of the tavern and drained his second tankard of ale. The room was packed with a shoulder-to-shoulder crowd; even so, he had found himself a niche. To his left was a noble and several of his villeins and before him a group of soldiers and a pair of cloth merchants. The noise of the crowd became a roar as the *jongleurs* took a final bow. Wulf joined in, shouting his approval. He had spent the day hunting, searching for some trace of the bishop's niece. After finding a stable for his horse, he had gone in search of food and drink. Entertainment was rare, and, like many others, he had been lured into the Red Rose by the shouting boys who ran about the streets advertising the play.

He bought half a roasted rabbit, drank his ale, and watched the play—though never far from his thoughts was the twenty-livre reward offered by the bishop. It was not enough to buy his freedom, but would pay for a new saddle and warm clothing for the coming winter. However, finding the bishop's wayward niece was proving to be more difficult than he had first imagined. He was convinced the girl was somewhere within the city's walls. He had expected to find her at the cobbler's shop; instead he found only the runaway serving girl, an old woman, a trio of unwashed children, and a young man, who though recovering still bore the telltale purple marks of the sickness on his arms and chest. Even so, he believed she was nearby, and that he had only to wait for the maidservant to lead him to her.

On stage the *jongleurs* were dismantling their props. The small boy skimpily costumed as Eve tripped over the curtain, took three exaggerated running steps, and dropped a sack filled with paper apples, which rolled and bounced across the stage.

Wulf chuckled, thinking that there was something oddly familiar about the boy, although he could not say what. Perhaps it was his flashing eyes and handsome darkness, reminding him of the Arab boys who lurked in Genoa's markets—little thieves who would steal the boots off a man's feet if given the opportunity. At the sound of voices, Wulf looked around. He saw he was not the only one who had noticed the boy. The noble, attired in rich blue lake velvet and standing only a few paces away, sent a villein to ask after the boy. Presently, he returned with the fat master of the *jongleurs*.

Several guildsmen halted beside Wulf and took up

a conversation. Though he could no longer hear their words, he continued to observe the exchange between the noble and the florid-faced *jongleur*. Judging from their actions, they appeared to be haggling over money. Wulf's interest wandered over the room and, seeing a tavern maid coming his way, he caught her by the arm, more or less, and sent her to fetch him another tankard of ale.

In the rear of the tavern, a full moon hung above the city's slanted rooftops. To Madeleine it appeared gaudy and too large, like a foolish linen prop, stiffened and painted orange. How, she wondered, was she to escape from this ugly make-believe, or even to undress or relieve herself without her sex being discovered?

Bresse came from the tavern's back door, his hulking form momentarily blocking out the lurid amber slash of light which poured into the tavern's garth from the kitchen.

He took Madeleine by the waist and swung her from the wagon. "You will be staying here tonight," he said. Madeleine was about to protest when Bresse's ham-like hand caught her by the neck and pressed her head against his paunchy stomach. He said, "Look keen, boy, and listen up to what I say. A gentleman is waiting for you. You do what he says and, on the morrow, you will be a richer lad and wiser, too." With that he gave her a shove toward the doorway where a grubby-faced man-at-arms waited to lay a bony hand on her shoulder and guide her back into the tavern and up a creaky staircase.

A feeling of utter panic constricted Madeleine's throat like a noose. What was she to do now? She had disguised herself as a boy to avoid the attentions of lustful men, only to discover there were no limits to some men's lust. Before she could think of a ploy, the grubby man-at-arms shoved her inside a dim room

115

and closed the door. She stood there shivering in the skimpy costume and straining her eyes to see by the light of a single feeble candle. Through the murkiness of the room her eyes conjured up the outline of a man's head and shoulders.

"Come here," a deep baritone voice coaxed.

Madeleine drew back against the door, her eyes as large as trenchers. The shadowy form laughed softly, rose from the bed, and crossed the room. "Why do you fear me, boy?" the virile voice asked. Madeleine breathed in sharply. The man's scent, musk, stung her nostrils just as his hands reached out possessively to grasp her by the buttocks.

Guiles de Luchaire! The sudden knowledge struck her with the force of a thunderbolt. She pirouetted from his hands, terrorized and frantic for a route of escape. There was but a single open slit of a window and beyond it the moon, fat and mellowed to a golden yellow, appeared to perch on the adjoining rooftops.

Madeleine sprang toward the window and, thanking God there was a roof below, teetered for a second on the embrasure then clambered onto the uneven tiles, ducking his grappling hands and scampering away. De Luchaire leaned full from the window, firing shouts and curses after her. The sound of his enraged voice echoing off the rooftops only served to spur her on; otherwise she would have been paralyzed by fear, for when she inadvertently glanced down, the dizzying height made her head float. She urged herself onward, slipping and clawing her way from one roof to another, and finally, on a roof lower to the ground, hung from a garderobe drainpipe and dropped with an unpleasant splash into a ditch. No sooner than her feet touched the earth, she was off and running as if the hounds of hell were snapping at her heels.

*   *   *

Wulf drank his third ale slowly. His thirst was now quenched and his stomach was full. With no *jongleurs* to entertain him, he wandered across the tavern to the gaming ring, where a large crowd of merchants gathered and noisily placed bets of as much as ten and twenty livres on a single roll of the dice. Wulf stood and watched. He had more practical uses for his money.

The tavern thronged with people of every description. Prostitutes mingled with foreign merchants, burghers, and thieves, and if one listened it was possible to hear as many as five or six different languages, though no one seemed to have any difficulty communicating.

A loud and unmelodic blending of voices drew Wulf's attention to the tavern doors, where five drunken Lombards sang at the top of their lungs and paraded in and out like a gang of demented children. Wulf finished his ale. He had lived among the Lombards for several years and he knew as surely as the sun would rise on the morrow, where there was a drunken Lombard there would soon be a knife fight.

He made a leisurely retreat through the tavern's kitchen. In the smoke-filled, low-beamed room the kitchen workers went on with their labors. None questioned his being there—in all likelihood they had not seen him through the haze of choking smoke.

He had only just stepped out into the garth and taken his first breath of decent air when he heard a commotion behind him. He stepped to one side and only narrowly avoided being run down by the noble in the blue lake velvet jupon and several of his villeins.

The noble cursed and ranted, craning his neck to scan the rooftops, and with a violent motion of his arms sent the villeins dashing through the maze of alleyways like hounds on a scent.

Wulf walked on, chuckling to himself over the comical scene in the garth and speculating on what

117

had transpired in the tavern's back rooms. He returned to the stable. No one was about, so he let himself in through a balky side door. He looked around but did not see the stable-keeper. Presumably he was asleep in the loft or, more realistically, lying drunk in an alley. Wulf drew a pail of water for the bay and helped himself to an extra ration of grain which he fed to Loki by handfuls as he fondly scratched the horse's ears. In the darkness of the stable, the boy returned to trouble his thoughts. He had seen the boy somewhere before. Not a boy of similar appearance, that very boy. But where?

Wulf kicked some fresh straw together and made himself a bed in the stall. With his saddle for a pillow, he closed his eyes, but could not sleep. Damn the boy. Where had he seen him?

Chapter Ten

Madeleine ran until her lungs ached. She was splattered with excrement, and even worse was her skimpy, ridiculous costume. Still, she had escaped and even the stench did not lessen the sweetness of her freedom. She knew her only hope of avoiding capture was to rid herself of the silly costume. She also knew if she returned to the house on the Rue Tannerie, Bresse would beat her and most certainly discover her sex. If only she could recall the name of the street where Albertine's little cobbler lived.

She halted in a refuse-littered alleyway, taking her breaths in ragged gasps and waiting for the stitch in her side to ease. "The rue du Domino," she murmured aloud, and prayed she was correct. She ventured from the alleyway and crossed to the church of St. Jean Au Marche, running a zigzag path through the graveyard with its rows of gravestones and phantom-like monuments. She did not stop until she reached the other side of the wall.

Madeleine did not know the little cobbler's name, only that a gaily painted wooden boot hung above the door of his shop. On the rue du Domino, she darted from one pitch-black doorway to another, at last sighting the red and yellow boot. First, she pounded her fists against the shop door in a futile effort to raise someone within the house. Then, creeping to a rear door off a tiny courtyard, she hammered away once more—this time rousing an old woman who poked her head from an upper story window and shouted at Madeleine to go away. Madeleine shouted back, pleading with the old woman to give her entry. Almost at the point of tears, Madeleine continued to beg, becoming louder with each entreaty. The ruckus brought a second woman to the window; she took one look at the comic figure below, let out a squeal of recognition, and then disappeared.

In only a moment, the door flew open and Albertine, clutching her night clothes about her, pulled Madeleine inside. After a joyous reunion, which woke everyone in the house, bath water was heated and clothes were found for Madeleine—those of the little cobbler's dead brother. Afterward there was much talk, and cheese and bread and wine were brought out.

Both Albertine and her little cobbler were opposed to her leaving in the darkness, but Madeleine feared for their safety if she remained—particularly after they told her that one of the bishop's guards had come to question them and search the house. Finally it was agreed by all that Madeleine should leave just before sunrise. The little cobbler gave her precise directions to lead her to the Artaud Gate and from there to the Priory of Notre Dame-en-l'Isle.

In the darkness, Wulf bolted up from the bed of straw. The bay snorted at his sudden movement and stamped restlessly. Realizing he had startled the animal, he quickly rose to his feet and laid a caressing hand on its neck to quiet it. "Of course," he told the bay, "It is not a boy at all. It is the dark-eyed girl." The one he had hauled upon his horse in the château's courtyard. The Lady Madeleine, the bishop's haughty niece. She had taken up with a troop of *jongleurs*, truly the last place anyone would have searched. Outside it was still dark. He waited. There was no use to search if he could not see. The time passed slowly, and the more he considered the situation, the more preposterous it became. There was only one way to settle it, and that was to find the 'boy'.

The light was sparse and darkness still clung to the city's streets when he and the bay left the stable. By that hour the troop of *jongleurs* might have been camped beyond the city's walls or moved on in the darkness. Wulf rode slowly through the market. Life there was only beginning to stir. Merchants crawled from their tents scratching themselves, and the air was smeared with the scent of cookfires and grease. He rode on toward the tavern. In the harsh light of morning, the Red Rose appeared even shabbier than it had the night before, with its crumbling walls and rotting shutters.

Wulf rousted the tavern keeper from his bed by hammering on the door and threatening to haul him before the bishop's court. The sleep-rumpled man protested his innocence with all the vehemence of a criminal. When at last he realized it was not a question of crooked dice, he swore upon the relics of St. Pierre's Cathedral that he did not know the whereabouts of the *jongleurs.* "I would not hire them again," he said. "Between you and me, I think they are a pack of thieves. I heard last night there were robberies on the rue du Mortier d'Or," and with a sly look, added, "I hear it happens wherever they perform." The tavern keeper, wishing to preserve his untarnished reputation as an honest and loyal citizen, then offered Wulf a tankard of ale—at no charge, of course.

Wulf declined. The sun was up and he had wasted enough time. He rode again through the market, then slowly past the cobbler's shop. All was as it should be. The cobbler was at his bench and the

121

former maidservant was working beside him. The old woman swept a storm of dust from the open door, and nearby the children were playing in the dirt. The sun was directly overhead and the sext bells were sounding as Wulf turned the bay back toward the market.

Earlier, Madeleine had cautiously slipped from the cobbler's shop. She had waited for the sky to lighten to a silvery shade of blue. Even so, darkness still clung to the post-and-beam buildings and the shadowy streets were deserted.

It seemed wisest to Madeleine to avoid the Grand Rue. By now, she felt certain her uncle had alerted his provost's guards. It was possible he had somehow guessed at her disguise, and even if he had not, Guiles de Luchaire was no doubt searching for the boy for whom he had paid so dearly and without satisfaction. There was also the danger of being spotted by the *jongleurs*. She knew enough of their thievery to hang the lot of them. Added to this was Madeleine's fear of becoming lost in the endless maze of intersecting streets and alleyways. To avoid such a catastrophe the little cobbler had given her descriptions of landmarks to guide her. Places, rather than the names of streets, for in some cases the names were known only to the street's inhabitants.

The day dawned bright and fair, and all along her route Madeleine passed sleepy housewives drawing water from wells and workers hurrying off to their trades. Madeleine walked at a steady pace, passing from busy working class streets to drowsy bourgeois neighborhoods. After a time she came upon a pair of pottery urns which guarded the entrance to a walled courtyard before a burgher's home on the rue Trieste. A tumble of flowers grew from one urn, while its mate had produced only an odd collection of weeds. The house was exactly as Albertine's little cobbler

122

had described it, complete to the small balcony and blue tiled facade.

A faint sound of voices drifted from the balcony into the pleasantly cool morning air, and somewhere down the alleyway a dog barked. The barking was soon joined by others and altogether the dogs raised a noisy serenade.

Standing in the shadow of the wall, Madeleine turned her eyes back the way she had come, thinking she must take the alleyway to the left. As she was considering this, the sound of running feet whirled her around. A half-grown youth hurtled past her in full flight. She gasped, startled as much by his face as by his sudden appearance, for she immediately recognized him as one of the *jongleurs*. She had not yet recovered when shouts sounded from the direction in which the boy had come, and the drubbing of hooves echoed along the alleyway.

For one terrible instant, Madeleine was immobilized by panic. Her gaze flitted from one sheer-sided courtyard to another. There was nowhere to hide. She stumbled against the urn and, looking up, realized the open courtyard before her was her only hope. She darted inside, praying she had not been seen by the house's inhabitants.

A trio of wooden barrels sat in one corner of the otherwise barren courtyard. Madeleine squeezed behind them, wedging herself into the very corner of the wall where she ducked down on her haunches, making herself as small as possible. The barrels had apparently held wine at one time, for their sharp fermenty odor hung in the humid air and all but took away her breath.

Curses and shouts rang out and the thunder of hooves grew ever nearer. The voices she had heard from the house were now on the balcony directly above her head. Madeleine sank still closer to the ground, clasped her arms about her knees and buried her face against the tops of her legs, hoping desperately that no one had seen her, and hardly daring to breathe.

Her worst fears were realized when the householder above her head cried, "Thief, thief!" and waved the horsemen into the courtyard.

Madeleine's heart leapt into her throat. They had seen her. A frenzied millrace of thoughts tumbled through her mind. She had seen her uncle's troops in the city's streets wearing the bishop's cross branded into their vest-like leather jerkins. She had also seen the brutal evidence of their harsh justice in the bloated corpses which swayed from the pillory. Would she be able to convince them of her true identity before they crushed her skull with their broadswords or strung her from the pillory as well?

The sound of clanging swords and stomping horses made a deafening racket, so loud that it seemed they were on top of her. They dismounted, shouting out comands and curses. But the trample of footfalls led away from, not towards, her. Hazarding a glance, she saw the last of them disappear around the side of the house. She gaped after them open-mouthed until it finally dawned on her—it was the boy! Obviously the householder had seen him fleeing. Seen him, but not her, because of the height of the wall. She took a deep breath and raised her head, expecting to see only horses. Instead she found herself staring into the broad back of a guardsman! She nearly swallowed her tongue.

It appeared he had been left to guard the horses. For a time he paced to and fro before the barrels, so close Madeleine could have reached out and touched him. Later, he broke a branch from a gnarled apple tree growing beside the kitchen door and scratched pictures in the dirt. When Madeleine looked again from the narrow space between the barrels, his back was to her and a large dark stain spread down the stones of the kitchen wall.

The sun climbed higher above the courtyard and

Madeleine, huddled behind the barrels, was miserable in the stifling heat. She waited for what was surely hours, for the sext bells sounded only moments before the soldiers returned empty-handed.

Madeleine waited long after the dust stirred by their horses had settled, then edged stealthily from her hiding place. She had crouched without moving for so long that her first steps were shaky and unsure and her legs felt as if they were pulled by strings.

With nervous backward glances, Madeleine made her way to the market. She felt safer there, where she could mix with the thronging crowd of peasants and townspeople and gape at the jugglers, musicians, and acrobats. The scent of spices wafted through the market, trinkets gleamed in the sunlight, and the flaunted colors of rich cloth delighted her eyes.

In one aisle, Madeleine saw a man selling cider and ale from a barrel. A cup of cider would have been heaven to her parched throat, but she had no silver coins and she could hardly purchase a cup of cider with a sapphire broach. She turned her head and tried not to think of her thirst.

A fat woman towing a child walked before Madeleine, blocking the aisleway between rows of wooden booths. Madeleine was anxious to be on her way and the woman's pace was maddeningly slow. At last, Madeleine managed to squeeze past the woman's broad backside when she stopped to inspect a bolt of linen.

Madeleine walked toward the rue Moyenne at a brisk pace. Near the end of the market square, the crowd thinned and there were fewer booths. A merchant and his assistants were unloading a string of packhorses before an empty booth. Madeleine cast a curious glance over the merchant's goods; sacks of salt perhaps, for they appeared to be weighty. She stepped gingerly past the line of horses, her downcast eyes playing over the pointed toes of her soft leather boots. Philippe's boots, she thought with a touch of sadness, and then considered how fortunate she was to have had a brother such as Philippe. She was certain he would have been pleased to know she remembered the sound of his voice, his laughter, and his mannerisms; it was those very memories which had enabled her to dupe the *jongleurs* and beat them at their own game of make-believe.

Gurgling pigeons scurried before her. Black and grey and white, they hurried off on fragile pink feet and with a sudden beating of wings took flight. Her gaze followed their ascent as they sailed over a booth draped with gaudy-colored cloth, where several men haggled over the price of pepper. One loudly accused the merchant of mixing clay with his product; another swore it was bits of donkey dung. The affronted merchant shouted back, evoking the name of every saint he could recall.

Several horsemen moved slowly toward Madeleine. The two in the foreground rode abreast on fine palfreys and, judging from their colorful, almost laughable parti-colored attire, were rich Lombard money lenders. The third horseman was a young soldier with fair hair, whose skin was burnt bronze and eyelashes bleached white by the August sun. He wore the bishop's cross upon his sweat-stained leather jerkin and the rough-woven shirt beneath hung open at the neck. Astride a dark bay horse, he moved slowly, purposefully, his eyes sweeping first right then left as if he were searching for someone.

Madeleine looked away quickly. Her knees felt as if they might buckle beneath her and she was trembling so that she feared it must be visible to all. She forced herself to walk on, hurrying a little to catch up to a group of peasants, hoping she might appear to be one of their group.

The large dark bay picked its way slowly through the knots of marketgoers. A merchant's wagon momentarily blocked its path; the horse sidestepped, then edged forward.

In a moment, Madeleine thought, he will draw even with me. She held her breath and set her eyes on the backs of the peasant family's heads. With a fearful sideways glance, Madeleine saw the horse's powerful flanks slide past her, saw the back of the soldier's head where his short-cropped hair grew several shades darker close to his skull.

She drew a breath through her parted lips. It was the Saxon. The oaf who had swung her onto his horse in the courtyard. Had he recognized her? Her heart thumped wildly against her rib cage and a sudden chill sent pinpricks of fear racing along her clammy skin.

When the gorup of peasants drew even with a cooper's booth, Madeleine ducked from sight, molding herself to the side of the booth and waiting for an interminable few seconds. Gathering all her courage, she peeked around the corner and, through the latticework of booths, saw he had turned his horse; he was coming back.

She leaned heavily against the rough-hewn booth, as if for support. With every heartbeat, he was coming closer. Still she could not decide. If she ran, she would give herself away. But if he had recognized her, and she waited, he would simply pluck her from the street like a lost coin. No, her only chance was to run and hope to lose him among the confusing network of alleyways.

She took a deep breath and darted from cover. From behind, she heard a shout, and with a fleeting backward glance saw the prancing horse lunge forward as people screamed and scrambled from its path.

Madeleine's stomach knotted with panic. She dodged from the blinding glare of the street to the blackness of a dank alleyway. Behind her, the loping stride of his horse pounded in her ears louder than the hammer-beat of her heart. Her lungs burned as if afire; the end of the alleyway hung deceptively before

127

her, looking as distant as the moon and stars.

Suddenly, her eyes seized upon a ragged clump of young trees—her salvation—whose leafy limbs blocked the far end of the narrow mud alleyway. With a final burst of endurance, she sent her legs plunging toward a small gap between the close-set trunks and the post-and-beam wall of the next house.

Wulf, intent on his quarry, was blind to the obstacle. At the last moment he saw it, and, frantically shifting his weight in the saddle, pulled up on the reins, shaving a plume of foam from the animal's neck. The bay skidded sideways and crashed into the trees, catapulting Wulf into a tangle of branches. The startled horse shied, reins dangling before it, and pranced backwards, snorting and stomping. Wulf pulled himself from the trees, catching a glimpse of the girl as she ducked around the corner of a thatched lean-to. He stood up, shook himself, and took out after her on foot.

She led him through a labyrinth of cluttered rear garths and poultry yards. It required little effort on his part to catch the exhausted girl, but just as he reached out to grab her by the billowing tail of her shirt, she veered away, dropped down on all fours and squirmed beneath a rail fence. As she did, a terrified chorus of squeals pierced the air and half a dozen pigs stampeded to the opposite side of the sty.

Wulf, unable to check his stride, lunged past her, then regained himself, and with his long legs easily leapt the rail fence. But no sooner had his feet touched down than they flew from under him in the sloppy mire and he went sprawling beside her.

With a yelp of surprise, Madeleine clawed her way to her feet, slipping and sliding and ducking his hands. But she got no farther than the length of his arm. He caught her by the shoulder and slammed her down in the sour-smelling swill, where she cursed like a drunken peasant and flailed her arms at him. Breaking away, she gave a mighty swing and clouted

128

him alongside the head.

He wrestled her back and forth, his ear ringing like a vesper bell. Again and again he grabbed the mud-slick girl, only to have her slip from his grasp. Finally he managed to pin he hands over her head. Madeleine fought against him with all her will, thrashing, tossing from side to side and howling like a cat, but she was unable to free herself.

He held her there until her fury seemed spent; more likely she had run out of air. He then pulled her roughly to her feet.

She sent him a hateful, daring glance and lashed out with her foot, catching him squarely in the groin. A searing pain jolted through his gut, nearly doubling him over. Seizing the opportunity, Madeleine wrenched free and sprinted toward the make-shift gate. The huddled pigs grunted and squealed in terror, scattering in all directions.

Wulf lunged after the girl. Before he had been careful not to harm her, but now with the pain still burning in his groin, he hit her with the full force of his body, bringing her down as he would a man. He shoved her face in the stinking mud, thrust her wrist to her shoulder blade, and straddled her. He was merciless. She would not get away a second time, he thought, and to be certain, whipped a cloth from inside his tunic and bound her hands behind her.

Several moments passed before he realized she was sobbing. Tears streamed down her muddy cheeks. It was her last defense, but her pitiable sobs could not begin to compare with the ache in his groin. He stood her on her feet and walked her back the way she had run.

She trudged before him. A hostile backward glance confirmed he was as filthy as she and he was limping—in that respect Madeleine felt somewhat avenged.

In one cluttered garth, an old woman with a bowl in her arms stepped from a doorway to feed her hens.

She had never seen two people so thoroughly covered with mud and stared at them as they passed by.

Wulf found the bay waiting patiently in the alleyway, idly stripping leaves from the branches of the young trees. He picked up the reins and lifted the muddy girl onto the saddle, then mounted, easing himself down behind her.

She turned her mud-splattered face to his. "Set me free," she begged, twisting herself in the saddle and promising, "I can make you a rich man."

Until that moment, he had not trusted himself to speak. "Be still," he growled, and, with a nudge of his heels, urged the bay forward.

In the market they drew more curious stares and at the town gate their stench wrinkled the noses of the guards, who laughed and traded comments about pig herders.

After they had gone a short distance, Madeleine began to squirm and complain in a whining voice that she had no feeling in her hands. "My fingers will fall off," she predicted, "and you will be to blame." He suffered her curses and accusations for a good distance, until his ears could no longer tolerate it, before he finally untied her hands.

Well beyond Troyes' walls, a slow-moving little fork of the Seine snaked through the sun-baked countryside. Wulf halted the bay in the leafy shade of overhanging trees. Madeleine, whose head nodded drowsily in the heat of the day, jolted awake and asked, "Why are we stopping here?"

"To wash off this filth," he told her, lowering her to the ground, then dismounting.

The idea was agreeable to Madeleine. She was glad for an opportunity to rid herself of the layers of stinking mud which had caked and dried on her hands and face—truthfully, everywhere. She crouched at the stream's edge and dipped her hands into the sun-sparkling water. The horse's shadow eclipsed her as it passed by, splashing into the stream and lowering its muzzle to drink. A school of minnows darted from the shoreline, flashing silver as they fled into deeper water and merged with the liquid shadows of the trees.

"Take off your clothes," he told her, shedding the leather jerkin. "Clothing is easier to wash when it is not on your back."

Madeleine raised her eyes from the stream, looking at him as if he had just suggested she set fire to herself. She was not about to shed her clothing and said as much. Her color deepened several shades when she saw he was nude to the waist and about to drop his leather hose. She turned her head.

She washed her face and arms, all the while staring into her reflection in the water. She heard the splatter and splash as he washed his clothing and heard his footsteps as he hung it to dry on a tree branch. She heard the horse, too, as it sloshed from the stream and began grazing a short distance away; heard its teeth ripping at the mature grass and the harsh swishing of its tail flailing against its flank.

She waded into the water, boots and all, and stood knee-deep attempting to wash the mud from her hosen and tunic. Wulf watched her cautious progress. She could not swim, he thought. It was not unusual, many could not. "Do you fear the water?" he called from mid-stream where he effortlessly treaded water. He ducked his head beneath the surface, emerging with an explosive splash, snorting and shaking the water from his hair.

"Yes," Madeleine replied, which was only half a truth. She could not swim, but she feared more for her modesty than from the possibility of drowning.

"You smell like a pig sty," he told her.

"My aroma is no concern of yours," she snapped irritably, her dark-lashed eyes marking off his distance from shore.

"It is if you expect to ride with me. Take off your clothes and wash. I will not look at you."

131

"Do you swear it?"

He gave an affirmative grunt.

With a sidelong glance, she saw the horse grazing nearby. "Turn your back," she commanded. When he had, Madeleine pretended to shed her shirt and hosen and, splashing her hands against the water, edged slowly from the stream. She saw his back was toward her. He had moved slightly downstream beneath the shade of the trees where a hazel shrub overhung the water.

At the shoreline, she turned and crept swiftly toward the grazing horse. With a rush, she grabbed at the trailing reins. But the bay threw up its large head with a snort and sidestepped away, swishing its tail.

She heard his voice boom. She did not recognize the words—a Saxon oath, no doubt—which prompted her to lunge at the dancing horse, only to have the obstinate animal prance aside.

From over her shoulder, she saw him come slipping across the mossy stones, naked and dripping wet. She bolted for the woods but he was on top of her, his hands reaching for any part of her he could grab, before she had covered half the distance. He caught her by the shirt, clamped his hands on her shoulders, and shook her until she thought her teeth would fall out.

He dragged her back to the stream, ignoring her screams, then shouted obscenities and dunked her into the water. Once, twice, thrice water surged over her head. She gasped and sputtered, throwing her arms against his in a futile attempt to escape.

"Close your mouth," he advised, "otherwise you will drown." Afterwards he shoved her under once more for the good of her soul.

Madeleine lurched to the surface and, with an explosive fit of coughing, staggered and fell backward with a loud splash. She sat there waist-deep, shaking with fury, blinking water from her eyes and sputtering the foulest language she knew.

"It is easier to wash your clothes when they are not on your back," he reminded her.

"I hope you rot in hell," she swore, narrowing her stinging eyes at him. She was infuriated to the point of blindness. The fact that he was naked as the day he was born did not even occur to her. Only in the moments which followed, when he, too, became aware of his nakedness, did he snap his wet shirt from the limb and whip it across his shoulders. The long-tailed shirt covered most of his dignity, but Madeleine noticed when he turned away from her to pull on his hosen that his behind was as white as a hare's backside.

Madeleine struggled to her feet and sloshed from the stream. As much as she wanted to cry, she was far too angry and stood there silently fuming.

He pulled on his boots, glanced over at her, and burst out laughing. Between brays of laughter, he tried to speak but his voice was lost.

Madeleine stared back at him as if he had gone mad. Only when she self-consciously took inventory of herself did she notice that the wad of material she and Albertine had fashioned into a manhood had come unwound in the water and grown to gigantic proportions in her soggy hosen. Her face flushed scarlet and she whirled around, tearing at the linen ties and flinging the traitorous material into the bushes beside the stream.

He was still chuckling when he eased himself into the saddle and hauled her unceremoniously upon the horse. When he took her by the thigh and swung her leg over the saddle, she protested with an indignant squeal. "Stupid lout! Take your filthy hands off me!" she shouted, jabbing at him with her fists. He dropped the reins and artfully dodged back in the saddle. His easy grace and mocking laughter antagonized her all the more.

Beneath them, the bay took the bit in its teeth and pranced sideways, crashing into the bushes. Wulf grabbed for the reins, but Madeleine cursed at him and batted his hands away. She had every intention of climbing off the horse.

His hands grappled after her, but before he could catch hold of her, she teetered atop the saddle on one hip.

"Careful," he warned with a gust of laughter, "You will fall on your head." When it seemed she would succeed in doing just that, he grabbed her by the shirt and anchored his other hand securely between her legs, on that part of her black as a stain, unseen, but imagined and infinitely fascinating to him. He gave her a jounce, as if he were judging the weight of a sack, then hoisted her, kicking and screaming, onto the saddle.

She flung curses at him and tugged furiously at the offending hand. "Ignorant shit of a peasant!" she shrieked. "Do you think you can handle me any way you please? I am not some tavern slut who keeps a little mouse beneath her skirts for every Jacques and Jean to pet!"

He understood her well enough, but was too paralyzed by laughter to obey. "*Souris!*" he all but choked. "A little mouse," he breathed, between guffaws of laughter and breathless, panting sounds. He was so amused that he was only vaguely aware of her determined efforts to twist his fingers backwards, and her boiling anger because she was having no success. He could barely speak for laughing and trying to hold the thrashing girl, who had abandoned all hope of breaking his fingers and now battered at his ribs with her sharp little elbows.

The bay tossed its head and side-stepped in a circle. A leafy branch brushed past his ear and cracked against his shoulder. He quickly took back his hand; he was in need of both, one to fend off her attack and the other to rein in the sidling horse before it raked them into a tree.

She continued to scream and thrash at him; the

stamping horse fought the bit. Two hands were not enough, but he, seeing again in his mind the enormous wad of cloth as it sailed through the air, was unable to curb his fit of laughter. "Not so much a little mouse," he wheezed, "but a full grown rat! Na," he said with a snort, "near long as my arm and the envy of even a Moor!"

Infuriated at being made the butt of his laughter, Madeleine swiveled her head round and spit in his hee-hawing face. He flinched, instantly sobered, his face white-edged and hard. She had no time to duck away. He grabbed a handful of cropped curls, jerked her head backwards, and kissed her squarely on the mouth, forcing open her startled lips and thrusting his tongue over hers. She was naught but a little castle and gown and deserved as much, he thought, for her snobbery and all the trouble she had caused him.

Madeleine twisted and squirmed, gouged and punched at him with her free hand, but he was too big—solid as the horse beneath them, and strong. She could not force him to release her and with his mouth on hers she could not even scream threats at him. She was powerless and the startling realization, coupled with a sudden push of fear, sent her heart to pounding, skipping like a stone across water.

Released from his hands, she lurched forward, clinging to the horse's tossing mane, strangling on her own saliva and coughing.

He dragged the back of his hand across his mouth and pressed her rigid shoulders to him. "Pax," he chuckled in her ear. "My silence for yours?" Knowing what he knew, however, he was confident she would not repeat the incident to anyone.

She wrenched from his grip, and, with an arrogant side-long glance, called him a lump of dirt. He gave her a smile filled with mischief and nudged the bay forward.

For the remainder of the journey, Madeleine, whose

135

ears burned with indignation, rode in sullen silence. She had been willing to dare anything to avoid returning to the clutches of her damnable uncle—now she was eager to be done with it. At least she would be rid of the mangy cur seated behind her. There would be another day, she promised herself. Her uncle would never succeed in bending her to his will. Never.

Chapter Eleven

The priest de Grailley walked swiftly from the chapel after reading Mass. A number of novices trailed after him as they, too, returned to the château and their studies. As he walked, de Grailley noticed one of the bishop's guards ride into the courtyard with a young boy seated before him. Drawing nearer, he saw it was not a young boy, but His Grace's niece, the Lady Madeleine. De Grailley covered the remaining distance at a run, shouting to the soldier, "Bring her inside at once. I will announce you to His Grace." He took the château's steps by twos and in his haste left the great iron-bound doors standing open.

Once inside the hall, word spread quickly and a number of servants came to gape and whisper. Madeleine glowered angrily at everyone and refused to be taken to her uncle until she had first gone to her chamber. After only a moment, de Grailley returned and beckoned to the Saxon. "This way," he said, "and be quick."

Seeing that her wishes were about to be thwarted, Madeleine rooted her foot to the stone floor of the hall and shouted curses at all of them. Wulf clamped a large hand on the back of her neck and shoved her before him. She twisted her head around, sending him a venomous look and snarled, "I hate you. If I

were a man I would beat you senseless with my fists."
He gave her another shove, propelling her forward.
"You do as well with words," he told her.

The door of her father's library loomed ahead and
there was no hope of escape. Even the darkness of the
passageway could not conceal her disheveled appearance. Her ill-fitting shirt and breeches flapped
against her thin frame. Her bedraggled cropped hair
was plastered to her head and her soft leather boots,
Philippe's boots, squished with every step, leaving a
trail of watery footprints.

Heribert, Bishop of Champagne, looked up as de
Grailley, leading the way, stepped aside to allow the
Lady Madeleine and her captor entry. Dubuc,
standing at the bishop's elbow before the map table,
raised his greying head, as did a pair of smooth-faced
novices, whose duty it was to hold down the corners
of the unfurled map.

Heribert stiffened at the sight of his niece,
regarding her with a look of profound disgust.
"Where did you find her?" he asked in a brittle voice.

"Troyes, Your Grace." To Madeleine he sounded
as proud and pleased as a boy who had won a May
Day race. "She had hidden herself among a troop of
jongleurs," he added with relish.

"A lie!" Madeleine screeched. Her dark eyes
bounded from one to another like a furious little
beast and her words came tumbling from her lips in a
torrent. "I was abducted, first by a band of thieves
who call themselves *jongleurs*, then by this dog of
yours!" She wrenched her arm from the Saxon's grip
and sent him a hateful look. "He has been crude and
insulting and has handled me roughly," she cried.
"You cannot know the abuses I have suffered."

Heribert swept from behind the table in his
flowing silken robes. "Silence," he thundered, and,
with a rapid gesture of his jeweled hands, dismissed
the pair of wide-eyed novices, who gratefully fled the
highly charged atmosphere of the room. Abandoned,

the leather map curled upon itself with a loud thump.

Heribert stared, appalled by his niece's unspeakably filthy appearance. She had deliberately and spitefully transformed herself from a desirable, lovely young woman into something less appealing than a village slut. Indeed, with her hair shorn like a shearling lamb's, it was difficult to judge her sex at all. "Look at yourself," he ground out. "You are a disgrace to your name."

Madeleine's anger exploded into words. "Water will wash this filth from my body, Uncle. But even the blood of Christ will not cleanse the greed from your soul!"

"Hold your tongue!" Heribert roared, his voice crackling with emotion. He very nearly struck her—his every instinct was to do so. It was with great effort that he checked himself, clenched his jaws, and lowered his voice to a civil tone. "Do not believe, my dear niece, that my patience with you is infinite. It is only through my love of God and the fact you are of my own blood that I have not abandoned you to your fate. Rather, I have endeavored to see you handsomely married, and for all my tedious labors, I have received only your ingratitude and insolence."

Madeleine's dark eyes blazed with unquenched fury, but fearing the consequences, she bit back her words.

Heribert noted well the defiant expression, so like his brother's. And like him, she was possessed of a single-minded determination and the cunning of a devil. He retreated to the windows, clasping his bejeweled hands behind his back and debating how he might still make good his arrangement with the Duke du Boulay. As his niece had so sarcastically pointed out, the filth could be washed away, even the hideously cropped hair could be hidden beneath a coif. Clearly, the problem would be restraining her until the marriage could take place. He had no doubt in his mind that at the first opportunity his willful niece would again attempt to escape; moreover, she might not be so quickly reclaimed a second time.

Dubuc, whose thoughts ran along a similar course, shuffled from behind the map table and suggested in an undertone that the lady be locked away until the wedding.

Heribert sent Dubuc an impatient glance and in a waspish voice replied, "The Duke of Burgundy would hardly accept a bride whose complexion rivaled that of a man condemned to the gibbet." He turned from the window, settling his eyes on the young mercenary. "By what name are you called, soldier?"

"Wulf, of Rügen, Your Grace."

"Dubuc, make note of it," he commanded. The reward was twenty livres and Heribert intended to make good the money. The young man had earned it. "Have you served me loyally, Wulf of Rügen?"

"Inasmuch as I am able, Your Grace."

Heribert considered this, then asked, "For what length of time have you served in my guard?"

"Since Martinmas, Your Grace."

The Widow Crozet and two serving women waited just beyond the door arch. The widow, Heribert's choice to hold the post of chatelaine and only newly arrived, was a woman of small stature, broad enough, but in all a head shorter than Dubuc. As for the two serving women, neither could be expected to handle a young woman as unruly and determined as his niece. Heribert's gaze settled again on the raw-boned young mercenary. He asked, "How have you pledged your loyalty to me?"

"Unto death, Your Grace," Wulf replied, somewhat puzzled by his question, for it was the pledge all liegemen swore.

"You would do well to remember it, for I commit my niece to your vigilance. From this day forward you are never to permit her out of your sight. If she

140

escapes, it is you who will pay with your life. Do you understand?"

Wulf inclined his head. "Yes, Your Grace," he replied, for any other response would have been unacceptable. Clearly, he was doomed to sit by the Lady Madeleine's chamber door until he developed calluses on his backside; that much he understood, but not how he was to keep sight of her from behind a closed door.

A copper tub was hefted up the stairs by the efforts of several household varlets and a line of serving women brought heated water from the kitchen to the lady's chamber. Wulf stood guard outside the door. He had looked over the room and was satisfied the Lady Madeleine could not easily escape. The chamber contained but a single window and it was of some considerable height from the ground. Later, the priest de Grailley found him there before the door and ordered him inside the chamber, much to the outraged cries of the widow and two serving women, who hastily moved a rich damask screen into place.

Wulf sat off to one side of the chamber on a bench near the hearth and stared at the toes of his boots. Madeleine's demure silence was far more eloquent than words. She sat shoulder-deep in the warm water looking pink and angelic and wearing a martyred expression.

Wulf, too, noticed her angelic composure. A man could not be expected to stare at his boots indefinitely, and he soon discovered that by angling his gaze slightly to the left he could catch an occasional glimpse of milk-white shoulder and firm little pink-nippled teats, a view which immediately quickened his blood and cluttered his thoughts with the normal urges and instincts of a young man his age. At the stream, his anger and the stunning cold of the water had kept him reasonably under control, but just then, with his eyes full of her, he felt monstrously uncomfortable. He stared again at his boot tops, praying he would not be asked to move, for at that moment, he was certain he could not walk.

His clandestine glances, however, did not go unnoticed. The widow saw right through his air of casual indifference. Her heart went out to the poor girl. She had not expected the bishop's orders to be carried out quite so literally and bristled with righteous indignation. "It is indecent," she said. "Such a cruel invasion of your privacy is shocking." She promised Madeleine, "I will speak to His Grace this very day."

Madeleine smiled gratefully, hoping to cultivate the woman's trust and loyalty. "Surely," she pleaded, "you will be able to dissuade my uncle from continuing this immoral situation."

The widow, sympathetic to her mistress's plight, agreed to do her very best.

Wulf heard their conversation. The Lady Madeleine's words only confirmed what he already knew of her. She was as deceitful as a Genoese merchant and treacherous as a Turk, and for all of that she and her uncle were well matched. As much as Wulf did not care to be a jailer, sitting in a warm dry chamber was by far a more pleasant duty than any he had known in some time.

Heribert had been expecting the Widow Crozet. Indeed he wondered what had kept her so long. He was well prepared for her indignant entreaties and immediately took her into his confidence.

"As you are a good and moral woman," he began, "I, better than anyone, understand your confusion." He paused and, leveling his gaze at her, went on. "I trust that what I am about to tell you will go no further than his room."

142

"It will never cross my lips, Your Grace," the widow swore in a hushed voice. She waited as if suspended at the edge of the table, in breathless anticipation of some dark secret.

"My brother's beloved daughter, the Lady Madeleine, has since childhood suffered from spells. You, of course, noticed her cropped hair?"

The widow nodded, rounding her eyes. "I thought it odd. It is not the fashion. Not at all becoming for a young noblewoman."

Heribert smiled benignly. "She cut it with a hunting knife, I am told."

The widow's mouth made a perfect "O." "Oh! A knife. The poor child. Is she mad, Your Grace?"

Heribert drew his long features into an expression of resignation. "I fear her affliction is far worse than simple lunacy." He hesitated and, choosing his words with great care, said softly, "She is at times possessed by demons. Ah, yes, it is to my eternal shame that one of my own blood is so cruelly afflicted, and though I pray daily for her deliverence, thus far it has eluded her."

The widow drew back with a sharp gasp, looking as terrified as if she had just discovered a rat in her pantry. Heribert, noting her reaction, continued. "When she is seized by these demons, she has the destructive force of a man and her senses are quite unbalanced. I could not in good conscience expose a frail and devout woman like yourself to harm. Hence the Saxon guard; all told they are a godless lot and of no consequence." In conclusion, Heribert cautioned the widow once more, adding, "The penalty for betraying my trust is harsh indeed."

The widow, Agnes Crozet, solemnly swore to carry the secret to her grave. And afterwards, whether from awe or fear for her eternal soul, would pass not one moment alone with the Lady Madeleine, but surrounded herself with serving women who knew naught of the lady's unholy affliction.

Before vesper bells rang that day, Heribert sent for the captain of his guards, Jean Paschal. The old soldier's iron-grey hair and military bearing lent him the appearance of being chiseled from stone. The keen coolness of the outdoors and the smell of horses clung to his mail and leather clothing.

There was a chill in the air that autumn evening and a servant had lit a fire in the library's hearth. Heribert settled into the chair before the massive table where his leather-and wooden-bound ledgers and books of accounts were stacked and arranged his robes about his feet to ward off the draft. He said a word of greeting to his captain, then asked, "The young Saxon mercenary who returned my niece this day—what do you know of him?"

Paschal slowly removed his gloves and placed them under his arm. "Practically nothing, Your Grace. He was among the mercenaries you purchased from Count Gianocarlo di Scalla."

Heribert was well aware of his purchase of one hundred and fifty men from the younger, foolish brother of the late prince. "Is that all you know of the Saxon? You are his commander," Heribert reminded him in a sharply reproachful tone.

Jean Paschal cleared his throat and addressed the bishop. "He wears a knight's sword, Your Grace."

Heribert raised a thinly-arched brow. "Is he a knight?"

"I have seen no proof of it."

The priest de Grailley stood at the far end of the room silently gazing from the chamber windows, where, beyond the thickly waved glass a spectacular sunset lit the low rolling hills of Champagne with shades of scarlet and purple.

"You doubt his worth as a man at arms?" Heribert questioned, somewhat annoyed by the evasive reply.

"No, Your Grace. He is able enough with weapons and an excellent horseman."

144

Heribert was becoming most annoyed. "What then? Out with it, man. I have other more pressing matters with which to puzzle my thoughts."

Paschal saw the rising impatience in the shrewd dark eyes, but still he groped for words. "He has a strange turn of mind. I do not trust him."

Heribert slumped back in the Italian chair and folded his hands on his chest. Dear God, the man was as wearisome as Dubuc. "I am in no mood for parables, Paschal. Explain yourself."

Paschal's eyes wandered 'round the room as if he were searching for a solution to his dilemma and might find the answer written on the walls. At last he said, "I cannot, Your Grace."

"Yet, you mistrust him?" Heribert's controlled tone rose with annoyance. "In Christ's name, why?"

"He is educated, able to read and put down letters. He is clever with words; he turns them to suit his own purposes."

"I see. Curious talents for a soldier." Heribert's interest was stirred. Few nobles could boast such talents; fewer lawyers, he thought bitterly, for the loss of Viezon was a wound that had never healed. Heribert toyed with the heavy gold and ruby crucifix which hung from his neck on a golden chain. "Tell me, Paschal, how did such an ingenious fellow come to the service of the Prince di Scalla?"

"From Kassa, as a prisoner of the Turks. At least that is the tale he tells."

"He is a Christian then?"

"So he claims. A knight of the Order of St. Mary the Virgin." Paschal said, adding that he did not believe him. "To my mind, he is more pagan than Christian and would sooner worship a tree or a stone."

Heribert was thoughtful for a moment. He had heard of the war-like religious order. Warrior priests who spread the word of God by the sword and were

145

ambitiously carving out an empire in the east. "He bows before the Holy Church, does he not?" Heribert remarked.

"Yes, Your Grace, when it suits him to do so."

"Then he is Christian as most," Heribert said, and with a wave of his heavily-ringed hand dismissed Paschal.

De Grailley, who had been gazing meditatively from the windows throughout the interview, came and leaned across the massive table. In a soft voice he said, "It seems our Saxon has the scruples of a Valois, as well as their blue eyes."

With haste, Guiles de Luchaire dismounted and tossed the reins at a waiting stable boy. Two burly villeins followed suit, leaving the boy to grasp after their horses' trailing reins.

Inside the dank-smelling hall, Sézanne's steward, Mirand, and the priest, Constanzo, awaited the lord. At their backs stood a dozen loyal serfs; among the group were two women.

"So this is what you have brought me," de Luchaire remarked, stripping off his riding gloves as he crossed the hall. He paced before the assembled peasants, looking hard into each face. Some were known to him, some not. No matter, they would soon afford him an ear and a hand in the house of de Moncelet.

"They are true to your cause, milord, and loyal unto death," the steward assured him, though the twitch of his jaw muscles betrayed his nervousness. If they failed, he would be held to blame.

The priest stood by silently. He viewed his lord's machinations as certain folly and had urged him, only that morning following Mass, to reconsider. "Let Avignon settle this dispute," he had all but begged. "Time will be your champion, not your enemy. Justice will be yours, for none could deny your right to the lady and her property. It is God's law and the king's as well." But his calls for reason were cast aside, and seeing the determined set of his lord's jaw, he wisely pressed his argument no farther.

It was near to lauds when de Luchaire, having made his choices, dismissed the group. When the last of them had filed from the hall, the priest, Constanzo, spoke out in opposition to three of the chosen conspirators . . . Oudart Gontier, his wife, and his elder brother. "They live in sin, milord, and such blasphemy can only bring your plans to ruin."

De Luchaire smiled, arching a dark brow. "Sin, Constanzo? What sin?"

A frown hardened the priest's mild features. "The woman is the elder brother's wife, yet she freely copulates with both. She makes no secret of it."

De Luchaire gave a hearty laugh. He, himself, had lain with Helayne Gontier. "The world is not a moral place, Constanzo. If it was, what need would there be of priests?"

From the shadowy recesses of the hall where he had sat patiently throughout the long session, Gédèon, the herbalist of de Luchaire's father, came forward wearing a smile on his wizened face.

Constanzo, seeing his lord had turned his back to him, took his leave.

Guiles de Luchaire glanced after the priest; to the herbalist, he said, "We will speak in my solar," and gestured to the old man to follow him.

A woman came to light the wall sconces and another brought wine to the lord, who had reclined on a chaise. "Well?" de Luchaire asked. He waved the women away and, taking up the tankard of wine, inquired, "Have you decided on a poison?"

Gédèon smiled and drew a fragile glass vial from his robes. It was no larger than a man's ring finger and sealed with a plug of wax. "Yes, milord." He laid the vial in the meaty outstretched hand and offered his assurances of its purity as well as its potency. He

147

then remarked, "A word of caution, milord. There is much mystery in plants. Ten lifetimes would not be sufficient to fathom all their properties. Oft as not an enemy is best dealt with by the blade."

De Luchaire looked up, a wry smile curling his lips. "I do not disagree, old Gédèon, but such a strike is not made in silence, and silence it must be." With that he sent the old man from the solar. Alone, he rolled the vial in the palm of his hand, his thoughts upon the Lady Madeleine. She truly was a mystery. She had snubbed him at their last encounter, only to shower him later with flowers. There was little doubt which husband she now preferred—he was certain she would come willingly. As for her fickle nature, he would soon curb that. For once she swelled with his child, she would be his without question or recourse.

On the orders of the bishop, a succession of coifs and veils was brought from Troyes for the Lady Madeleine. Until and unless she agreed to conceal her unfashionably cropped hair, she was not permitted to leave the upstairs chambers.

For a week Madeleine stubbornly refused to cover her hair. If it was ugly and unfashionable, then let the Duke of Burgundy choose another bride.

Madeleine spent her time working the colors of her mother's vast tapestry. Her stoic Saxon guard never left her side, but sat on a bench by the window, silent as a stone. Madeleine preferred it. Deep in her own depression she sat pale and impassive before the tapestry. She never spoke to him, other than to ask in a mechanical voice to be escorted to the garderobe or in certain other instances when she was obliged to make some reply.

On Sunday, the priest came and served communion to Madeleine and her guard. Afterwards, she crossed the passageway to her sisters' room and began working on the tapestry. It was stuffy and her guard opened the chamber window. The bittersweet scent of the autumn day wafted through the room like a siren song, dissolving Madeleine's unrelenting reserve. The Saxon, too, was restless. When he was not gazing from the window, he moved about the large chamber like a man kept waiting for an appointment. Presently, he came and looked at the section of the tapestry she had completed.

It was lovely—gold, blue, green, scarlet, and many other vivid colors, with cherubs chasing butterflies in and out of a garden where garlands of delicate flowers were woven amid the flight of brightly plumaged birds. "It is beautiful," he said, more to himself for he expected no answer.

Madeleine sent him a scornful look. "What do you know of beauty?"

"I have eyes," he replied in a good natured tone.

Madeleine continued to stitch. Her hands flew rapidly over the design. She was well aware of his eyes, disturbingly blue and clear as the sky on a cold February day. They suited him, she thought, with his thatch of pale Saxon hair, his odd accent, and bland but pleasant face. At first she had despised him, but as the days passed there seemed less and less a reason. She was certain he was as bored with her company as she was with his. "Where have you come from?" she asked, suddenly tiring of the silence.

He had not moved away, but remained before the tapestry. "Your bishop's city of Reims, milady."

Madeleine knew as much and sent him a dark glance. She tied off a thread, deciding a gentler shade of green was needed for her design and chose a wachlet shade from her basket. "I did not know Saxons were bred in Reims," she said.

He ignored her sarcasm and, watching as she threaded the needle, assured her that Saxons were bred in much the same manner as anyone else and such a happening would not be impossible.

The shade of green displeased her as much as the facetiousness of his reply. She was tired of sewing and put her needle away, announcing, "I would like to walk in the garden." Her self-imposed exile was ended. She returned to her chamber and, though it galled her to do so, covered her hair with a coif.

He watched her from across the room. It was his pleasure as well as his duty and he marveled at how simply and becomingly she wrapped the silken scarf about her cropped hair. The filmy whiteness framed her small oval face, making the great dark eyes all the more vivid. Her reflection in the silver-framed Venetian mirror was one of lovely innocence. Wulf could almost believe in Old Erna's tales of *doppelgangers*, for at times it seemed there were two Lady Madeleines: the one who fought in the mud with the gusto of a peasant and the serene, delicate creature before him.

They walked out into the sun-speckled garden. Madeleine strolled along the paths, thinking there was a sadness about the fall of the year. It was the last of something beautiful and she could not hold back the memory of the happy hours she and Albertine had shared there in the garden.

Her guard, never more than half a dozen steps behind her, paused to break a tender tip from a willow branch and twirl it between his teeth as he followed along.

To Madeleine it seemed a lifetime had passed since those carefree days spent with Albertine. She could not bring back the days, not with her tears or longing or even gold, and she wished she had been happier then. The thought that her own father's brother had brought her this latest misery with his schemes and plots was like a poison which ate at her soul. At times it was too much to bear.

She suddenly halted and, turning her pale face to her guard, said, "You are no better than a dog. You are large and disagreeable, you sleep barring the door, you break wind, you snore, you follow me everywhere. No," she said spitefully, "a dog would be a better companion. At least it would amuse me."

He halted, took the willow sprig from his teeth, and, with the expression of a scolded boy, smiled. "Milady does me an injustice."

Madeleine walked on. "Oh, have I overlooked one of your loathsome habits?"

His smile deepened. "No, I think not."

"Then what?" she snapped. Her expression, like her voice, was strained and nervous. What did she care for his feelings? No one had ever spared hers.

"Unlike myself, a dog cannot reason or speak."

"You do it so seldom, I was unaware of your ability."

He clenched the sprig between his teeth. "Milady should learn to blunt her tongue. She may cut herself one day."

"My aim is always true," she said, narrowing her dark eyes.

"That may well be, but His Grace does not bleed as easily as I."

"His Grace is treacherous as a snake. I doubt he has any blood; nay, green bile like all the other devils of hell." She turned quickly with her dark brows drawn into a severe line and asked, "Why do you serve him?"

"I am a liegeman, bound to serve him until I may buy my freedom or he chooses to set me free."

"Until you are dead then."

"In all likelihood. At least until I am of no further use."

Madeleine paused beneath the cool green shade of the trees where the ferns grew thick and the air smelled of moss. "You will not repeat my words?" she asked, though her manner was brusque rather than pleading.

"That His Grace's veins are filled with green bile? No," he said with a grin, "it is an apt description."

Madeleine smiled to herself, suddenly amused. She was accustomed to the attention of admiring males, though it had never before affected her so profoundly. She led him as far as the pear orchard, stepping lightly beside him and pointing out the burnished fruit ripening in the lazy sunshine. She spoke wistfully of summers past and the honeyed taste of the golden pears.

"Would a pear please milady?" Wulf offered, basking in the glow of his victory, for she had spoken to him—not kindly perhaps, but acknowledged him at least.

Beaming, she turned to him and said, "Yes." But when he reached to pick a golden fruit, she caught his sleeve, saying, "No." He looked at her, confounded by her indecision. Only when she explained, "I wish to grasp it with my own hands," did he smile and, in his oddly accented French, point out the obvious. "Milady's stature does not permit." It was true, the pear dangled far above her head and no matter how she stretched she would have been unable to reach it. "Would you be so kind as to lift me?" she asked with a flutter of lashes and a coquettish smile.

He hesitated for only as long as it took to clasp his hands around her small waist, for how could he refuse so charming a smile and the opportunity to hold her in his arms once more?

She gave a joyous little laugh as she ascended in his arms, all at once magically taller than he. The pear orchard was as she had always known it, yet in that glorious moment, suspended above the ground, everything appeared different. The mild breeze touched her face and lifted her soul and for an instant she felt free as a bird. Laughing, she clutched a pear, held it out for his approval, and pointed to another, even larger, golden fruit peeping from a cluster of waxy dark green leaves. "May I?" she pleaded. He lifted her higher still so she might pluck the second pear, then lowered her gently to the ground.

She held out the largest pear, an offering of peace. "This pear is for you, Wulf of Rügen," she said shyly, and, looking into his blue eyes, asked, "Was I a great burden on your arms?"

"No," he answered, "milady is slight, a pleasure to hold." He could have added *when she was not cursing and kicking,* but he did not. It was a time of new beginnings, and that was good.

Madeleine held the fragrant pear to her nose and sniffed its spicy scent. "Am I permitted to walk as far as the mill?" Wulf judged the distance. He saw no harm in it. He had already allowed her to lead him too far, and he fully expected to be berated for his lack of common good sense and caution.

"There are shade trees by the mill pond," Madeleine prattled on. "We can sit and eat our pears and watch the geese." She told him she had gone there often as a child, told him of the geese and how they chased the miller's dog. But as she walked, her words came back as ghosts to haunt her and she was overcome with sadness once more.

Earlier that clear September morning a boy with curly, reddish hair and dressed in the rough clothing of a countryman's squire approached the château on a small shaggy horse. At the gate the boy produced a letter, folded and sealed, from his coarse-woven tunic and said he had been instructed by his master to deliver it to the Lord de Moncelet.

"The Lord de Moncelet is dead," the guard told the boy, and motioned to the *charrettes* in the courtyard being readied for a funeral procession. The boy's round brown eyes shifted quickly away. He crossed himself and, turning his freckled face to the guard, asked, "Who then is the new lord, for this letter is his."

Puzzled, the guard did not know how to answer the boy's question. Was the Lady Madeleine the new lord? He had never heard of such a thing. Or was His Grace, the bishop, the new lord? Glancing around, the guard saw two of his fellows loitering by the armory and called them to him. He explained about the letter and asked for advice. The trio could not agree and one, tiring of the discussion, went to seek the captain of the guard.

Paschal sent the boy to de Grailley, who rapidly read the letter. It was a request by a steward to give employment to the bearer, his squire, whom, because of the shortage of food, he could no longer feed.

To be sure, there was a shortage of servants at the château, and de Grailley, who had personally taken charge of such matters, looked the boy over with a severe eye. He was perhaps sixteen, though he claimed to be but fourteen and tall. He had a sturdy look about him and a willing manner. De Grailley told him he could stay and work for several days. "Perhaps you will be suitable," he said, promising nothing. "We will see." De Grailley folded away the letter and called the chief squire to take the boy in his charge and acquaint him with his duties.

Chapter Twelve

The truce of the pear was doomed to last no longer than the honeyed taste of the fruit upon their tongues. Returning to the château, Madeleine saw the iron-bound doors of the hall open to the afternoon. Servants rushed in and out and all around her there was a beehive of activity. From the doors, she saw three *charrettes* had been pulled into the courtyard and a number of servants were busily engaged in draping the cumbersome wagons with black cloth.

When she questioned a household servant, she was told the *charrettes* were for a funeral procession. "Whose funeral?" Madeleine demanded. "The Lord de Moncelet and his family, milady," the broad-faced girl replied. The words struck Madeleine like blows. Her heart felt as though it had been wrenched from her breast. Why could he not leave them in peace?

Madeleine hurried to the library in search of her uncle, but found only Dubuc and several young clerics rummaging through account books. Dubuc looked up like a startled rabbit from a mildewy volume, advising, "His Grace is at the chapel overseeing the disinterment."

As much as she could not bear the thought of what she might see, Madeleine made her way to the chapel. Entering the doors, she was overcome by a wave of grief and remorse and stood supporting herself with a hand on the font as she gathered her scattered wits. She found her uncle hovering at the top of the stone stairs of the crypt. He stepped to one side as several servants hoisted the first coffin to the floor of the chapel. In those few brief weeks a layer of dust had settled upon the polished lid. Below, in the crypt, a lamp glowed in the blackness and the pungent odor of decay wafted up to mingle with the smell of incense and candle wax.

Madeleine, whose face was white with grief and indignation, argued passionately against transporting the bodies of her family to the cathedral, only to return them. "In Christ's name," she cried, "leave them in peace!"

Heribert signaled to her guard with his eyes, then turned his back. At the foot of the altar a man's head and shoulders appeared to rise from the stones of the chapel floor. The man called out to another below and a second coffin was lifted up the stone stairs of the crypt.

Wulf, as he was bid, walked the Lady Madeleine from the chapel. Outside, she threw off his arms, angrily accusing, "You kept me from the château so I would not see his handiwork."

Wulf denied it. "I knew nothing of his plans." It was the truth, but she would not believe him. Afterward she was haughty and unresponsive as before, and there was only silence between them.

Madeleine, if she was to eat, was required to take her meals in the hall where she and her guard were seated among her uncle's novices. Heribert sat in her father's place of honor, the priest de Grailley to his right, and Dubuc to his left. Religious discussions dominated the conversation. Madeleine sat in icy silence, eating little of anything, nourished only by her bitter hatred of her uncle.

On the Sunday of St. Getulus a solemn funeral procession approached the city of Troyes. Heribert, Bishop of Champagne, robed in purple and azure and surrounded by a tide of black-clad clergy, rode before the coffins of his brother's family. Close on the ranks of the clergy and black-draped *charrettes* a detachment of soldiers followed. Fearing armed intervention by the Baron de Luchaire, the bishop's guards were heavily armed. Though they wore mail and bristled with weapons, all had removed their helmets and rode into the city bareheaded to symbolize their mourning.

The black-draped *charettes* jounced and swayed along the rutted road, each drawn by a trio of horses harnessed in tandem and decorated with plumes and rosettes.

In the city, crowds gathered at street corners to watch with somber faces; some wept, while others knelt in prayer.

Madeleine, looking pitifully small and sad seated on her dappled mare, followed closely behind the coffins. For this occasion she was dressed in mourning and wore a black velvet coif and heavy black veil. The texture of the veil was such that she could hardly see the fluttering black draperies of the *charrettes* directly before her as they jolted past the market square and the Church of St. Jean au Marche. Her guard rode at her horse's flank. A black cloak, borrowed from the count's wardrobe kist, concealed his sword, leather clothing, and mail; like the soldiers of the guard, he, too, had removed his helmet and carried it under his arm.

At the Cathedral of St. Pierre, the voices of the choir echoed from the vaulted ceiling and through a haze of incense, candles blazed upon the altar. The biers of Count Étienne de Moncelet and his family were borne up the steps of the cathedral and placed at the foot of the altar.

Wulf lifted the Lady Madeleine from her horse.

The cool morning breeze riffled the veil; beneath it her face was pale and expressionless as a waxen mask.

A young novice, supporting a rod from which a heavy golden triptych swayed, walked before her. She followed blindly, tears blurring what little vision she was permitted through the weighty veil, and the smoky haze of frankincense and myrrh drifted before her eyes like souls of the dead.

She took her place to one side of the coffins and stood very straight and still, her full lips tightly compressed and her hands folded in prayer. Wulf took up a position several paces from her, placing himself between her, the choir aisle, and the arch of the chapter house door. Earlier, he had heard her weeping as the serving women came to assist her with her clothing. He had seen her reddened face and her eyes swollen from crying and now could not help but feel sympathy for her.

On the morrow Madeleine looked from her window. She saw the *charrettes* standing in the courtyard, bereft of horse and harness, with black banners hanging lank in the morning stillness. A haze of dew streaked the coffins. It was hideous to see, to know that all she loved was there, left to stand, abandoned like so much useless baggage. Her tears and shouts were ignored. It was not until late the following day that the coffins were again lowered beneath the chapel.

Madeleine retaliated in the only way left to her, by steadfastly refusing food or even water until her hated uncle should again lay her family to rest. Her guard was forced to suffer with her. He said nothing; it was not his place to speak, though two days without food set his stomach to grumbling.

The funeral her uncle had forced upon her was but another stone to weigh down her heart. She would never forgive him. Afterwards, she went about with downcast eyes, affecting an appearance of great tragedy, a feature, Wulf observed, which only served to heighten the rebellion smouldering in every exaggerated side-long glance of her dark eyes. Whether her despair was truly felt, or yet another of her deceits, he could only guess.

She was a puzzle, one moment laughing and the next a tragic figure. At times it was almost comical. He understood, at least in part, for she was helpless to choose her own fate. She had his sympathy, yet he was wary of her. She drew him to her like a lodestone. She could not be trusted, of that he was certain, though knowing it did little to dampen his desire.

Several days passed in silence. Madeleine stitched on the tapestry. The suffocating depression which had settled over her threatened to snuff out her very will to live. She neither ate nor slept and was overcome with gruesome thoughts of death and grief for all she had lost. Painfully, she recalled each smile upon her mother's face, her father's deep voice and warm hand, her brother, and her sisters. Her monstrous guilt tore at her soul like hounds harrying a hart. She was reminded of all the little cruelties she had perpetrated, said, or thought. Moment by moment her remorse built, until she felt her heart would surely burst. She made an anguished little cry, snatched up a round of kermes-colored wool, and sent it spinning across the chamber.

Wulf had balanced himself on the bench, angling his body so that he could prop his boots on the window embrasure. The bench was hard, sadistically so, for any length of time and he had spent much of the day shifting from one uncomfortable position to another. He was dozing, not quite asleep when the sudden motion . . . the color red . . . roused him. He pulled himself from the bench, retrieved the yarn, and, crossing the chamber, placed it in her hand.

She flung it in his face. There was no one else on whom to vent her misery. He stared at her for a moment, then stooped to retrieve the round yarn once again and calmly place it on the tapestry before her. The hurtful, hovering silence shamed her more than words. She quickly turned her head, no longer able to stanch the tears spilling over her cheeks.

He stood there woodenly, mute and helpless, seized by an emotion he could not put to words. Gently he touched a hand to her shoulder. She was trembling, or perhaps it was his hand that trembled? He dared not speak, fearing his voice, like his hand, would betray what he felt.

Madeleine twisted away, recoiling from his touch, and screamed at him. "Leave me be! I do not need your kindness nor your pity!"

Wulf's trembling hand fell to his side and without a word he returned to his place by the window.

Day after dreary day, she stitched out her misery in the vaunted scarlets and golds until one morning she drew her gaze across the breadth and length of the vast tapestry deciding, if such a place as heaven did exist, it must be as the tapestry: a bountiful garden filled with pure and brilliant colors that, perversely, she would never know. For what was in her heart was sin beyond redemption.

She thought of the days in the chapel when she had prayed to die, cried out for punishment, believing her wicked pride and selfishness had brought the sickness. Was this then her punishment, she wondered, her accursed uncle? Surely he had stolen her joy, her very will to live, just as he had stolen all else his greedy hands could grasp. It was too much to bear.

What did the future hold but endless wretchedness? She saw with a terrible clarity the long staggering hours of her days, to live a life of pain and then to die. And if she was to die, and since all mortals were thus doomed, *momento mori*, should not the hour be of her own choosing? For if she could not live life as she chose, she would choose death. At least then she would be free, gone to infinite nothingness . . . dust in the wind.

Such thoughts haunted her for days. Not the act itself—that she had considered with the coarse practicality of a peasant woman. She had no access to poison, she feared the dark weight of water, and knives were painful. But there was a way.

All morning she had worked silently on the tapestry, brooding upon the past, fueling her despair. She heard the bells toll sext, and with exacting care laid out her needles and arranged the rounds of brilliant wool. Madder and wode, wachlet, kermes and lake, the colors blurred before her teary eyes. It would not do to cry, she told herself and, drying her eyes, glanced across the chamber. Her guard lounged on the bench beneath the window, his legs braced against the embrasure at an improbable angle. She knew he would do all in his power to stop her. Not from any great concern for her, she assured herself, but rather his basest instinct—that of his own survival. Her uncle had sworn to kill him if she escaped. How, she speculated, would His Grace view her death? And in a humor dark as her intent supposed that he might discuss it endlessly over roasted pork and racks of lamb as he did mortal sin and grace and charity. More likely, she concluded, it would go badly for her guard.

The Saxon was a loutish oaf, she argued. There was no love nor kinship between them. Yet in her heart she did not wish him harm, certainly not death. The thought suddenly irritated her. Let him shift for himself, she decided, just as she had been left to do. No one had mourned her fate, him least of all.

Madeleine stood up, straightening her back. The low, nagging pain was a monthly occurrence heralding her flux and the one misery for which she could not hold her uncle accountable. She slowly

161

smoothed the creases from her gown and announced, "I would like to walk in the garden."

She heard a sudden indrawn breath, a grunt. He had been asleep. The bench squealed against the floor as he lifted his large frame from the wickedly uncomfortable seat, collected his sword, and followed her across the passageway; a scowl was stamped on his face.

Before the mirror, she placed a coif on her head and wrapped the scarf snugly 'round her throat, then lead off down the snail-curl of steps. The route she took was unfamiliar to him and led generally toward the armory.

Midday brought a flush of activity to the château. The aroma of food wafted through the passageway and a steady stream of servants pressed past them.

Madeleine saw them coming along the passageway, just as she knew they must. They moved in a long line like a black cord knotting and stopping, ill-assorted yet identical in their black cowls with prayer books clutched in their hands and their low gossipy voices like the sound of bees.

As they drew even, Madeleine slowed her pace with halting steps. When the black of their cowls and the ruddy pink of their faces filled her eyes, she lunged into their midst, sliding past the startled and bumbling young men as effortlessly as an eel.

Wulf was caught in the tangle of novices and had to shove his way free before bounding after her at a full run. He saw only a glimpse of her fleeing form, the fluid green of her skirts as she darted round a corner. He raced along the passage, searching out its rooms. The passage ended abruptly in a large vaulted chamber stacked deep with stores.

He stood for a moment catching his breath and considering the possibilities, deciding that amid the clutter she might hide herself till Christ-tide. "Idiot," he cursed himself softly. She was deceit embodied; she could not be trusted, not for an instant. Moreover he was a fool to allow himself to be manipulated by a female, an admission which angered him even further. He stood there running his hand through his hair. Where was he to begin his search? Once he walked past her hiding place or turned his back, she would slip behind him and be gone.

The sound of voices and the trample of feet swiveled his attention to the passageway. He saw the priest de Grailley coming, at a run with a horde of novices at his heels.

De Grailley had heard first hand of the lady's misadventure with the novices and, peering into the cluttered room, inquired in a winded voice, "Is she here?"

"Yes," Wulf replied, for he believed she was though she would not be easily found, even with their help. This was a fact he pointed out, suggesting, "If we move as one, keeping in a line, she will not slip past us."

De Grailley, seeing the wisdom of that, placed his novices and the search began.

Halfway through the cluttered chamber Wulf noticed a recess in the stones and beyond a coil of steps. He asked the novice at his shoulder, "Where do they lead?" The boy shook his head—he knew not. But another, with a fine haze of yellow fuzz above his upper lip, replied in a crackling voice, "The tower, sire."

Wulf vaulted up the slanting stone steps at a reckless pace, driven by an unknown though all-consuming urgency, taking the course of the stair by twos and threes until it seemed the blood would burst from his veins. At the summit he plunged into a turreted room of no particular size—four men could not have comfortably stood abreast. He saw the barren room all at once. An open door arch faced the walled city of Troyes and slotted window openings marked the remaining walls. Beyond was a circular walkway and a waist-high wall.

As he bounded through the door arch, he caught sight of her balanced precariously on the parapet. There was no time to consider her motives. Did she intend for him to witness her death? He thought not, judging from her helpless expression. Rather she had lost her will and now wavered, trembling and terrified, atop the stones. He did not call out to her, he could not; there was no air in his lungs. He closed the distance in long, running strides, caught her by the waist, and pulled her to him.

Moments before, Madeleine had raced upwards, dizzy with exertion, and in the first frenzied rush of passion, like a soldier screaming into battle, bounded onto the parapet. She swayed to and fro, free, deliriously free, one with the sky and the breeze, until her gaze tumbled down, down the long expanse of cruel grey stone.

Eternity floated before her stunned and staring eyes, and death, that which she had rushed to meet, no longer held a charm. It was not freedom she saw, but the hard-packed earth—hideous reality, the primitive horror of putrefaction and decay. She gasped, clawing at the air, too numbed by fear to move or utter a sound.

Swept into his arms, she sobbed, clinging to the warmth of his body with desperate clutching hands. She was miraculously safe with the scent of his skin in her nostrils and the feel of his solid arms about her.

Her wracking sobs staggered him backwards into the stones of the watchtower. He sagged against the reassuring roughness of the wall, his blood pounded in his lips and in his fingertips, and his trembling knees threatened to buckle beneath him. "Bête à bon Dieu," he breathed, crushing her in his arms, and with more force then he had intended. "Stupid little ladybird," he repeated, his voice no more than a whisper. "Did you think you could fly away?" He held her until she could speak. Even so, her voice came in great hiccuping sobs, wracking her small shoulders and shattering her aura of haughtiness.

She felt ashamed, certain that she must look a fool, gasping like a fish out of water. She averted her face and pushed against his arms so she might breathe.

A voice came from the top of the stair—the novice. Wulf did not see his face, only the pale patch of tonsured crown. "Have you the lady?" the boy called in his uncertain voice.

"Yes," Wulf answered, and, mustering a more natural voice, said, "She admires the view. Tell the priest she is safe."

Madeleine would risk but one trembling hand to unwind her coif and dab at her eyes and dripping nose; the other gripped his fingers like a vise. Even later as she ventured a look from the tower, she was unwilling to release the warm safety of his hand. "It is a different view," she said, regaining a measure of her composure. The golden tones of late summer colored the countryside and great white blocks of sheep swarmed over the meadows—more sheep than she had ever seen. "My uncle should be well pleased." Her cheeks pinked and she sounded more herself with each word. "It seems he has stolen all the sheep in France."

"Not all," Wulf smiled, "though not from lack of effort. He will reap twice the riches; he will have their wool as well."

Madeleine's dark eyes raised to his inquisitively.

"Last evening in the hall, the novices who sat opposite spoke of it. One had cyphered the weight of the wool by estimating the number of sheep. The other questioned his figures."

"I close my ears when I am in the hall," she remarked in a tart voice, recalling the discussion but not the subject. She looked away, her dark brows drawn into a frown. "I would like to walk in the garden now," she said, and abruptly took back her hand.

As they descended the stairs, they heard excited shouts and cries of "Huzzah." Victorious cheers, not for their success at locating the Lady Madeleine, but for a huge rat, routed by the search and which several novices had cornered and were in the process of bludgeoning with staves taken from a litter.

De Grailley, seeing the lady safe with her guard, made a sign with his hand and returned his attention to the novices bashing away at the rat.

Once in the garden, Madeleine's eyes filled anew. How glorious it was to be alive—to see, to feel. She inhaled deeply, and again, until she was giddy on the sweet scent of grass and trees and sunlight. She walked, looking at everything as if for the first time. She saw the fine delicate shadings of green and bronze, the clear chromatic yellows of the changing leaves, the soaring arch of mild blue sky, and the white mist of trailing clouds.

At the mill pond, she sat in the grass plucking wildflowers and winding their spindly stems into a wreath. Nearby, Wulf leaned against a tree, watching the breeze raise a cat's-paw on the pond's smooth surface and the geese sunning themselves on the grassy bank. After a time, he went and crouched beside her, balanced on his haunches. It was awkward to sit with the sword on his hip. His gaze ranged to the meadow, the browing horses, and the parti-colored tents of the encampment. A haze of smoke drifted from their cook-fires.

Madeleine saw his shadow lying on the grass. She did not raise her eyes from the wreath of bright *immortelles* and dusky green leaves; but said, "Swear you will not mention the tower to anyone. His Grace will lock me away in my chamber. The garden is my only pleasure." When he made no answer, she looked up swiftly to meet his eyes, pleading, "Say you will not tell?" Hardening her features, she warned, "He will punish you if he hears of it."

Wulf had long before come to the same conclusion. "I have forgotten the tower," he said, "as I pray you have." His gaze shifted once more to the encampment: the gaudy tents, and browsing bays and chestnuts.

She smiled, twining a final bloom into the garland, then nimbly rose on her knees and stretched out her arms to place the wreath in his hair. His first reaction was to pull away, but her dazzling young-girl smile drew him back to let her perch it on his head.

"It is your reward," she announced in a clear sweet voice, and, tilting her head to arrange the wreath, declared, "For you are noble as a Roman." Though at that moment, with the wreath in his tousled hair and his merry eyes, blue as borage flowers, she thought him more like Pan.

He laughed. He had no defense against her. She was a puzzle and there was no understanding her— not her impulsive nature nor the unpredictable strangeness.

She drew back as if offended. Her smile cramped and with a look of sudden displeasure she scampered to her feet and left him sitting there on his heels. He called after her, called her by name. It was a liberty he should not have taken and only later realized he had. Bewildered, he bounded up and strode after her, his sword rattling against his hip.

The days were golden, fair, and warm. One afternoon, the Widow Crozet and her seamstresses sat where the fountain splashed amid the yews and the surrounding flower beds blazed with color.

A short distance away in the shade of the arbor, Madeleine read silently. The air was sweet with the scent of roses, blowzy and past their prime. A petal fell upon the laboriously hand-scribed page. Madeleine pressed her finger to the fragile thing and, holding it to her nose, sniffed its sweet aroma. She raised her eyes and saw the widow and her women and felt a bitter twinge of resentment that the widow Crozet should be sitting in the place of which her mother was fondest, basking in the sunlight and feeling its warmth upon her bones. Madeleine frowned into the sunlight. The stinging sharpness of her grief brimmed her eyes with tears and put a catch in at. She looked away, fixing her gaze on the page. The rose petal, forgotten, drifted to the ground.

Nearby, Wulf stretched lazily in the grass. He had lain his sword and belt aside, more at ease without the thick leather belt to pinch his spine, and folded his arms beneath his head, dreamily contemplating the tumult of high white clouds that chased across the sky. Demons and dragons, lofty barbicans, and galloping steeds raced through the heavens. A prince wearing a towering crown, altered to become a fish with a peacock's tail, and a moment later a whimsical pig with feathered wings. In that way he had amused himself for the better part of the afternoon. Occasionally he would pluck a blade of grass, clamp it between his teeth, and slowly extract the last tangy sweetness of summer.

The fickle breeze shifted to the east and the sounds of the shearing; loud masculine shouts and bleating of sheep drifted across the rocky stream bed, up the curve of the hill, and into the garden. With the sound came the combined stench of the sheep and the soldier's encampment. Wulf noticed the rank smell at once, as did the Lady Madeleine. She looked up suddenly from her book with a wrinkling nose and disapproving frown. It seemed to Wulf that she meant to say something, though only a startled yelp escaped her lips as a full-grown ewe exploded from the hedge, an arm's length away, and blundered past at a full gallop.

Dumbfounded, Wulf lurched to his feet, thinking

he should do something. But not knowing what, he continued to stare open-mouthed, his amazed eyes following the ewe's frantic zigzag course. A peal of laughter sounded behind him as three more full-fleeced sheep thumped past his legs, nearly toppling him.

Thunderous shouts and thudding footfalls approached from beyond the hedge. The sheep, in full stampede, sliced through the lacy ferns, trampling the sweet smelling lavender, bounded over the low-ivied wall, and dove headlong into the yews.

Only then did the widow and her women catch sight of the roving sheep. A chorus of screams floated on the air as the women, abandoning all, skipped and jigged among the panicked sheep. The fleeter of foot made toward the safety of a stout wall where espaliered altheas grew in perfect symmetry. But the widow, refusing to desert her hoop and thread, ran afoul of the largest ewe.

The widow's blood-curdling screams only served to further confuse the animal. They dodged and danced and for an instant it seemed the ewe was bent on trampling the terrified woman. Around and around they went in a dizzy circle until the widow lost her footing amid the gillyflowers and went down with thrashing legs and shrill cries, imploring the Virgin to save her.

Shouts and crashing footfalls preceded half a dozen or more guardsmen who burst into the garden in pursuit of the wayward sheep. Among them were Wulf's two comrades, and he, weak with laughter, raised an arm in salute as they sprinted past. Beside him, clutching her book to her bodice, the Lady Madeleine laughed tears as several of the widow's women extracted her, unharmed though smudged with grime, from the bed of flattened gillyflowers.

Helayne Gontier came from the château's kitchens by way of the garth, as she did most days, with a tray of refreshments and tankards of spiced cider for the

169

Lady Madeleine and her guard. She paused for a moment at the entrance to the garden, distracted by the uproar and confusion.

In the heat of the commotion, Madeleine and her guard were unaware of the serving woman's approach. Helayne placed the tray beside the arbor and waited, wondering how she might speak her piece to the Lady Madeleine without the guard's close attention. As she debated, a troop of guardsmen returned with the balky sheep in tow. Helayne could not have better arranged it herself, for the Saxon's two comrades trailed behind the others and sighting them he stepped away from the lady.

Helayne watched with a keen eye as the trio, the curly-headed Latin, the black-faced Moor, and the Saxon greeted one another with hearty good-natured blows, spoke loudly as men do, and laughed. That was the moment she chose to lean close to the lady's ear and whisper, "I am sent by one who knows your true heart."

Madeleine's eyes blazed with hope. Albertine, she thought. It must be she, for who else could know her heart?

"Follow me from the garden tomorrow."

Madeleine's eyes darkened. "But there is my guard."

"All is arranged," she whispered. "Put your trust in me, milady," and with a quick nervous smile, she withdrew. On the footpath to the garth, Helayne glanced back to see the Saxon still talking with his friends. They parted with laughing and jests. "We are guarding sheep," one called after him, "while you, you lucky hound, have a pretty lamb to watch!"

In the hall as the meal was served, the religious discussion swirled around Madeleine. Her Saxon guard ate heartily, as he did at every opportunity. Later she could not recall what she had eaten, if at all. She treasured her secret, turning over and over again in her mind the serving woman's words. Albertine, she thought, had not forsaken her. Soon she would be beyond her vile uncle's grasp.

The widow did not come to attend Madeleine that evening, but the serving women came, and one, as she turned back the bed linen, made mention of the incident in the garden. Not one of the women broke a smile, yet it seemed all fought back the urge to do so. Madeleine saw their amused glances and thought them as cruel as herself. Her mood was generous that night and prompted her to ask politely after the widow's well being. More amused glances were exchanged before she learned Madame Crozet's only true injury had been a bruise to her knee and a blow to her much inflated self-esteem.

When the women had gone, Wulf secured the door as he did every night, banked the fire, and snuffed the single candle. Her voice came at him from the darkness. "The Moor and the other, have they long been your comrades?" Madeleine asked from the immensity of the bed.

"For some time, yes, milady," Wulf said, nudging the pallet against the door with his boot to block the draft.

"Do you value them above all others?"

"As friends, of course." He shed his shirt and lay down, settling himself between the furs.

"I valued Albertine above all others; she alone knew my true heart."

"Milady has other serving women." He wadded up a section of the fur and laid his head back. He was accustomed to using his saddle for a pillow.

"They are all in the service of my uncle," she replied. "I may trust none of them."

He could hear her moving about on the bed, the soft sounds of pillows being plumped. "I, too, am in the service of your uncle," he reminded her. He was as puzzled by her line of conversation as he was curious to know where it would lead.

"At least I may speak freely before you," she

sighed, falling back among the pillows. "You would not betray me?"

"My first loyalty is to my lord bishop, but no, I will not carry your words to him."

Madeleine lifted her face from the pillow. "But you would keep his commands?" she asked, knowing his answer.

"I am sworn to do so."

"Yes," she agreed, and in the next breath announced: "Tomorrow in the garden I will read aloud to you."

It seemed to him she would say more. He waited, staring into the vacant blackness at the ceiling, but she said nothing, nothing at all. After a time, he fell asleep.

Beneath the exquisitely bound volume of amusements, Madeleine carried a small brocatelle pillow. In the kitchen the women plucking birds and stirring pots saw the Lady Madeleine pass by in her wine-dark gown. Her guard, with his close-cropped fair hair, trailed at her heels like a faithful hound. He followed her through the kitchen, sniffing the aroma of food and casting an observant eye over the preparations for the evening meal.

Before the arbor, Madeleine turned to him, a shy smile upon her lips, and offered the pillow, saying, "It is for your head so you may lie in comfort."

The heady scent or roses slowly dying with the summer spiced the air. Her kindness, like the overpowering odor of the roses, took him unaware. How strange she was; the demure smile, which he knew or at least suspected, was surely motivated by something aught than a genuine concern for his comfort. Still, he accepted gratefully and, looking full into her eyes, cautioned, "I may come to expect smiles and pillows for my head."

Madeleine pressed her lips into a frown and turned

away, reminding him, "You must listen quietly while I read. It was our agreement." She seated herself beneath the halo of red roses and arranged her skirt. She had no heart for what she must do. She opened the book. The playful breeze lifted a page, she pressed it back and, setting her dark little brows in a straight line, began to read.

He put aside his sword and belt and lay down on the sun-warmed grass. The pillow beneath his head smelled of her perfume and the enticing scent coupled with the sight of her among the roses crowded his thoughts with amusements far more sensual than those set down in her monk's scribed book. With consummate care he noted the velvet darkness of her brows and lashes, the sheen of moisture on her pink-flushed skin, and, above all, her lips, moistened and about to speak. Lips that were pink and full as pillows. He watched each motion, watched them plump and part and sigh until he could all but feel them on his flesh.

She looked up suddenly, aware of his acute stare. "Does something trouble you?" she asked, a dot of red upon each cheek.

He blinked, startled that she might somehow read his thoughts, and smiled defensively. "Forgive me, milady," he said. "I did not mean to stare."

She quickly looked away, her emotions in a state of flustered uncertainty, and fixed her gaze upon the swirling script. "I thought perhaps you did not care for my selection," she said, careful to avoid the clear blue eyes. Her conscience ached.

"No, truly, I was entranced," he assured her, which was not entirely a lie, and lay back, fixing his eyes on the distant fern fronds and the sparrows squabbling in the tall grass.

The sun had passed its meridian when Helayne Gontier came to the arbor with the tray of spiced cider. She served the lady's tankard, then the guard's. Before she turned to go, she sent the lady a secretive smile from beneath her round straw hat, then tucked the tray under her arm and swept from the garden.

Madeleine continued to read. Her guard, lying in the dappled sunlight, listened to the pleasant rise and fall of her voice. Several times Madeleine touched the cider to her lips, but she could not bring herself to drink, fearing the serving woman may have unwittingly switched the tankards. The two were identical. Her Saxon guard drank. In wary, stolen glances she saw him twice take a swallow of the cider.

After a time she noticed his head nod. Though he jolted awake a moment later, yawned, and stretched his shoulders. Madeleine looked up from the brilliant colors of the illuminated page, reassuring herself that it was but a sleeping draught. Albertine would never be so cruel as to use poison. As for her uncle's punishment, she preferred not to think of it. Surely her guard was of a size and age to care for himself. "My story has made you weary," she remarked.

"No," he assured her, and with yet another yawn, rubbed his eyes and blamed the heat of the afternoon, remarking, "Your voice is soothing and the sun too warm." He lay back, resting his head on the pillow.

She read several more lines and, hazarding a glance, saw he was asleep. She waited, then rose stealthily. In her haste she had forgotten the book, which nearly slipped from her grasp. She fumbled with the pages and set it aside with a pounding heart. Looking about the garden, she saw no one.

The clear, trilling *ka-de, ka-de* of a songbird floated on the breeze and as if by magic she saw the serving woman, with a second straw hat clutched in her hands, step away from the dense mottled green and yellow leaves of the maple hedge and beckon her to follow.

He fell through wispy clouds of mist . . . falling, falling. The sudden slap of his hands against the ground woke him. He lurched to his knees. He saw at once the arbor seat was empty, the Lady Madeleine gone. He staggered to his feet, overturning the half-empty tankard of cider. His head felt as if it had at that moment grown ten sizes larger and he was nearly bowled over by a violent dizziness.

The cider, he thought, certain it had been drugged or poisoned. In Lombardy he had seen men die of poisoning. The revulsion relived in his memory sent pinpricks of fear coursing along his spine. He rejected the thought, thinking he must alert the guards, and prayed he might yet be able. A surge of anger heaved in his chest and scalded his throat like gall. No sound came from his open mouth, none he could hear for his ears seemed deaf, and so he ran toward the château.

Where the maple hedges ended, currant shrubs clumped and straggled over the garth wall. There, by chance, he saw straw hats bobbing through the oat field beyond the garden plots. Yellow disks which merged and pulled apart and floated before his eyes. One or two, or three or four, he could not judge, for all he saw contorted and writhed in loathsome parody, doubled and trebeled and blurred into nothingness.

In his confused state the guards were forgotten; his thoughts seized upon the serving woman beneath the straw hat, certain in his tortured mind that if he found her he would also find the lady.

He plunged down the hill toward the vegetable plots, stumbled through the turnip field on legs made of water, then crashed amid the oats. The lush panicled seed heads slapped against his thighs, thrashing back at his passage, winking in the sunlight and stabbing at his eyes with sharp spears of refracted light. The field ended at a copse of trees where, amid the crazed lattice-work of leaves and branches, he saw the straw hats dip and bob to merge with the woods and melt into thin air like a mirage. He followed to the road. A trickle of traffic plodded past. He stood swaying in the woody brush, staring at the scene and doubting his own senses.

There was the road before him and he had been too close on their heels to have missed seeing them mount horses and be away. But where was there to hide? The uneven course of the ditch that shouldered the Troyes road supported little more than a sparse growth of brushy shrub, weed clumps, and nodding thistle. Yet they had vanished. Had his eyes deceived him? Had he come too far?

A tumbril loaded to its topmost slats with sacks of dyestuffs creaked toward him. Only then did his drugged and disordered mind grasp what surely must be the answer. But was she fleeing to Troyes or east and away? Had her plot been hatched with the aid of the disgruntled baron he wondered? Did she now consider him a more attractive suitor than the Duke of Burgundy? Was the ginger-headed maidservant involved, or was it an ally of which he had no knowledge?

Upon the road he halted merchants and peddlers, thundering threats and fiercely interrogating the fearful yet protesting tradesmen. He accosted a peddler with a line of pack horses and a merchant driving a cart laden with bolts of silk cloth.

A guard pacing the château's wall sighted the altercation on the road and alerted his commander, reporting, "A madman wearing the bishop's cross is halting all upon the road, assaulting merchants and making a ruin of their goods!" A madman surely, for his lumbering gait and ranting voice bore witness to the guard's words.

The dye merchant danced about, wringing his hands. Half his cargo lay on the road, bursted sacks of tansy and woad, and still the crazed soldier searched. The poor merchant was near to apoplexy when an eastbound cart, covered to the elements, drew even with the tumbril.

A woman wearing a straw hat sat beside the driver. Her eyes widened at the sight of the soldier and she

176

nudged the driver, urging, "Put the whip to the horses."

Wulf saw her face, distorted and blurred, and not for an instant, but enough to recall the bitter taste of the cider. He lunged at the horses, throwing up his arms to turn them. Both animals shied away with flattened ears and white-rimmed eyes, bucked wildly and, straining at their traces, angled the cart sideways in the road.

The bearded driver hauled at the reins and shouted curses at the wild-eyed soldier. Wulf flung himself at the cart's foot rail, grasping after the screaming woman. She fended him off with a straw basket, all the while screeching for the driver to use the whip. Taking the reins in one hand, the driver kicked at the soldier and grabbed for the whip. The cart geed and hawed.

Wulf clung stubbornly to the foot rail, his arms plunging after the hem of the woman's skirts as she retreated into the blackness of the cart's interior.

With a bounce and a leap, Wulf launched himself onto the cart. The driver dropped the reins and met him head on with the whip. They grappled hand to hand with blows and kicks until Wulf drove his elbow into the man's throat and tore the whip from his hand, clouting him with its base. He would have chucked him off the cart, but the panicked horses, with a free rein, lurched forward. The driver fell backwards into the cart and Wulf was pitched onto the road.

He hit solidly, jarring his every bone and knocking the air from his lungs. Even that could not compare to the killing pain in his eyes and the sudden uncontrollable agitation within his body. He felt aroused as if by madness and seized by a raging impulse to clutch and grasp and tear to pieces all within his reach. His disordered mind struggled to hold a single thought—the Lady Madeleine! He must find her. He would not be done. She was there in the cart, for there was nowhere else.

Clawing at the dirt, he swayed to his feet and bounded headlong after the jolting cart. A faded rug, rotted by the elements, hung from the cart's end, concealing the interior. Orange-red, it dangled, bouncing, wag-tailing with the motion of the cart, just beyond his reach. He felt it brush past his outstretched fingertips. Again he hurled himself toward the cart, this time catching the knotted fringe and tearing the rug free of its wooden frame.

Through the painful murkiness that clouded his vision, he saw only the flash of a blade and, an instant later, felt the crushing weight of an adversary. They sprawled, rolling in the dust with snarls and grunts, locked in a vicious struggle like dogs fighting to the death. Wulf did not need his eyes to drive the dagger into the man's chest and with such force that afterwards his blood-slick hands could not pull it free.

The pair on the cart might yet have escaped, had it not been for the deeply-furrowed surface of the road and the cartman's reckless haste. Good's carts were cumbersome and heavy and never meant for such foolhardy punishment. A wheel lost to the furrow cracked like thunder and disassembled. The cart careened wildly to one side, plowing a rut in the road as it skidded to a halt.

From atop the cart, the woman shouted frantically and pointed to the soldier closing ground, and then, with a shrill cry of alarm, to the distance where a troop of mounted guardsmen drove a cloud of dust into the air. The driver drew a dagger from his clothing and threw himself at Wulf with the fury of a cornered beast. He was not as adept or quick with the blade as his comrade, though despite his awkward bulk, he was not easily disarmed.

Helayne Gontier watched in stupefied silence. Seeing all was lost, she leapt from the cart and, lifting her skirts, fled toward the ditch and a brace of thicket.

The bearded driver was also desperate to be gone and landed several stunning blows on the berserk soldier but Wulf fought like one possessed. In a fit of frenzy he clamped the driver's neck in the crook of his arm and drove his head into the side of the lopsided cart. Released, he dropped like a sack of grain.

A trio of guardsmen leapt from the dust stirred by their horses and collared Wulf, pinning him face down on the road. Jostling horses and men milled around the wreckage. Their captain alighted from his saddle, cursing and shouting questions. With a guardsman's boot on the back of his neck and his mouth in the dirt, Wulf could make no reply. The pain in his eyes was rapidly becoming unbearable and a dizziness like nothing he had ever experienced swept over him in waves.

The captain sent two guardsmen after the woman and continued to question Wulf. "Are you drunk then? Answer me!" he blustered. "Mad or drunk? For what have you done but wrongly attack innocent merchants? One is dead, or nearly so by your hand, and this one knocked senseless!"

Wulf heard his dire threats and felt his boot against his ribs and though he fought against it, his mind tumbled into confusion. He could not force his spinning thoughts to put together the words in *lange d'o-ïl*. They rolled from his tongue in a garble of Jute and Saxon and heavily accented Lombard . . . unintelligible to all.

By then a clutch of curious onlookers, passing merchants, and peasants had gathered to stare and mumble among themselves.

A young guardsman, curious as to the cart's cargo, climbed inside. Immediately he called out, "In here! Help me!" As the carpets were cast aside one by one, it was clear what cargo had been bound east toward Sezanne. His Grace's niece, the Lady Madeleine, trussed and rolled up snug as a louse in an Arab carpet.

She tumbled from the carpet, sputtering and coughing and beating a cloud of dust from her skirts. A length away, a pair of guardsmen pulled the belligerent Saxon to his feet. He dragged them around like a dog with a rat until a third snatched up a broken board from the road and whacked it across his shoulders. The blow staggered him but did not take him down. Only then was Madeleine aware of her guard's presence. She ran to him, shoving at the guardsmen. "Stop it!" she screamed. "He is my guard!" She clutched his hand and, at a glance, saw he was covered with blood, bleeding from his nose and jaw and a dozen other scrapes. "Take us to His Grace!" she demanded. When the captain did not immediately move to do so, she screeched at him, "At once!" It was precisely the captain's intention, though he proceeded at his own pace.

Madeleine was near to hysteria, certain that her guard was blind. His eyes were wholly unnatural, no longer blue but black as empty holes. She would not be silent and determinedly pelted the captain with her shrill curses. It was poison, she knew, for once they had her in the cart the brazen witch had laughed in her face and confessed as much.

Up the stone steps and into the hall, Madeleine clung to Wulf's blocky fingers. In frantic glances she saw his color change from white to grey. Taking two steps to his one, she attempted to steady him while entreating the back of the quickly-striding de Grailley to fetch His Grace's physician. In desperation she shouted, "He is sick to death, do you not hear?"

Wulf did feel sick, worse with every labored breath. He was all but blind and his head reeled with vertigo. The odor of boiled cabbage met him in the passageway. He could endure no more. Green and greasy, the stench enveloped him like marsh gas. He gagged and swallowed hard, leaned his shoulder to the wall, heaved once and spewed the contents of his

180

stomach onto the stones in a noisy, sour-smelling stream.

The sound spun de Grailley 'round on his heels. He halted, shouted for a guardsman, and sent him running along the passageway. He then turned to the lady and, observing her stricken expression, took her by the arm, ignoring her balking gait and loud protests, and swept her through the door of His Grace's study.

Heribert moved swiftly to extend a protective arm and draw his niece inside the chamber. To de Grailley, he said, "What foulness is this?" While de Grailley imparted all he knew of the affair, Heribert seated Madeleine deep in the ornate Italian chair. "Have you been harmed?" he asked.

Madeleine, speechless for once, buried her face in her filthy hands and mutely shook her head.

"From what I have learned, it appears to be the handiwork of the Baron de Luchaire," de Grailley stated, coming to stand at the chair's back. "Apparently," he said, "we have taken his threats too lightly. He means to carry off the lady, that is clear."

The gutteral sound of wretching echoed from the hall. Heribert looked toward the door, a frown screwed upon his face, then inquired as to his guardsman.

"I have sent for Brother Umberto," de Grailley replied, and clearing his throat, added, "As best I can determine, he has been poisoned. It seems there has been a conspiracy in our midst, directed by the Baron de Luchaire and aided by a serving woman of this house."

Heribert took in the words, nervously fingering his ruby crucifix. "Have you the woman?"

"No, Your Grace, she has escaped. There were two men involved as well; one is dead, the other nearly so."

"You believe de Luchaire is responsible?"

The awful wretching from the hall roused Made-

181

leine from her tears. "They said as much to me!" she blurted in an anguished voice.

Heribert's gaze fell upon his niece huddled in the huge chair. "You resisted them, of course?" he posed, interrogating her at length. His tone stung her very soul.

"Yes," she sobbed. "Yes." Her voice was little more than a whine, as mean and miserable as she felt. When she no longer heard the wretching from the hall, she craned her neck to see, then attempted to rise, frantic to know if her guard lived or died.

De Grailley, perceptive to his bishop's sudden glance, grasped the Lady Madeleine's small shoulders and sat her down firmly in the chair.

"You had some hand in this, did you not?" Heribert said accusingly.

Madeleine's face crumpled at his railing tone. "No!" she wailed, bursting into sobs.

Heribert turned away with a derisive hiss and went to stand before the windows, his jeweled hands clasped at his back.

The loud brabble of serving women, the clunk of wooden pails, and the sloosh of water upon the stones echoed from the hall. Heribert fingered his rings, considering the fact that the Saxon's death would be unfortunate—a pity, though not a complete tragedy; guardsmen were plentiful. A flurry of motion at the door shook him from his reverie.

The widow came with several serving women to lead the Lady Madeleine away to her chamber. On their heels came the physician, Umberto. With long, lank strides he entered the chamber. "Your Grace," he said, bowing slightly.

Heribert acknowledged him, asking, "What is your judgment?"

Umberto smiled and informed him most pleasantly, "Your prisoners are now both with Satan, I presume."

"The guardsman?" Heribert pressed with some urgency.

"I believe he will survive. His size was in his favor and I do not think he drank as deeply as was intended. More would have killed him. It is a violent death."

"Poison, then?"

"Oh, yes," Umberto said cheerfully. "I am fair certain of the substance. Some call it dwale. In Sienna it was known as belladonna. The ladies of the prince's court used it to doctor their eyes—to induce a lustrous look of love or so I am told. A vain and foolish enough practice, though it is poison only if ingested." Then with characteristic delight, he proceeded to describe the symptoms, concluding, "The pupils of his eyes are much dilated, mayhap you noticed?"

"I did not see him," Heribert remarked through tight lips.

"No? Well, it is not blindness. It will pass, just as the convulsive vomiting, hallucinations, and incoherent speech."

At the rear of the chamber, several scriveners sat hunched over their tables. The candlelight made pale circles of their inquisitive faces.

"I have moved the guardsman to the lady's chamber and left a novice to sit with him," Umberto advised, adding with assurance, "He should be right in a day or two." He turned to go, paused, and as an afterthought addressed de Grailley. "See he takes no wine or ale for several days."

When the dark had mostly worn away, Madeleine padded from her bed. She stood above his sleeping form and peered at him intently for any sign of life. Once she had determined he was still alive—in truth, she thought he looked none the worse for being poisoned—she woke him with a nudge of her pale foot.

He bolted up with a sudden jerk that sent her back a step. She stammered for a moment, disconcerted, her thoughts in a muddle, then quickly said all she had rehearsed. "I believed it was Albertine and her cobbler who sent the serving woman. Albertine would never be so heartless as to poison anyone. A sleeping potion, but no more."

He glared at her, though more from the misery in his stomach than actual malice.

"I believed it was so!" she said insistently. When he made no response, she pressed her lips into a grimace, turned, and ran back to her bed. With a furious swipe, she closed the bed drapes and flung herself down amid the sheets, her fierce pride stinging from his curt, unspoken rebuff.

The widow and her women soon arrived and Wulf dragged himself to his feet. His stomach was remarkably sore and his disposition no better. Half the night he had wretched and heaved, bringing up nothing until it seemed even his boot heels ached.

In the garderobe he squeezed the bridge of his nose. It was sore. He then drenched his face with water from the barrel. His head ached with a fury; even so, he decided he would live. He saw only one of everything and that was a definite improvement. He rinsed the foul taste from his mouth and considered her words. Just then, with his temples pounding and his stomach twisted in knots, it seemed far more likely she had not intended to kill him quickly; no, rather a painful, lingering death. He gargled a handful of water and spit it out in a fine mist, concluding she and her apology, if indeed the fit of temper was meant as such, could be damned.

For the better part of two days, there was an armed and angry silence between them. He had a great deal of time to think and after his bile had settled, concluded she had probably told the truth for a lie would have cost her pride just as dearly and with less reason.

Each day he felt less of an invalid. His appetite returned, though not his fondness for cider.

On a warm, still afternoon the bee skeps were robbed. Madeleine, while walking in the garden, saw the peasants gather in their odd attire. She debated for a moment, despising to ask yet longing to go, as if in doing so she might have again, at least in memory, the days gone by. "Look. They are going to rob the bees," she said, so that he might hear. "Albertine and I often helped," she intimated. She added, "It would please me to watch," making it clear by her inflection that it would equally displease her to be refused.

He agreed. He was not by nature spiteful. The skeps were close by, near the pear orchard. Not a far distance, not beyond the watchful eyes of the guards on the wall nor the one now placed in the tower. But no, none of that was why. It was because she had deigned to speak to him.

From the safety of the orchard they watched the peasants descend among the woven straw skeps like sleepwalkers through the drifting smoke. Unearthly wanderers without a hint of peeking skin, gloved and cinched, moving beneath straw hats draped with fine netted cloth.

One carried a smoking pot which jounced and swayed at the end of a limber pole, another a leather-sided bellows. And with each wheezing breath, "Humf, Humf," the bellows chuffed clouds of rolling smoke to lull the angry bees.

Wulf watched, fascinated, as Madeleine described how the honeycombs must be removed through the bottom of the rounded skeps and why some honey must be left to feed the bees in winter. For though the bees did not stir from their skeps, they still had to eat. She told him of the fat and fertile queen who dwelled inside and of the yearly swarm. And later, laughing in the drifting smoke, she told him of the winter days when she and Albertine would run to brush away the snow to see if mice or woodpeckers had attacked the skeps, for both were enemies to bees. Her simple knowledge of nature, her lilting tone, and the sweetness of her smile charmed him completely.

The long-haired youth seated upon the tufted leather hassock strummed the lute softly, humming to himself. His lord, Guiles de Luchaire, sat drinking at the heavy-topped table with two cronies recently come from the Paris court. The boy paused to take a sip of wine from the tankard by his side. As he did, his bored gaze followed two young varlets as they crossed the hall, arms laden with wood for the kitchen fires.

There in the hall amid the daily routine of the house, de Luchaire and his guests had spent the better part of the sweltering late-summer's day. Their discussion touched on many topics—most notably the sickness, the fate of France, and King Philip's foolishness. Since all were in hearty agreement, it was a jolly conversation interrupted only by an occasional round of laughter and calls for more wine.

At one end of the hall food was being prepared and a thin stratum of acrid blue smoke hung just below the beamed ceiling. A number of serving women drifted about the table carrying jugs of wine. Guiles de Luchaire caught the waist of one girl who was younger and prettier than the others. "Sing for us," he bade the girl, and dropping his hand from her waist gave her rump a pat. She shrank back shyly, but there was a smile on her lips.

"Sing! Sing!" the two knights chanted.

Laughing, the slender, brown-haired girl sat the wine jug on the table and went to the boy who sat with the lute. After a brief whispered exchange, he took up the lute once more. The colorful ribbons decorating the instrument tumbled over his sleeve as he struck the first melodious notes.

De Luchaire turned to his friends with a smile. "She has a most charming voice."

The round-faced knight grinned broadly. "All about her is most charming," he said, openly ogling the lissome girl with the chestnut hair.

"Will Foquet and I be forced to fight over her?" the hard-faced knight to his left remarked in a jesting voice.

De Luchaire, who did not fancy her favors that night, gave his permission with a curling smile. "Make a torte of her if it pleases you," he suggested. He was known by all at court as a debauchée. It was a well-deserved reputation, as his cronies could attest.

The girl's sweet voice and the simple notes of the lute filled the hall. As her voice faded over the last lingering notes, the conversation at the table turned to other topics.

"Our class is dying, chivalry is dying," the hard-faced one commented morosely.

The round-faced knight emptied his tankard, saying, "I have heard of a powder from the east that when touched with fire can propel stones with a speed beyond reckoning. It destroys walls as well as armor."

The other nodded in sad agreement. "It is a fierce thing, this powder."

"No man of honor would stoop to such a weapon," de Luchaire insisted; the horrors of Crecy were still fresh in his mind—the bottomless mire, the air stitched black with arrows. But it was the sound he recalled most, the deafening roar of thousands of men and horses coming together to the death. His line of thought was soon given form by his friend.

"The English will. They used it at Crecy."

"I did not see it," de Luchaire returned.

The round-faced Foquet added his voice. "Nor did I."

"No, nor I," the other agreed, "but there are those who swear it happened and soon it will be the end of all we know.''

The colicky cries of a babe echoed through the noisy hall. A serving woman entered, bouncing a child in her arms. She went by stops and starts, attempting to soothe the squalling babe, while struggling forward with two larger tots clinging to her skirts. She sat on a bench near a table where loaves had been left to rise.

"Is that the babe?'' the round-faced Foquet asked, peering through the smoke, for the Baron of Sézanne's marriage, a profitable one, had been made at court.

De Luchaire inclined his head. "My heir,'' he scoffed, remarking, "He is as bandy-legged as his dam. The other two are my bastards.'' Then with a short laugh, he posed, "Why is it bastards are always the stronger?''

"They are freely made,'' the hard-faced one responded with a laugh.

"Truly said,'' the other remarked with a hand slapped against the table. "My wife is homely as a hedgehog. I asked for twice the dowry and got it!'' he said with a loud guffaw. His laughter was taken up by the others and the discussion turned randy as any overheard in a tavern.

Within the hour de Luchaire and his guests' conversation was again disrupted, this time by the appearance of a shaggy-headed villein. He was roughly dressed and dragged the smell of sheep with him as he approached the table and mumbled into his lord's ear in hushed tones. A dark look stormed across de Luchaire's features. For a moment it seemed he would give voice to his sudden anger, but he did not. He sent the villein away and once more took up the conversation.

Crickets chorused in the meadow as Guiles de Luchaire stepped into the night. His guests had retired to entertain themselves with the little *chanteuse*—conveniently, for he had matters to attend to that night and made haste through the dew-damp grass.

"Yes, yes," the old herbalist agreed, his hands raised in weary supplication. "The drug was not strong enough or he drank too little. Did I not warn you this could happen? Too much brings immediate seizures and would have drawn attention, too little renders a man like a maddened bull. Had he drank the proper amount he would have slept peacefully for eternity, but how was I to . . ."

"Enough!" de Luchaire angrily bit off his words. "I am bored with your whining excuses. You have failed. I should have the hide from your back!"

The old man licked his lips in silence, his darting tongue not unlike a snake's. "All is not lost, milord. The two you value most are free from blame. There will be another day," he added hopefully.

From the door, de Luchaire pinioned the frail form in a black stare. "I go to make other plans. Pray you they meet with more success."

Chapter Thirteen

On the feast day of the Nativity of the Blessed Virgin several courtiers in the service of the Duke du Boulay arrived from Nevers. Their spokesman, a certain Baron Legoix, a middle-aged man with longish lank brown hair, spindly legs, and an oddly-shaped mouth, first spoke privately with the bishop, then joining the others of his parted attended Mass in the château's chapel.

Madeleine, dressed in a gown of blue and white samite, noticed the men enter the chapel and wondered who they were. Wulf noticed them as well. He had not been informed of their coming and watched them intently until he felt satisfied they posed no threat.

Following the Mass, Madeleine was called to her parents' solar, which her uncle now used as a sitting room. There in the room, the walls hung thick with tapestries, she was presented to the duke's courtiers. She smiled and spoke politely but her eyes did not smile and her voice was cold as frost.

The courtiers were impressed by the Lady Madeleine's vivid dark beauty and her elegant bearing. But Legoix, taking the bishop aside, voiced his concern about the girl's obvious youth. "Is she old enough to conceive?" he whispered. Heribert assured him she was, adding that his niece was in robust good health.

As he spoke, Legoix gazed across the chamber. His appraising eyes, swaggering stance, and slyly-spoken asides flared Wulf's anger. When he could tolerate it no longer, he met the courtier's eyes with a hostile stare; the smirking man looked away.

Later, over quantitites of fine wine and richly sauced game birds, the terms of the dowry were again discussed. It was merely a formality since the Duke and His Grace, the bishop, were both well pleased with the agreement. There remained only the question of the portrait. Heribert saw no need for it. "You have seen my niece with your own eyes, *mes seigneurs*. To my mind, the sight of a loyal courtier is by far more accurate than an artist's interpretation."

But Legoix was adamant. "A portrait would convey the lady's child-like innocence," he insisted. "One perhaps with her long hair flowing over her shoulders, for that is the fashion," and suggested an artist who was popular at court.

Heribert paled at the suggestion, replying that the cost would be outrageous. He would be expected to pay and having seen the artist's work, questioned its accuracy. However, he told the courtiers, among his novices was a boy whose rare talent far outshone any court artist. Heribert hastened de Grailley to fetch the novice and samples of his work, holy portraits of the saints, were exhibited to the courtiers.

Darkness had fallen when the bishop and his guests gathered in the hall to sup. Flames leapt in the hearth and, in the center of the hall, a novice stroked the strings of a harp. The courtiers, seated close to the bishop, were red-faced and laughing from too much wine. Their loud voices and hearty laughter rang throughout the vast room.

On this evening, the novices concentrated on their food for the subject of religion had been set aside. The discourse was a great relief to Madeleine, though she considered the leering Legoix equally boring.

Serving boys attended the table, offering a variety

of meat dishes, vegetable mélanges, fruits, and breads. Madeleine took very little of what was offered and ate practically none of it. The laughter and bantering conversations of the courtiers rang in her ears, annoying her and drowning the sweet notes of the harp. Their high good humor thoroughly irritated Madeleine, making her more depressed and miserable with each passing moment.

When the pastries, cakes, and comfits were brought to the table, a serving boy whose tousled, sandy-colored hair curled around his freckled face, bowed and, bringing his face near to Madeleine's ear, held out a tray of sugared cakes. He murmured, "The kitchen woman says these are your favorite."

Madeleine raised her eyes in surprise. Squires were not permitted to initiate a conversation with their superiors, but her cross look lightened when she saw the boy's broad smile. It was an infectiously merry smile and Madeleine, unable to repress it, smiled back, lifting a sugary cake from the tray.

The boy was about to move off when Wulf, whose attention had been momentarily drawn to the other end of the lengthy table, fixed him in a formulated stare. He disliked the boy's manner even more than his shifty appearance. "What have you got there?" he asked.

The boy continued to smile, but the corners of his lips twitched slightly. "Sugar cakes, sire."

"Eat one," Wulf commanded in a soft but firm voice, and pointing one out, instructed, "This one."

Madeleine, nibbling on her square of white-dusted cake, turned and stared at Wulf with disbelief.

The boy's eyes darted nervously. "Sire, I am not permitted to eat in the hall."

"Eat it," Wulf repeated, this time in a more menacing tone. Seeing no other alternative, the boy popped the square of cake into his mouth and choked it down. As he did, Wulf took a cake from the tray and motioned him away.

ENJOY ALL THE PASSION AND ROMANCE OF...

Heartfire

ROMANCES from ZEBRA

After you have read HEART-FIRE ROMANCES, we're sure you'll agree that HEARTFIRE sets new standards of excellence for historical romantic fiction. Each Zebra HEARTFIRE novel is the ultimate blend of intimate romance and grand adventure and each takes place in the kinds of historical settings you want most...the American Revolution, the Old West, Civil War and more.

SUBSCRIBERS $AVE, $AVE, $AVE!!!

As a HEARTFIRE Home Sub-scriber, you'll save with your HEARTFIRE Subscription. You'll receive 4 brand new Heart-fire Romances to preview Free for 10 days each month. If you decide to keep them you'll pay only $3.50 each; a total of $14.00 and you'll save $3.00 each month off the cover price.

Plus, we'll send you these novels as soon as they are published each month. There is never any shipping, handling or other hid-den charges; home delivery is always FREE! And there is no obligation to buy even a single book. You may return any of the books within 10 days for full credit and you can cancel your subscription at any time. No questions asked.

Zebra's HEARTFIRE ROMANCES Are The Ultimate
In Historical Romantic Fiction.
Start Enjoying Romance As You Have Never Enjoyed It Before...
With 4 FREE Books From HEARTFIRE

TO GET YOUR
4 FREE BOOKS
MAIL THE COUPON BELOW.

Heartfire Romance

FREE BOOK CERTIFICATE

GET 4 FREE BOOKS

Yes! I want to subscribe to Zebra's HEARTFIRE HOME SUBSCRIPTION SERVICE. Please send me my 4 FREE books. Then each month I'll receive the four newest Heartfire Romances as soon as they are published. Free for ten days. If I decide to keep them I'll pay the special discounted price of just $3.50 each; a total of $14.00. This is a savings of $3.00 off the regular publishers price. There are no shipping, handling or other hidden charges. There is no minimum number of books to buy and I may cancel this subscription at any time. In any case the 4 FREE Books are mine to keep regardless.

NAME

ADDRESS

CITY   STATE   ZIP

TELEPHONE

SIGNATURE

(If under 18 parent or guardian must sign)
Terms and prices subject to change.
Orders subject to acceptance.

HF 102

GET 4 FREE BOOKS

HEARTFIRE HOME SUBSCRIPTION
SERVICE
P.O. BOX 5214
120 BRIGHTON ROAD
CLIFTON, NEW JERSEY 07015

Madeleine's eyes flashed angrily. "Did you think they were poisoned?" she asked in a mocking voice, infuriated with him for bullying the boy.

He looked at her without a trace of remorse. "It blends as easily with dough as with cider. There are merchants in Troyes who are not pleased with the prospect of paying taxes to the Duke of Burgundy," he said, pushing the last morsel of cake into his mouth.

At first stung by his sarcasm, Madeleine suddenly realized she had never given a thought to such matters. She turned away and, looking down at the remaining chunk of cake, decided she did not want it after all.

Late in the evening the bishop and his guests were still at their conversations. Weary servants leaned against the walls in feigned readiness, while others brought more wine. The harpist had long since deserted the hall. He had trailed out with his brethren to prepare for devotions and to rest his aching fingers.

Madeleine, too, had retired to her chamber where the Widow Crozet and three serving women waited to undress her and carefully fold away the heavy silken gown. Only during this time, and when the women came of a morning to dress her, was Wulf permitted to see to his own needs.

Inside the tower room that served as garderobe, a polished steel mirror hung above a wooden chest and basin. Beside it a supply of fresh water for washing was kept in a wooden barrel and where the room corbelled outwards were the lavatories. All waste fell to a ditch below.

When Wulf returned from the garderobe, a serving woman was attempting to brush the lady's cropped hair. Holding the brush in her outstretched hand, the girl made a helpless shrugging gesture with her shoulders, insisting that the brush stimulated the hair and made it grow more quickly. But Madeleine rose impatiently from the stool before the silver-framed Venetian mirror, replying that she did not care if her hair fell out since perhaps then the Duke du Boulay would choose some other unfortunate woman for his bride. She then climbed into the huge bed and in a peevish voice told them all to leave.

Wulf banked the fire in the hearth and pulled his rush-filled mattress before the door. The pair of fur rugs he slept between had belonged to Madeleine's brother, the late young lord, and glowed soft and brown in the dim light cast from the hearth.

King Death moved through the broken shadows, his tattered shroud trailing after him. He floated, dancing on the moonlight to some unheard, macabre melody. With a beckoning, skeletal hand he summoned up the putrefying corpses of her parents and siblings. They rose as phantoms in the swirling blackness. Matted hair fell in clumps from her sisters' withered heads, exposing the skull beneath the skin. Toads and great white worms attacked the faces and entrails of her parents' rotting flesh as they swayed to King Death's tune. Around and around Death danced, then slowly turned his hideous, grinning face on her and reaching out a knotted, bony hand beckoned her, "Come!"

Madeleine awoke with a scream, chilled to her soul, her eyes wide with horror. Moonlight flooded into the room, casting monstrous forms upon the chamber walls. She leapt from her bed with a cry and fled across the cold stones. At the door, she collided with a shapeless black hulk which sprang up like a snare and seized her with such force that only a breathless sob escaped her parted lips.

It was not the cold, hard grip of King Death, for the warm and living arms encircling her had a familiar scent. Madeleine struggled to speak, croaking, "Save me! He is here, it is King Death!" Having found her voice, her words gushed out in an endless terrified stream. "King Death has come for me!" she wailed, shaking the black, furry form. "He is here, I have seen him!"

Wulf clasped a hand over her mouth, silencing her, and in a voice still thick with sleep, said, "There is no one here, only you and I."

Madeleine would not be convinced and shut tight her eyes, mumbling into the moist warmth of his palm, "No, no, he is here!"

Groggily, Wulf shrugged away the fur and pulled his shoulders to a more comfortable position. "Open your eyes," he coaxed and, tilting her face, asked, "What do you see?"

For Madeleine the horror was as real as the sound of his voice. Cringing, she opened one eye, then the other. She saw no skulking King Death nor mouldering corpses, only the chamber bathed in moonlight. "He was here!" she insisted, shaking his muscular arm.

"A dream," he told her. "No one was here." His tone was more amused than chiding. Madeleine blinked and, salvaging what she could of her dignity, remarked, "I did not have such dreams when Albertine slept in my bed. I was warm with her beside me. Now I am chilled to my bones. Cover me with your fur," she begged. "I am cold enough to die."

"Can it be you are afraid of King Death?" he teased.

"No," she snapped, for a lie better suited her purposes. "I am cold," she insisted, "and you are warm as a hearth. Let me stay?"

"Where is your modesty tonight?" he asked, his hands acutely aware of the soft flesh beneath the loose folds of the night dress.

"You cannot see in the dark," she told him, for there was little light; she could make out only his dim outline, and therefore reasoned her modesty was safe.

"Blind men do," he said with a soft laugh, hauling her against him and smoothing his hands over the sweet curve of her hips.

"Stop it!" she demanded, wrestling with his

195

hands, startled more by the profound upheaval of her senses, the intense excitement generated by his touch, than the playful mauling. "No!" she lashed out, angry that he should affect her so and with no deeper feeling on his part than the soft taunting laughter. Indignant, she shoved against his chest with the flat of her hands, threatening, "I will return to my bed."

"Then go," he told her. "The fur is not large enough for both of us, not unless we lie together."

"Swear you will not touch me again?"

He made no reply, but turned his back to her and lay down. Satisfied, Madeleine snuggled against him, molding her back to his. She felt safe and blessedly warm, though she could not sleep. The unexpected touch of his hands had stirred a storm of emotion within her.

The sound of his jabbing at the logs in the hearth with the flat iron poker caused her to stir beneath the furs. She saw him crouched, sitting on his heels, before the hearth in only his hose. Tongues of flame licked over a fresh log.

He came across the room toward her. She closed her eyes, pretending to be asleep. He dropped to his haunches and brushed her shoulder with his fingers. "Milady," he said softly, "best you return to your bed before your women come."

Madeleine jerked as if burnt, threw back the fur rug, and ran to her bed, tossing the bed covers into the air and covering her head. She did not mention the nightmare nor thank him for gallantly rescuing her from the clutches of King Death, but afterwards she did speak to him and with a bit more warmth.

The artist, a young novice in the service of His Grace, was thin and very fair and the skin of his delicate long hands appeared almost transparent. He was waiting for Madeleine and her guard at the door to a small chamber behind the library. His arms were filled with equipment and brushes and a stretched canvas leaned against the passageway wall.

A gust of musty air greeted them as they entered. The room was used for storage and the upper half was cluttered with furnishings.

The young artist chose a spot opposite a pair of long arched windows. He was from the south, Arles, and spoke a *Langue d' Oc* of sorts. At times his timid voice and soft provincial accent obscured his words. He set up his tools methodically rather than artistically and from the jumble of furnishings salvaged a stool on which to sit while he worked.

No fire had been set in the hearth and Wulf, seeing the Lady Madeleine was shivering, called down a passing household varlet and sent him to fetch an armload of logs.

Since hours of posing were required, a chair was brought from the clutter for the Lady Madeleine. No sooner had Wulf positioned the chair in the chosen spot than the artist pointed to another, more ornate, chair with an upholstered seat and back. It was necessary for Wulf to move several heavy chests and a large *prie-dieu* in order to reach it.

Each day for two weeks, Madeleine sat for hours in perfect silence. During these sittings the only sounds were the crackle and hiss of the fire and the rapid strokes of the artist's brush upon the canvas.

There was little to occupy Wulf other than to feed logs to the fire and daydream. His gaze often fell on the Lady Madeleine. He thought the thoughts all young men think and when he had made himself sufficiently uncomfortable, often to the point where he feared it was noticeable, he would go stare from the window or watch the artist from Arles paint. Wulf was by no means an artist, though he looked at the world with honest eyes. The portrait was her likeness, he decided, but there was little life to it. More like a holy picture, flat and rigid—an oval face and dark hair which, on canvas, had miraculously lengthened and flowed freely over her small shoulders.

On the day the portrait was completed, a cold rain pecked at the greenish glass and somber clouds swept across the horizon, darkening the chamber. The young artist, obviously pleased with his endeavor, asked the Lady Madeleine her opinion. A mistake, for she looked at it from far and near and from a dozen other distances, made a *moue,* and then declared, "The nose is much too long."

The rain kept them prisoner in the château for days. Madeleine worked long hours on the tapestry. Out of sheer boredom, Wulf neatly wrapped the loose yarn of the basket into tight balls. At times she would ask his advice on colors, then smile politely and use the one she intended all along.

The despised portrait had been sent along to Nevers by courier. Twice Madeleine had quarreled with her uncle, but it had done nothing to relieve the quiet fury which brewed inside her like dark clouds before a storm.

It was the insufferably boring suppers in the hall which tested her endurance beyond mortal limits. Wulf sat uneasily beside her at the bishop's table while she seethed with irritation. She ate hardly at all. She was too thin, Wulf thought, but he knew enough of women to keep his thoughts to himself.

One evening Madeleine brought out the game of draughts with which she and Albertine had passed the evening hours and asked if he could play. He could, he said, though truthfully he did not fancy games. He spread the fur rugs before the hearth and each evening they sat in the flickering light and played the game of strategy.

Wulf enjoyed the company of women more than did most men. His earliest years had been spent among doting women and so he had grown to associate their ways, the smell of their skins, their soft voices with contentment and comfort. What he would not have admitted, even to himself, was that he was so beguiled by the Lady Madeleine he would have gladly sat in the rain for the pleasure of having her speak to him.

Madeleine allowed him the opening move. There was an initial exchange of pieces. She sacrificed one. He moved, unwisely it seemed, and she captured three of his pieces. Afterward he was more cautious. She smiled to herself and set a white piece as an inviting decoy. He ignored it. Did he not see it, she wondered? He moved another piece. She had no choice but to capture it. She nimbly retrieved the piece.

She was so certain of victory that she did not perceive the glint of skullduggery in the slanted blue glance. In an instant she realized the strategy of his foolhardy sacrifices. She had fallen into his trap and was now powerless to avoid the rout of her game pieces. He, Madeleine decided, would pose more of a challenge than Albertine. The next game she played with more finesse.

Late of a cool evening, Madeleine looked up suddenly from the board and asked, "Is my nose overlong?" She appeared so youthfully serious that for a moment he said nothing, fearing he would smile. "No, milady. It does not appear overlong to me. I believe it suits your face well."

"Soothly?" she asked, unconvinced.

"Soothly," he repeated, no longer able to repress a smile.

She cocked her head and laughed. "You would not lie to me to spare my feelings?"

"No, milady." His smile deepened.

"On your honor as a knight?"

"That I cannot give," he said in his bland tone.

"You have a knight's sword; are you then a thief?"

"A knight without land or rank is little better than

a thief. His honor, like his sword, is easily bought."

"You are a younger son without an inheritance?" she asked, temporarily putting aside the question of her nose for one she found more intriguing.

"Not a son, a bastard, and not of my lord but his daughter."

"You must have had his blessings? Otherwise how could you be knighted?"

"By his own hand," he said evenly, adding, "There was no ceremony. His sons lay dead and he, too, was dying. He held the sword and said the words only because he could not die with the thought of a stranger holding his lands."

"Then you have both land and rank," Madeleine determined.

"And may claim neither," he said with a bitter smile.

"What is there to prevent you?"

"I am not free. There is a ransom to pay and failing that I would be declared an outlaw by the church— unable to lay claim to rank or land."

Madeleine recalled the ransom he had spoken of in the garden. Her dark eyes danced with curiosity.

Over the days she slowly wheedled the story from him. First he spoke about his mother, who he said was very young and was sent to a convent after his birth to atone for her sins—then about the old midwife, Erna, who had kept him. When he was old enough to understand, she told him he had been born to the Lord Hasso's young daughter and was unwanted, a disgrace, because she had been raped. And with a laugh she had confided that it was not so much rape as the Lord Hasso wished to believe it was. She said it was a soldier in Hasso's pay, a Jute, who had planted the seed in the daughter and that Hasso had killed him for the wrong he had committed.

When Madeleine asked to hear more of the tragic tale, he said he knew no more. No one had told him and he had not asked.

Madeleine's questions were endless. She wanted to know what sort of life he had led as a child. He told her that at eight he was sent to live with the priests. They taught him to read Latin and pray and at ten he took the vows of the Order of St. Mary the Virgin and afterward became a squire to Hasso's youngest son.

Intrigued, Madeleine asked what vows he had taken. He smiled good naturedly and recited them for her amusement.

"But those are the vows of a priest," she exclaimed. "May you never take a wife?" Her thoughts dashed off in all direction.

It was not exactly so, but near enough, for without his freedom he could never claim Rügen. Still smiling, he said, "A vow of celibacy means little to a boy of ten."

"But you are no longer a boy."

"No," he agreed. It was a vow he had broken as often as kept. He set his gaze beyond the window where the burnished hills glowed orange and russet in the fading light.

Madeleine had heard many scandalous tales of priests and priories, even those in Avignon. "Have you never been tempted?" she pried, needing desperately to know and in the same instant wished she had not asked.

"Me?" he mumbled, turning to her with a vague smile on his lips. "I am a sinner."

In the hall, Madeleine took her place at the lengthy table. She sat stiff as a statue and molded her small features into an expression of great forbearance.

A long line of novices filed into the hall with a shuffling of feet. De Grailley, awaiting the bishop's entrance, noticed the Saxon had not yet taken his place beside the Lady Madeleine and seized the opportunity to draw him aside. He said, "Scrape the stubble from your face and bathe; there will be guests in the château on the morrow." Wulf silently nodded and took his seat.

He glanced round the room, feeling mildly affronted. Soothly, his clothing was rough, perhaps he did smell of horses and he often put off shaving, but he never failed to wash himself. He had never forgotten the words old Erena had drummed into the skull of a small boy who was delighted to learn he could direct a stream of piss. *Take care of your schwanz and your teeth. Keep them clean,* she had told him, *otherwise the ones will fall out and the other fall off and then you might as well put a knife to your throat.*

In the garderobe he washed as he always did and scraped the stubble from his jaw. It was a chore to shave with only a minimum of light, a crude straight blade, and polished steel mirror. The alternative was a beard which itched and moreover was a convenient place for lice to nitt.

On the morrow, as the prime bells rang, the Lady Madeleine and her guard, bathed and scented, heard Mass in the chapel.

After returning to the château, they were brought before the bishop, the courtier Legoix, and the priest Evarrard. Madeleine, recalling her first meeting with the priest and the mortification she had suffered at his questions, flushed with anger.

As she entered, she overheard the closing sentences of their conversation. The Duke du Boulay had been injured in a tournament in Bourges and had been advised by his physicians not to travel even the short distance to his own bed in his château at Nevers. Madeleine could hardly contain her joy. Surely the wedding would be postponed and, she thought gleefully, perhaps he would not recover.

The men turned as she crossed the chamber. The heavy tapestries adorning the solar's walls were predominantly green and amber hues and all within the room was tinted with an odd patina.

Legoix bowed and said, "Madame, as much as it displeases me to be the bearer of bad news, it is my duty to inform you that His Excellency Roland du Boulay, Duke of Burgundy, has been injured in a tournament and will be unable to take his place at your side in the Cathedral of St. Pierre on the twenty-eighth of this month." He paused, expecting the young woman to inquire as to the seriousness of the Duke's injuries. She did not. Legoix cleared his throat. "Despite his painful indisposition," he intoned, "His Excellency has proposed a proxy marriage in order that you, madame, may not suffer too lengthy and tiring a betrothal." In a time of such calamity, life was uncertain and the Duke of Burgundy did not wish to hazard the loss of the much-needed revenues he would gain from the Count of Troye's lands.

Madeleine remained stiffly quiet. After a moment, Heribert spoke, putting an end to the embarrassing silence. "It is agreeable, of course." Heribert had much to gain as well. He said, "Each day my niece expresses her deep longing to be united with His Excellency in marriage."

Madeleine choked with fury and, turning her flashing eyes upon her uncle, pressed her fingers to her lips making a sharp coughing noise.

Without a word from Madeleine, the date of the proxy marriage was set as before for the twenty-eighth of September, the feast day of St. Wenceslaus.

By afternoon, all arrangements had been completed and the courtier Legoix and the priest Evarrard, whom Madeleine learned was to become her confessor, hurriedly left the château to carry the news to Bourges.

Madeleine felt as if a noose was closing on her throat. For days she moped over her tapestry or on pleasant afternoons wandered through the garden like a ghost. She was petulant and cross to her serving women and snapped irritably at her guard. He could do nothing to please her and was left to shrug and follow after her, wearing a glum expression.

The Duke du Boulay, no more or less vain than other men, had sent a likeness of himself—a miniature enclosed in a golden Florentine frame which depicted him as a lithe and youthful knight suited in flawless armor astride a white horse. The head, however, appeared as if it had been severed from another body and set upon the shining knight's gleaming shoulders. It was a paunchy face with protruding eyes, a long humped nose, and straggly moustache.

Surely, Madeleine thought, the artist had flattered him, for all artists did if they wished to please their noble patrons and live successfully. She set the miniature face down on her trousseau chest and never looked at it again. The thought of marriage to such an ambitious man left her sick with despair. She did not wish to sacrifice her youth and happiness in endless pregnancies to supply heirs for a pompous Valois duke who connived to be king.

The days passed in misery for Madeleine and each evening she was subjected to the smug face of her despised uncle.

Heribert swept into the hall, followed by his protégé, de Grailley. Old Dubuc trundled after them. Once seated, Heribert led the prayer and, following the benediction, announced the topic for the evening meal was *humility*.

As he spoke, a parade of servants trooped from the kitchen bearing a stuffed roasted piglet, a tray laden with game birds, a mélange of stewed vegetables, various crusty breads, and honey-soaked pastries.

"Humility is a virtue that must be practiced daily, for only through humility are we acceptable to God." Heribert smiled, and lifting his eyes from the tempting feast before him, said, *"In spiritu humilitatis—suscipiamur a te, Domine."*

Madeleine watched those around her consume the meal. They seemed to be creatures possessed only of elbows, hands, and mouths, all moving in unison. They chewed, slurped, sucked, and munched. One raised a goblet, then another, and so on down the length of the thick-topped table. It required little imagination to picture them as noisy pigs at a trough and had she not been in such a foul mood she would have found the scene thoroughly comical.

Her uncle's long-winded dissertation, she noticed, did not affect her guard's appetite in the least. Like the novices, he, too, was young and hungry. Perhaps his prowess at pushing food into his mouth was better founded than theirs, for he was the tallest man at the table; only de Grailley and her uncle approached his height. She liked the thought of his large body and it was a thought which occurred to her more often than she was willing to admit.

Once again Heribert's voice intruded upon her thoughts. "Our humility," he said, "ensures that we are acceptable to God. However, the sacrificial action of the Mass depends upon divine pleasure for its fulfillment. Only through a perfect spirit of humility do we invite the blessings of our divine Majesty.

"Our Lord Jesus Christ was an exemplar *par excellence* of the virtue of humility. During every moment of his life, he practiced self-denial and self-abasement. His life was directed toward only one aim, his sacred passion and death. If we are to truly emulate him, then we must know well the ways in which Our Lord humbled himself."

"His passion and death, a choice in which He was not bound," a novice from Artois said.

"By the place in which His body was laid, and that His Soul descended into hell," another added.

A third, managing to swallow a cud of pork, replied, "The shame and mockeries He endured."

A frail novice, whose jaws were distended with food until he looked not at all like himself, said, "By delivering Himself up to man's power. And as He Himself said to Pilate, 'Thou shouldst not have any power against Me, unless it were given thee from above.'"

"Excellent," Heribert commended his novices. "Following this example of Our Lord we are bound to teach humility to mankind, but do we ourselves practice this virtue to the extent we hope to instill it in others? We must let the words of our Divine Lord sink deeply into our hearts . . ."

"Eat your food," a hushed voice urged in Madeleine's ear.

Madeleine, whose thoughts had been turned inward, looked crossly toward the sound of the whispered words and blinked into the sidelong glance of her guard. Presumptuous cur, she thought, suggesting that if he was so concerned *he* could eat her food. He could eat the soup bowl for all she cared!

He shrugged and, returning to his meal, mumbled, "It is a sin to starve yourself when there is food before you."

To which Madeleine contemptuously replied, "I cannot eat in such an atmosphere. I am filled to my nose with words. I have had several helpings of sin ladled with humility; there is no room for food." She was sick to death of the endless stupid discussions. Was it not enough to be held a prisoner, to be used as a pawn by her uncle and men like him, men who cared only for wealth and power? Her angry pulse pounded against her temples and the rage rising in her throat threatened to smother her. She could not bear it another moment, any of it.

At the opposite end of the table, Heribert suddenly raised his hand, bringing the discussion to a halt. Looking far down the table's length, his eyes settled upon his scowling, dark-headed niece. "Is there something you wish to say, Madeleine?" He had not heard his niece's words, but her expression of displeasure was plain to see. The novices seated near

206

her had heard and it was she, not the spirit of God, which filled their thoughts.

"No," Madeleine said in a constricted voice, wanting to scream out that he was naught but a stinking hypocrite. Instead she jolted to her feet, bumbling against the table. "I feel ill," she cried, and swaying a little, gathered her skirts and ran from the hall.

Heribert, taken by surprise at his niece's abrupt departure, sent a questioning glance to her youthful guard. Indeed, all eyes were on him. Wulf, not knowing what else to do, glanced after the slight, fleeing figure. Clearly, he was expected to follow.

He rose to his feet, grumbling under his breath at having to abandon his half-finished meal. The passageway was empty. He had no clue as to where she had gone. As he stood there deliberating, a serving girl came toward him from the kitchen carrying a tray of pastries. "Have you seen your mistress?" he questioned.

The plain-faced girl with a kerchief knotted tightly at the back of her head gave a quick nod and responded, "She passed through the kitchen, sire."

Wulf walked swiftly into the heavily beamed kitchen where a warm fog of food filled the low room. He found the servants taking their meal, some seated and others standing. A fat woman drinking a bowl of soup wiped her mouth with the back of her hand and informed him that the mistress had rushed out into the gardens without a word. Half a dozen others hastened to tell a like story.

From the kitchen stoop he viewed the broad expanse of the gardens where the gentle green hues blended in the approaching twilight. He did not see the Lady Madeleine.

He swore softly and started out, a fierce frown upon his face. She had slipped away like a shadow. There was no trusting her, not even for an instant. He belched, tasting his food for the second time. His gut rumbled. He was in no mood to play her little game of fox and geese. He strode toward the stable which he felt certain was her logical destination.

But at the stable all was quiet. The old stableman was nowhere to be found and the lady's dappled palfrey was in its stall contentedly swishing flies.

He stepped outside. Beyond the meadow, the tethered horses of the bishop's soldiers grazed quietly. The encampment lay on the opposite side of a small stream which bordered the vegetable plots and the orchard. Smoke from the cook-fires curled above the ragged patchwork of tents and the distant sound of voices carried on the still air.

He turned, surveying the tree-lined walkways of the garden, now quickly fading in the twilight haze. She could be anywhere, he thought. She may have ventured into the forest, but no, even she was not so foolish as that; she would have taken a horse. She seemed much attached to the dappled mare—he doubted she would leave her pet behind if she intended to flee to one of her father's estates or to a kinsman, though none would offer her shelter and defy a bishop of the Holy Church. He belched once more, experiencing a burning sensation in his throat.

He was convinced she was close by, in all probability watching him from a hiding place in the gardens and hoping to lure him away from the stables. The thought galled him to his soul. He debated over which action to take. If he did not return with her shortly, the bishop would call out his guard and he would be punished for his failure.

He was about to set off into the garden when he heard a rustling behind him. He whirled round, his gaze sweeping past the steaming dung heaps to a patch of tall weeds which marked the boundary of the stable yard. The dense growth swayed gently in the still air as if an animal moved within. He crossed the soggy yard in long strides.

Madeleine, crouching close to the humid earth, held her breath. He was coming straight for her. She had only one chance at freedom and that was to break and run. If she could but reach the woods and hide herself in the deep undergrowth, neither he nor all her uncle's soldiers could find her before the sun set. She gathered her skirts and bolted from the brace of weeds like a hare pursued by hounds, veering off to the left around the back of the stable and down a grassy slope.

He sprinted after her. The rapid-fire pounding of his footsteps raised a rash of gooseflesh on her sweaty skin. In another twenty bounds, he was close enough that she heard his panting breath and could all but feel it on the back of her neck. From the edge of her field of vision, she saw him gather to lunge.

She lurched sideways, nearly losing her balance but avoiding him. She heard him curse loudly, then heard the pumping sound of his pursuing footfalls. She ran blindly; her lungs burned with exhaustion and the calves of her legs ached with every stride.

Only when the stable reeled into view did she notice she was running not toward but away from the woods. With every stride she was losing her momentum. She darted once again into the tall weeds. Burrs clung to her skirt and snagged at her sleeves. A blackberry cane ripped at her hand, but she ignored it. With a gasp of relief, she realized she no longer heard him close behind her. It was then that her eyes caught sight of him hurtling toward her. He had circumvented the weedy patch and come in on her flank.

She gave a yelp of surprise and threw herself to the left. A dung heap rose up before her like a mountain. She skidded in a futile attempt to avoid it, lost her footing, and went down in the mire. With a violent motion, she pulled herself to her hands and knees. Sputtering and cursing, she attempted to rise only to slip and fall again into the sour-smelling, fermenting ooze of manure.

He stood above her, panting and laughing so hard he burst into a fit of coughing.

"Bastard!" she shrieked and flung a handful of manure at him.

Convulsed with laughter, he sidestepped the wad of dung.

Madeleine clawed her way to her feet with murder in her eyes and charged full at him. He held her at bay with a long arm. She thrashed out with her feet, swearing at him with the fury of a drunken peasant, ranting that he was naught but animal shit, no better than what she had fallen into, and wishing him burnt at the stake a dozen times over. In a frenzy of frustration, she threw herself on the ground and refused to budge.

Red-faced and still chuckling, he offered her his hand. She spat on it. He wiped his hand on his hosen, offering it once more, and in a remarkably good-natured voice asked, "Will milady accompany me into the château or does she prefer to be dragged?" He had no intention of dirtying any more than his hands.

Seething with rage but fearing he would carry out his threat, Madeleine struggled to her feet. She took three steps forward, spun on her heel, and slapped her filthy hand across his face—then stomped off toward the kitchen, clutching her grimy skirts with a stinging hand.

He followed her into the kitchen wearing a smear of manure and the angry white imprint of her hand on his cheek. In the kitchen, the servants gaped and stared; as she entered the passageway, she heard their whispers and snickering laughter at her back.

Sick with embarrassment and her own stench, Madeleine turned at the stairs, but Wulf clamped a large hand on her shoulder and roughly pushed her towards the hall. She turned on him like a wild animal, her hand drawn back to strike again. He

210

caught her small wrist and, whirling her about, raised it to her shoulder blade and with another shove propelled her forward. She balked with every step, whining that he was hurting her and threatening to scream. Only her uncle's appearance at the door arch silenced her.

"What in the name of St. Anthony is this?" he thundered, grimacing as the stench invaded his nostrils.

"Milady lost her footing on her way to the stables," Wulf said in a voice as bland as his northlander's features.

"Get her away from me. De Grailley!" Heribert shouted to his young curate. The pale, hawk-nosed young man immediately rose from his seat at the table. "Have the serving women bring water to their mistress's chamber."

De Grailley, whose pallor rivaled that of a corpse, nodded and disappeared down the passageway with swift strides, his black robes flapping after him. Heribert snorted with disgust and turned back into the hall away from the noisome stench. By the time Wulf had maneuvered his rebellious mistress up the stairs, he was as filthy and stinking as she.

In Madeleine's dim chamber, a line of serving women brought water and filled the cumbersome hammered copper tub. They hustled their mistress behind the lavishly embroidered screen, all talking at once and clucking over the ruined gown.

Wulf took the flint striker from where it sat on the stone mantel and lit a fire in the hearth. Slowly the room warmed.

The drone of female voices and the splatter of water took him back to another time when he lay by the fire in Erna's smoke-filled hut and read the future in the cracked and roasted hulls of nuts and dreamed. Erna had taught him about the old ways; she told him of the forest gods, of trees who walked like men, and the meanings of the runes.

One of the serving girls brought him clean clothing, then a basin of water with which to wash. He lifted the clothing; it was not his—he had no other clothing save for what he wore on his back. The shirt was of a fine cotton cloth and the hose-like breeches were of soft Italian leather. When he glanced again at the hearthfire, orange and yellow flames had enveloped the logs.

He stripped the dung-fouled clothing from his body and washed. A servant girl with thick blondish braids stepped away from the damask screen, her arms filled with towels. She stood there a moment looking at him. Wulf's eyes met hers. The girl's cheeks flamed with color and she stepped quickly behind the screen.

Chapter Fourteen

A week passed uneventfully. Couriers shuttled between Bourges and the château. Heribert received a delegation of priests and clerics from Reims who brought news from the King's court, rumors concerning a successor to the ailing King Philip.

Madeleine sulked in her chambers. She did not wish to play draughts nor walk in the garden where the spider webs hung heavy with dew and the first tawny leaves of autumn littered the paths. Day in, day out she sat before the tapestry, working like one possessed, stitching out her misery in its flaunted colors.

In accordance with her uncle's wishes, she continued to take her evening meals in the hall where her ears were subjected to the endless religious discussions of his novices.

On the feast day of St. Paul, the saint favored above all others by the bishop, a groaning table was set and the finest wine brought from the cellars.

Heribert made a grand ceremony of the blessing of the food, then delivered a lengthy dissertation on the life of St. Paul.

As the meal began, the matter of Madeleine's approaching marriage was again broached. Dubuc, in his eternally befuddled manner, mentioned the Duke of Burgundy's request to have his bride remain at the Château de Troyes until he should return to his city of Nevers. "Would it not be more a comfort to have his wife by his sick bed in Bourges?" Dubuc suggested.

"No, Dubuc," Heribert answered shortly and, lifting his wine goblet, remarked with a rueful smile, "Not in his present condition." A hushed murmur of laughter swept along the table.

Madeleine, who was now required to sit beside Dubuc within her uncle's hearing, rose so suddenly that the sleeve of her gown brushed the elderly cleric's face. Her dark eyes burned upon her uncle and she impudently replied, "Why not simply send my purse and tax ledgers? I am certain they would comfort the Duke far better than I."

Heribert scowled back at his niece and sharply reminded her of her position. "If you wish to remain at my table, you will keep a modest tongue." Heribert's reference to 'his table' was like fat flung into a fire.

"This is my father's table," Madeleine hissed. "Mine now that he has been called to Christ and mine to voice the opinions I choose."

"Enough!" Heribert shouted her down. "I will not endure your insolence." His gaze swept to the Saxon. "Remove your mistress to her chamber," he commanded.

Wulf, as he was bade, took the Lady Madeleine by the arm. His action prompted yet another outburst.

"You are the worst of hypocrites," she screamed into her uncle's face. "A common felon." She threw off her guard's hand, accusing, "You have plundered my inheritance and held me prisoner against my will!"

"Silence!" Heribert screeched, leaping to his feet. "Remove her at once!"

Wulf found there was no civilized way to control her. After a short scuffle, he clasped her in a great bear hug, pinned her flailing arms to her sides and carried her kicking and screaming from the hall. He heard a ripple of voices behind him, but not what was said.

He sat her on her feet before the coil of stone steps. As he did, she stabbed an elbow into his ribs and swore at him. "Boot-licking cur! If he had bade you slit my throat, you would have obliged him with a smile!"

Wulf stared at her; a muscle in his jaw began to twitch uncontrollably. Like the proverbial patient ass, he could be driven only so far. In a voice thick with reproach, he asked, "What ultimate good has your foolish tantrum accomplished other than to send us both from the hall with empty stomachs?"

The tone of his voice, not his words, cut her to the bone. Her face crumpled before his eyes and she burst into tears. She whirled on her heels and bounded up the stone steps, bawling like a weanling calf.

He stumbled after her, totally bewildered and feeling somehow betrayed by his glans. What had he said? Only the truth.

Madeleine heard him behind her, taking the steps by twos and threes. At the top of the passageway he caught her arm and, stepping into the dark shadows, drew her after him, cinching her against his body. The maneuver was accomplished with such alarming swiftness that it left her breathless. She did not struggle, though tears spilled from her eyes and she stubbornly refused to look at him.

Leaning over her, he murmured her name and dropped his head close to hers. His lips brushed past her face and he whispered, "Do not hate me." Her hair smelled of roses and the feel of her body pressed to his, her soft warmth, went to his head like May wine. He was so drunk with the thought of her that he no longer recognized his own voice when he said, "I am not free to speak in your defense, just as I am not free to say what is in my heart. Believe that I would willingly give my life for you, Madeleine."

His words, and the passion behind them, brought

her face to his. Only a breath separated their lips. With no remaining will to resist, he kissed her full on the mouth, sliding his tongue over hers, taking her breath for his and molding her to him.

At first, Madeleine had been too startled to respond, but now slid her arms around his neck and strained against him. For weeks, his calculated glances and the lingering touch of his hands had filled her with a confusion of desire and frustration. But at that moment, with the feel of him hard against her and the answering throb of desire in her own lower body, the craving she felt as well as the means to satisfy it was no longer without form or substance, but instinctive and obvious as the hunch in his leather hosen.

She made no effort to end the kiss, which filled her with a soaring sense of pleasure; neither did she rebel when his hand encircled a breast and the other slid to caress her smooth rump. She made only a soft sighing sound in her throat and moved against him without a thought or a care as to where it might lead.

A sound on the staircase jarred Wulf to his senses. He wrenched his mouth from hers and took a step backward, holding her at arm's length, his breath whistling through his teeth and a dazed look in his eyes.

A serving girl carrying a candle before her topped the stairs. She bobbed to curtsy and hurried past, entering Madeleine's chamber. If the passageway had not been deep in shadow, she would have seen he was trembling like a stag in rut, his face pale as ashes.

He did not trust himself to look into the Lady Madeleine's eyes and walked her before him, with good reason, to the chamber door.

From the direction of the stairs, the Widow Crozet and two serving girls followed. At the door he stepped aside so they might enter.

Madeleine turned to him, her lips still stinging from his kiss and her eyes wild with excitement, but

216

saw only his back retreating down the passageway.

The iron-strapped hinges of the garderobe were well oiled. Wulf stepped into the darkened passageway and saw a young squire, not six paces from him, poised beside the door to the late young lord's chamber. His back was to Wulf; he had neither seen nor heard him and his eyes were directed down the darkened passageway where a pale slice of light shone beneath the Lady Madeleine's door.

"Why are you here?" Wulf challenged. The boy gave a startled grunt and whirled to face him. "A priest sent me, sent me to fetch a book from the young lord's *prie-dieu,*" he quickly replied.

It was the curly-headed squire who had proffered the sugar cakes. Wulf was surprised by his height—he had not appeared to be so tall by the table. He looked older as well, Wulf thought, but no less shifty. Wulf took several steps, placing himself between the boy and the stairs. "Which priest?"

The boy swallowed, the knot of cartilage in his throat bobbed from his collar. "The tall one," he said, "with the hooked nose."

De Grailley, Wulf guessed from the boy's description, and in truth the boy did have a book in his hand. After a moment Wulf said, "Then why are you standing here? Go."

The boy darted past him and down the stairs. Only when Wulf saw his head vanish beneath the top step did he realize that the boy had no candle. Wulf walked back to the young lord's chamber, opened the door, and looked inside; blackness swirled before his eyes. He pulled the door to and walked toward the pale slice of light considering, even if cats could read, one would have had difficulty locating a book in so dark a chamber. A thief, Wulf thought, but decided to say nothing for the time being, imagining the squire would give himself away to others soon enough.

The Lady Madeleine was in her huge bed and the draperies had been let down. The Widow Crozet and the serving girls waited just inside the door. Judging from their impatient expressions, they had waited far longer than pleased them.

Wulf dragged his rush-filled pallet before the door and banked the fire. Not a word passed between him and the Lady Madeleine. He lay awake all night, reflecting upon his lack of self-control. It was, he thought, a form of madness and could only bring him grief.

On the morrow he acted as if the kiss had never occurred. After a time Madeleine began to doubt her senses. She did not understand and tormented herself with questions. What manner of Virgin's knight was he to kiss her with such tender passion, crush her to him until there was nothing to be imagined, tantalize her with touches and words . . . and then deny it? When she smiled at him, he politely looked away. The restrained touch of his hands and the distant look in his blue eyes hurt her beyond reason.

The pleasant autumn weather returned with fair skies and crisp mellow days. Taking advantage of the respite in the weather, Heribert walked in the garden. However, his time was never spent aimlessly. Dubuc and de Grailley strolled along by his side engaged in a conversation concerning the stewardship of Viezon.

The rich lands had already been wrested from Cardinal Gaspard by the Duke of Burgundy's forces and following the marriage vows, Viezon became the property of the Bishop of Champagne. In the present political climate, Heribert felt confident the cardinal would not be foolhardy enough to retaliate, not while the Duke of Burgundy stood so near the throne of France.

Unexpectedly, Heribert came to an abrupt halt. Dubuc stumbled into de Grailley and murmured an apology. Heribert frowned into the sun. He asked, "Is that my niece by the stable?" Dubuc lifted his white head, craning his neck to see over the hedges.

De Grailley, who was taller, confirmed it. "Yes, Your Grace," he replied, hastening to add, "I saw no reason to deny the lady's request; the guard is with her." Heribert turned and walked on, again taking up the conversation.

In the warm afternoon the air of the stable was heady with the scent of fresh hay. Madeleine petted and cooed over her dappled mare. She had secreted a handful of comfits in her gown and offered them, one at a time, watching as the sugary candies vanished into the mare's velvety muzzle.

Wulf walked to the bay's stall, raised the rail, and slid inside. The horse pricked its ears and, swinging its head 'round, greeted him with large inquisitive eyes. He laid a hand on its sleek hide, felt the instant shiver of response and the tensile strength of muscle and bone. "I have not forgotten," he said in reply to the soft snorting and the brown muzzle bumped repeatedly against him. He teased the bay for a moment, then opened his hand filled with salt he had pilfered as he passed through the kitchen. The bay sucked and slobbered over the salt while Wulf looked on fondly and rubbed its face from muzzle to forelock.

Inspecting the stall, he saw there was clean bedding underfoot, a pail of water, and hay in the manger. From all appearances the bay was well cared for and, he noticed, putting on fat from standing idle.

The old stableman hobbled up carrying a hayfork and leaned against the stall. "I turn him out each day with the others," he said. Then with a grin he noted, "He's putting on fat."

"Yes," Wulf smiled. "How many coins will that cost me?"

"I am a generous man," Onfroi replied with a snagged laugh, which could be taken either way.

Wulf stroked the bay's handsome arched neck. "You have done good by him," he told the old man.

A feminine voice interrupted their conversation. "Is he a tournament horse?" Madeleine asked. From where she stood there was no doubt as to the horse's gender.

At the sound of her voice, Wulf turned. His eyes clouded with annoyance and he said, "No," as if she should know better. "He was bred for speed, not battering."

Onfroi smiled down at his tattered boots and, shaking his grizzled head, collected his hay fork and hobbled away.

"Does he belong to you?" Madeleine posed, studying the horse anew. It was a tall animal, bay but nearly black with long graceful legs and wide-set intelligent eyes.

"Yes," he said, crouching to run his hands over the bay's legs.

"What is his name?" When he did not reply immediately, Madeleine slipped into the stall and placed her face before Wulf's. "Surely you have given him a name," she persisted.

"Loki," he said finally, moving from the stall and holding the rail aside for her to pass.

At the stable doors, Madeleine raised a hand to shield her eyes as she stepped into the bright sunlight. In the kitchen garth she saw a group of young household servants, girls and boys, energetically laughing and talking. She stood there watching while behind her in the stable her guard settled his account with the old stableman.

From among the group of youths, a hand raised in a salute. Madeleine saw it was the curly-headed squire and that he was smiling gaily at her. His tousled hair was a copper color in the sunlight and he was standing beside a tall serving girl whose blondish hair was plaited into two thick braids which were wound on either side of her head. Madeleine raised her hand, returning the smile.

Sensing a presence behind her, she turned to find

her guard, his gaze fixed on the crowd of youths in the garth. "He has at least a pleasant manner," Madeleine said and, lifting the hem of her gown, picked her way through the stableyard. Wulf followed in silence.

Later that day, Dubuc laid down his stylus and rubbed his weary eyes. The ink pot before him gradually came into focus. He cleared his throat and said, "Your Grace, I must speak with you."

Heribert, preoccupied with an apparent inconsistency in a steward's ledger, looked up irritably, his long aquiline face halved by the candlelight. "What is it, Dubuc?"

"Your Grace," Dubuc began anew, "I feel I must speak out concerning your niece." His voice teetered hesitantly, then strengthened. "Would she not be more secure with a guard of her own gender?"

Indeed, Heribert thought, she would be gone on her willful way. He raised his eyes and in a peevish tone remarked, "You question my wisdom, Dubuc?"

The cleric shook his jowls. "Never, Your Grace. It is only that I know not what view the Duke of Burgundy may take of a deflowered bride."

Heribert eyed his cleric with a mingling of impatience and amusement. "What is it you are trying to say, Dubuc? Do you know something I do not?"

"No, Your Grace," Dubuc stammered. "But a healthy young man and a young woman as lovely as your niece left alone in one another's company . . ." he paused, approaching the subject with his usual diffidence. "The natural order of the world dictates . . ."

Heribert cut short his words. "Spare me, Dubuc; I have deeper mysteries to unravel."

After a moment of silence, Dubuc said, "Your Grace, a bride distended with child would hardly pose a mystery."

Heribert continued to frown over his ledger. "Not at all, Dubuc," he said in a weary tone, "but a situation welcomed by a man unable to sire an heir."

The cleric made an astonished face not unlike that of a gossipy woman. "Roland du Boulay, the Duke of Burgundy, is impotent?"

"Yes," Heribert murmured, and, raising his voice slightly, remarked, "afflicted with the English pox." It was laughable, Heribert thought, that the French had labeled the venereal affliction the 'English pox' and the English had responded in kind, referring to the affliction as the 'French pox.' To Heribert's mind it was God's vengeance on whoremongers and justly so. "The Duke of Burgundy," he said, "cannot further his claims to the throne so long as he remains childless."

"Your Grace," Dubuc timidly interrupted. In the flickering light, the cleric's smooth pink forehead creased into perplexed furrows. "The issue of a Saxon?" he questioned.

Heribert raised his eyes from the ledger and, with a smile, reminded his cleric, "We are all one in the eyes of God, Dubuc."

A hammering on the chamber door, it seemed upon his very skull, brought Wulf to his feet. Dazed and stupid with sleep, he kicked the pallet of rush and fur rugs aside. He answered the door in only his hose-like breeches. Like most soldiers, it was his habit to sleep in them, for the moments a soldier spent struggling into his hose might well cost him his life.

A curly-headed squire holding a candle in one hand waited on the other side of the door. In the haloed light, the sprinkle of freckles on his face stood out like script on a page. Wulf recognized him at once as the young thief and, in a voice that was more of a growl, asked what he wanted.

The boy's round eyes darted nervously down the passageway and his youthful voice was slurred with urgency. "My lady must come to the stable at once." And speaking louder, so that his words would carry across the chamber, said, "Her dappled mare is down and dying and the old man said I should fetch her."

Madeleine gave an anguished cry and sprang from her bed. She was at the door in her night dress before Wulf could send the boy away. When Wulf refused to allow the Lady Madeleine to leave, the boy jabbered that the mare was in great pain and the old man thought the lady might comfort her.

Madeleine wept, entreating Wulf so pitifully that he, not knowing how else to quiet her, agreed though grudgingly. In the dark he threw on his shirt and boots. Madeleine quickly wrapped a velvet cloak about her night dress and pushed her feet, stinging with cold from the chamber floor, into a pair of embroidered slippers.

Together the trio, with only a single candle to light their way, descended the snail-curl of stone steps, made their way down through the passageway to the kitchen and out into the utter blackness of the garth.

The squire led the way, his hand cupped before the candle to preserve the flame. Where the currant bushes tumbled over the garth wall, the squire snuffed the guttering flame.

From behind him, Wulf heard something rush, singing out of the blackness. He half turned, instinctively raising an arm to shield his head. His arm, rather than his skull, took the brunt of the blow which sent him sprawling to the ground with the lights of the firmament spinning before his eyes. A searing white-hot pain coursed through his arm and a wave of nausea washed over him.

Madeleine saw only a pair of arms drop over her. A terrified yelp escaped her lips but before she could cry out again, a foul tasting rag was thrust into her mouth. The taste of it gagged her. She scuffled, thrashing with her feet. It seemed there were two of them, for while one held her, another pulled a coarsely woven sack over her head and trussed her inside.

Wulf had lost all sense of direction. The sounds faded, then returned as if from a long distance; a scuffling of feet, a shrill muffled cry. And though he could not see her, he knew it was Madeleine's voice. From the darkness above him, he heard a loud panting sound as another blow struck his leg, shooting it through with pain. He rolled on the ground, flinging himself to one side as the cudgel sliced through the blackness once more and thudded into his side. He opened his mouth to cry out, but no sound came from his throat. Blind with pain, he threw himself aside with a violent thrust of his feet. Something parted the blackness before his eyes, he jerked his head to one side and felt a rush of air as the cudgel brushed past his ear and cracked, splintering against the wall of the garth. Shoving himself with his feet, he threw his back to the stone wall. His eyes cleared and he saw the flash of a naked blade as his attacker hurtled toward him.

With all the strength he could muster, Wulf raised his legs and kicked, slamming his feet into the man's groin and knocking him backward into the blackness with a loud groan.

Wulf groped blindly in the dirt for whatever he could lay hands on that could be used as a weapon—a stone, anything. With his right hand—his left was useless—he grasped a length of the broken cudgel and swayed unsteadily to his feet. He saw the man now, caught a glimpse of the mail he wore beneath the cleric's robes as he grappled on all fours in the dirt for his lost dagger.

A light appeared in the kitchen door arch and shouts rang out. The man in the cleric's robes saw the light as well and heard the cry of alarm. When he looked up, he saw Wulf's long body coming toward him armed with the blunted cudgel. The man scrambled to his feet and ran.

From the direction of the armory, lanterns bobbed in the darkness and answering voices rang out. More shouts sounded from the garth, followed by the trample of running feet.

Wulf did not wait for them, but lurched toward the woods, calling for them to follow. "This way," he yelled, his voice more of a croak. "They have the lady," he called, and with another hoarse shout directed, "their horses are by the woods." He had not seen them, but he was certain they must be, for it was only reasonable to assume they would be bound for Sézanne.

Off to Wulf's left there were answering calls from the meadow and a dozen or more soldiers splashed through the stream.

Soldiers from the armory overtook Wulf on the rise above the woods. One sighted the kidnappers as they made for their horses and the others swarmed after him.

The metallic clash and clanging of swords echoed up the rise. At the edge of the woods, Wulf sagged against a tree. It hurt him to breathe. Not thirty paces away the vicious struggle continued. He closed his eyes, but even so the spiraling streaks of color shot before his eyelids. He raised his head and blinked and, through the whirling lights, saw the squire wrestling with a large unwieldy bundle, attempting to hoist it onto the back of a horse.

Wulf lunged forward, weaving between the trees, and with the good arm flung the cudgel into the startled horse's flank. The horse squealed, rearing on its hindquarters and reeled away, crashing through the brittle leaves.

The squire threw down the bundle and clutched at the horse's trailing reins, but he was not quick enough. Wulf expected him to turn and run after the frightened horse; instead he drew a dagger from his tunic and, crouching down, stalked forward.

From behind the squire, Wulf saw Harun—rather, only the whites of his eyes and the flash of the long steel blade. The Moor swung the sword with both hands so that he nearly hacked the squire in half, spilling out his bowels like a gutted fish and splattering Wulf with his blood. The smell of it, the sticky warmth, made him sick.

Harun and he, though with one hand he was of little help, stripped away the coarse woven sack, freeing the Lady Madeleine. Wulf pulled the filthy rag from her mouth. Only then could she answer him. She was not hurt, she insisted between coughing and spitting the awful taste from her mouth. Harun freed her hands; she struggled to her feet, nearly falling over her night dress and cape which had wound about her legs. She could not help but glimpse the squire's crumpled body; she shuddered and turned away, clinging to Wulf's blood-spattered shirt.

By then the grounds were crawling with soldiers and servants. Smoking lanterns spotted the darkness and a babble of voices carried on the chill night air.

The bishop and de Grailley trudged over the hill wrapped in fur-lined robes. A household varlet with a lantern swinging in his hand trotted before them. Heribert questioned Madeleine. She appeared stunned and frightened, but uninjured. De Grailley noticed that her Saxon guard had not fared as well. "Your arm appears to be broken," he told Wulf. Harun had said the same a moment before.

Only one of the kidnapper's horses was found in the woods. Later the bodies of the two men and the squire were laid out before the armory.

In the smoky light of the kitchen, Wulf saw that it was true; his arm was broken. It had already swollen several sizes, stretching taut the wide sleeve of his shirt, and hung at his side numb and useless.

A crowd of servants accompanied him and Madeleine up the stairs and into the chamber. He found a stool and slumped down; his entire body was wracked with pain. Amid the confusion, it all seemed unreal to him. His rush pallet was moved before the fire, someone had brought a basin of water, and a young squire was attempting to strip the shirt from his back in a most ungentle fashion.

"No!" Madeleine sharply reprimanded the boy. "You will have to cut the sleeve." She sent the squire to fetch Wulf's knife from where it lay beside his leather jerkin and sword. She then wrenched the cloth from the hand of the serving girl with the thick blondish plaits and began sponging the blood from Wulf's face. The serving girl stepped back and, catching the eye of the girl holding the basin, smiled.

Heribert appeared at the door and with an impatient wave of his jeweled hand sent the servants scurrying from the room. De Grailley followed him inside.

Wulf, made suddenly self-conscious by Madeleine's attention, pushed her hand away. He attempted to rise, but Heribert motioned him down with a vexed gesture. "I should have you horsewhipped for your stupidity," he hissed. "Once more, because of your negligence, my niece was nearly carried off by de Luchaire's villeins." The violent diatribe was interrupted only once when Madeleine cried out that it was she who insisted on going to the stable and her guard had agreed only because he knew how dearly she loved the mare. Heribert commanded her to be silent and ordered her to her bed.

For his part, Wulf had fully expected to be punished and considered himself fortunate to escape with no more than abusive words.

Heribert's physician, the priest known as Umberto, hemmed and hawed at the door arch. At last the bishop noticed the physician and motioned him inside. He was followed by a stout novice and a teenaged squire with a pimpled face.

"I am through here," Heribert said with a last terse glance at the Saxon. After a brief aside with the physician, he walked swiftly from the chamber, de Grailley at his heels.

Umberto first asked the young Saxon about his general state of health. Though it pained him, Wulf managed to twist his lips into a smile and reply, "Not good."

"Ah, but you are breathing," Umberto reminded him, also with a smile, "and that is surely a good sign." He then asked him specifically about the injury, listening with great patience, often asking further questions. Where did he experience pain? Had he coughed and brought up blood? Was his arm numb? Could he move his fingers? Considering all this, Umberto turned his great domed head to the fat intent face of the novice at his side and instructed him to examine the young man's ribs.

The novice's touch was considerably gentler than Umberto's, but even so streaks of light flashed before Wulf's eyes.

"They are broken," the novice determined and, laying his ear to the Saxon's chest and back, asked him to breathe deeply. After what seemed an eternity of agony to Wulf, the novice ventured, "There seems to be no damage to his lungs."

Umberto then examined Wulf once more, pressing a huge ear to his chest and back. "Quite correct." Umberto commended the novice and turning to Wulf, remarked, "Your ribs are indeed broken. Unfortunately there is little which can be done other than to allow nature to heal them. And now," he smiled, "the arm."

They lifted Wulf's arm, the novice first, then Umberto; they felt the arm and discussed it among themselves.

The pimple-faced squire watched closely. He had

carried the physician's case into the room and now stood beside it, craning his neck to see. Physicians, he decided, were more on the order of torturers, for the arm was no better; it still appeared large as a log and beads of perspiration stood out on the soldier's forehead and above his lip.

At length, Umberto congratulated his student; to his patient, he said, "The bone is not seriously misplaced; it will heal straight." From the case, the novice took a rectangle of cloth and fashioned a sling from it. While he was industriously engaged in trussing up Wulf's arm, Umberto sent the squire after a cup of wine.

When the boy with the pimpled face returned, Umberto took a small pouch from his robes and shook an amount of white powder into the wine, swirling it with his finger. "Drink this," he said, and held out the cup to the Saxon.

Wulf, cautious as well as curious, asked, "What is it?" But the priest gave him only a smile and a one-word reply. "Paradise."

Once they were alone, Madeleine brought several cushions from the bed, arranging them beneath his head and shoulders to make him more comfortable. Afterward, she sat on the floor beside him. "It is my fault," she wept. Tears spilled down her cheeks and she made no attempt to brush them away.

His head seemed to float; it was a great effort to turn his eyes. "You could not have known," he said. His tongue felt thick, as if it were fashioned from leather. "I did not. I went like a sheep to the hacker." He spoke the words slowly. The pain had gone, but so it seemed had his ability to put thoughts together. "I feel foolish," he managed.

She looked back with tearful dark eyes. "My uncle will send another guard," she sobbed, burying her face in her hands.

He fixed his eyes on the delicate hands, the pale

face. It was becoming more and more difficult to focus his eyes. "Would that be such a tragedy?" he asked.

Unable to speak for weeping, Madeleine nodded and after a moment, sobbed, "Yes."

He wanted to reach out to her, but at first even his uninjured arm refused to obey. Then like a man who gropes for something in a dream, he reached out his fingers and touched her dark hair where it curled about her forehead. He said, "It would be best."

Madeleine turned to him with wide and wounded eyes. She did not understand. His fingers brushed her glistening cheek; he tried to smile. "You are all I see, you are my every thought." His lips could no longer form the words; he was so very tired. "I should not be alone with you," he said. He would have said more but the words died in his throat.

Madeleine took his hand and pressed his fingers to her lips. For a long moment she sat there breathing in the scent of his skin, wanting desperately to tell him of her feelings but unable to find the words. When at last she turned to him, she saw he was asleep. She was still there, huddled beside him when her serving women came tapping at the door the next morning.

Chapter Fifteen

Agnes Crozet gathered half a dozen serving girls to accompany her to Troyes. She did this on a weekly basis and it was an honor to be chosen.

The widow inspected each serving girl, looking her up and down to be certain she was dressed morally, had washed her face and freshly braided her hair. Agnes Crozet would tolerate no coarse or unseemly behavior, loud laughter, or idle talk. Each girl was assigned a task and woe be to her if she failed to complete it within the allotted time.

In the courtyard, two *charrettes* waited. The sky had lightened to a silvery blue, but in the shadow of the château's towers it was still dark. Frosty puffs of steam rose from the mouths of the drivers and the snorting horses.

As the *charrettes* jounced toward the walled city, Agnes Crozet's thoughts were heavily occupied by the approaching marriage of the bishop's niece, more particularly the feast which was to follow. Many of Champagne's lesser nobles, as well as the powerful bankers, financiers, and burghers of Troyes, were expected to fill the banquet hall of the old palace. The palace lay within the city's original crumbling Roman walls. Built in the old style, the former château of the Counts of Troyes was now used only for ceremonial occasions.

That day the Widow Crozet carried with her the bishop's instructions to the drapers, specifically describing the decoration of the banquet hall.

With the rising of the sun, the city of Troyes thronged with activity. Work at the cloth halls began with first light, and dyers, weavers, and stretchers hurried to their work stations. In the street before the halls, wagonloads of raw wool and woolen and silk cloth were being unloaded. Competition was fierce and bargains were struck amid a confusion of tongues.

The Widow Crozet looked sharply at the tall girl with the thick blondish braids. There was a sauciness about Odette Marsi that the widow disliked. She was, however, a conscientious worker and the widow had no valid reason to complain.

Odette's task was to deliver the order to the bakers. the order was a particularly large one and included the bread, pastries, and comfits to be served at the wedding feast. Odette bade the widow well and hurried off, dodging the early morning shoppers, peasant women with baskets over their arms, burly workmen, and the ragged chase of children. The route she took would eventually lead her to the bakers, but first, there was a rendezvous she had to keep.

Guiles de Luchaire crossed the room to where his clothing lay, took a gold livre from the blue lake jupon, and tossed it onto the chest of the sleeping boy. The teenager lay on his back with his mouth open. Startled, he bolted up in the bed, squinting and batting his eyelids.

"Leave me now," de Luchaire bade him and moved to stand before the slotted window. Though the tone of his voice was not harsh, the boy understood that it was a command. He leapt from bed, collecting his clothing and struggling into it as he crossed the room. The robed figure silhouetted against the pastel colors of the morning sky neither turned nor spoke again.

At the bottom of the rickety stairs, the teenaged boy turned the gold piece over in his hand and tucked it into his coarse-woven cloth jerkin. He wasted no time in exiting the Red Rose Tavern. He went swiftly through the kitchen and threw his weight against the door.

Odette Marsi staggered back a step, emitting a grunt of surprise. For an instant she and the boy eyed one another; then without a word, the boy bounded into the garth and was gone.

Odette warily entered the kitchen and, finding no one there, crept into the passageway. At the foot of the stairs, she halted, looked anxiously around, then tiptoed up the stairs. The red door was at the top of the landing. Odette hesitated, then tapped once at the door. She was new at intrigues and very nervous; Jean had always kept the rendezvous in Troyes.

The door jolted open. Odette drew back with a breathless gasp, exclaiming, "Milord de Luchaire!"

"Quickly!" he urged, taking her by the arm and towing her into the room. "What news is there?" he demanded, standing before her with his hands anchored on his hips. Of his kidnap plot he had heard nothing and, seeing the girl rather than Jean, suspected the worst. He was not a tall man but broad and heavily muscled and to the girl he appeared almost God-like with his roughly chiseled features and black eyes. "What of the other night's business?" he questioned.

"They are all dead, killed by the bishop's guards," she reported, and, lowering her eyes, said, "Jean was all but hacked in half."

Failure, or perhaps the boy's fate, stirred a muscle in de Luchaire's heavy jaws. He moved again to the window, resting his hip against the embrasure. He said, "There are rumors that the Duke of Burgundy

233

will soon be master of Troyes."

Odette inclined her head. "The Lady Madeleine is to marry the Duke on the day of St. Wenceslaus. It is to be a proxy marriage."

"Proxy?" he questioned, reaching out a hand to draw the girl near. "Where did you hear this?"

"In the kitchen, milord. They said the duke was injured in a tournament at Bourges and is confined to his bed."

De Luchaire was thoughtful for a moment. Folding the girl's hand in his, he asked, "You are Dorée's sister, are you not?"

The fact that the lord had noticed startled her into a moment's silence. "Yes, milord," she stammered. Blood rushed to her face. A faint lingering scent of musk rose from de Luchaire's velvet robe, stirred perhaps by the heat of his body. Odette was keenly aware of the scent and also of the sight of his muscular chest. The thick mat of crisp black hair which curled from the open neck of the robe sent her pulse to racing. Even as a child, Odette, whose kinsmen were stewards on the de Luchaire lands, had gazed longingly at the young lord of Sézanne. She had burned with envy when he took her older sister as his mistress.

"I had no idea you were so lovely, so like Dorée," he smiled, and leading her to the bed, bade her sit beside him. "Tell me about your mistress," he said.

Odette could barely speak above her pounding heart. "She is unhappy, I think."

"Dissatisfied with this match her uncle has arranged?" de Luchaire prompted. Odette was completely in his power, he thought. He was not surprised or even particularly flattered. Guiles de Luchaire had never had any difficulty in making conquests among the fairer sex—even the worldly and polished ladies at court came easily to his bed. Only Madeleine de Moncelet had resisted him. At first he had found her haughty provincialism and cool self-possession almost ludicrous, a challenge, until she had made it perfectly clear that nothing about him pleased her. She had looked down her nose at him as if he were naught but a fool, a mawkish boy. Perhaps it was this slap at his masculinity, as much as her rich dowry, which drove him to possess her.

The heat of de Luchaire's thigh against hers made Odette dizzy. She felt suddenly weak. "Yes, milord. I have heard her speak against the Duke of Burgundy with my own ears." She gave a quick smile and in an uncertain voice, said, "I believe no man would please her." Odette had disliked the Lady Madeleine from her first days at the château, deciding the strange, unpredictable girl who was at once shy, surly, and quickly offended was not fit match for her Lord de Luchaire. Odette herself hoped to become Guiles de Luchaire's mistress just as her sister had been. Dorée had lived in Paris with the young lord and it was there she died giving birth to a stillborn. Jealousy prompted Odette to report, "The Lady Madeleine has cut her hair to spite her uncle. It is short as a squire's and now her uncle forces her to wear coifs to conceal it."

Guiles de Luchaire raised a slanted eyebrow in amusement. "It does not lessen the worth of her dowry," he said, his tone philosophical. In truth, the revelation excited rather than disappointed him. It had been the lady's lithe pubescent body that first caught his eye. With her hair cropped she would appear almost boyish.

De Luchaire's inscrutable smile was not the reaction Odetete had hoped for. She said, "Did Jean tell you of the bishop's mercenary? He is with her constantly and sleeps inside her chamber."

He had been told of the guard. He, too, thought it an odd arrangement, but Jean had assured him that the Lady Madeleine was hostile toward the guard. In Jean's words, "I would treat a dog with more kindness."

"He is young and tall," Odette supplied. "And more than once I have seen her look at him fondly."

"The way I am looking at you, demoiselle?" he smiled, his hands taking liberties. Odette blushed and sighed with pleasure as Guiles de Luchaire's strong hands sought her out beneath her clothing, caressing her and bidding her to disrobe.

Afterward, as they lay tangled in the bedclothes, he told her she must be his eyes and ears at the château. "Every few days a beggar will come to the kitchen garth. He will make himself known to you and you will tell him all you have seen and heard."

Odette left the tavern with glowing cheeks and rumpled clothing. Her senses still throbbed from the brief but violent lovemaking. In her heart she was certain that she, Odette, Marsi, would be Guiles de Luchaire's mistress. He had said as much. And despite his plans to carry off the Lady Madeleine and purposely get her with child so as to force a marriage, she would never be his love.

For several days Madeleine sat nearby. She passed the hours reading aloud to Wulf. When their meals were brought, she cut his meat for him and poured his wine.

One night after the servants had banked the fire, she sat with her head close to his and asked him endlessly about the house which would be his, its rooms, his lands, and his dreams for the future.

He did not lie to her. Rügen was a poor fife—poorer, no doubt, than the humblest of her father's holdings, but nothing he said seemed to discourage her.

"We will go there together," she told him. "You will not regret it. I am capable at gardening, I read, and cypher; I know how to bake bread and I could amuse you, I think."

He listened with amazement to her stream of words, allowing himself to be drawn into her fantasies. He did not realize that for months these dreams of living a quiet country life had been her only comfort. As she spoke, she gazed at him with sparkling eyes.

I am a fool, he thought, to listen. He had never known such a female. It was a little frightening one moment to feel certain of his superiority and the next to feel a bumbling fool. For just when he had convinced himself she was naught but another witless girl, she astonished him with her cleverness and muddled his mind until he was blind to everything but her.

As the days passed they returned to the routine of their lives. He no longer carried his arm in the sling; the awkwardness of it annoyed him. The swelling had gone but his arm was still weak; he could not flex the muscle nor make a fist.

One chilly afternoon in the garden, Madeleine spoke to him again of her plans. He gently interrupted her and, with an embarrassed smile, explained that as much as he wished she was his to love and keep, she was not nor could she ever be. He did not mention the Duke of Burgundy—there seemed no need; instead, he said, "I am nothing. A knight without rank or land and scarcely a chance of attaining either. Most likely I will never be free. I will spend my life fighting other men's battles and that is how I will die."

"I will buy your freedom," she said in an authoritative tone. "My uncle cannot refuse me access to my inheritance."

"To purchase the freedom of a mercenary? You know as well as I that is foolish."

She looked at him coldly. "No. You spoke differently by the fire."

He did not deny it. "The fault is mine," he said. A gusty breeze sent a shower of golden leaves fluttering from the willow; several settled upon her scarlet coif. Wulf plucked the bright leaves one by one from the velvet material, confessing in his bland, brutally honest way, "By the fire such thoughts pleased me: to think I might spend my life with you; to see your smile, hear your voice, and know they were meant for me alone. As much as I wish it was true, it is not and can never be. A foolish dream, nothing more."

The color drained from Madeleine's face and her dark eyes appeared deep as wells. He reached out to touch her, but she pulled away and ran from the garden.

In the evening light a haze of mist hung just above the slow-moving waters of the Moline Canal. Beyond the canal, houses stood shoulder to shoulder in the gathering dusk. The amber glow of oil lamps appeared in doorways and windows and the musty scent of leaves drifted on the dank, chill air.

Guiles de Luchaire covered the distance in swift strides, entering an alleyway near the Rû Corde. He halted before a tall house, cramped among a score of others which stood in the shadow of the Dominican friary. At the door he bid his squire wait. He entered without ceremony as a man enters his own house and quickly ascended the stairs. He made his way to the third floor and there, in a small apartment in the rear of the house, found Salvatore Orsini, the astrologer.

Orsini was not alone in the room. With him was a small, shriveled boy who sat cross-legged on a rope sling bed. De Luchaire hardly noticed the boy, who was half concealed by the deep shadows in the room, and addressed Orsini impatiently. "Do you have it?"

Orsini smiled indulgently. "But of course, milord. Salvatore Orsini is a man of his word." And with the practiced gesture of a magician, he led de Luchaire's sharply pointed black pupils to a chest draped with a square of red velvet on which a pentagram had been worked in silver thread.

Guiles de Luchaire looked to Orsini, made a tight smile, and in an undertone said, "Let me see it." It was difficult for him to bridle his intense excitement. He knew Orsini would ask twice the price if he guessed the true depth of his feelings.

The astrologer, complaisant as always, lifted the cloth with a flourish. He was an oily old liar and had learned long ago how to please and dupe the wealthy. Orsini had garnered a small fortune selling charms to ward off the plague and elixirs to cure it. Rumors of a recurrence of plague in the city was as good as gold in his purse.

De Luchaire motioned him with his fingers to bring the gold ring. "You are certain it has been done properly?" he asked as Orsini dropped the ring into his open palm.

"Yes, milord." A lipless smile wreathed his face in wrinkles. "The ring has lain within the heart of a hanged man these three days while the full moon held sway. If you doubt me, ask Paulo. It was he who carried the corpse away, opened its chest, and sat with it those three days."

De Luchaire's glance fell on the brown, shriveled boy. He saw it was not a youth at all, but a hideous little deformed man the size of a dwarf. Repelled by the little man's malevolent appearance, he turned back to Orsini. "And the other?" he questioned. "It has been done?" He wanted his money's worth; it was costing him dearly enough.

Orsini nodded. "The words have been said." He bowed slightly and extended his hand, assuring the Lord de Luchaire, "No maiden's heart can resist such a powerful amulet."

Guiles de Luchaire slipped the ring onto a chain and put it around his neck, lifting the collar of his jupon so that the ring fell against his bare flesh.

He paid Orsini and took his leave. On the stairs, a long shadow passed before him; the queerness of it sent his heart to pounding. To his left was a window whose shutter was rotted through in spots. He half convinced himself it was a trick of the moonlight, but he fled the house like a man who had met a ghost and with his squire returned to the canal where a servant waited with their horses.

Madeleine's time was again monopolized by fittings and seamstresses. Her uncle, the bishop, had viewed the wedding gown sewn for her marriage to Guiels de Luchaire and declared it totally inadequate. The Duke of Burgundy stood in line for the throne of France and nothing less than a state gown would be appropriate.

Madeleine's Saxon guard lurked in the background, appearing bored. When he was not gazing from the window, he drifted idly about the room or sat by the hearth in one of the large Italian chairs with his leg casually hung over the arm, cracking and munching hazelnuts and tossing the shells into the fire.

His arm had mended, but it was still weak—tender, just as his ribs were. The evening before in the hall, the Lady Madeleine had inadvertently bumped his side as she took her seat. He said nothing, but the pain sent lights dancing before his eyes.

Madeleine no longer fought against her fate; it seemed pointless. Even he, who had sworn his love, had deserted her and it was that which she found unbearable. She went through the château without a smile or a pleasant word, wearing a look of cold resignation upon her features with her Saxon guard following along after her like a man condemned to purgatory.

Alone together in her chamber it was no different. Wulf, tormented by guilt, was left feeling somehow responsible for her unhappiness. If by chance he met her tense cold gaze, he looked quickly away, bewildered and confused by her anger.

What was it she expected of him. That he should make love to her? Wrest her from her uncle's grasp and the Duke of Burgundy's betrothal? Take her north with him to a place he had last seen as a boy nearly eleven years before? Why could she not understand? He was not free. He would be declared an outlaw, condemned, and though Rügen was far from the world, perdition would surely follow. They would be pursued, besieged. But the most frightening thought of all was that if he had his freedom, he would have dared all the rest.

Out of his unswerving devotion to the cause of Christ, Heribert invariably sang the prime Mass at the château's chapel. After which he breakfasted lightly, then entered the library where his clerics and scriveners sat in readiness to receive the host of people who waited in the barren reception room directly across the passageway from the library.

Among the throng of petitioning burghers, merchants, lawyers, and peasants who waited rubbing their numbed hands and stomping their feet in the dank chamber was François Larousse, seneschal of Troyes. Larousse had been appointed by the bishop's late brother many years before and his loyalty, honesty, and moral reputation were without a stain.

Larousse, shivering in his fur-lined cape, was the first to be ushered into the bishop's presence. The unwelcome news he brought from Troyes troubled the bishop's mind and hardened his voice. "This discontented rabble you speak of, who is their spokesman?"

"They have no leader, none that I might name," Larousse said, and in a graver tone cautioned, "At least not yet, but it is only a matter of time. Since the pestilence subsided, they have poured into the city from the countryside. They possess nothing save the clothing on their backs, consequently they have nothing to lose. Without direction, they will do no worse than rob travelers, start brawls in taverns, and be content to murder one another. But in the hands of certain individuals, they could become a dangerous weapon, an army. Even the normally placid peasants and workers have become infected by their discontent and demand higher wages and better living conditions."

Heribert grimaced. "What are you saying? That I am surrounded by treachery?"

"Not treachery so much as the matter of your niece's marriage to the Duke of Burgundy." Larousse had not planned to put it so bluntly, but he knew no other way to say it. "It is known to all that Burgundy taxes his nobles and lands to the limit; the people fear he will do the same here." Larousse looked down to his large hands folded in his lap and in a quiet voice said, "The individuals I spoke of are well known to you and highly placed. I do not believe the majority would betray you, were it not that the Duke of Burgundy is a hard master."

"The marriage contract is signed," Heribert said coldly, thus ending the matter.

Larousse shrugged. "Alas, Your Grace. Then the problem is in God's hands." A tall man though bent with age, Larousse rose slowly to his feet. He had fulfilled his sworn duty; he had warned his lord. If the bishop chose not to heed the warning there was little he could do aside from return to Troyes and guard his own interests. Dismissed, he backed from the chamber.

Several days later, Heribert called his provost to the château and questioned him. Falkes Delouvrier was more evasive than blatantly dishonest. Heribert

242

knew him to be ruthless, greedy, and brutal . . . the very qualities he had deemed necessary to restore order to the city in those first troubled days after the sickness had subsided. He also knew Falkes De-louvrier well enough not to trust him; there were others as well—Guiles de Luchaire and several of the grasping Lombard bankers. They would all bear watching.

At vespers, de Grailley quietly entered the chapel, made his obeisance, and knelt close by his bishop's side. In a voice softer than a whisper, he said, "The laundress informs me that your niece's monthly flow has begun."

Heribert's fingers paused on the beads of his rosary. He drew a deep breath, a sour smile upon his lips, and remarked in an equally hushed tone. "I would find little humor in it if he, too, were impotent."

De Grailley responded in a murmur. "I do not believe that is the problem, Your Grace."

"Oh?" Heribert stared hard at his young curate, then focused his eyes on the altar and the statue of the Blessed Virgin bathed in candlelight. He had done everything in his power to foster their mating. "What then in your estimation is the problem?"

The hawk-nosed young priest lowered his head and whispered, "I suspect they have yet to couple."

Heribert's long face twisted in amusement. "I am well aware my niece is a shrewish little termagant. Are you suggesting my Saxon mercenary is a saint?"

De Grailley, having no ready reply, set his gaze upon the altar.

"Yes," Heribert chuckled, "perhaps that is the answer," and took up his prayers again, his fingers moving rapidly over the silver beads.

Chapter Sixteen

The home of the banker Alessandro Tanzenetti was located in a quiet square off the rue du Bardi. The surrounding homes were equally large and grand, belonging to an assortment of bankers, financiers, and the city's wealthier merchants.

On that gloomy September afternoon, the gates of the Tanzenetti courtyard were closed, unusual for so early an hour, and two male servants stood huddled in their cloaks as if on guard. A drizzle of rain polished the cobbled stones of the leaf-strewn courtyard.

In the richly carpeted second floor reception room a fire blazed in the hearth and the soft glow of oil lamps illuminated the magnificent tapestries of religious scenes which adorned all but one wall, where Tanzenetti's fine collection of daggers and swords were displayed.

The somewhat strained conversation of the men gathered inside the room reflected the fear and uncertainty of the times. They and generations of their families had labored to raise themselves to a class apart: the bourgeoisie—bankers, financiers, and merchants who had gained wealth, power, and influence to match that of the nobility. Despite the war and famine they lived in luxury and garnered huge profits. But the world was turning, and not in their favor. First, the pestilence had come; then civil unrest; and now the specter of exorbitant taxation to those who could best afford it . . . the rich. Such a future did not set well with the disconsolate group gathered in Alessandro Tanzenetti's grandly appointed reception room.

In recent months there had been discontented rumblings from the workers and peasants. Their numbers had been thinned by the pestilence and those who remained demanded higher wages, more rights, and better living conditions. The merchants and bankers knew these demands would have to be met if they were to avoid disaster, but were they also expected to pay fealty to the Duke of Burgundy? It was common knowledge that Roland du Boulay was heavily in debt. His military adventures and lavish life style demanded more and more money be extorted from his holdings. It was roundly agreed that he would bleed the city white. "We shall all be poor as cloth menders," one merchant sadly predicted.

"The peasants are accustomed to suffering," a merchant said scornfully. A banker added, "We have methods to quiet the peasants in Lombardy." Still another remarked in a humorous tone, "I would like to see the Duke of Burgundy convince my wife that she does not need twenty new gowns a year."

Across the room some sat at a table while others stood before the hearth sipping wine and arguing over what had initiated their miseries. The pestilence was foremost on their lips, followed by the English. "Who can deny that the English are responsible for all our misfortunes? Was it not they who made a battleground of France?" a broad man with a full beard insisted.

"No, no," another disagreed, shaking his bald head. "That is not it at all. It is our own nobles who caused the problem in the first place. They have taxed us beyond all limits to finance their vainglorious crusades and wars and raised large armies of soldiers and fattened them on our profits while we starve."

Falkes Delouvrier, Provost of Troyes, had been standing in the background listening. "Surely you exaggerate," he said in a tone thick with sarcasm. "You do not appear to be starving to death, any of you." His fierce gaze bore down on the soft, fleshy faces of the men dressed in velvet and brocade. "Were it not for the soldiers you so readily slander, you may well pray the pestilence take you for who would protect your fine white hides when the peasants tire of carrying you on their backs?"

Falkes Delouvrier had no use for the likes of those in whose company he had passed the afternoon. In his estimation they were leeches, blood-suckers, whose deaths would be mourned by no one. Delouvrier was no longer young at forty-five. He had seen the glory of the old days when there were but four classes: nobles, military, clergy, and serf. A man understood his place in such a world but the world had changed, and now there was no understanding any of it.

The banker Tanzenetti, paunchy in his saffron velvets, excused himself and rose from the table where he had been engaged in a conversation concerning the domination of the cloth market by English wools. He hastened from the delicate Florentine table to the window and, pressing the corner of a tapestry aside, gazed into the courtyard. The blabber of discussion went on without him. After a few moments, he said, "He is here." Behind him the drone of conversation halted; men rose and chairs were shuffled.

Guiles de Luchaire appeared at the door, flanked by two of his most trusted villeins. He entered smiling and confident, removed his riding gloves, and glanced around the room graciously receiving introductions and words of encouragement from all present.

"We have a common cause, gentlemen," de Luchaire told them. "It is justice." All agreed the Baron of Sézanne had every right to make good the betrothal contract signed by the late Count of Troyes, particularly when de Luchaire promised to levy no new taxes or fines and to put the interests of the merchants first.

Delouvrier, the bishop's provost, was a man with no loyalties other than to himself. He saw de Luchaire's plot as a means to vastly increase his own wealth and power. With de Luchaire as master of Troyes, he could then reclaim his estates and promote his own interests in the market place. His sons would profit as well, for de Luchaire had promised to make the post of provost hereditary.

Though Delouvrier had been drawn into de Luchaire's machination by greed, he wanted no hand in the actual murder of a bishop of the Holy Church. For such a heinous deed, a man could expect no mercy in this world or the next, neither could he be buried in hallowed ground nor could Masses be said for his soul. Delouvrier had been certain that his only sin would be one of omission. For although he had agreed to dismiss his troops into the tender care of Troyes' tavern keepers, who would be paid in advance to fill them with wine and ale, he would do so only after the bishop had entered the church. If Guiles de Luchaire moved swiftly and surely there would be no provost's guards to oppose him.

Delouvrier listened, sipping his goblet of wine while de Luchaire vilified the Bishop of Champagne and urged the support of all present in his plot to murder him in the cathedral and kidnap the Lady Madeleine de Moncelet, thus preventing the unholy alliance between the houses of Champagne and Burgundy.

247

One among the group mentioned the possibility that the Duke of Burgundy might well respond to such an affront by marching upon the city of Troyes while others feared that if the daring plot failed, the bishop, who was well known for meting out justice with a swift sword, would hang the lot of them from the pillory. But de Luchaire boldly dismissed such fears. "There is no chance of failure," he responded, swearing before all, "None but Heribert de Moncelet's corpse will hang from the pillory on the day of St. Wenceslaus."

Long before the lauds bell sounded, Madeleine was awakened by an invasion of serving women with candles and oil lamps. She sat up blinking at them and was immediately hustled from the warmth of her bedclothes by the Widow Crozet while a line of chattering serving women filled the copper tub with pails of steaming water. Several vials of fragrance were added to the water and the air was redolent with the scent of roses.

While Madeleine bathed, the bed was hastily made and the weighty silk gown was laid out, a feat which required the combined efforts of five women.

Agnes Crozet stood in the midst of the feverish preparations, making certain that everything went accordingly. In her brief time at the château, Agnes had risen to a position of importance.

Madeleine did not like her—not her patronizing tone nor her slavering obedience to her uncle's slightest wish—and directed her bitter complaints at the widow. She complained the room was too cold and the water too hot, but the widow and her women were so busy gabbling among themselves that no one paid her whining complaints any mind. And so she said no more about the heat of the water or the chill of the room. Instead, she asked, "Where is my guard?" Twice more she asked, louder each time, before she received an answer.

"Nearby, milady," the Widow Crozet replied in a vexed tone and directing her strident voice across the room, shouted at the girl attempting to unfurl the veil of the coif. "Carefully! You are clumsy as a cow!" With swift steps she crossed the room, shoving the girl aside to see if any damage had been done to the fragile silk veil.

"You have not answered my question," Madeleine called irritably, glowering at the widow's back as she inspected the veil and further chastised the white-faced girl.

A serving girl holding a towel over her arm whispered, "He is being given instructions, mistress."

"What sort of instructions?" Madeleine frowned. The girl was uncertain. She shrugged but said no more and Madeleine turned her ill humor on the widow, demanding an answer. Agnes Crozet gave a harried sigh, conceding, "He is to be the proxy groom."

The cruelty of it stung Madeleine's heart like a nettle. How like her uncle, she thought, to choose him as the instrument of this final humiliation. "Why?" she asked sharply.

"I was not told why," the widow replied and stepped away to see to yet another matter.

The serving girl washing Madeleine's back leaned forward, and murmured, "They fear the groom will be struck down; the people of Troyes do not wish to become slaves to the Duke of Burgundy."

It seemed to Madeleine that the girl would have said more, but a severe glance from the widow silenced her as effectively as a gag. No matter how Madeleine balked and threatened, she could learn no more from the widow and none of the serving girls dared to speak.

The widow applied rouge to Madeleine's cheeks and lips, kohl to her eyes, and directed the cinching and lacing of the heavy silken gown. The coif was then placed on Madeleine's head. The widow fretted over it. She was not satisifed until she was certain not one sprig of bluntly cropped hair strayed from the heart-shaped silken coif. At last she stepped back and, folding her hands before her, smiled. Madeleine saw the self-satisfied smirk on the widow's smooth colorless face and that, too, annoyed her.

De Grailley had come before the lauds bell rang and escorted Wulf to the chamber of the late young Lord de Moncelet. A tub of water, no longer warm, awaited him. He was told to bathe and shave and then was left alone. Presently de Grailley and two squires returned with clothing. Only then was Wulf informed he was to be the proxy groom.

The squires laid out the clothing while de Grailley instructed him on the ceremony. Wulf, with the assistance of the two squires who were truthfully more of a hindrance, dressed in the clothing of the former Count of Troyes, Étienne de Moncelet. Wulf's height prevented him from wearing the wedding garments fashioned for the courtier, Legoix, whose chosen apparel was of white and gold brocade. Nothing so frivolous could be found in the count's clothing kisk; de Grailley decided on a brocaded jypon of black and scarlet trimmed in fur, black velvet hosen, a ceremonial dagger, a golden belt and tall, soft leather boots.

Wulf scowled at his image in the mirror, thinking he looked like a gaudy, foolish popinjay. It was then, at de Grailley's bidding, that one of the squires doused him with a cologne made of herbs and juniper berries. The concoction smelled sharp and cold as a wintry day and caused him to sneeze. De Grailley, intensely aware of the time, did not wait for the fit of sneezing to abate, but in a repetitious tone went over the instructions once more, having the Saxon repeat his vows aloud.

Servants, courtiers, novices, and clergy crowded the hall. From the wall sconces, candles blazed in the early morning darkness and beyond the high arched windows layer upon layer of ominous purple clouds stacked high upon the horizon, silhouetted by the first rays of light.

Wulf and the two squires assigned him that day by de Grailley stood to one side of the huge hearth, more or less out of the path of activity.

The bishop had not yet made his appearance, but Wulf saw de Grailley enter the hall from the direction of the lord's chamber. The young priest paused briefly to speak with the courtier Legoix and several of his group, then to a trio of Dominicans who had arrived from Reims the day before to meet with the bishop on church business. A second group of Burgundy's courtiers was engaged in a lively conversation puncuated by raucous bouts of laughter.

Heads turned and the crowd shifted. The movement drew Wulf's attention to the far side of the vast hall where Madeleine and four serving women appeared. To the young squires she was simply the Lady Madeleine, though the richness of her attire held both spellbound for a moment before they returned to their hushed conversation.

Wulf's gaze followed her closely—nothing about her escaped his eyes. Her vivid beauty, the shimmering white silk gown, like a vision from one of Erna's tales of long ago: the hauntingly lovely snow maiden who came swirling from the white fury of winter storms to blind men with her dazzling beauty and lure them away to die in the snow. Perhaps he, too, would die, he thought, die of longing. In the last days his desire for her had heightened unbearably to the

251

point where the mere thought of her caused him pain, crudely physical as well as mental. There was an easy cure for the one—a moment to himself and several strokes of his hand; but for the other, his aching heart, there was no remedy.

In the courtyard, servants steadied the nervously stomping horses of the wedding party. A blustery wind buffeted man and beast and sent an endless chase of brittle leaves swirling into the air. Before the armory, thirty of the bishop's guards sat mailed and mounted in full battle gear awaiting the appearance of His Grace.

Above the spires of Troyes, pyramids of black clouds massed upon the horizon, blotting out the sunrise. The wind howled past, filled with the musk of earth and leaves, oddly warm for so late in the year.

The exodus from the château began. A *charrette* was brought to the steps for the Lady Madeleine and her women. As Madeleine stepped from the château's iron-bound doors, the tempest caught her veil, whipping the fragile silk material forward like a billowing cloud of smoke and threatening to lift the heart-shaped coif from her head. She and her serving women battled the buffeting wind and their flapping gowns. Four women were required to carry the elaborate gown's lengthy train and struggled mightily against the wind, at last hoisting the gown and themselves into the upholstered interior of the *charrette*.

Heribert, Bishop of Champagne, and his mounted clergy led the procession from the courtyard of the château. Their billowing robes, lifted by the gale, lent them the appearance of a flock of kestrels hovering in the face of the wind.

The *charrette*, with servants astride the long team of horses, fell into place behind the clergy followed by Legoix, the courtiers from the house of Burgundy, and the priest, Evarrard, who rode at the side of the proxy groom. The bishop's guard rode out last, accompanied by the harsh discordant jangle of mail and weapons. Once beyond the château's gates, the guard deployed itself in a defensive line.

Baleful black and purple clouds churned above as the procession wound its way into the walled city. Along the Grand Rue uneasy knots of townspeople and peasants gathered in the rising wind. They had not come to cheer, but watched in angry, guarded silence.

At one point a squalid mob charged into the street, bringing the procession to a halt.

Madeleine was terrorized by the angry men with gaunt faces and the hate-filled fury of their shouts. She drew back in her seat; as she did, a face leapt at her from the crowd: the villein who had ridden into the courtyard and whom she had driven away with stones. Before she could look again, he turned away and was lost in the throng of milling, shouting men. It was he, she was certain, and recalling de Luchaire's vow was gripped by a cold, numbing fear. She turned frantically in her seat, struggling against the confines of the heavy dress, attempting to catch sight of her guard. The wind stung her eyes, blurring the images of the riders so that the colors of their gaudy clothing seemed to flow together. Only Wulf's Saxon-colored hair stood on end by the gale set him apart, for custom dictated that a groom come bareheaded before God.

The bishop's guards quickly routed the ragtag group of malcontents with curses and the flat of their swords, clearing the Grand Rue. After a moment the *charrette* lurched forward and the procession continued.

On the plaza before the cathedral, mounted soldiers of the Provost's guard cleared a path through the grumbling crowd, saluting the procession with their lances. Banners fluttered and snapped in the wind and the throaty iron bells of St. Pierre's shook the air with their tolling.

Heribert, Bishop of Champagne, dismounted and walked forward in victory. All was as he had wished it to be. He cast his gaze over the plaza, his eyes sleek with confidence. It was with a spirit of thanksgiving that he entered the ornate doors of St. Pierre's. There, before the eyes of God and men, he would seal his bargain with the Duke of Burgundy.

The wealthy of Troyes and the nobility lined the aisles of the cathedral. The extravagance of their finery dazzled the eye—jewel-hued azures, blues, and greens. Furs gleamed in the candlelight, as did mantles of velvet and silk, edged in ermine and miniver, and richly embroidered surcoats of gold and silver set with jewels.

Though the aisles were packed, it seemed to Heribert that all were not in attendance; the niche of the banker, Tanzenetti, was empty. It was but a fleeting thought, for Heribert's mind was occupied by the ritual which lay before him.

As the solemn Mass began, a choir of novices took up a hymn. Their youthful voices echoed from the stone walls and down the graceful colonnades and soared to the highest point of the cathedral's domed arch in a glorious crescendo.

With his greatest victory at hand, Heribert, Bishop of Champagne, robed in a silken cassock the color of the molten sun, stepped to the altar and sang out the Kyrie in a splendid Latin voice.

The cathedral blazed with the illuminated glow of a thousand candles. Bathed in the unreal light, the painted waxen figure of Christ upon the cross took on the luster of living flesh and blood.

Beyond St. Pierre's walls and sweeping buttresses the storm, which had darkened the skies and quenched the light of day, broke with a fury, unleashing a torrent of rain. Thunder crashed above the heads of those assembled and blinding flashes of forked lightning lit the magnificent stained glass windows with bursts of sudden but transient brilliancy.

The words of the Holy Gospel and the voices of the choir became one with the booming thunder. Wulf stood woodenly at Madeleine's side, hearing only the pounding of his own heart. Like a creature moved by strings, he knelt beside Madeleine to receive communion.

As the Mass progressed, the priest Evarrard, looking pig-eyed in the candlelight, stepped forward and thrust a golden tray before the Saxon. "Take the ring," Evarrard said in a lisping undertone.

Wulf plucked the damnable golden band from the tray as he was bid and awkwardly slipped the ring onto three of the fingers of Madeleine's left hand, repeating over each, "In the name of the Father, and of the Son, and the Holy Ghost." Smoke rolled from the golden incense pots, thick and narcotic, stinging his eyes and burning his throat. At last he fitted the ring onto her third finger and in his broad-voweled accent pronounced, "With this ring I thee wed." Until that moment he had not fully comprehended his loss of her. She would be taken from him, just as all else in his life had been taken.

With a deft motion, Heribert blessed the couple then stepped forward in his flowing golden robes and bestowed the kiss of peace upon his proxy groom. Wulf, in turn, embraced Madeleine. Her lips were still and cold as stone.

It was done; before God she was the wife of Roland du Boulay, Duke of Burgundy. Lost to him forever. Seeing her pale face in the candleglow, his heart was seized by a helplessness beyond remedy. "No." He said it aloud without realizing he had, though only Madeleine heard. She pressed her cool hand tightly in his and met his eyes with a look of passionate devotion that all but stopped his heart.

A drum roll of thunder shook the air followed by a

crashing blow. A volley of shouts rang from the rear of the cathedral and all eyes were riveted upon the ornate doors. After the third successive blow, the brass hinges groaned and gave way before the assault of four mailed horsemen armed for battle and bearing a log wrapped with chains and borne between them as a battering ram. Casting the log aside, the horsemen reined in their mounts.

With a wild clattering of hooves, Guiles de Luchaire entered the cathedral followed by twenty or more mounted villeins.

Heribert's long jaw dropped in disbelief. Regaining himself, he hurled his powerful voice down the nave and, raising an arm as if to summon the wrath of the almighty, shouted, "God is witness to your heresy, Guiles de Luchaire!"

De Luchaire leaned forward in his saddle and bellowed back, "Usurper, do not speak to me of God. Your black deeds speak for themselves. I have come to claim that which is rightfully mine. Concede or die!" De Luchaire, helmeted and mailed, was recognizable only by his massive shoulders, his blue lake surcoat, and shield.

Heribert's aquiline features twisted in a fit of rage. "Swine!" he shrieked. "Eternal damnation is what you shall have. Return to Sézanne and await your excommunication!"

The bitterly hostile exchange and the premonition of where it would lead bristled the hair on the back of Wulf's neck. Closing his hand on Madeleine's silken waist, he took several backward steps, drawing her toward the chancel door arch. From where he stood, he saw no other route of escape.

Those who crowded the cathedral also sensed the approaching violence and shifted back, seeking protection among the forest of supporting columns. Fearful, angry voices rose from the crowd and were directed toward de Luchaire. "Take your battle elsewhere," one merchant cried. "Innocent people will be killed," others chorused. If de Luchaire heard, he paid no heed. He raised himself in his saddle once more and, in a tone calculated to intimidate, shouted, "It is you who will answer to God, Heribert de Moncelet. Make your peace and prepare to die!"

With a single practiced motion of his hand, de Luchaire slammed shut the hood of his visor, drew his sword and set his heels into his horse's flanks. The wild rolling drumbeat of their horses' iron-shod hooves reverberated from the cathedral's stones. The horsemen, riding in battle formation, bore down on those who had sought the safety of the columns, cutting a swath through the terror-stricken merchants and their families. The crush of bone and screams of the dying rose above the clamor. The horse of one villein stumbled upon a tangle of maimed bodies and went down thrashing, pinning the rider beneath its weight.

Heribert grasped his jeweled chalice and, herding his servers before him, hurried toward the chancel door arch, all the while screeching for his niece to follow and extending a beckoning hand.

Wulf carried Madeleine forward on his arm, thrusting her toward the narrow door arch which was barely visible amid the ornate rood screens.

At the door arch Madeleine cast a terrified backward glance over her shoulder. The unwieldy weight of the gown and her inattention sent her blundering into the iron fretwork of the screen. She pulled herself from the cold embrace of the metal only to discover the train of her gown was hopelessly tangled in the spiral coils and twists of iron.

Seeing that his niece was trapped, Heribert together with his servers darted from the chancel to tug frantically at the train of the gown until the material gave way with a rending sound and they swept Madeleine into the safety of the chancel and barred the door.

Wulf's attention had been directed elsewhere in a

desperate search for a weapon. He had glimpsed Madeleine vanish into the chancel and the heavy door close after her. He did not notice the shredded remains of her silken train impaled on the rood screen. With little to choose from, Wulf grasped an iron candle standard, braced its base against the stones, and angled it horse-high as one would a pike.

He glanced to his right and his left and saw perhaps fifteen or twenty of the bishop's guards close ranks at the altar rail. Dead men, he thought, all of them. They would be cut down like sheaves of wheat. They were fools to stand and fight, but it was too late to do otherwise.

The horsemen rode into them full tilt, towering above them like goliaths and blackening the air with their broad swords. They met in a calamitous crash of bone and flesh. The altar rail was reduced to splinters by the stampeding horses. Blows and slashing strikes rained down from all sides.

Wulf angled the makeshift pike, only to duck beneath it an instant later to avoid the swing of a broad sword aimed at his skull. A horse reared up before him; iron-shod hooves passed over his head. Two other horsemen collided before him, their horses shrieking and wild with fright. The guardsman beside him screamed and sagged against him as a sword bit deeply into his shoulder, showering Wulf with his blood.

Wulf pushed the falling body aside. The clang of weapons and trample of horses deafened him. He took up the makeshift pike, forcing every thought from his mind save one: he did not want to die. Before he could brace the candle standard, a horse lurched toward him, the rider hunched over its powerful neck and his broad sword in mid-swing. Without time to brace the iron rod against the stones, it served only to bisect the path of the blade. The sword and the standard met with a shower of sparks. The stinging impact jarred both weapons from the hands of the combatants and sent them cartwheeling away into infinity.

Wulf dropped to the ground, grappling for a fallen sword; there were many to choose from. He pulled one from beneath the body of a dead guardsman. The scene before him was appalling; heaps of mangled bodies and downed horses littered the floor of the cathedral and the stones beneath him were slick with blood.

De Luchaire and his villeins regrouped, wheeling their horses for another pass. Some among them, having lost their broad swords in combat, drew estocs, thrusting swords, from before their saddle bows.

The horsemen approached as a wall, trampling men beneath their horses' hooves. To Wulf's left a shrill scream exploded in his ear followed by the wrenching sound of crushing bones and tearing flesh. A horse fell thrashing before him on the blood-slick stones.

Believing the horsemen had passed him by, Wulf rose, drawing the sword with him. The color brown filled the whole of his vision as the roomy chest of a large bay loomed before him, so close he glimpsed the whorls of hair upon its hide—horse and rider in mid-air going over him.

He staggered backward, dragging the sword with him, and with all his strength thrust upwards, sinking the blade into the man's groin. The rider pitched to one side, toppling from the horse and tearing the sword from Wulf's hands. The horse hurtled past him like a hot wind; as it did, something, the iron stirrup perhaps, struck his face a heavy blow and he tumbled into blackness.

Amid the carnage, Guiles de Luchaire signaled to his remaining few horsemen. He had intended to cut down the bishop's guards on the first assault; his failure had been costly. Soon the bishop's guards and those soldiers of the provost who had proceeded to the old palace would be alerted and pour into the cathedral. He had lost the advantage and, reining in his horse, raised a gloved hand.

Shouts of "Murderer, murderer!" arose from the stunned and horrified survivors. Women wailed over dead husbands and children and the screams of the maimed and dying were like those of souls in hell.

Heribert, ashen-faced and shaken, appeared at the chancel doorway. He strode to the altar and, raising both arms, shouted to his few remaining battered guardsmen. "Enough! Let them pass!" Heribert wanted no more blood spilled in his cathedral, no more innocent men, women, and children trampled. He raised his voice and, casting the words as if they were stones, shouted, "For your crimes you will burn in this world and the next, Guiles de Luchaire!"

At the doors, Guiles de Luchaire sawed at the reins of the large tawny-colored chestnut. Wheeling the animal around, he pointed an accusing finger at Heribert de Moncelet, responding, "The crime is yours and I will yet have justice!" With a shout and a flurry of flying hooves, de Luchaire and his few remaining villeins left as they had come.

A scant dozen of the bishop's guards who had come afoot from the old palace and a paltry few of the provost's soldiers entered the rear of the cathedral through the chapter house. It was through questioning the soldiers of the provost that Heribert learned of Falkes Delouvrier's treachery. And a short time later, when Delouvrier came forward with smiles and palliations hoping to appear less blameworthy, he addressed the bishop. "It seems Your Grace is beloved by God, for all has ended well."

They were the last words Delouvrier would utter. Heribert had him struck down and his body dragged out into the street and left bared to the rain.

A sergeant of the guard and several soldiers were sent to rout the provost's troops from the taverns. Silver coins to each who reported; death to those who did not.

Wulf swayed to his knees and eventually staggered to his feet, surveying the mayhem surrounding him. He put a hand to his buzzing head; when he took it away it was covered with blood. He did not know if it was his own or that of the men he had fallen among. He could recognize only one of the dead guardsmen; the others were covered with congealed blood or too badly maimed.

Madeleine pushed her way from the chancel with only a single thought on her mind—to find Wulf. She freed herself from the restraining arms of a well-meaning novice, who had served at the Mass, and picked her way through the dead and dying.

De Grailley saw her go, struggling with the heavy gown as she stepped down from the dais of the altar. He did not call out or attempt to stop her. In truth he was struck dumb by the sight of the carnage. Of the bishop's near twenty gaurds who had remained in the cathedral, only five battered survivors stood on their feet. Beyond, a number of Dominican clergy, the cream of Champagne's lesser nobles, and Troyes' merchant class lay dead and broken on the cathedral floor.

After a terrying few moments, Madeleine sighted Wulf and, straining against the weight of her gown, embraced him; she cared not for the white silk gown, the hem of which was already soaked with blood. She grasped his hand and though it was sticky with blood, it was warm and real and alive. She led him to the font where she dipped her veil in the holy water and washed the blood from his face. For a long while neither of them spoke.

Heribert sent his priests through the wasteland of cries, moans, and weeping to give absolution to the dead and dying and comfort to those who had survived. With his next breath, he ordered his newly chosen provost, Pascal, to arrest the banker Tanzenetti and numerous others which he named.

Madeleine's serving women crept from the confessionals where they had taken refuge and stood near the altar weeping and praying, adding their voices to the uproar and confusion.

Townspeople, peasants, and workers heard of the massacre and thronged through the driving rain to see for themselves, gathering outside the cathedral until troops were sent to disperse them.

Legoix and Burgundy's courtiers, though thoroughly shaken, had miraculously escaped serious injury save for the priest Evarrard, whose mangled corpse was found near the altar.

Heribert, surveying the destruction, tallied the toll in lives as well as damage to his beautiful cathedral. He was sorely tempted to cancel the wedding feast. De Grailley, however, advised against it suggesting, "Might it not appear the Baron of Sézanne has won the day after all?"

Outside the walls of St. Pierre's Cathedral a wind-driven rain swept the plaza, sheeting down and bouncing from the cobbled stones. The old palace stood at the extreme edge of the city's original Roman wall, a scant three hundred paces across the plaza and down the rue de Vieille Rome. Its steep stone turrets sailed with the rolling clouds, high above the irregular rooftops of the close-crowded houses.

To the right lay the old city with its Jewish district, priories, abbeys, and homes of wealthy burghers. To the left, beyond the Moline Canal was the Artaud Gate and the new city, sprawling westward with its cloth halls, tanneries, taverns, and market stalls. Like a sentinel, the Viscount's tower stood against the stormy skies, stark and bleak as a mountain rising from a raging sea of rain and mist.

A number of servants wrestled against the wind to raise canopies supported on long staves beneath which the wedding party and guests made their way across the open plaza. The awnings and those beneath them were alternately lashed and buffetted by the wind and rain.

All arrived at the hall disheveled and soaked to their skins. Many of the guests, particularly those who had journeyed to Troyes, had for several days been in residence at the old palace. Although they were able to change into dry clothing, many were reluctant to abandon their finery and don traveling clothes, which as a rule were drab and serviceable.

In the superior lighting of the hall, the bridal pair's blood-spattered clothing made a grisly sight. They crossed the hall to the dais, appearing like corpses risen from the dead, and took their place at the banquet table amid whispers of doom and ill omens.

Inside the thick walls of the old palace, hearthfires blazed at either end of the vast hall. The air, heavy with humidity, was made stifling hot by the constant stoking of logs onto the fires. Musicians played and lines of dancers moved across the rush-strewn floor while beyond the old palace's open doors, flickering torch-light lit the plaza as the dead were carried from the cathedral.

The guests, unaware or uncaring, drank wine with abandon. Laughter rang above the music and the sons and daughters of lords and wealthy merchants, with their flushed faces and soggy clothing, who had an hour before seen the face of death, danced gaily.

Upon the raised dais, Madeleine sat still as a statue, neither smiling nor speaking. The forced merriment of the guests and the songs of the troubadours could not dispel her morbid thoughts. The image of Guiles de Luchaire rigid in his saddle, his brutish head thrown back and thick shoulders thrust forward, struck her heart with dread. Would she never be free of him? In her fearful state of mind, she felt that no less than some fated doom existed between them. A covenant, which demanded for its fulfillment the death of one or the other.

Madeleine did not turn or hint by her expression that she had reached for the hand of her guard. Instead, she found his thigh. Wulf's large hand quickly folded over hers. He did not look at her. There was no need; her offered hand was enough.

Pascal entered the hall, water dripping from his mail and surcoat. He went directly to His Grace, seated on the dais, and dropping his head close to the bishop's ear, reported the arrest of the banker Tanzenetti. A confession had been wrung from him as had the names of the other conspirators. The majority had been taken into custody.

Heribert, who had in the heat of his anger sworn to hang the banker Tanzenetti from the pillory, now had second thoughts. The Tanzenetti family was among Lombardy's most powerful, related by marriage to Princes. In light of this, Heribert deemed it wiser to return Tanzenetti to his family in dishonor. They would deal with him, thus sparing the city of Troyes their ill feelings.

As to the others, Heribert ordered them held in the cells of the provost's hall. They were all men of great wealth and it occurred to Heribert that perhaps justice would be as well served through fines. Legoix, who sat beside the bishop, was in hearty agreement, and one of his entourage—a thin, sickly youth—proposed a toast.

Music and laughter floated through the torch-lit hall. The dancers, the musicians, the gaudy colors of their clothing dissolved before Madeleine's tear-filled eyes. She would not have noticed François Larousse in his ermine-trimmed jupon of murry-colored velvet had he not stumbled as he stepped onto the dais and crashed into the table. The look of fear in his eyes was terrible to see and his voice burst from his mouth in a wail. "Your Grace, it has come again. I feared this. Oh God most merciful, it is the pestilence. Two kitchen workers have collapsed. I have seen the black buboes upon their flesh with my own eyes. All must flee!"

From a dozen other sources the word spread like wildfire. Songs and laughter deteriorated to shouts and screams as the terror-stricken guests departed into the rain, caring not for their baggage and in some cases not even for one another.

Unwilling to wait for the *charrettes* to be hitched, Heribert called for horses. The chapel bells were sounding compline as the sodden procession entered the courtyard of the château.

Wulf lifted Madeleine from her horse; it was all he could manage not to stumble with her, for the gown, now thoroughly soaked, weighed thrice its ungodly weight. A north wind had followed on the heels of the storm and the falling rain was cold as ice. Madeleine sagged against him, exhausted, her eyes smudged with fatigue. She leaned heavily on his arm as he guided her up the château's steps.

The widow and half a dozen serving women waited to escort Madeleine to her chamber. Her four attendants trailed after her in their limp and dripping wet red velvet gowns. Their hair straggled into their faces and they wept uncontrollably as they attempted to tell the others of their ordeal.

From the hall, male voices called for wine and rehashed the battle in the cathedral. Legoix and his entourage supplied personal accounts of derring-do and miraculous, much exaggerated, escapes from death, all amid shouts of encouragement and loud laughter.

In the garderobe, Wulf leaned slack against the washstand applying handfuls of cold water to his aching face. The stunning cold of the water temporarily anesthetized his gashes and contusions. The lump above his eye was the size of an egg. By the light of a single candle he inspected his wounds in the polished steel mirror. It felt much worse than it looked. Tomorrow, he thought, it would be the reverse.

As he returned to the chamber, he pushed the events of the day from his conscious mind. Even so, he knew he would not sleep. It had always been that way for him. He was still a boy when he had fought his first battle. It was little more than a skirmish but he had fought it for weeks in his dreams and so it was with each battle since.

The widow and her women waited with their candles outside the chamber door. Seeing him emerge from the garderobe, they moved leisurely toward the stairs, leaving the rustling sound of their whispered conversation and the scent of candle wax in their wake.

The draperies of the Lady Madeleine's bed had been pulled to and the only light was that cast by the leaping flames in the hearth. He turned to secure the bar on the heavy oaken door; when he turned back, she was standing before him.

She clung to him, sobbing softly. He closed her trembling shoulders inside his arms, felt each heave, bruised cry, and momentary recovery. He was like one struck dumb, without words to say and, as always, bewildered by the sudden fury of her emotions. In his embrace, she was like a fragile bird entwined in a snare, her heart beating furiously against his chest.

When he was able to speak above the painful lump which had risen in his throat, he asked, "What would you have me do?" For he would have promised to catch the moon for her, anything to quiet her anguished cries.

She buried her face in the brocaded jupon, whose intricate raised designs were stiff with blood. "Love me," she cried. The words tore from her throat like a sob.

"I do love you," he said in a voice that to him sounded foolish and brimming with the tender honesty of a small boy.

She pressed deeper in his arms, so that it seemed he

266

could feel the blood coursing through her veins. Tears glistened on her upturned face and the words she spoke fell from her lips like sighs. "Lie with me tonight," she begged. Her eyes were large and shining and there was nothing in the world he wanted more. His freedom, perhaps, but freedom was too abstruse to compare with the heady reality of her supple body pressed to his.

He cupped her face in his hands and kissed her, a kiss filled with promises and sweetly fatal, for now they were lost to reason—helpless as a leaf upon the water, compelled by the wild delirium of their passion.

It was Madeleine who unloosed the bodice of her linen night dress and offered her breasts to him. Small impertinent breasts, tender and milk white as pearls with tightly whorled pink nipples which slid erect and glistening from his lips.

He shed the jupon, while with trembling fingers Madeleine fumbled over the ties of his hosen. She had seen him nude by the stream and that was the image she had carried in her thoughts: his slender, muscular body, narrow hips, sturdy long legs, and his maleness before him. But it had not awed her as it did at that moment when loosed from the velvet hosen; it rose before her fully erect and blooming from its foreskin.

Neither would recall what words they said, nor exactly how they found themselves amid the clutter of their abandoned clothing. They fell into bed and into one another's arms, caring for nothing, knowing only the intense delight of their entangled limbs.

His hands sought her out, his lips wetted her with kisses, and without a hint of shame, she spread her legs, accepting him as eagerly as a bitch in heat.

Only when he entered her did she cry out, startled that love should rend and pierce. But the pain was less than her desire and the feel of his flesh in hers filled her with a wondrous hurt.

They moved as one, their eyes glazed with pleasure. The heaving sighs which escaped their lips were like the song of the wind and their undulating bodies rose and fell to life's eternal rhythm. One, until their peaking passions grew to frenzy, ignited into pure flame and exploded like a white-hot star, spewing out its brilliance into the night.

For a moment they lay together still joined and damp with perspiration. The chamber was heavy with the scent of their lovemaking, the doughy musk of semen and blood.

It occurred to Wulf that he should unlatch the window but there was little chance of discovery and at that moment it mattered not so much as the whispered words of love and warm embraces. Wanting her as he had for months, he could not slake himself of the taste and feel of her; rousing her with kisses, he ran his fingers between her legs to fondle those lips slick with his sperm.

The touch of his fingers left her lower body throbbing with excitement and the madness took her again. For that was how it seemed to Madeleine— madness—to desire the weight of his body, the pressure, the punishing pain of his penetration for a few moments of intense pleasure.

She would have begged him, "No, not so soon," but wherever he touched or kissed stirred her with desire and the feel of his hardened shaft rubbing against her leg left her aching for the need of it inside her. Her hands moved fitfully over his body, touching him, clasping his shoulders, his back, searching for a way to draw him nearer, but he would not be rushed.

He took her slowly, deliberately, and filling her, gathered her in his arms to rock her with each rhythmic thrust until she moaned and wrapped her legs about his body. He felt her waves of pleasure come and hastened to meet her in a climax that left them both limp and exhausted.

Chapter Seventeen

A slanting shaft of cold gray light from the chamber window woke Wulf. The fire, forgotten in the heat of their lovemaking, had fallen to ash and the bed where they lay was smeared with the evidence of their adulterous act.

Denied the heat of his body, Madeleine awakened and not finding him there beside her, sat up with a muffled cry of alarm. She was frantic until she saw he was before the hearth rekindling the fire.

He smiled at her and, rising to his feet, lifted her abandoned shift from the floor and brought it to her.

After a discussion of how best to conceal their guilt, they decided to wrap the soggy, blood-spattered gown inside the sheet. Later, on His Grace's orders, the serving women took the bundled gown to the seamstress so she might salvage what she could of the brilliants and seed pearls.

Upon opening the bundle, the seamstress found the gown's train had been torn away and the hem was stiff with blood. She clucked to herself, thinking the water-marked, blood-stained silk was beyond use.

When the laundress came to collect the sheet, she pointed to its center and the dried stains of mucus and watery brown blood. "Where did this come from?" she asked with a grin.

The fat-cheeked seamstress raised her head and

looked at the laundress as if she were simple. "The gown was lying upon it," she replied, and to the woman's smirking face, repeated, "The gown, where else?" and once again went back to snipping brilliants from the front panel with a small hooked knife.

Where else indeed, the laundress chuckled to herself and bundled the sheet under her arm. She had washed enough sheets in her life to know better and wondered if such information might interest His Grace.

Later, Wulf followed his mistress into the crisp October morning. The breeze held a chill, but the sun was climbing in a cloudless sky, warm and yellow as marmalade where it lay upon the walkway. At the quince hedges she took his arm impulsively but he lifted her hand from his sleeve at once and sent her a warning glance.

Madeleine looked up with a puzzled expression. He smiled at her and signing with his eyes led her gaze toward the windows of the tower. "Your uncle sends a guard to stand watch."

"To watch us?" She said it only half-believing him, and hastening her step drew beside him where the thick blue junipers spilled over the rock terrace and perfumed the air with their aromatic scent.

Wulf slackened his stride to allow her to keep abreast of him, advising, "He reports all that he sees." He took several more strides, his gaze fixed on a thicket of young elms directly ahead.

"And what might he see?" she asked, glancing back, deciding it was clearly too distant and the trees too close-set for him to see anything.

No sooner had the words passed her lips than Wulf took her by the hand and pulled her after him into the thicket, where he cinched her to him with his arms, nuzzled her throat, and whispered close to

270

her ear, "Our lustful behavior."

She laughed for the sheer joy of being alive on such a morning and encircled by his arms. She tiptoed up to kiss him and afterwards looked at him oddly and giggled, declaring, "You are ugly as a toad. I do not recall your face being so swollen last night."

"Perhaps not in comparison," he chuckled, and leading her by the hand, walked deeper into the islet of trees. Leaves crunched beneath their feet. In another few paces they reached a small sunlit clearing.

Madeleine gathered her skirts and plopped down in the warm, fragrant leaves. Wulf sat down stiffly beside her, easing his spine against the rough bark of a young tree. His head ached with a fury as did his entire body.

Madeleine reached out her hand and tenderly touched his swollen cheek bone, asking, "How is your face this morning?"

"It is painful." He winced, but smiled at her and did not draw away from her touch.

"Your eye is more red than blue," she observed, looking closely, a frown upon her small face.

"I can still see from it," he told her in a playful voice, shutting his good eye as if to demonstrate and planting a kiss on her forehead.

"I hope that kiss was not meant for my lips," she said in a merry, bantering tone.

He pulled her into his arms and hugged her against him. "No," he laughed, "I ache too much for lovemaking." A foolish gesture for the pressure against his ribs sent a sharp pain through his chest.

"I, too, am tender," she confessed with a flutter of dark lashes, "and where you might expect." She stood up suddenly as if embarrassed by her admission and, turning from him, plucked a burnished leaf from a sapling. "Why did they return to Nevers without me?" she asked, stripping the golden leaf to its veins.

"So as not to break my heart." He said it in jest, murmuring, "Although it, too, feels bruised."

"I am serious, Wulf. Why?"

He shrugged, and that, too, was hurtful. "Perhaps the Duke of Burgundy has not yet returned to Nevers or they fear de Luchaire or the plague."

Madeleine made a pouting grimace. "They are all equally hideous." She cast aside the skeletal remains of the leaf and plucked another. From where she stood she could see the mill pond and hear the honking of the geese. "My uncle could have sent guards to escort me."

Wulf came and stood beside her. The geese swam into view. "Your uncle has precious few to guard himself," he said, "and you know as well as I, whose backside is dearest to him."

"But he will send me away eventually."

"In time," Wulf agreed.

She looked up through her dark lashes and smiled. "Time enough for us to be away?"

"Time enough," he repeated. But the smile had faded from his lips and his gaze shifted away.

Following morning Mass in the chapel, Legoix and his entourage, along with the body of the priest Evarrard which had been hastily sewn in a leather sack for transport, departed for Nevers.

Heribert, heartened by the laundress's observations, delayed the departure of the Lady Madeleine, now the Duchess of Burgundy. He named a date early in December at which time, he assured Legoix, Roland du Boulay would not only receive a lovely and charming bride, but one who was also conveniently pregnant with an heir.

Heribert was in a high good humor for the remainder of the day. The fact that his bargain with the Duke of Burgundy could still be salvaged was in itself cause for rejoicing. However, the news he

272

received from Troyes on the following day was less hopeful.

The pestilence was spreading inside the city at an alarming rate and this second pandemic threatened to be even more devastating than the first. Although the most damaging blow came several days later when Pascal, newly appointed provost, arrived at the château to report the banker Tanzenetti had been found dead in his cell. It was plague and though his family had been informed, no one had come for the body. Many of the others had died as well. Heribert, realizing there was scant profit in holding dead men for ransom, ordered Pascal to release the survivors for the time being.

Days passed and prayers were offered in the château's chapel for the deliverance of the city from the evil sickness.

Each morning at Mass, Madeleine prayed for the souls of her family and for the souls of those who had been taken by the plague. It often depressed her to be there in the chapel, though of late, her dark moods did not linger.

In the hall roasted pork and game birds were brought to the table followed by vegetable dishes and stewed pears and cakes. The discussion was subdued that evening—the moral state of a soul, piety, and death.

Madeleine thought it morbid and closed her ears to their words. She was relieved when the meal was ended and she and her guard were permitted to return to her chamber.

They played several games of draughts. After a time, Madeleine raised her eyes from the game board and smiled at him. Sitting as he was, it was impossible for her to ignore the hunch in his leather hosen. Without a word she placed her hand on his thigh, smoothing her fingers over the telltale bulge.

"It is a better game than draughts," she suggested shyly, her hazel eyes at once vivid with delight then retreating beneath a thick fringe of dark lashes.

He smiled at her, his pupils dilating in the firelight until it seemed they might eclipse the clear blue iris. He brushed his fingers over her cheek and buried his large hand in her tousled hair, feeling the smoothness of the skull beneath, and was struck by the wonder of it all. Flesh and bone, no more than that, but with the power to turn his thoughts to confusion. From the first, her unexpected sensuality had stirred him as no other ever had.

He cradled the curve of her skull in his hand and covered her lips with his, sliding his tongue over hers. With his other hand he loosed the chafing leather hosen.

Madeleine stared at the impudent thing, marveling at the sleek efficiency of it as it lengthened before her eyes. In the revealing light of the fire the sight of its reddened cap swaying before her like the head of a viper momentarily immobilized her. She touched it hesitantly. It bucked and she drew back with a giggle. "What magic makes it rise?" she asked, her cheeks high with color.

"You are the magic," he told her, and guiding her head with his hand brought her close and kissed her once again, stealing her breath and planting a trail of damp kisses down her throat. "Hold it in your hand," he coaxed. "Kiss it," he whispered.

She blushed, uncertain yet wanting to please him, and did as he asked, touching her lips to it cautiously and drawing her tongue along its length. He spoke softly, instructing her. When she took the swollen cap into her mouth and sucked on it as she would a bone, his features became fixed as those of a mask and his breath came in moaning gasps.

He pushed her away, but not quickly enough, and came with a shudder of release into a cloth drawn from inside his jupon. He brushed his lips against her ear, telling her how he loved her. She sat there considering what she had done, her mouth tasting strangely of salt and musk, unable to understand why it had pleased him so.

Wulf cleansed himself, wadded the cloth, and tossed it into the fire which greedily consumed it. Drawing her into his arms, he nuzzled her throat. "Listen," he murmured. "Do you hear them? My sons and daughters dancing in the flames."

Startled by his words, she looked at him. "Why do you say such a thing?"

He smiled, remarking, "It is God's jest, not mine, to make the mighty king and the humble peasant from the same gout of slime."

Madeleine did not understand and in a perplexed voice asked, "The fluid is what begets a child?" Despite Albertine's elucidations on love, Madeleine was not exactly certain how such things occurred. Suddenly her eyes grew large as trenchers. "I swallowed some," she gasped. "Will I come with child?"

He could not keep from smiling at the innocence of her expression and pulled her deeper in his arms. "No," he laughed softly. "Not from what you have swallowed and most likely not from what I have put inside you."

A million questions crowded upon Madeleine's tongue, but his hands beneath her night dress drove every thought from her mind.

Wulf found in her a perfect lover, unabashedly willing and eager to please. For himself he could not have enough of her. He knew full well she belonged to another, but for a time he had held her heart, held her in his arms, and given her measure for measure the passion she had given him.

Inside the château, the pleasant routine of life went on undisturbed while reports from Troyes grew more desperate with each passing day.

Pascal reported that soldiers of the provost had begun to desert. He had captured some and hung them from the pillory to serve as a warning to the others, but even so they continued to slip away. Before he took his leave, Pascal advised the bishop, "Close the château; permit no one entry. The world beyond these walls is bedlam. God have mercy on us."

The days grew shorter and there was the scent of frost in the chill morning air. For several years past the winters had been harsh and with the advent of the cold primal darkness there was an uneasiness among the people—fears from a time older than human reckoning. Even those who scoffed felt a sense of disquiet. People talked of it in half-whispers.

Some said the evil pestilence was an omen and the world would soon end. They had seen the falling stars with trails of sparking fire, seen the blood upon the horned moon, and the two-headed snake the miller's children found.

The people feared, and so it was on La Veille de la Toussaint that the bishop led a devout procession. With mitre, crozier, and smoking incense pots he blessed the château's grounds and those within its walls and banished the forces of evil.

Those assembled for the Mass which was to follow watched as the torches made a moving line of illumination against the unrelieved blackness of the landscape.

Snug in her cape of miniver, Madeleine met her guard's eyes with a tender, secret smile. The cold and darkness no longer held fear for her. She would lie in her tall Saxon's arms, safe and warm forever.

Later they made love and fell asleep on the pallet of rushes and fur. Uncertain of what woke him, Wulf raised himself on one arm and gently shook

Madeleine's shoulder. "Go to your bed," he urged in a voice dazed with sleep.

Madeleine stirred, murmuring "Yes," then snuggled deeper in the furs. Wulf pulled himself from the pallet and added several logs to the dying fire. His leather hosen lay nearby; he hiked into them and crossed the room, opening the window to relieve his bladder. Completing the ritual, he returned to the fire and roused Madeleine. He stood her on her feet and tickling her thoroughly, dropped the ample night dress over her head. She giggled and thrashed, for a moment lost beneath the voluminous linen frock, all the while cautioning him not to tickle her and insisting she must go to the garderobe.

"The chamber pot is across the room," he pointed out. He did not relish the thought of a long walk down the drafty passageway in only his hosen.

Madeleine protested and with a giggle declared chamber pots undignified, but he had a way of gently mocking her that always left her blushing. At last she relented. Still grumbling, she squatted over the pot and then clambered into the huge bed, complaining she was deathly cold and begging him to come and keep her warm.

He leaned over her on the bed, and, bracing himself with his arms, said, "That would make a pretty picture for your women to find on the morrow."

"They cannot enter until you unbar the door," she reminded him.

He smiled. It was true enough, but he said, "Go to sleep," and playfully covered her head with the bed clothes.

Wulf pulled his pallet before the door and lay down. It was a long while before he slept. Perhaps his conscience bothered him, though he could not keep from wondering why the bishop had placed such infinite trust in him . . . and so unwisely.

Why had he not chosen a guard from among his

novices? Or several? One to watch the first and a third to watch the other two. Instead it seemed His Grace had done all in his power to tempt him. Wulf knew there were substances which could be mixed with a man's food to render him impotent; Carlotta di Scalla had once boasted of dosing her husband with such a substance to keep him from her bed.

What concerned him even more was Madeleine's insistence that he take her north. He had nothing to offer her, even less than a hand-to-mouth existence, for the poorest borel had at least a hut above his head. He had tried to explain it to her in such a way that she would see the impossibility of it. But she was deaf to reason and he could not bring himself, rather the fire in his glans would not allow him, to say no to her, though his own common sense and decency told him she would despise him for it later.

Some evenings they would talk for hours about many things. One night he told her about the northern forests, the lakes bright as mirrors, and the broad grassy plains of his lord's lands, and how in the spring the mists rolled in from the East Sea and turned all to silver. He told her, too, of the North Star and that it would one day lead him home.

"You are the lord now," she reminded him.

He smiled. A smile for her, the thought. He knew there was little hope he would ever hold Rügen or, for that matter, lay eyes on it again.

Later when he held her quietly by the fire, he asked in a thoughtful tone, "Have you ever wondered why your uncle leaves me with you?"

"You are my guard."

"Yes," he said, though it was not what he meant. Pressing his lips to the nape of her neck, he asked, "Does he not suspect?"

She turned to face him. "Why should he? We have given him no cause."

Wulf said no more on the subject. Only when he lay alone on his pallet did he decide it was his own guilt and not a question of the bishop's motives. He would never have dared make love to the Lady Madeleine, fill her again and again with his seed, had it not been for the others. He had known an assortment of serving girls and the Prince di Scalla's widowed sister by marriage.

In truth, the serving girls occasionally came with child but he was not the only man with whom they shared their favors and none had come complaining to him. As for Carlotta di Scalla, he had been her lover, one of them, her blue-eyed pet. She had not conceived. Once she told him that she had paid a midwife to insert a golden ring into her womb so that she would not be cursed with a succession of pregnancies. Perhaps it was true.

He knew of such things, for Erna had done a brisk business. Of all, he recalled most being sent to fetch stones for her—smooth round stones the size of lingonberries. He did it often. She was very particular and at first he found few that suited her. He learned quickly, as children are apt to do for praise, and soon there were few she rejected. She would wash them and dry them in the sun and put them by threes, always three, into women who wished to have no more children. Whether or not it was successful he could not recall.

The season changed. The château, closed to all, became a world unto itself—a microcosm spinning to its own rhythmic beat, waking, eating, sleeping. The dinners in the hall, Heribert noted, went undisturbed. His niece ate her food without complaint, complacent as a cow. Her ill temper had mellowed to the point where, at times, he could not help but be amused, and yes, somewhat awed by his own innate wisdom. His choice of the Saxon had been a stroke of genius. It had taken only that, nothing more, to content her youthful passions and quell her rebellious nature. Human nature, Heribert concluded. How easily one could draw a metaphor to the beasts of the field, but that of course was a dangerous thought which he at once dismissed.

They played a game of draughts to pass the time. Their silent concentration was interrupted only by the sizz and crackle of the fire. When all in the château were surely abed, Wulf dragged the pallet before the door. Madeleine gathered up the draught board and playing pieces. She heaped the fur rugs on which they had made their seats into her arms and carried them to the pallet.

As he crouched to stoke the fire, Madeleine dashed across the chamber and threw open the window. "There are stars tonight," she announced in a voice bubbling with child-like anticipation. "You must show me your North Star." She turned suddenly, her dark brows drawn into a frown. "Or do you only tease me?"

He stood up, dusting the soot from his hands. "No, I do not, truly." He came and stood behind her in the chill draft. "There," he said, directing her gaze with his hand. "That is the North Star."

Madeleine raised her eyes skyward. The stars appeared distant beyond comprehension, twinkling like candles lit for Mass. "There are so many," she breathed, suddenly awed by the multitude of stars blazing against the absolute blackness of the night sky. "How do you know which star is your North Star?" She wondered aloud. It seemed unfathomable to Madeleine. How small she felt in the face of such immensity!

He drew her close and said, "By those that bound

it. See the pattern they keep? Like dipping bowls, one large, one small. Look to the larger," he instructed. "Do you see the base of the bowl? There," he guided her. "Now see there are two stars in perfect alignment. Do you see them?"

She nodded, believing she did.

"Now follow them. They point always to the North Star."

She sent a quick look over her shoulder, her eyes filled with wonder and her cheeks flushed from excitement or the cold. "Who taught you to read the stars?" she asked.

Her animated expression, the bright eyes, brought a smile to his lips, though truthfully he was more interested in steering her toward the bed than recalling his days in Lombardy. He said simply, "An astrologer in the pay of my Lord di Scalla. A man too fond of wine and the sound of his own voice." He did not tell her of the youth eager to learn about the stars, the youth who believed the astrologer was the wisest man in all the world. Nor did he say that for all his wisdom the astrologer had failed to foresee the lord's murder and ultimately his own. He much preferred to draw her warm supple body close to his and plant a kiss at the base of her neck. His one hand teased the nipple of a small firm teat, while the other pushed beneath the voluminous shift with practiced familiarity.

Madeleine squirmed, making a soft mirthful noise in her throat, a laughing pretense. For when his fingers riffled the dark feathery rise of her pubis she leaned against him, making herself available to his hands. Only when he nimbly reached between her legs to tickle her did she jig from his touch, pulling him after her to the bed.

Deep in the jumble of bed linen she wrestled his arms, giggling wildly. He, too, was laughing, though in truth he made more a panting sound, as both were mindful to be silent.

Tangled in the sheets, he neatly pinned her beneath his weight. "What will you do now, Souris?" he laughed, grinning down at her.

Her dancing eyes met his. "You are a big loppy hound," she teased.

"One who pleases you," he prompted, releasing her wrists and dropping his head to nuzzle her neck, what little of it he could find amid the mire of bed linens.

Her cool hands groped over his bare shoulders. "Yes," she whispered, "my only one," and arched against him, unashamed.

They kissed and touched and too soon felt the aching need. Her fingers tugged at the ties of his hosen. Their fingers bumbled together, his hand and hers fumbling between them.

Abruptly he raised himself on one arm. "The bed," he mumbled, "we cannot here." It was true; they dared not risk spotting the bed linen. If the laundress guessed, everyone would soon know.

Madeleine lifted her head. Her eyes were as dazed as his. "Why did we move the pallet before the door?" she moaned.

He blinked, thinking it was done and therefore useless to discuss. "Where is the towel?" he asked breathlessly.

She spied it on the chest, lying beside the carved containers of rouge and kohl, the vases of perfume, and the water basin for her hands and face. She slid from the bed and dashed to fetch it. As she did, he rolled onto his back to strip off the leather hosen. They clung like a second skin.

On her swift return Madeleine shed her shift, hopping away from it. She fell upon the bed naked, giggling like a loon at their predicament and shivering from the cold for the chamber window stood open to the night.

He fought the hosen like a foe, momentarily trapped and wearing a silly pickerel grin. With a mighty tug, he freed himself. He looked across the bed and laughed out loud, or nearly so, as Madeleine bounced up between the pillows, displaying the towel. She made an extravagant gesture, the sort employed by *jongleurs*, and with a joyous silvery laugh exclaimed, "Now we may love to our heart's content."

He dropped the damnable leather hosen onto the floor and, turning back to her, was halted by the sight of a large white moth fluttering and beating against the bed drapes.

"What is it?" Madeleine asked, perplexed and curious to know what had captured his attention so completely. She curled onto her side, following his gaze. "Oh, how beautiful," she cooed, rising to her knees to better see the wondrous creature. She had never seen a moth so large or quite so lovely. Its silvery wings appeared dusted with pearls, unearthly bright and almost luminescent in the unsteady light cast by the fire. She marveled over each thick feathery antenna and snowy wing. All at once she turned to Wulf, her voice edged with alarm. "She will fly into the flames!" The thought of the lovely creature blighted and scorched sickened her.

"They seek the light," he agreed smiling. "Some say they are angels lost in the dark." He made a sudden lithe movement, and, rising on one hip, reached to cup the moth inside his hands. "Perhaps she will tell us?" He held the creature to Madeleine's cheek, murmuring, "Feel the softness of her wings."

"It is soft as snow," she smiled. "No, softer, like angel's wings." Turning her eyes to his, she said, "We should set her free."

They stood before the window, naked, like celebrants in a pagan rite. "Fly away, Velvet Wings," Madeleine whispered as he opened his hands and released the moth into the night. For a long moment they watched her gliding, fluttering course in the moonlight before returning to the warmth of the bed

283

and one another's eager arms.

With each coupling, each sweet coming together, Madeleine had gained greater pleasure from his body and from her own as well. The frequency of their lovemaking led to deeper pleasures, tenderness, and inevitably to innovation. To Wulf it afforded the luxury of restraint. No monk in his meditations could have been more intent as he strived to hold in check his peaking passion until he brought Madeleine to climax and climax again before he took his release with her.

He shifted his weight and, sliding free of her, rolled onto his back. He lay there in the tangle of bedclothes, listening to the thudding cadence of his heart. Madeleine snuggled her way into his arms, wanting his caress and soft words. She pressed her lips to the thatch of fair hair on his chest, murmuring, "Do I please you?"

His head lolled on the pillows and he smiled back at her through half-closed eyes. "If it was possible to die of pleasure, I would lie here beside you a corpse wearing a dead man's skin and a dumbstruck face."

She raised herself on one arm, chuckling, "Am I so fatal?"

His languid gaze swept to the curve of her hip and back. "I swear you are. Look what you have done."

Madeleine's gaze met his and she smiled with wide, bright eyes. "Oh, I do not think he will succumb," she said, smoothing her pale hand through his crisply curled hair to fondle the fat, lazy thing. "See?" She sent him a dazzling look. "He twitches. He will soon be resurrected."

Wulf laughed softly. "Not this night. Here, lay your head close to mine."

"Why?" she asked in a teasing voice, but lay down with her face to his.

"So I may kiss you." He did, fondly, the way one might kiss a child; then, with his lips brushing hers, he said, "I will love you always."

"And I, you," she replied, troubled by the strangeness of his tone. Perhaps it struck a chord deep inside—fear that he, too, would desert her—and prompted her to seek his reassurance. "We will go north soon?"

He put her off with words, as he always did. He did not lie to her, though he did not say the truth.

Later, lying on his pallet, he could not sleep for mourning the loss of her. Soon she would see the truth and turn against him, despise him for what he had done. It occurred to him that in her anger she might confess their sin. But, no, she would only hate him. A worse punishment, for he would be forced to live out his days with the knowledge of it.

Toussaint, the feast of All Saints, came and passed, and with another gray dawn came Jour des Morts, the day of All Souls.

For weeks the passing bells had sounded as each church of Troyes spoke. It was no different at the château's chapel, where clanking bells heralded the high Mass sung for the souls of the dead.

The harsh calls of crows echoed through the autumn woods and in the plot beside the chapel, rain fell upon the tumbled earth of eight freshly filled graves: soldiers of the bishop felled by the pestilence and put into the sodden ground before their bodies cooled.

Chapter Eighteen

The second onslaught of the pestilence put a temporary halt to Guiles de Luchaire's vengeance upon the Bishop of Champagne. Where de Luchaire had formerly been able to muster fifty able villeins, he now had less than thirty at his disposal and had taken to recruiting wandering men-at-arms.

The disastrous battle in the cathedral and the sickness with its lurid dark swellings had combined to dwindle his forces. The pestilence with its promise of a swift and horrible death threatened his holdings as no army could. One steward after another sickened and died and the peasants could be held to the land only by the threat of force.

A beggar astride a fine palfrey with a crutch dangling from his saddle bow made a queer sight. The villein who hailed him from before the gatepost of the imposing château Sézanne called him by name. The beggar dismounted and in a normal gait entered the château. He had no need of his crutch, other than as a disguise, and the villein who had greeted him brandished the crutch to several of his comrades, each hobbling about on it amid laughter and rough horseplay.

In a parlor off the main hall, where a boy strummed on a lute, Guiles de Luchaire reclined on a

286

chaise before a crackling hearthfire. His recovery from a wound suffered in the cathedral was nearly complete. Cushions had been heaped behind him and his half-eaten meal sat off to one side on a small table. The room, with its thick walls, was dank and dim. After the ragged villein entered, a stout woman came with a candle and lit the wall sconces.

De Luchaire's injury, though not severe, had become fouled with dirt and the resultant fever had laid him low. The villein noticed his lord was much improved and because of his own empty stomach, also noticed his appetite was hearty.

Guiles de Luchaire continued to eat as his villein reported all he had seen. He listened, his expression darkening. "You were not able to speak with Odette?"

The villein shook his head. "By the bishop's order no one may enter the gates of the Château de Troyes. They fear the sickness. I have seen the bishop's guards rout beggars, cutting them down with no more thought than if they were vermin." This was an act which in the past the villein would have found no cause to criticize.

"You are certain the Lady Madeleine is still held in the château?"

"Yes, milord. I have seen her walking to and from the chapel with her guard." In the early morning darkness, he had dared to draw near enough to view the courtyard, retreating before the sun rose.

De Luchaire had him describe her, then asked, "And the guard?"

"Tall and fair-headed," the villein replied.

De Luchaire frowned and sipped at his goblet of wine. "The guardsman who stood as proxy in the cathedral?"

"It is likely," the villein agreed. "My eyes were on the lady more and it was yet dark," he said, regretting he had not looked more closely.

"You must find a way to reach Odette," de Luchaire remarked, setting the wine aside. "Without her information, we are blind."

The villein folded his filthy felt hat as he spoke. "There is a way, milord. While I lay hidden I saw a pair of Dominican brethren, pilgrims, stop at the château's gatehouse. The guards would not give them entry to the château, but sent them to the kitchen garth and there a serving woman brought food to them. I and another dressed in Dominican robes could do likewise."

"And if you are questioned?"

"The brethren I saw were not. No one save the woman and the guards who directed them spoke a word."

"Would Odette recognize you in a Dominican's cowl?"

The villein's weather-tanned face creased in a grin. "With or without it, milord."

De Luchaire said no more. He directed his gaze across the room and, snapping his thumb and forefinger together, motioned to the boy who was absently plucking at the strings of the lute. The youth looked up suddenly and silenced the instrument by laying the flat of his hand on the strings.

"Fetch me my priest," he bade the boy. And to the villein he said, "Take yourself to the kitchen and fill your belly. I will call for you later."

De Grailley celebrated the high Mass on the Day of St. Euverte, a week to the day before the bishop's departure for Reims.

Heribert watched closely and with great pride as his young protégé prayed for salvation and peace. Not the peace of the world, but the peace of God—a peace free of evil and sin. De Grailley was Heribert's natural choice to steward his holdings, those lands

288

and fees which came to him with his niece's marriage to the Duke of Burgundy. In de Grailley, Heribert felt confident. The young priest was well versed in dealing with matters of administration and his loyalty and devotion were above reproach.

After de Grailley had sung the triumphant song of the Preface and glorified God in the Sanctus, *"Te igitur, clementissime Pater, per Jesum Christum Filium tauum Dominum nostrum, supplices rogamus ac petimas, uti accepta habeas et benedicas haec,"* he beseeched God, the most merciful Father, to accept and bless the sacrifice of the Mass.

In the silent prayers of the Canon, he prayed for the Bishop of Champagne, under whose direction he labored, and sought God's blessings upon the bishop whose responsibilities were great and whose trials and tribulations were manifold.

That morning before the lauds bells rang and while the château was still in darkness, de Grailley had fetched the Saxon to His Grace's chamber and witnessed the bishop present the young guard with a parchment drawn by the scriveners the day before to which the bishop had applied his holy seal. It was, in essence, the Saxon's freedom and required naught but the Duke of Burgundy's seal to render it binding—a seal to be set upon the safe arrival of the Lady Madeleine, Duchess of Burgundy, in Nevers.

To de Grailley's mind it seemed Roland du Boulay, who wanted no hint of bastardy to taint his heir, would be far more likely to have the Saxon killed later and silenced forever rather than allow him to return to his lands, no matter how far to the north. When de Grailley voiced his thoughts to the bishop, His Grace agreed. "A wise man would," Heribert remarked, smiling. "The stain of murder will be on his soul, not ours."

Before the altar, de Grailley devoutly inclined his head and prayed to the saints that God, through their prayers and merits, would look kindly upon his petitions and grant peace to the souls of the departed. "Grant that we may in all things be made secure by the aid of thy protection. Through the same Christ our Lord. Amen." Then he sang out, *"Hanc igitur oblationem servitutis nostrae . . ."*

Approaching the most holy moments of the Mass, Heribert's breast swelled with thanksgiving to God. Though much had fallen before the onslaught of the evil pestilence, opportunity had arisen from the ashes of destruction and through God's grace he would return to Reims to victory.

There remained only the matter of delivering his niece into her husband's arms. To this end Heribert had ordered the covered *charrette* made ready. The time of his niece's monthly flux had come and gone without event and he would not risk sending her such a distance astride a horse. He had further instructed the Widow Crozet to choose two able serving women to accompany his niece to Nevers. For his niece's protection he chose a dozen of his most able and hardened mercenaries. Regrettably, he could spare no more.

The resurgence of the pestilence had taken a heavy toll among his troops and reports and rumors of lawless marauding bands who sacked unprotected villages and ambushed and murdered travelers had reached his ears, disturbing his peace of mind. This concerned Heribert far more than the sworn vengeance of Guiles de Luchaire, of which no more had been heard. Whether the pestilence had claimed him or he had at last conceded defeat was no longer an issue, for de Luchaire's betrothed was now an irreclaimable bride.

Heribert observed his niece and her guard receive Communion. The mellow candlelight of the altar revealed a rosy coloring high on her cheeks. She glowed of good health and she had gained weight, which suited her very well. Awed by the majesty of God's works, the miracle of life itself, Heribert returned his gaze to the altar and through his prayers humbled himself before God.

That night, the widow ushered her women from the chamber. Wulf set the bar on the door and went to where Madeleine knelt at her *prie-dieu*. At the touch of his hand, she looked up and smiled. They spent the evening in each other's arms, making love in the firelight.

Afterwards they lay together damp with perspiration, his erection lost, her thighs glistening with his sperm. He stroked her and told her that he loved her. In the flickering light his eyes were soft and blue as the sky on a summer's day and the intensity of his whispered words brought tears to Madeleine's eyes.

There was a strangeness in his manner—a sadness, a quiet desperation, as if he would never hold her again. Perhaps it was a single word, a certain hesitation in his voice that first gave form to her suspicions. For weeks she had denied her fears, convincing herself he would truly take her north with him and that they would have all their lives to love.

All lies, she thought, her heart aching. For now she heard it in his voice and saw it in his eyes; he had lied to her.

"It was never your intention to go," she accused, "nor to take me with you."

"You knew I was not free to go," he said, shifting his gaze to the dying fire.

"Liar!" she cried.

His eyes met hers, his brows drawn into an anguished frown. "No. I did not lie to you."

"Oh, yes! Oh, yes! You swore you would take me with you and once your claim was granted, we would marry."

"No, I did not. I said only that I loved you and that

291

is the truth."

"You said all I have repeated."

"I said I wished I might, no more than that," and taking her by the bare shoulder, Wulf said, "Think for a moment, Madeleine. You are wife to the Duke of Burgundy. Do you not realize he would follow you to the ends of the earth to possess your dowry?"

She angrily flung his hand from her shoulder. "You are a seducer, an adulterer!"

The firelight blazed up in his eyes, cold and hard as ice. "If it pleases you," he said in a curt tone, "though the sin is not mine alone." He told her all, for she had guessed the better half.

"How long have you known of my uncle's intention to send me to Nevers a week hence? And do not lie to me!"

"This day, before High Mass."

"Why did you not tell me?"

"I wanted to hold you one last time," he said honestly, glancing away to avoid the dark accusing eyes, the pale face, and bitter twist of her mouth as she spoke the words.

"Coward! I am ashamed to think I cared for you!" She snatched her night dress from the floor and, covering her nakedness, fled across the chamber and flung herself into bed. She burrowed beneath the bedclothes like a mole. Even so, he heard the sound of her muffled weeping.

After a time he went and leaned over her and called her name softly. She struck a blow at him, blunted by the heavy woolen coverlet. He went away without another word, back to his pallet.

In the garderobe he removed the stubble from his jaw with a small, straight-bladed knife. The handle was fashioned from antler and the blade was of a type used by physicians to let blood—an instrument far more effective for slitting throats than dispatching whiskers. His thoughts strayed; his hand slipped. The sting of the blade jerked his attention back to the dull luster of the metal mirror. He had nicked himself. It was no larger than a pinprick, but the bright red surprise of his own blood shook him back to reality. Once she had hungered for his touch; now she shunned him, hated him for the coward he was. It was ended. She would never be his, he reminded himself, and, rinsing the blade in the basin, continued to scrape at his face.

Chapter Nineteen

On the third day of December 1348, a great procession of wagons, soldiers, and clerics trundled past the gatehouse of the Château de Troyes. They moved beneath a leaden sky and into a wind cold and sharp as a dagger's blade.

Several hours' journey found the travelers at the village of Ste. Savine, where the wind-blown leaves cluttered the hedgerows and curious peasants came from their huts to stare.

A *charrette* and a goods wagon escorted by a troop of twelve heavily armed guardsmen turned away from the main body of the procession and onto the old Roman road. Their eventual destination was Nevers.

Throughout the weary day, a single horseman followed the smaller party at a distance. The sun set quickly and early that time of year and as the afternoon drew to a close, the horseman spurred his mount. Skirting the party, he galloped ahead to where his lord, Guiles de Luchaire, twenty mounted men, and eighteen bowmen lay in ambush. The fact that the bishop's escort numbered only a dozen men ensured his lord's resounding success, for he had expected a much larger force.

Rocked by the sway and jounce of the *charrette*, the two serving women, Odette Marsi and a small matronly woman, whom the Widow Crozet considered to be of sound and practical judgment, drowsily nodded their heads.

Odette woke with a sudden start. Outside, the gray light of a day was fading and, seeing her mistress was fast asleep, she pushed aside the window-covering to peer at the countryside. It would be soon, Odette thought, viewing each turn of the road, each rise, with a sharpening sense of anticipation.

Wulf and another of the guardsmen had ridden ahead of the party all day, scouring the roadsides for danger. Hour after weary hour they plodded onward. For all their vigilance, they sighted only an occasional bird.

The folded parchment, stowed carefully inside his leather jerkin, crinkled with his movement as he turned in his saddle to glance back at the *charrette*. Madeleine had not spoken a word to him since that last evening before the fire. Her icy silence tortured him. Never had he suffered such pain and self-abasement over a female. The guilt, admittedly, was his. He had fallen victim first to her charms and then to his own lust, knowing full well to love her was folly. She could never be his and the inevitable result would be the pain and longing he now felt. Her carefree smiles and loving glances that had been for his eyes alone had turned to icy, hate-filled stares for which he had no defense.

Ahead, the bleak, frost-burnt forest closed in a deep tangle of thickets. He called out his intention to rein his horse toward the road, thus avoiding the brindled snare of thorns and interlacing vines. That there was no answering call did not at first pierce his consciousness. Directly before him a crazed geometry of barren branches barred his path. He leaned low over his horse's neck and, raising an arm to shield his head, moved forward.

A hail of arrows launched from the roadside underbrush rained down upon the party. Wulf saw at least five guardsmen topple from their horses and another go down as his horse fell under him. The lead horse of the *charrette* sagged in its harness, panicking the remaining horses and sending them squealing and blind with terror into the ditch. The *charrette* lurched forward, swayed precariously at the road's edge, then crashed into the ditch, coming to rest on its side.

The air vibrated with the thrum of arrows. Wulf, shielded to some extent by the latticework of branches, hugged the neck of his shuddering horse. Several arrows fell around him. Another, its distance spent, struck his arm and tumbled harmlessly to the ground.

The cold air exploded with the screams of men and horses. With a thunderous crash, twenty heavily armed horsemen burst from the dense brush and charged into the destruction, swinging broadswords and axes. Their leader, garbed in a surcoat of blue lake, hacked a path toward the overturned *charrette*.

Wulf drew his sword and took up his shield. He did not give a thought to the worn helmet dangling from his saddle bow, and kicking his heels into the bay's ribs, joined the half-dozen beleaguered guardsmen defending the *charrette*. In the frenzied and brutal disorder of panicked horses, broadswords, and axes, Wulf battered his way toward the *charrette*. Twice the blue lake surcoat flashed before him, and both times he was prevented from striking a blow by the unrelenting onslaught of a florid-faced youth swinging an axe. Wulf's shield was slammed against his still-mending arm again and again, each blow an agony.

The youth, though clearly inexperienced, fought with the reckless fury of a demon. In a bold move, the youth swung his horse into Wulf's bay and rearing in his stirrups, flailed the axe. The youth's daring but foolhardy maneuver fully exposed his mid-section. Wulf's blade pierced him at the waist, just below his mail vest, pitching him from the saddle and into another horseman.

Inside the *charrette*, all that was mobile shifted violently to one side. The three women screamed and pulled themselves from a tangle of arms and legs and twisted clothing.

Bruised and dizzy, Madeleine crawled toward the rear of the *charrette*, scraping her hands as she pounded on the balky wooden door. Odette scrambled after her, clambering from the ditch on all fours just in time to prevent the Lady Madeleine from fleeing into the forest.

Odette grabbed her first by the hem of her cape, then by her shoulder. Madeleine turned on her like a furious little beast, kicking and clawing. The pair went down, tumbling in the ditch, screaming and hissing. Odette, unquestionably the larger and stouter, struck Madeleine's jaw a blow with her fist.

Stunned but infuriated, Madeleine paid her back in kind. And before Odette could lay hands on her again, Madeleine kicked her solidly in the chest, knocking the air from her lungs.

In an instant, Madeleine was on her feet and running. Branches whipped at her clothing and stung her face. A thunderous crashing sound overtook her, and, with a sudden jolt, it felt as though her spine snapped. She was pulled through the punishing tangle of branches and onto the back of a lunging horse. She screamed, struggling until she realized the hand that clutched the reins was as familiar as her own.

Wulf shoved her face to the horse's neck and, leaning over her, sent the bay forward, laying down a path through the brittle thicket. The din and clangor of the battle echoed through the barren woods. At one point, they heard curses and shouts and the crash of swiftly moving horses behind them.

The sun set quickly and the sounds of the horsemen died away. Wulf reasoned de Luchaire would not pursue them in the dark and let his exhausted horse choose its own pace—a walk.

Where the trees thinned he descended a brushy slope and, coming upon a shallow brook, sent the bay splashing along its course for a while before veering off to higher ground.

Madeleine sat perched before him. The punishment of the afternoon had taken its toll. Her every muscle ached and the pommel of the saddle had battered her until she was tender.

They rode in silence, neither hazarding a word. The woods were very still, frost-scented and smelling of leaves in the chill of a December night.

When Wulf spoke his voice was hoarse from the long silence and more of a whisper. He asked if she was hurt. She would not answer him in words, but shook her head, resisting the arm that attempted to ease her back against him for warmth. He said, "There is no hope of finding shelter for you," and after a pause, "A fire would only betray us. If we are out of the wind, it will be some comfort at least." Madeleine made no reply. She was willing to follow his instructions, but stubbornly refused to speak to him.

He found a place for them by the creek, where the spring rains and swift-fed waters had eaten away the stony bank and made a cave beneath the overhanging roots of a large tree. He unsaddled the bay and wiped him down as best he could with handfuls of dry grass gathered at the bank's edge. There was water aplenty standing in quiet little pools, but scarcely anything for the bay to browse. He tethered the horse close by and ducked beneath the tree roots where Madeleine lay curled in her cape, shivering.

She flinched at the touch of his hands and glared at him when he offered her a place inside his arms. "Hate me if it pleases you," he told her, "but do not be a fool. The air is killing cold tonight." He had learned long ago that lying full upon the frozen

298

ground was a fool's bed. It was far better to set one's back against a bank or a tree, with the knees flexed, so that a cape made a cozy tent.

Madeleine reluctantly allowed him to position her between his knees. She lay back in the curve of his body, blessedly warm. The stirred memories brought tears to her eyes, but the hatefulness in her heart would not let her cry; had he not sold her for his freedom?

Wrapped in their capes, beneath the tangle of roots, they fell into a fitful sleep. The noisy clatter of a woodpecker above their heads woke them.

Madeleine relieved her bladder behind a bush, and at the creek dipped her hands in the numbing cold water and splashed her face. A splattering sound behind her caused her to swivel her head. She saw the foam of urine on the ground and, raising her eyes, caught him in the act. She turned her gaze back to the creek. In the cold light his maleness was small and shriveled—not the swollen hard shaft of the firelight.

She rose to her feet and stretched her aching body. Her empty stomach grumbled for food. She regretted now that she had refused the comfits offered by the mousy serving woman, but in her present state of mind she was prepared to starve before she uttered a word of complaint.

With Madeleine again seated before him, he followed the meander of the creek until the dense growth thinned to mature trees. They rode south, generally, through forest, hearing only the sighing of the wind through the bare branches and the muffled slur of leaves beneath the bay's hooves.

Several times Wulf sought out higher ground to rest the horse and scan the silent woods. If de Luchaire followed, there was no sign of him.

By late afternoon the forest gave way to pasture land. Beyond the haze of barren treetops open fields stretched beneath a sky layered thick with clouds, gray and mottled as the scales of a fish.

Wulf was certain that Madeleine must be as hungry as he. She refused to speak and his every attempt at conversation had been met with an armed and icy silence.

He chose a downward-sloping track and turned the bay toward the open fields. Where there were fields, there would logically be peasants to work them and, hopefully, food and shelter.

As they topped a rocky clef in the hill, they came upon a boy carrying a bundle of sticks on his back. His unkempt brown hair hung lank to his shoulders and his eyebrows grew in a straight line. He stared at them with wary black eyes before heaving his burden to the ground.

He did not speak but bobbed his head in response to Wulf's questions. At first, Wulf thought him a mute. But when Wulf asked, "Whose lands are these?" the boy replied in a frail voice, "The Lord Hourdibaught's," and with a gesture of his scrawny arm pointed beyond the crest of the ridge, advising, "His château be there."

"They are my mother's kinsmen," Madeleine said, although she did not address Wulf directly. She knew there would be food and shelter for them but said no more, thinking he could be damned and do as he pleased.

The boy had called it a château. But when they saw it, the rambling timber-and-limestone structure was more of a huge manor house, and ill-kept. They would have thought it uninhabited had it not been for the curl of smoke rising from the chimney.

Wulf set the bay toward the house through a thickly overgrown field. The skeletal stalks and dry seed heads of bull weed and thistle swayed above the frost-burnt undergrowth. A tangle of brambles clawed at their boots and burrs snagged the hems of their cloaks.

Halfway through the field Madeleine turned to him with astonished eyes. "It is music—do you hear it?" She would not have broken her spiteful silence except that the distant eerie sound, coupled with the deserted appearance of the house, filled her with a sudden overwhelming sense of foreboding.

"It is the wind," he replied. He heard nothing but the rustling crash of the horse through the dead weeds.

"No, music," she insisted. He did not reply. The bay forged onward laying down the brittle stalks. The scent of food reached Wulf's nostrils long before he, too, heard the plaintive notes of lute, pipe, and drum.

As they drew nearer, they saw the doors stood open to the chill of the December dusk and that a throng of people danced and laughed and sang before a blazing hearth.

At the door no one questioned their presence or even noticed them. The musicians played above the voices and laughter and the dancers swayed to and fro.

"There is my aunt," Madeleine exclaimed, noticing her mother's elder sister, Beautrice, seated on a bench near the hearth. Without another word Madeleine dashed off, threading her way through the merrymakers. Wulf watched after her for a moment, then collected the bay's reins and led him away to the stables.

Madeleine breathlessly embraced her aunt and kissed her cheek. "Madame-ma-tante, do you not remember me? I am your sister Isobel's daughter, Madeleine." But the face so like her mother's remianed indifferent, staring with lifeless, unblinking eyes as if she neither saw nor heard. In her hands she clutched a rosary and her lips moved silently as she twirled the beads between her trembling fingers.

Madeleine drew back, repelled by her strangeness and, looking helplessly around the crowded hall, saw a male cousin among the dancers—a young man who would have been her sisters' age.

She caught his arm as the line of dancers swayed past, and dragging him and his fat partner to one side, questioned, "Who are these people?" He laughed, making a sound that was more of a squeal. "The spirits of the dead," he replied in a shrill voice, and whirled away with the fat girl in the russet gown and pleated coif.

Madeleine's startled gaze darted after them. She wandered across the room like a lost lamb and, when she could not locate Wulf among the throng, a cold unreasoning terror gripped her heart.

The moment she saw him standing in the open doorway, she ran, dodging the dancers, and clung to his arm; she gazed up at him with large, grateful eyes as if his appearance was a blessing from God. At the first opportunity, she whispered in his ear, "They are all mad."

Gazing over the crowded hall, Wulf saw that the merrymakers, staggering to and fro and laughing unrestrainedly, were so immersed in their own self-indulgence that they were not even aware of his and Madeleine's presence. "Drunk," he replied softly, side-stepping a tipsy woman dancer who careened into a stork of a man garbed in a green and gold jupon.

Wulf made his way to where a large pot of wine and spices bubbled over a brazier beside the hearth-fire. Earthenware bowls lay scattered over the long trestle table; judging from the stains of food and wine, all appeared used. He chose a bowl and held it over the flames with the fire tongs.

Madeleine watched, thinking him as addled as the others. "What are you doing?" she asked anxiously. He merely shrugged and replied, "God roasts sinners in hell to cleanse their souls," and with a sudden smile, reasoned, "Perhaps it serves as well for bowls." She smiled back at his foolishness and hung at his elbow, unwilling to lose sight of him for even an instant.

While their bowl cooled, he took his dagger and sliced a slab of meat from the overdone carcass of a young hog spitted in the hearth. Rivulets of fat trickled into the flames, spitting and hissing while they stood before the brazier dipping wine into their bowl.

The long table was littered with crumbled cakes and chunks of bread, the ruins of more than one meal. And though much remained, the stains of spilt wine, assorted bones, and the dregs of vegetables looked too unappetizing to tempt even a crow.

The musicians and the dancers went on indefatigably as if they were possessed, driven by some irresistible compulsion to strum and dance until they dropped.

Balancing the bowl of wine, Madeleine followed Wulf to a bench by the far wall. She sat beside him and silently chewed on her share of the greasy pork, washing it down with gulps of steaming spicy wine.

An old man, laughing and breathless, whose face was scarlet from exertion, teetered before them. Wulf, biting a chunk of pork from his dagger, looked up invitingly. "Sit down, grandfather; catch your wind."

The old man gave a drunken grin and flopped down on the bench beside Madeleine. He introduced himself as a physician and told of his life in Paris and how he had traveled south with a company of nobles and thus came to share in Lord Hourdibaught's hospitality. "They all fled from the sickness," he said with a broad gesture of his arm. "I told them it was useless. The disease is everywhere. It abates, then returns with a vengeance. They cannot hide from it anymore than they may hide from their own scent."

"Have they not yet found a cure for it in Paris?" Madeleine asked, for the finest physicians in the world were in Paris or so she had always heard.

The old man's face convulsed in laughter. "In Paris, yes, every trickster sells one, madame," he brayed. "But no, there is no cure, no cure for the wrath of God. With these eyes I have seen the sickness kill within hours, at times almost instantly. They spit blood, their tongues blacken, and they die."

"But it is not here?" Madeleine asked with terrified eyes.

"No," he smiled, "but the night is yet young, madame."

Madeleine edged closer to Wulf, pressing her thigh to his. He continued to chew on the pork, asking the old man a host of questions. By what route had he traveled and what were the conditions to the north? It made no sense to Madeleine to talk of roads and wars and truces. Finally, she made a motion to rise. Wulf pressed his hand over hers and with his eyes bade her stay.

She remained at his side amid the dancing and debauchery. Time and again her gaze fell upon the tragic visage of her aunt. She was seated as Madeleine had first viewed her, her face pale as death, unmoving save for her fingers plucking at the beads and her lips feverishly mouthing the words of salvation.

The old man went on as tirelessly as the dancers until without warning, and in the middle of a word, his chin dropped upon his chest and he was silent. Madeleine sent Wulf a terrified glance and tugged at his hand. "He is dead!" she gasped. "Only asleep," he advised with a smile. Madeleine saw it was so; the old man's chest and protruding belly, which were one, rose and fell with each breath.

"We should go now," Madeleine urged. She said it thrice, each time more vehemently, before at last he answered. "There was rain falling when I settled Loki in the stable. Here it is at least dry." He drew a square of cloth from inside his leather jerkin and scrupulously cleaned the dagger.

"We cannot sleep here," she insisted with a fearful look, recalling the old man's words.

"We will find a quiet place," he promied and,

leading her eyes with his, indicated the darkened passageway at the opposite end of the hall. From the stable he had noticed a rear door not twenty paces across a small garth. The door to a storeroom perhaps, he thought, and reckoned it should be at the end of the passageway. Convenient if they should have to leave quickly. He replaced the dagger in its sheath and rose from the bench, knowing she would follow.

The dancers flowed rhythmically across the hall to the haunting melody of lute, pipe, and drum. Caught in their midst, Wulf took Madeleine's hands and in an undertone asked, "Do you know the ways of dancing?"

"Yes," she breathed, impatiently pulling at his hands. She wanted only to be away from the mad chase of skipping, swaying lunatics.

He held her fast, confessing, "I have never danced." She looked at him first with disbelief. Did he mean to join in their insanity? Then she pleaded, "Please, this place frightens me."

"Dance with me this once," he coaxed. "Show me how it is done." He looked very young with his wide-set blue eyes and boyish smile.

She would have refused had it not been for the sight of her small hands in his. How large his hands were, young and strong. And yes, she thought, vulnerable, for death cared not for youth or strength.

The dancers swirled around them and with a shudder Madeleine understood. It was fear she saw in the faces of the dancers and fear that echoed in their trilling laughter. How many, she wondered, in a few days hence or even hours, would lie dead without a priest or mourners to bury them or a grave to call their own?

Madeleine raised her eyes to his, and, in the glittering brevity of a glance, like something found unexpectedly, realized she had never truly known love until that instant. The sudden rush of emotion brought tears to sting her eyes.

She stepped lightly away, drawing him after her, smiling through her tears. He was awkward but willing and Madeleine could not help but laugh at his enthusiasm.

Across the hall they galloped, Madeleine clinging to him with both hands, until he swept her nearly off her feet with a boxy flourish and into the darkened passageway. She staggered against him, her every sense reeling, and in a merry breathless voice, giggled, "I never thought of you as clumsy." He hugged her to him in a rough caress and, laughing softly, agreed that Saxons were seldom known for their grace.

Directness of purpose, perhaps, for looking back she saw he had steered her across the hall and into the darkened door arch—away from the mad chase of dancers. Even so, a shiver of fear passed through her.

No light entered from the long, slotted windows and the darkness of the passageway was absolute. Madeleine groped after him through the dark, gripping his hand. Down the length of the passageway the music and laughter faded and mingled with the restless sighing of the rain.

At the end of the hall they entered a room cluttered with what appeared to be a tumble of furnishings. Across the room's length, Wulf tried the door and stepped out into the swampy garth. Keeping beneath the dripping eaves, he moved a short distance from the door and relieved himself, advising her to do the same. In the brief moments when Madeleine hiked her skirts and squatted, careful so as not to dip her gown in the mud, she saw the night was as bleak as he had said: wet and cold, and no less forbidding than the passageway.

She did not mention leaving again, but followed him silently back into the passageway and settled beside him on the cold stones. From where he sat beneath the open slotted window, he could see the

306

stable and any sound would carry well on the damp air.

Madeleine huddled against him. He made a place for her under his arm. Against the warmth of his body, she was no longer cold. Her bladder was no longer uncomfortably full; she was neither hungry nor thirsty, yet the maelstrom of thoughts which spun through her mind tortured her. She turned to him, whispering in the dark. "What will become of us?" For a moment he said nothing; then, pressing her head against his chest, he brushed her forehead with his lips. "We will go to Nevers. You, milady, will be the Duchess of Burgundy and I will be a soldier."

She raised her face to his. "No, you will be free."

"I will never be free," he said softly, his words warm against her face.

Her eyes opened wide in the dark. "But the parchment; my uncle?"

"Without the sight of you, what purpose would my freedom serve? I will stay and offer my sword to your Lord Burgundy."

"No, not for my sake! No, you must not! I could not bear to see you, knowing we might never share more than a glance, a word."

"If it is all I may have, it will be enough."

Madeleine pressed her face to his chest, crying, "Better if I were to die here and now."

"Do not say such words."

"It is true. They could not quarrel over me then. They would have all they wanted and no more use for me, no more than if I were a dead goat."

"Shhh," he murmured and drew her deeper in his arms. But she would not be silent. "They are to blame. Because of them, I hated you, believed you had sold me for your freedom!"

He trailed his lips over her cheek, her ear, saying, "You were never the price. I would give my life for you, Madeleine."

307

In the dark, her lips sought his and the hand she had set on his thigh moved instinctively to cover his maleness.

He pulled his lips away and closed his hand over hers. "Not here," he breathed. "There will be another time, a place, I promise." As much as he longed for her, he could not dispel the thought of a drunken reveler stumbling over them in the darkness.

In the recess of the slotted window they slept huddled in their cloaks. Wulf was not certain what woke him, the rain striking his shoulder or the sounds from the hall. Not music and laughter, but the solid crack of furniture colliding, shouts, and groans. The sickness had come.

He closed a hand over Madeleine's mouth and whispered close to her ear, awakening her and pulling her to her feet. "It is time we leave," he said and with no other explanation hustled her down the passageway.

They ran through the drilling rain to the stable. Madeleine watched dumbly as he saddled a chestnut mare. "That is not Loki," she blinked, still thick-headed from sleep. "No," he smiled. "It is your horse; do you not recognize it?"

Their horses sloshed from the mire of the garth. Through the darkness and scissor-slant of rain Madeleine could see nothing of the house. Later, as they entered the woods, she asked why they had left in the darkness. He told her what he had heard. His words sent a shiver of horror through her. She thought of her aunt's pathetic face and . . . Tightening her fingers on the reins, she asked no more questions.

By midday the sharpening wind had blown away the rain and polished the sky a deep pewter gray. In the forest the leaves mushed to pulp beneath their horses' drubbing hooves and from the barren trees, blackbirds called.

The gentle rolling hillocks gave way to rocky ground which in places rose steeply through the sparse woods. At evening, the creeping blue cold numbed their hands and faces. When they stopped to rest their horses beneath the vast gray sky, Wulf lifted the wineskin from his saddle bow and offered it to Madeleine. From the weight of the skin, she suspected it was barely half-full. She took only a swallow and passed it back. He also took but a single swallow and replaced the cap. He asked if she was too weary to ride further; he could see that she was. Her face was pinched and colorless from the cold and her hands in his were like ice. "No," she said, "let us ride until dark."

As they traveled, the forest was broken by high meadows overgrown with gorse and briar thickets. They rode on until darkness closed around them and it seemed they were two alone in the vast dark world. Single-file they plodded down a hillside dense with cedars. Madeleine crouched in her cape, cold and exhausted. She had no feeling in her hands or feet and there was no way she might shift in the saddle to ease the ache low in her back. When her mare halted abruptly, she nearly toppled from the saddle.

She raised her chin from the moist warmth of her hooded cape to see Wulf's back before her and her mare nosing Loki's hindquarters.

Wulf turned in his saddle. "There is a campfire beyond that stand of cedars," he said softly. "Wait here." Without another word he prodded the bay forward. It was all Madeleine could mange to keep her horse from following. The obstinate mare tossed her head and gnashed the bit between her teeth, determined to follow the stallion. Madeleine's brain was numb as her hands and feet and slow to grasp his words. She watched him go, suddenly frightened at being left alone in the dark.

Nestled among the cedars, the orange-red eye of a

fire glowed against the night. Wulf moved closer. He had neither seen nor smelled the smoke and that puzzled him, but as he closed ground, the reason was clear. A north wind blew, and that same north wind sent the smoke rolling away close to the ground. He saw the scene fully now: the leaping fire, the carcass of what appeared to be a sheep spitted over it, an old shepherd, a dog, and perhaps two dozen browsing sheep, half-concealed by the darkness and the close-set cedars.

Wulf motioned Madeleine to follow. When she drew close to his horse's flank, he nudged the bay with his knee. The horse picked its way down the hill. The sleeping dog, at once aware of the riders, leapt to its feet and barked furiously until its master called it back to his side.

The old shepherd rose from his haunches, adjusted his mangy sheepskin cape, and stepped forward to welcome them. "Warm yourselves," he offered, and boasted that he was roasting his finest, fattest ewe. "What does it matter?" he said with a low laugh. "I will soon be dead and the loss of a good ewe will be of no consequence to me." The dog hung at its master's leg, warily watching the strangers dismount.

"Dine with me," the shepherd insisted, relating how he had always desired to eat at the same table with a knight and his lady. "'Tis a pity I have but rocks for furnishings," the shepherd said, and, with a gallant gesture, offered them their choice of stones.

They shared the last of their wine with him and ate their fill while the shepherd regaled them with tales he had heard from passing troubadours.

The morning dawned cold and gray with a raw wind whipping at their capes. They awoke to find their horses contentedly cropping the meager grass. But of the old shepherd, his dog, and flock there was no sign.

Madeleine stretched and, with eyes squinted against the morning glare, edged close to the remains of the fire. There was still some heat in the blowing ash and she warmed her hands. The night seemed long ago, like a dream or a half-forgotten memory. Glancing around, she saw naught but a few gnawed bones and the circle of cold stones.

As they rode through the morning, the sky cleared and sunlight burst through the last fleeting clouds. They passed a handful of peasant huts, all deserted. Scrawny chickens scratched the frost-burnt ground and a pig rooted in a withered garden plot.

Before one thatched hut, an old woman sat humming to herself, rocking to and fro. Her thin white hair riffled in the breeze like the fluff of a weed pod and her gaze was set in another world. She seemed neither to see nor hear them. From the open doorway, they saw an old man lying on the floor, hands folded upon his chest; laid out beside him were a young man, a woman, and two small children, all dead.

Later they came upon a road marked with wagon ruts and, from all appearances, heavily traveled. Wulf was wary of the road, for in such rough country it was only reasonable that de Luchaire would search there first.

It was not long before they overtook a peddler and his pack horses. Bundled to his nose against the cold in an assortment of multi-colored clothing, he looked more of a wandering jester than a merchant. He was bound for the cardinal's city of Clamecy, he told them, adding, "It is but a scant distance south." His nose was red from the cold—or a lifetime of imbibing—and he invited them to ride along with him, commenting that he would be glad for their company and conversation.

"Clamecy?" Wulf asked the peddler a second time to be certain he had not misunderstood. He marveled at the distance he and Madeleine had covered. Surely, he thought, de Luchaire would have grown weary of the chase long ago and returned to Sézanne.

Late that December afternoon they rode into Clamecy with the peddler. At the town gate, guards halted all who approached. One guard, a skinny, slack-jawed youth whose straggling auburn hair flowed from beneath his helmet and bounced over his shoulders, passed among those queued before the gates. There were peasants returning to the city with their cattle, a pair of foot-sore brethren on a holy pilgrimage, and several merchants, their assistants, and pack horses. The guard examined each with narrowed eyes, questioning, "Are you ill? No one who is ill may enter the city." At last he came to the peddler, the young soldier, and his wife. The guard's eyes lingered a moment on the pretty face framed by the white coif, then signaled to the soldiers manning the gates to allow the group to proceed.

Inside the gates, Clamecy bustled with the daily routine of living. Wood smoke scented the chill air and the aroma of food hung in the streets. Wulf and Madeleine bid the merchant farewell and went in search of a stable for their horses.

They found one not far from the town gate—a low-beamed structure whose interior was dark, humid with the heat of horses, and fragrant with hay and manure. A man and several boys were at work clearing fouled bedding from stalls and forking it into a rickety hand cart.

The stableman advised them they would find no lodgings in the city. "It is filled to overflowing," he said, explaining, "Our cardinal has returned from Avignon. He is a holy man and people have come from far and wide to seek sanctuary from the pestilence. You are fortunate to have come on this day," he told them. "Tonight there will be a holy procession and all may join in with their prayers to protect our city from the evil sickness." The burly stableman with his large head and bushy brows went on to say that it was the holiest of days for the bones of St. Martin would be carried through the streets.

Wulf listened to what the man had to say, paid him in silver coin, and instructed him to feed and water the horses, but not to unsaddle them. The stableman nodded his large head; he would do as the soldier asked. But as they turned to leave, he said, "Stay and be blessed by our cardinal. If you cannot find lodgings, I have a storage room you may let reasonably; it is there in the rear of the stable."

"If I can find nothing else," Wulf replied, though his intentions were to fill the wineskin, which he lifted from the saddle bow and slung over his shoulder, to take a meal at a tavern, and be on his way.

"At least we would have privacy," Madeleine whispered hopefully, for in the taverns and inns all slept in one great room. Wulf steered her into the street. "This time of year it is probably stacked with raw sheepskins," he told her, pointing out that not only would it stink abominably, but their clothing would hold the stench for days. "We will find a place in the woods and you can help me to build a fire. You will be twice warm," he promised with a smile and squeezed her cold fingers in his.

They made their way through the crowded streets. Near the square, a group of snotty-nosed children shouted and chased hoops. Farther along the street, they noticed people crossing over to avoid a tall house which abutted a tinner's shop. As they drew even, they saw a strip of black cloth hanging from the door, marking it to all as a plague house.

The square was jammed with people. Dogs ran about yapping and there was a babble of voices and boisterous activity. The aroma of roasting nuts hung in the air. Hawkers sold chestnuts while others sold apples from willow baskets and a man carrying a lantern sold candles to the faithful. Crowds had already gathered on the plaza before the cathedral and also before the many taverns. Participants in the procession milled before the church; many carried huge masks, large enough to cover a man's head and shoulders. Some masks were fashioned in the likeness of animals, while others were meant to portray saints. And those men who posed as saints carried tall stilts and wore long gowns which had been tucked into their belts so that they might walk about without their stilts.

Neither Madeleine nor Wulf had ever seen anything quite like it and, after purchasing several apples and a pocketful of chestnuts, stood watching and munching like children at a fair.

After a time Wulf reminded her, "The wineskin must be filled." But Madeleine, with a merry smile, begged to watch a while longer. She was still cold and exhausted, but the colorful scene before her and the excitement had raised her flagging spirits.

It pleased Wulf to see her smile and so he remained. He scanned the square, noting there was no shortage of wine and ale in Clamecy. He counted six taverns from where he stood and many of the onlookers, as well as members of the procession, were heartily drinking and reeling about unsteadily.

Guiles de Luchaire pushed his way through the crowd and stood before the tavern with an ale tankard in his hand. Several of his villeins followed him out into the chill winter dusk and watched as the procession took shape.

Before the cathedral all manner of persons swelled the crowd: priests, brethren, altar boys in flowing robes, and men carrying large kettle drums. The cathedral was as large and as grand as St. Pierre's, though much of the cloister and a section of the tower were still under construction.

Moment by moment the light of day faded as reed torches dipped in pitch were lit and candles appeared like bright clear stars. A gilded litter bearing a statue of St. Martin and borne by eight robed brethren emerged from the cathedral's ornate doors. A second litter, much like the first, held a golden bejeweled

314

reliquary box.

Trumpets sounded on the plaza and the cardinal appeared on the balcony of his residence. A cheer went up from the crowd, then all fell silent as the cardinal blessed those below. Afterward the procession marched from the square with the deafening accompaniment of pipe, drum, and holy chant. Many of the onlookers rushed from the sidelines to join in, adding their voices and the flames of their candles to the din and the blaze of torchlight.

Guiles de Luchaire's interest was captured by two cloaked figures who crossed the square by an oblique path in the wake of the procession. Obviously a man and a woman and young, for the man's hand was clipped protectively on the woman's shoulders as lovers were apt to do. The man was tall. Halfway across the square, he lowered his head to speak to her. She looked up and it seemed to de Luchaire that she was laughing, though he could not make out the sound above the voices of the crowd behind him.

The woman walked beside the man with a light, smooth step and though both wore cloaks with hoods which all but covered their faces, there was something familiar about the tilt of her head, the set of her small shoulders, and the confident step. De Luchaire was suddenly alert. It was she, he felt certain. The cold and the barrenness of the countryside had forced them into Clamecy, just as he had hoped. He turned and motioned to several of his villeins who hung nearby, lounging against the tavern wall.

Madeleine talked as they strolled toward one of the taverns. The sign which hung above the door arch of the stone-and-timber building caught Madeleine's eye and coaxed a laugh from her. It was lopsided with peeling paint and displayed the profiles of two women joined at the back of the head, one more homely than the other, and named, appropriately enough, "Two Faces." Madeleine pointed to the sign. "Look," she giggled, "Their noses are even longer than the nose the artist from Arles gave to me."

Wulf agreed, remarking it was a pity. "Such a nose would be useful for traveling at night," he teased with a smile. "We could hang a lantern from it."

"At least my nose would be warm," she laughed, remarking that at the moment her nose was so cold she could hardly feel it. The thunder of drums drew Madeleine's attention to the top of the square where torches blazed and the clergy, with holy relics, led a throng of faithful toward them. "If we do not hurry," Madeleine urged, "we, too, will be marching."

The pair took two steps forward, then, without warning, Wulf's hand tightened on her shoulder and brought her to an abrupt halt. Silly goose, she thought, smiling up at him.

Only then did she see Guiles de Luchaire and two villeins, swords drawn, coming toward them. From the corner of her eye she saw three others approaching.

"Step away from him," de Luchaire ordered, moving swiftly to within striking distance, motioning Madeleine to him with his left hand.

Madeleine looked into the square face jutting beneath the soft felt lithrope with great dark eyes that grew larger as she stared. She did not stir, but remained as if her feet were rooted to the ground, knowing the instant she stepped away they would cut Wulf down there before her eyes. They were six and he had not even a sword in his hand.

De Luchaire took a step forward. Wulf could do naught but watch helplessly. "Step away," de Luchaire repeated. His voice hardened and his eyes shifted to Madeleine, a tight hard smile on his lips. When she shook her head in refusal, he reached out with his left hand and gripped her shoulder with an iron grasp. "You were pledged to me by your father's hand. You are my wife and after tonight there will be no doubt of it," he said with gloating satisfaction.

Madeleine's first impulse was to shout at him that he was too late—there was no virginal bride to consummate. Instead, and perhaps unwisely, she threw off his hand, shouting, "You have no need of a wife; young boys suit you better. Have you forgotten the boy *jongleur* who leapt from the tavern window?" she screamed, and tearing the coif from her cropped hair, spat, "I have not forgotten!"

De Luchaire's features contorted with rage. His heavy hand struck Madeleine full in the face, knocking her to her knees.

In that instant Wulf lunged at him, seizing the arm that held the sword, and with all his strength thrust the sword upwards into the startled face. The hilt struck de Luchaire's jaw a stunning blow and sent him sprawling backward onto the ground.

Wulf spun 'round, grasped Madeleine's arm, took two running steps, and veered into the pitch black alleyway beside the Two Faces Tavern.

The villeins sprang forward, swords at the ready, but with their lord down howling with pain and fury and the lady in the Saxon's arms, they hedged fearing if they struck at the Saxon they would maim the lady as well.

De Luchaire swayed to his feet, cursing and roaring with rage, his battered jaw bleeding freely. "After them!" he bawled, and, ranting like a madman, sent half his men 'round the square in hopes of blocking their escape. With his remaining men at his heels, he charged into the alleyway.

The foul-smelling passage between the tavern and the close-set and shuttered houses was cluttered with obstacles which reared up from the darkness to check their headlong pace. They dashed through a maze of intersecting alleyways, poultry yards, pig stys, cattle pens, and drainage ditches.

A chill surged through Madeleine—the terrifying feeling of strained muscles and of her feet stumbling over the ground. She must run faster and faster, she thought, and though her mind urged her on, her body refused. She sagged against Wulf; her heart pounding and a strange thundering sound ringing in her ears. Her breath came in explosive gasps; she could no longer swallow. But Wulf's hand, which had not loosened its grip on her wrist from the moment he had turned on de Luchaire, pulled her forward.

Behind them the shouts and plunging footfalls gained ground, and before them the roar of voices and slow roll of drums reverberated off the night air.

Wulf slowed his pace, changing directions abruptly, and dragged Madeleine after him into a garbage-filled alleyway. Plainly, she could run no farther. He, exhausted as well, could not carry her. It seemed their only hope was to lose themselves in the mélée of marching people. Through the narrow gaps between houses they caught glimpses of the torch-light blazing against the darkness.

They burst from the alleyway and into the twisting, gyrating mob of masked celebrants and gigantic saints who stomped along on stilts. The light of their torches cast fantastic shadows upon the walls of houses and a cloud of fiery glowing sparks floated on the smoky blackness. Wulf clasped Madeleine to him as the chanting mob engulfed them like swimmers in a surging sea and swept them away.

De Luchaire and three villeins plunged from the alleyway a moment later with curses and oaths. At first they attempted to battle their way through the throng of humanity with fists and elbows but saw it was useless. "Keep sight of them!" de Luchaire shouted as he, too, was swallowed up and carried along by the momentum of the mob.

Wulf saw the other three villeins at the foot of the square attempting to search the crowd as it flowed past. But where the street narrowed they, too, were swallowed up and swept along. Glancing back into the mad crush, Wulf thought he caught sight of de Luchaire. If it was he, he had made no progress through the sea of people.

Clutching Madeleine to him, Wulf strived mightily to reach the edge of the chanting crowd. As the procession snaked toward the cathedral, it made one final turn past the square. When they drew even with the tinner's shop, Wulf and Madeleine slipped away into the shadows, running the route they had earlier walked from the stable.

With their goal in sight, a single lantern burned in the rear of the stable, Wulf and Madeleine stepped into a darkened doorway of a nearby shop and waited. They heard no pursuing footfalls, only the pounding of their own hearts. In the distance the roar of the crowd and the hellish glow of their torches moved on through the night.

The boy heard them enter the stable and stirred from his pallet in the straw. He asked the man if he wanted to let the storeroom. Wulf did not answer him, but sent him straight away for their horses.

The boy scratched himself thoughtfully and watched after them as they cantered away. He returned to his pallet, shaking his head and thinking that only a fool would ride out in the darkness, for everyone knew the night was filled with evil spirits looking for souls to claim.

The town gate reared before them blacker than the night, wicked-looking with its pointed Gothic towers and thick blunted walls. The guards had gone, lured by the magic of the masked procession or the free-flowing wine and ale of the taverns.

Wulf dismounted and, passing the bay's reins to Madeleine, opened the gates so that she and the horses might pass. He then threw his weight against the massive wooden doors and sent them creaking on their hinges to close with a rumble. In a moment, he made his way over the wall and dropped soundlessly into the frost-dead undergrowth.

"Do they follow?" Madeleine called in aloud whisper. "I saw no one," he said, taking the reins and swinging onto the bay. "They will be after us soon enough," he predicted, turning his horse. "Stay close. Once we are in the forest, we will have the advantage."

On the plaza before the cathedral, people fell as they marched. Shouts of "Plague!" rang out, and by twos and threes and fours the procession dispersed. Fearful voices and sputtering torches marked the paths of their retreat into the darkness.

De Luchaire and his villeins filtered through their terrified numbers, searching for two among the masses of people, halting and demanding of this masked celebrant and that, "Remove your mask, show your face!"

They searched Clamecy's taverns and stables. At length, they shook the stable boy from his straw pallet. The cheeky boy hemmed and hawed, angling for a silver coin. De Luchaire promptly cuffed him alongside the head for his impertience and questioned him as if he were a felon.

De Luchaire's face darkened with rage as he listened to the boy's words. "I will follow them into hell," he swore angrily. He strode purposefully from the livery and hastened to return to the tavern where his horses were stabled.

His villeins struck out after him, falling into step. "Milord," one called, "how are we to follow in the darkness?" From his expression, the villein was less than eager to ride out into the night. For was it not there that the priests had driven all the evil in Clamecy? His sliding glance met with mute agreement from his fellows, who strode along shoulder to shoulder, though none dared voice his fears.

At the tavern, the horses were saddled. Nursing his wounded jaw, de Luchaire followed the old Roman road south, believing the Saxon would not dare stray from the road in the darkness. De Luchaire led his uneasy men as far as Oseille, a small village south of Clamecy, before turning back defeated.

Late in the night they came upon a shabby tavern. De Luchaire demanded food and drink and sent his villeins to roust half a dozen merchants from the room above and cast them out into the damp chill night.

The elderly proprietor kept his silence. The noble's rage was fearsome to see and unabating, and the man feared for his life and his family's safety.

All night long Guiles de Luchaire drank wine, feeding his raving fury as a draft feeds a flame. For hours he paced to and fro in the smoky, earthen-floored tavern. He knew full well Avignon's reply, if indeed the case had been presented, would come too late. By all reports, the pestilence had devastated Avignon. He cursed and swore at fate. The marriage would be consummated and she a wife and likely with child long before he could reach Avignon to plead his case and return to claim her. Only then did it occur to him like a flash of sudden summer lightning. He need not go to Avignon—Avignon was in Clamecy—a part of it, at least. If he could but sway the cardinal to his mind, he might still have his prize as well as the Lady Madeleine to humble as he pleased.

When the morrow dawned with gray skies and drizzling rain, he roused his men with curses and the tow of his boot and set out for Clamecy.

Chapter Twenty

No angelus rang in Clamecy; silence and the cold, predictable drizzle shrouded the city. No living creature stirred and it seemed that the revelers of the night before, with their mindless chants and flaring torches, had marched away into the darkness and followed the moon beyond the mountains. The deserted streets were cluttered with debris; a pair of abandoned stilts propped against a naked tree, litters of blackened torches, rain-spattered masks, and the sodden bodies of those felled by the sickness. The dead stared with glazed eyes: men and women with an arm flung at an improbable angle, a leg askew, as if they still struggled to escape death's terrible judgment.

Guiles de Luchaire saw the fearful looks that passed among his villeins. They were loyal men, hardened to battle and feared no man. But how were they to deal with an enemy who could not be seen nor heard, one that came as the wind, without casting a shadow or leaving a print? Even Guiles de Luchaire felt the icy touch of fear and urged his horse forward.

The cardinal's walled residence stood to the rear of the Cathedral of St. Martin's as-yet-uncompleted cloisteer garth. At the gates, Guiles de Luchaire demanded an audience with the cardinal.

The stone-faced guards made no reply. Presently, a

young priest appeared on the wall; gesticulating wildly with his arms, he shouted, "Go away! Go away! His Excellency sees no one!" The stout priest with receding fair hair and the face of a dissolute cherub refused to carry de Luchaire's message to the cardinal and again shouted, "Go away!"

Choking with impotent rage, de Luchaire damned the name of de Moncelet. Only then did the young priest relent and asked to hear the name once more. "Wait," he told the noble and hurried away. In a short time, the stout young priest reappeared and instructed, "You must first disarm yourself, and only you may enter."

De Luchaire passed his sword and dagger to a villein and entered the gates. From the portico, the young priest peered anxiously through the rain. "Are you in good health?" he called. His voice, like his hair, was thin as a thread. As de Luchaire followed him into the residence, the priest explained, "His Excellency believes the seeds of the sickness are passed from one to another by the breath. No one may approach directly, but he will hear your plea." De Luchaire did not understand, but nodded in agreement. The more the priest said, the more peculiar it all sounded.

He followed the stout young priest through a labyrinth of dark passageways and at length entered a cavernous vaulted chamber filled with fire and smoke. At the center of the vast room two blazing bonfires sent flames leaping high above the heads of those present. To one side of the room long lines of servants passed logs hand to hand to feed the greedy blazes.

The heat of the fires could be felt from as far away as the ornate stone door arches and a fierce draft drew through the room, so that the robes of all in attendance were slapped against their legs. The bonfires howled like living things, bathing all in their infernal radiance. The windows—which were of the old style, slitted and open to the weather—belched rolling plumes of smoke.

De Luchaire squinted into the flames, catching only a brief glimpse of a fat man in scarlet robes seated upon a gilded throne-like chair. The man's shining red face glistened like a lump of lard melting in the sun.

The stout priest sidled close to de Luchaire, made the sign of the cross, and noting the cardinal's upraised hand, said, "His Excellency will hear you now."

De Luchaire, gauging the distance—a hundred paces, surely—made no attempt to conceal his skepticism. Nonetheless, he drew in a deep breath and at the top of his lungs presented his case.

After a great deal of shouting back and forth, Cardinal Gaspard was satisfied that Madeleine de Moncelet was indeed the niece of his old enemy, Heribert, Bishop of Champagne. The cardinal, a crafty man, saw de Luchaire's *affaire du coeur* as a means to censure his old enemy, Heribert de Moncelet, before the Pope—as well as put an end to the ruthless Duke du Boulay's pretensions toward the throne of France or, at the very least, gain profit from it.

Without lifting his immense backside from the purple velvet cushions of his gilded chair, he motioned to a pair of elderly clerics who stood nearby and summarily orderd a troop of his guard to be sent to seize the Lady Madeleine de Moncelet and return her to Clamecy. What he did not make known was that once he had acquired the lady, he had no intention of releasing her. Not, that is, until he had at his leisure determined and weighed what price each of the lady's husbands might set upon her worth. For as far as he could determine, both du Boulay and de Luchaire had a valid claim. Gaspard smiled his crafty smile and envisioned the return of Viezon to his estates, the lion's share of the market stalls of

Troyes, road fines and taxes, and sweet revenge. It was such thoughts that warmed his heart on a winter's day.

Guiles de Luchaire, exhilarated with his success, bowed and backed slowly from the room. He turned at the door arch, dizzy with victory, and walked into the clammy cold of the passageway.

In less than two hours a troop of thirty mounted guardsmen had been recruited and outfitted and sat astride their fretting horses before the armory, which was located at the far end of the courtyard of the cardinal's residence. The red combs of their light steel basinets shone vivid scarlet in the drab gray afternoon.

The captain of the guard, a thick-set man of middle years with a bulbous nose and ruddy face, swiftly crossed the courtyard, past the stone fountain and the cold ragged collapse of water to where a groom steadied his restless horse. With a brusque nod to the groom, the captain mounted and led his troop from the cobbled courtyard to join ranks with the horsemen beyond the gate.

Guiles de Luchaire drew his horse abreast of the captain's and at a canter the horsemen rode from the cardinal's city of Clamecy.

A short distance from the city's walls, the captain, a local man familiar with the countryside, divided his troop and sent them to scour the woods as far south as Pont Payant, the toll bridge, where the old Roman road crossed a fork of the Loire.

Though he bristled at the captain's presumptive manner, de Luchaire agreed to follow the road; it would have been his choice in any case, for the cold and drizzle penetrated even his fur-lined cape and he was certain the Lady Madeleine and her guard would seek shelter from the weather.

Wulf and Madeleine rode for hours through the

darkened woods, hearing only the wind in the trees and the reedy calls of owls. With the cold gray dawn came rain, a light drizzle that pecked at their hands and faces. Numbed by the icy cold, Madeleine was little aware of her bruised cheek and bloodied lip.

It was still raining when they stopped to rest their horses. Wulf brought a handful of dry needles from deep beneath a grove of pines and lit a fire with the flint striker. For the first time in days Madeleine was magically warm. The heat of the fire sent her cheek to throbbing and she was reminded of the nightmarish confrontation with Guiles de Luchaire.

Wulf tethered the horses and moved about apprehensively. He knew it was foolish to light a fire, even at such a distance from the road, but Madeleine had been chilled to the bone and he could not bear to see her shiver any longer. He, too, was cold and after a time, he came and crouched beside her by the fire.

When the numbness had gone from her fingers, Madeleine opened the small gathered purse which hung from her belt and took out a tiny polished mirror. Slowly she ran a finger over the bluish welt on her cheek then tenderly examined her swollen lip. "All that I said was true; that is why he struck me," she remarked. Until that moment, she had not told Wulf of her experience with de Luchaire as a boy *jongleur* in the upstairs room of the Red Rose Tavern. They talked of it, and eventually laughed when he told her he had seen the performance that night and had walked from the tavern's back door only a moment after she had fled over the roof.

Wulf added more wood to the fire. It was damp and hissed and spat like an angry cat, but slowly burned. They lay in each other's arms by the fire with both cloaks wrapped around them for warmth. They talked for a time, with her dark hair against his cheek and her warm breath against the hollow of his throat. Hugged close and anchored by embracing arms, inevitably they kissed and, knowing so well the ways to pleasure one another's body, soon teetered on the brink of passion.

No, he told himself. It was neither the time nor the place. His body said otherwise—his pounding heart, the tightening in his groin. He tore his gaze from hers and, looking beyond the clearing in the pines, saw only the soggy woods. Silent, save for the muffled sounds of their horses. But there was the fire to lead de Luchaire to them, and it would be far too late by the time the horses whickered a warning.

"Yes," Madeleine whispered, looking up at him with darkly hazeled eyes that sparkled and danced like brook water. "It may be for the last time," she pleaded.

He kissed her, but not with the urgent passion of the moment before and, brushing his lips over her cheek, murmured, "Not like this, lying on the wet ground with your skirts over your head and me in my boots. It is not the way I would want it to be."

"It is better than nothing," she began in a tormented voice. "And nothing is what we—." He silenced her with a kiss and, nuzzling her ear, promised, "There will be a time for us. Now try and sleep. We cannot risk a fire much longer."

Madeleine sighed and looked away with tears glistening in her eyes. All the shattering emotions of the night before returned to tear at her very soul. "You will not let him take me?" she sobbed, thinking what would her life be worth in the hands of Guiles de Luchaire. Particularly when he discovered that she was not the virgin of the betrothal contract, but with child. At least she suspected she was, for her last flow had been in mid-September. Would he beat the child from her womb? It was all too obvious who had fathered it. Or would he kill it the moment it was born? The thought terrified her beyond reason. She had said nothing to Wulf of her condition; she could not, believing it was kinder if he did not know.

"No," he said. "Guiles de Luchaire will not take you."

"Promise me that you will use your dagger on me, give me a merciful death."

He lowered his head, bringing his lips close to her ear. "You are not going to die."

"Promise me," she cried.

"I will not let him take you; I promise you."

Madeleine huddled in his arms, soon falling into an exhausted sleep. Wulf dozed, waking every few moments, never really asleep. After perhaps an hour, he woke her with a gentle shake of her shoulder and they set out again, riding south. Wulf believed it to be south, though he had little more than his inborn sense of direction to guide him.

The rocky track rose steeply, slick and treacherous. From the crown of the wooded hill they saw a village, like an island in the misting rain, where a huddle of steeply rising and falling rooftops and an untidy sprawl of outbuildings surrounded a small rustic church. Emerging from the dripping trees, they followed the track downward into the raw-smelling wood smoke and the winter mud.

As they approached the village they glimpsed the Roman road, hidden from their view till then by the clouds of mist and stand of black-barked trees.

The mired mud of the village streets was thronged with people, carts, and tumbrils of every description: travelers, for they were far too numerous to be local folk. Some wore the clothing of wealthy burghers, others the rough weave of country men and peasants. They shouldered past one another, haggling with villagers who demanded dear prices for the most meager scraps of food, a cup of milk, or wine. Desperate men and women in full flight from the ravages of the pestilence, fleeing death only to meet it unexpectedly in the gray December chill.

They saw men, women, and children lying sick,

328

others dead in their carts, flesh blackened and mouths agape. The milling crowd seemed neither to notice nor care. Madeleine turned her face from the appalling scene and fixed her gaze on the pale golden mane of her chestnut mare: flyaway and flaxen, crimped as a little girl's hair loosed from its braids.

A single tavern stood in a muddy lot well back from the village's thoroughfare. Abandoned carts littered the lot, sunk to their wheel hubs in the mire, and the lean-to stable overflowed with the horses and mules of travelers.

Wulf dismounted, slung the wineskin over his shoulder, and handed his horse's reins to Madeleine, astride the mare. She had agreed to wait with the horses, but now regretted it. Seeing she was afraid, Wulf lifted her from the mare and tethered the horses to a rough-hewn timber projecting from the tavern's overhanging eaves.

He took her hand and together they went inside, pressing their way through the crowd. Wulf had silver coins with which to pay, gold if necessary, and hoped to fill their wineskin.

In the rear of the smoke-filled room a large man with a beard worked continuously, filling wine cups from a cask. Wulf threaded his way through the crowded tavern with Madeleine trailing behind, gripping his hand. Against one wall, where a hearthfire blazed, Madeleine spied a fat child turning the crank of a large circular spit laden with roasting birds. She nudged Wulf and with large ravenous eyes led his gaze to the ambrosial golden carcasses, whispering, "I am so very hungry." But he only nodded and continued on his way.

Coming in from the rain, they had not doffed the hoods of their cloaks; water puddled where they stood. While Wulf held the wineskin for the portly man to fill, Madeleine peered from beneath the deep hood. The humid air of the room reeked of wet wool clothing, grease, and wood smoke. There were women with babes in their arms, old men and women, young men, and half-grown children, all noisily eating, drinking, talking, and laughing until the discordant drone of their combined voices seemed a language all its own.

Madeleine glanced about the room. A shade of blue caught her eye and an involuntary shiver raced along her spine. She did not at once connect the two, though the color drew her gaze back. She saw a group of men, soldiers, for she glimpsed mail beneath one's cloak. Each held a roasted game bird and greedily gnawed at the carcass. One among them stepped aside to ogle after a young woman as she passed by, and the man standing opposite him threw back his head and laughed.

For a moment, Madeleine was too stricken to move or utter a sound. Her eyes leapt to Wulf. She saw his large hands securing the wooden cap of the wineskin and pushed against him, tugging at his arm.

He swung the wineskin over his shoulder and smiled down at her. "I have not forgotten—my stomach is also empty. How many game birds can you eat? An even dozen?" he teased.

"No," was all Madeleine could coax from her dry throat, but the look of abject terror on her face said much more.

Wulf raised his eyes and looking over her head saw Guiles de Luchaire surrounded by perhaps seven or eight of his villeins. Without a word he laid a hand on Madeleine's waist and guided her slowly toward the door, his every sense strained, waiting to hear their shouts at his back.

At the door, a man burst in dragging a gusty sigh of rain. He looked them squarely in the face. For an instant, he planted himself directly before them, then pushed his way past. Madeleine held her breath, certian she had seen a spark of recognition in the man's dull brown eyes.

Outside the rain peppered down, drilling the mire

330

and bouncing off the building's low eaves. They waded through the slosh to their tethered horses. Wulf lifted Madeleine onto the mare, then mounted the bay. As they rode off, Madeleine cast a fearful backward glance at the tavern. She saw the hide-covering of a window stripped away and Guiles de Luchaire's face framed in the opening. "He has seen us!" she cried.

De Luchaire and his villeins raced through the slop of the garth to their horses and were away. They had lost precious moments. For all their hard riding, they were rewarded with but a distant fleeting glimpse of the pair as they recklessly descended a brushy hillock and plunged into the deep woods at its base.

There was little hope of tracking them in such rough terrain; the rocky ground yielded precious few prints despite the rain and muddy conditions. A mile or so distant from the sighting, one of de Luchaire's men stumbled upon a set of tracks midway across the face of a hill; two horses traveling swiftly. The villein proudly showed off his find and the hunt began anew.

The steady rain which had been a nuisance now teemed down in blowing waves, obscuring the distance. The unmistakable whickering of a horse came too late. Guiles de Luchaire and his villeins exited a wet hollow to find themselves face to face with a detachment of the cardinal's guards commanded by the florid-faced captain.

"Mayhap milord has lost his way?" the captain drawled sarcastically. But when the noble in the blue lake cape made a stinging reply and motioned his villeins on, the captain shouted, "Hold fast!" His menacing tone and the fact that his men drew arms left no doubt as to his intentions. De Luchaire reined in his mount. "I am in pursuit of the lady and her guard," he bellowed through the falling rain, impatiently relating the incident at the tavern and insisting, "They came this way."

The captain was equally adamant. "And I tell you no one passed this way. More likely it is our tracks you followed, or your own. For while you are fool enough to chase your tail in circles, the road's course is open and runs steady and level straight for Nevers."

After several more heated exchanges, Guiles de Luchaire, in a savage state of mind, angrily galloped away. As much as he was tempted to take to sword and humble the insolent captain, there was some merit in what he said. A young girl could not long endure the hardships of weather and the rough terrain. She would soon be exhausted and the gentle course of the road, food, and shelter, would lure her and her guard out for the taking. And on that occasion, Guiles de Luchaire would make certain the cardinal's troops were not present to interfere. "I have lost faith in the cardinal's motives," de Luchaire told his most trusted villein. "For once he holds the lady, and that seems his intention, he holds her property as well. What is there to prevent him from demanding a ransom?"

"We could have taken the captain and his troop, killed and been done with them," the villein said with a confident air. De Luchaire smiled. "Yes," he agreed, "but first, let them chase the lady into our arms."

Chapter Twenty-One

At evening, layer upon layer of ominous dark clouds draped the sky. Darkness was falling when they sighted another, smaller village at the foot of the mist-shrouded hills. Here there were few travelers, and, it appeared, fewer inhabitants. The village, they later learned, was called Trémière and its tavern leaned beside a sluggish, silt-filled stream. Beyond the tavern yard, a small knot of wandering peasants, looking like ragged birds in their layers of tattered clothing, crowded around the orange glow of an open fire.

The tavern keeper was a jittery, garrulous little man with a beak of a nose and bright sharp eyes. He had only four paying guests and was overjoyed to see two more enter his tavern.

While Wulf and Madeleine devoured a hash made of rabbit and vegetables served with coarse bread and ale by the little man's plump wife, he crowded in beside them at the rough-planked table and subjected them to a constant stream of chatter. The peasants, he said, were a nuisance. They had no coins, and moreover they were fools to leave the warmth of their huts to wander around in the cold world. "I once asked a poor borel why he had left his home," the little tavern keeper said. "He told me, 'I do not want to die.' Can you imagine," the little man laughed,

333

"the comings and goings, if death could be so easily avoided. The world would be a fine stew indeed, with no one to raise the crops and no roof to call one's own."

When the meal was finished, Wulf stood up and announced his intention to see to the horses. He had not necessarily trusted the young boy who led the bay and the mare away to feed and water them properly. "By all means," the little man said. "See if my grandson has done his work; I have been looking for a reason to thrash him for days."

Madeleine heard the man's jesting words and saw Wulf step away from the table. Not wishing to be left behind, she sopped up the last bit of gravy with a morsel of bread and shoved it into her mouth, making a motion to rise. "Stay where it is warm," Wulf said, laying a reassuring hand on her shoulder and advising in a soft voice. "It is safe here."

In the stable, Wulf found no reason to complain; the bay and the mare were content with a generous portion of grain and hay. Walking through the drizzle, Wulf returned to the tavern.

As he entered, he noticed the tavern keeper talking to another of his guests, a bearded young man. A button peddler from his appearance, for his parti-colored jupon was sewn end to end with samples of his wares. Wulf sent Madeleine a smile from the door and went and sat down beside her on the bench before the hearth, dropping a large arm around her. She laid her head against him and in a moment was fast asleep.

After a time the tavern keeper came from the lively conversations across the room and stood warming his backside by the fire. "Your wife looks to be all in," he remarked. "Did you ride from Clamecy today?"

"No," Wulf replied, offering nothing more. He, too, had been drowsing in the warmth of the hearth, but now he was alert.

With a gesture of his gray head, the tavern keeper said, "The peddler there told me that many have died in Clamecy, and those who have not are searching for the young daughter of a noble, a headstrong girl, who has betrayed her betrothal vows and run off to God knows where." He then went on to tell how the cardinal's troops had come to the tavern where the peddler last rested. "Came at first light, cracking heads and questioning all they found." The little man gave Wulf a sly smile and tucking his tongue in his cheek, ventured, "The lady's lands must be rich indeed. Why else would a man chase after her? For the world is full a'plenty with foolish young girls, and all with the knack for raising a man's fancy," he chuckled.

Wulf smiled good-naturedly at the man's jest. He had thought Madeleine asleep, until he felt her hand close over his. There was no danger of her being mistaken for the daughter of a noble, he thought. Not in her mud-spattered clothing and with her head wrapped in a soiled coif. She looked for all purposes a soldier's wife. She wore no jewelry save for the plain gold band.

The tavern keeper continued to talk. At long last his plump wife came to lead him to bed with a candle. The other guests had long before trailed off to the floor above, where all slept in a single large room.

"Come," he gestured. "Bring your pretty little wife."

"She is asleep," Wulf said, looking up from where Madeleine's dark lashes brushed the curve of her cheek. "She shivered all day from the cold. Best I keep her here by the fire. I will feed the logs for you tonight," he offered.

The tavern keeper had no objections, and a small boy, another grandson, whose nightly chore it was, beamed with joy.

It was yet dark when they rode from Trémière. Frosty puffs of steam floated from their mouths and from the flared nostrils of their horses. Shivering in the early morning stillness, they rode south again, avoiding the old Roman road.

Much of the land they crossed was cleared for pasture and plow. From a distance they saw a patchwork of farmsteads, peasant huts, and cattle sheds with thatched roofs. Smoke rose from the squat chimneys and there was further evidence of human habitation in the neat wood stacks and orderly garths.

Perhaps, Madeleine thought, the sickness had not yet touched this valley and life went on as it always had—unchanging, its monotony broken only by the seasons.

Madeleine found it increasingly difficult to think of anything other than the hunger which gnawed at her stomach. As she rode it seemed she could recall every bit of food she had refused with a wrinkled nose or turned aside: pickled fish, thick slices of juicy lamb, black puddings, sausages, ham, not to mention sugar-dusted cakes and comfits. At this point, she decided, she would even devour a bowl of turnips, which she detested.

Wulf, riding at a slow, steady pace beside her, steered his horse close to her mare and held out an apple. The shiny red apple with its overlay of bright yellow speckles danced before Madeleine's eyes like a vision. She looked up suddenly, her eyes wide with surprise. "From Clamecy?" she asked in an astonished voice.

"I kept it for you," he said.

She drew her dark brows into a peeved expression. "Why did we not eat it this morning?" She could not decide if she was pleased or angry.

"If we had," he said with a bland northlander's smile, "I could not offer it to you now," and dropped the apple into her hand.

"I will share it with you," she called, smiling despite herself.

He reined his horse away, and as he did flashed a smile filled with mischief and pulled another apple from his cloak.

Madeleine gave her mare a nudge with her knee and moved up beside him. "What else have you hidden in your cloak, Monsieur Tromperie?" she accused with a laugh.

"Only my love for you," he called back with a wink. Madeleine rolled her dark eyes and made a grimace which instantly dimpled into a smile. "I have seen little proof of it," she teased.

"Be content with your apple," he told her. He motioned ahead with his hand and said, "Do you see the copse of trees where the hollow ends? We can rest our horses there." She nodded and, holding the apple to her nose, sniffed its spicy fragrance.

Across the field, a narrow strip of alders and elms marked the boundaries of the hollow. They ate their apples, drank a little wine, and passed an hour among the trees—time enough to rest their horses and their own stiff muscles. The wind had laid down, though without a fire it was bitterly cold.

Madeleine rose from where she sat on a fallen tree trunk, shaking the weed seed and chaff from her skirts. The hawk they had been watching wheeled higher in the leaden sky and glided away toward a line of distant trees.

As they prepared to leave, Wulf looped the strap of the wineskin over the mare's saddle bow, instructing Madeleine to take some wine if she began to shiver. She agreed, only to please him. She would not drink it, she decided, but keep it for later, just as he had kept the apples.

Warmed by the wine and the bit of nourishment, they rode on beneath the low-hanging clouds through weed-choked meadows and still woods with only the sounds of their horses and the scrunch of leather and jangle of harness to break the silence of the winter's day.

A rain-swollen stream halted them. On either side the steep banks had been eaten away by the churning water. Madeleine gazed across its muddy span. "It is not so very wide," she said in a heartening voice, though the thought of the cold, dark water filled her with dread.

Wulf dismounted and walked to the edge of the crumbling bank. At best they would emerge soaked to their skins; at worst, Madeleine's mare might stumble and unseat her. In the murky rolling water he would have little chance of finding her. The stream was no wider than a village street, but surged past swift and deep.

"We cannot cross here," he said finally, taking the bay's reins and swinging into the saddle. "Downstream there will be a riffle," he predicted, and prayed there would be. He did not mention the bridge the tavern keeper had spoken of, south of Clamecy on the Roman road where the toll was twice what an honest man could afford to pay. The price of the toll was of little consequence—rather that the road and most certainly the bridge would be watched.

For it was entirely possible that de Luchaire also knew of the bridge. Perhaps, Wulf speculated, it had been the bridge and not his skillful backtracking which had drawn off their pursuers. Had de Luchaire abandoned the chase so that he might set a trap at the toll bridge? At the time Wulf had not given it much thought; he had been too pleased with his own cleverness, but now it returned to gnaw at the back of his consciousness like a dog worrying a bone. He was still weighing the dangers as he led off downstream.

Further along the stream's winding course, they sent their horses through a brace of willows. The springy reddened switches lashed back at their passage, thoroughly thrashing them. Madeleine suffered her way through the entanglement, following closely as she dared.

Then, through a haze of willow switches, Wulf sighted the Pont Payant, and there, directly in their path, though he could not yet see it, would be the Roman road. They were forced to cross onto the road—there was no other way, unless they chose to return upstream and search for a shallows there. A backward glance at Madeleine caused him to reject the thought completely. Her pale face was pinched from the cold and she sat with her back painfully braced in the saddle.

From the stream's edge the ground rose steeply so that even as he drew nearer, his view of the road and a portion of the toll house was obstructed by the crest of the hill and the screen of barren willows. They continued on, making a gradual ascent. Presently, they entered a clearing where the trees had been thinned by axes and the ragged stumps jutted from the soft earth.

Voices carried on the damp air. Wulf's bay pricked its ears sharply forward and snorted. In another few strides, Wulf caught his first clear glimpse of the toll building and the weathered sheds surrounding it. His view of the road was still obstructed by the close-set trees.

A peal of laughter swiveled his attention to a cow shed from which four children suddenly emerged, dodging and chasing one another in play. A moment later, a woman stepped clear of the toll house's side door and called to the children and from somewhere near, but out of sight, a horse whickered.

Wulf cautiously reined in the bay. Madeleine, on the mare, drew even with him. "What is it?" she asked in an anxious whisper. He gave no reply. His gaze swept past her toward the road. The bay moved restlessly beneath him; he tightened his grip on the reins and waited, listening, grasping for sounds.

*   *   *

Guiles de Luchaire made a swift movement with his hand. "Wait," he said, his voice a harsh whisper. "Let them come closer." In a shed opposite, a villein poked his head from a doorway inquisitively, then stepped swiftly back into the shadowy interior.

Guiles de Luchaire leaned his shoulder against the worn boards of a lean-to shed and watched closely the progress of the two riders. A little thrill of excitement raced through him.

He and his villeins had ridden at an exhausting pace all night in order to reach Pont Payant by dawn, thus ensuring that the cardinal's guards would not be present to interfere.

A tight smile tugged at the corners of de Luchaire's lips. He was confident that once his trap was sprung, the Lady Madeleine and her Saxon guard would have no opportunity to slip away as they had in the past. He continued to watch with the silent intensity of a hound crouched to spring on its prey.

From his vantage point, de Luchaire saw the two riders top the crest of the hill, press through the undergrowth, and set their horses at a walk toward the toll building. He drew in a deep breath of cold air, eased his sword from its scabbard, then edged to the corner of the shed, motioning his villeins to follow.

The sound of horses coming at a gallop wrenched de Luchaire's gaze back to the road. His jaw dropped in disbelief as he saw ten or twelve of the cardinal's guards, the presumptive red-faced captain at their lead, thunder toward the toll station.

De Luchaire let loose a string of obscenities and charged from between the sheds like a raging bull. His villeins swarmed after him.

He caught only a glimpse of his prey as they wheeled their horses from the road, galloped up a rise, and vanished into the woods opposite the toll house, the cardinal's guards in hot pursuit.

"Bring the horses!" de Luchaire bellowed.

*   *   *

Madeleine's chestnut mare bolted after the stallion, stretching out her neck and straining for more speed. A blur of tree trunks and limbs flashed past. Madeleine kept her head close to the mare's neck to protect her face from the lashing branches and hung on, trusting the mare to follow the bay.

Ahead, a weedy meadow ended blindly at the foot of a rugged hillside. To the right, the land dipped through a small wood then stretched away to broad grassy fields where without a doubt, the guardsmen would run them to ground.

Wulf chose the hill, shifting his weight in the saddle as the bay flung itself upward through the thorny bushes and loose rock. Madeleine's mare, close behind, crashed through the thicket, stumbled, regained her footing, and struggled up the last stretch of rock and underbrush.

Clearing the summit, they plunged down a steep slope, the thunderous crash of the guard's horses at their backs. Below, the thick brush gave way to open forest—an old woods, populated by immense oaks and carpeted deep with leaves that dulled the staccato beat of their horse's hooves. Windfalls of tangled limbs and rotting tree trunks littered the forest floor. The winter landscape blurred before their eyes and the wind stole their breath. Wulf hazarded a backward glance and saw the guardsmen charging down the slope.

The oaks thinned, giving way to thicket, and another hill loomed before them. Wulf veered away, sending the bay into the deep underbrush where a valley, cleft by a rocky creek bed, nestled between two hills.

They clattered into the creek. Water stood in shallow pools, mirror bright, riffling over the flat mossy rocks. They crossed the creek's meandering path three times in only a short distance, their horses never slackening their pace until they ran headlong into a dense snarl of brambles. A limb cracked against Wulf's knee and the tangle of wild vines and brambles closed in, slowing their progress. Deep in the thicket, the sounds of the guardsmen grew fainter. They had fallen behind.

To their left the ground rose steeply from the thicket. Wulf aimed the bay toward the hill; Madeleine followed. The chestnut mare lunged gamely upwards over the low brush and clumps of rock.

At the crest, a broad ridge descended abruptly to dense undergrowth and beyond open meadows. The steep, almost sheer descent left Madeleine breathless and near to panic.

Halfway down the rock-strewn slide, the mare slid to her hocks, caught herself up, and lurched on, lifting Madeleine out of the saddle for a heart-stopping instant, only to be slammed down again, jarring her teeth together.

In the open meadow, Wulf gathered the bay's reins, slowing its stride, and, falling back, came even with Madeleine. When he glanced over with an encouraging smile, he saw her face was white as whey except for two flaming splotches of color high on her cheeks.

They galloped across the weedy meadow and into the forest. Beneath the shelter of the trees, they followed the wood's ragged perimeter, making a half-circle and returning to within sight of the hillside they had so recklessly descended. There, deep in the underbrush where a canopy of wild vines and brambles closed above them, they halted their heavily lathered horses and dismounted.

Madeleine closed her eyes and pressed her forehead against the mare's slick neck. The sound of approaching horses seemed to come from directly above them. Madeleine looked up with a startled gasp and saw a mêlée of riders break from the crest of the ridge and pour over the hillside, taking the path they had ridden into the meadow. She stroked the mare's slobbering muzzle, praying to God they would not be seen, praying the cardinal's guards would not too soon discover the ruse. She looked uncertainly to Wulf, standing close by the bay's head, and saw his face was marked by dozens of angry red welts where twigs and brambles had lashed him. Her face, too, stung fiercely. They exchanged weary smiles and raising their eyes, watched the scarlet combs of the guard's helmets flow across the meadow and into the forest.

They had not long to wait before they again heard the unmistakable thunder of horses upon the hill. Guiles de Luchaire and his villeins burst over the ridge and charged down the rock-strewn slope in a disorderly stampede.

In the meadow, they reined in their horses, ignoring the trampled path of the guardsmen, and milled about like hounds who had lost a scent. After a brief shouted conversation, de Luchaire split his group, sending several after the guardsmen. Then he and the others galloped off, making a broad curve back toward Pont Payant and the Roman road.

Wulf and Madeleine waited until they were out of sight, then followed the thicket to where the woods opened again to large trees. They rode fast, driving themselves and their exhausted horses unmercifully in an attempt to cover as much distance as possible before the guardsmen and de Luchaire realized they had lost them and retraced their tracks.

Within the hour, they sighted the stream once again: yellow with silt, swift and broad where it flowed through the flat soggy meadows and gently rolling hills.

They crossed at a shallows, where the muddy water swirled thigh-high across the rocky stream bed.

After they had crossed the stream, Wulf turned in

his saddle and saw horsemen coming across the meadow at a gallop. A trio of riders. Three who had not been led astray, or more likely had happened on them by chance. The scarlet combs of their helmets marked them as Cardinal Gaspard's guards.

Clearly his and Madeleine's exhausted horses could not outdistance them. He would face them here, or later. He turned to Madeleine. "Go," he told her. "Keep to the forest."

"No!" she shouted back, guessing his intention. "I will not leave you!"

He yelled at her. "Go!" and when she did not obey, threw his heavy gloves at her horse. The mare shied, throwing up her head. Angrily, Madeleine swung the sidling mare around and kicked her to a canter. She twisted, bouncing in the saddle, to glance back; tears blurred the whole of her vision.

Wulf reached to his shoulder, unclasped his cloak, and let it fall. His thin metal basinet with its bent nasal hung from his saddle bow, as did his shield. He lifted the helmet and dropped it into the tall, withered grass. A helmet could not protect him, and moreover the bent nasal would only block his vision. He drew his sword—the one Hasso had laid on his shoulder with its silver ravens and runic prayer— took up his shield, and wheeled his horse toward the stream.

He poised atop the mud-slick embankment, bracing himself for what was surely his death. His only chance, and it a remote one, was to meet them mid-stream. The water would hinder his movement as well, but there were three of them and hopefully, like too many cooks, each would have an arm in the other's face.

They were much closer—close enough for Wulf to see the plunging forelegs of their horses tear out chunks of turf and send them flying into the air. One among the guardsmen, astride a white-faced bay, held a lance couched at his side. Close to the shore line, he cast it away and drew his sword.

Wulf stabbed his heels into the bay's side. Loki's powerful hindquarters thrust them down the muddy slope and into the water, sending up a plume of spray. Wulf had planned well. He and the riders met in mid-stream with a clash of swords. The rude, disorderly struggle churned the thigh-deep water of the shallows into a froth as they hacked away at each other.

The white-faced bay went to its knees on the slippery stones, collided with a dun-colored horse, and with a squalling scream went down atop its rider and lay thrashing in the boiling water. Wulf saw the horse go down, saw the water sheeting upwards, but of the rider there was no sign.

Every blow upon Wulf's shield jarred his newly mended arm, shooting it through with pain. He could not much longer support the weight of the heavy shield, for it weighed down his bridle arm until he could hardly maneuver. He shook the shield loose and flung it into the face of the rider on the dun-colored horse.

The dun reared, slid backwards, and went down with a shuddering splash, but the unseated rider was on his feet almost at once, both hands on his sword.

Wulf and the man on the chestnut slashed away at each other, knee-to-knee or nearly so, neither gaining the distance needed to deliver a deadly blow with the heavy swords.

Wulf saw the man afoot struggle forward, waist-deep in the churning water, and raise his sword. His target: the deep chest of Wulf's bay. Wulf spun Loki round on his hocks. The bay rose heavily onto its hindquarters as Wulf brought his sword down on the crown of the man's helmet. A glancing blow, but enough to cleft the thin metal basinet and send the man to his knees like a slaughtered beef in a circle of black blood.

Something sharp slashed Wulf's leg. He towed

desperately at the reins. Loki staggered backward with a scream, sliding, scrambling to gain a footing. Wulf raised his eyes to see the chestnut bearing down on him, its nostrils blood red and its jaws pried apart by the bit.

The sword came at him in a whining black arc. He lunged forward, his sword before him, and with a thrust drove past the leather buckler and pierced the man's side, peeling away the mail vest and flinging the man backward from the hurtling chestnut.

Wulf tore at the reins, but too late. The momentum of the plunging horses brought them together in a bone-wrenching collision.

The chestnut wheeled away, going down on its side, shrieking with fright and struggling wildly to rise from the muddy froth.

Wulf's bay kept his footing, but the force and sheer weight of the chestnut swept the lighter horse downstream into deeper water. Wulf gave the animal a free rein. The bay laid back its ears and stretched out its neck, straining against the current, clawing for a toe hold. At last the horse stumbled into the shallows where it halted, snorting and trembling from head to foot.

Of the three guardsmen, Wulf saw only the chestnut's rider, lying face-down near the shore line, his buckler beside him. An ever-widening wallow of blood spread into the murky water. The other two were gone, mayhap drifted into deeper water in time to bloat and come to rest downstream. Their horses were on the opposite bank calmly cropping grass. The white-faced bay's forelegs were skinned to the bone.

Wulf sheathed his sword and dismounted. The icy water bit into his leg like salt. He limped from the stream, leading the bay after him.

From atop the embankment, Madeleine burst out tearfully, "Jesu, Maria!" Her voice broke with emotion and tears streamed down her cheeks. She took the embankment at a run, sliding most of the way, muddying her skirts from hem to waist. "I thought they would kill you," she cried, throwing herself against him and nearly bowling him over.

He staggered back a step at her unexpected weight, then clutched her to his side, too exhausted to berate her for disobeying him. They and the bay clambered up the embankment.

At the top, he coughed and spit; his mouth was dry as dust.

Madeleine had not noticed his leg until that moment. She was frantic. "It is horribly deep," she wailed, trying to examine his leg as he walked.

He halted, dropping the bay's reins. "It is nothing." He could hardly speak for the dryness of his throat. He was more concerned with his horse, who moved off and began greedily ripping grass.

There was no use to argue with her. She would not be satisfied until she had tied her silk scarf around his leg. He wanted to walk over to the bay, but had not the strength. He waited, watching the blood soak through the flimsy scarf.

Across the stream, a horse whinnied. The bay raised its head and pricked its ears toward the sound. Wulf crouched beside the bay and ran his hands over its legs. He could find no serious damage, other than the slash on Loki's right flank which he reckoned to be from the same sword swath that had ripped his leather hosen and the meat of his leg.

Madeleine pulled the wineskin from her saddle bow and hurried back to where he stood. He downed a swallow. For a moment, he thought he would wretch.

There was a chill in the wind. He had not felt the cold before, and now it seemed to blow through his bare bones. When he turned to speak to Madeleine, he saw she had gone to fetch his cloak and helmet from the grass.

He was grateful for the cloak. He slung the helmet

by its strap from the saddle bow, thinking it was useful as a drinking bowl. They found only one of his gloves.

"Where is your shield?" Madeleine asked, holding the mare's reins in preparation to mount.

"Gone," he replied. He made a cup of his hands for her knee, and lifted her onto the mare.

Chapter Twenty-Two

In the gray between-light of the cold December dusk they sighted a mill silhouetted against the rose-hued sunset, a structure of post-and-beam and stone, whose water wheel was stilled. They approached at a cautious pace, following the fringe of woods which bounded the islet of cultivated fields and country paths.

When darkness closed, they ventured from beneath the trees and into a weedy field of unharvested barley, long ago gone to seed and lain down by the wind and rain and frost. A covey of partridges burst from cover before their horses with a wild beating of wings.

From the mill there was no hint of life, no scent of woodsmoke nor mellow glow of lamplight. The pig sty stood empty and the door of a slant-roofed shed nearer the mill hung open, its rusty hinges creaking a protest to the breeze.

In the miller's garden plot, rotting cabbages peeked among the weeds and cockleburs.

An elm, whose girth would have required the arms of several men to span, spread its barren limbs before the mill cottage door. Close by, the tree's rough-barked trunk was a bench fashioned of creek rock that in another season would have made a pleasant retreat.

Wulf found the cottage's door unbarred. From

astride the mare, Madeleine called to him in a whisper. "Where have they gone? Will we find them lying dead?" Her face was bright with fear, envisioning still more blackened and putrefying corpses. There seemed no end to it, and, at that moment as she sat weary and trembling from the cold, the horror overwhelmed her and tears stung her eyes.

He told her to wait with the horses. He dismounted, drew his sword, and limping, slipped inside. It was not the dead he feared, but those who had sacked the sheds and others with a like intent.

He stood with his back braced against the thick door, waiting for his eyes to grow accustomed to the dimness. Slowly, images took form: a trestle table, benches, a stool lying on its side, and in one corner, a loom. To the left of the living quarters were a stable and storage rooms, separated from the family's hearth by only a rail fence. A common enough sight, for most country folk lived side by side with their beasts.

He took several steps into the room. As he did, something rustled from the shadows and leapt past him. He threw up his arm, bringing his sword with it. His every muscle tensed, only to glimpse the fleeing form of a cat, whose long tail floated after it. He stared into the shadows, suddenly light-headed and feeling mildly foolish. After a moment, he lowered the sword.

Moving cautiously, he looked over the large room with its lime-washed walls. In the deep hearth, a blackened iron pot hung amid the cobwebs. He wiped the dirt of spiders from his hand and walked to where the board floor corbelled above the mill pond. At his feet was a trap door and pails for hauling up water. He climbed to the loft and found it bare to the walls. Returning to the foot of the wood-slab stairs, he spotted a low doorway off to his right and rooms beyond. But they, too, were empty, still as dust.

It was difficult for Wulf to fathom that fear alone could drive a man from so comfortable a home. He would have traded his soul for such a home and Madeleine to share it. As he moved about the hollow rooms, he wondered what fate had befallen the miller and his family. There had been a child, for in one room he found a cradle.

Making his way into the stable, he pushed wide the doors with a rumble and squeal of rusted hinges. He saw Madeleine's head jerk at the sound and heard her startled gasp. He grinned at her from the shadows and motioned to her to bring the horses.

She halted at the door so he might lift her from the mare. "They are not lying dead in their beds?" she asked, her cheeks red with cold. When he did not answer at once, she hung at the door. "Are they dead?" she asked again, and louder, refusing to enter until he answered her.

He reached past her for the horses' reins. "There is no one, living or dead—a cat somewhere." The horses moved into the stalls. He closed the doors to the cold and began unsaddling them. His hands moved familiarly over the horses, his every movement practiced.

Madeleine stood nearby, craning her neck and peering into the shadows. Wulf pulled the saddle from the bay and turning, noticed her curious expression. She was looking for the cat, he thought, and said, "He is hiding, I expect; we met in the dark."

She turned, smiling. "You frightened him."

"Yes," he agreed, stripping off the mare's saddle and hefting it onto the stable rail. "My heart is still pounding at my ribs."

With each passing moment, the shadows grew deeper within the heavy beamed structure. Before the blackness was complete, Wulf broke the three-legged stool apart and with the flint striker started a fire. Later the miller's benches would follow the stool

351

into the hearth.

He brought up half a dozen pails of water through the trap door and together they filled the large iron pot which swung from the hearth.

A search of the premises netted them only a few handfuls of grain, a chipped earthenware basin, a pitifully small stub of a candle, and a worn scrap of soap that smelled of lard and rosemary.

They fed the grain to their horses. They watered the bay and the mare in silence and rubbed them down with handfuls of straw. Wulf cleansed the bay's wound as best he could. Given time it would heal.

As Madeleine rubbed down the mare, she noticed the animal's right foreleg felt hot to her touch. She had learned something of horses from Wulf and asked gravely if the mare would go lame.

He crouched beside the mare and ran his large hand over the foreleg several times. "It is the muscle," he said finally, rising to his feet and giving the mare a pat upon the neck.

Madeleine looked on anxiously. "Will she go lame?"

"No, I do not think so."

Madeleine smiled with relief and tenderly stroked the mare's forehead. "She is a willing creature. I would feel badly to think I brought her harm."

Wulf smiled and gave the mare another pat of his hand. "She will be fair enough." It was a sin, he thought, to ride good horses into the ground, but they had had no choice in the matter.

In the warmth of the fire they shed their muddy clothing. Their hands and faces were etched with grime and a wealth of weed seeds and chaff had inexplicably found its way inside their garments.

They shared the scrap of soap between them, playfully, for both knew where it would lead. And though Madeleine's sexual arousal was not so blatantly evident as Wulf's, nor so impudent as to bob between them red-capped and stiff as a rod, yet the touch of his hands on her bare flesh as he soaped her end to end, left her breathless and shivering with excitement.

Madeleine lathered the fair hair of his chest, running circles through it with her fingers. Here and there, a blue-seamed scar showed beneath the meager froth of suds. Frolicking with the soap, she lathered his shaft. "If I had one of these," she giggled, aiming it purposefully, "I could lie in bed and pee into the chamber pot across the room."

"You are a braggart," he laughed, and taking the soap from her, touched the sudsy scrap to her nose.

Madeleine reached for the soap, wrestling it from his hands and insisting she must properly cleanse the gash in his leg. It bled anew, sluggish and dark, just as he predicted.

"It is sore deep," she frowned, fretting over his loss of blood and all because of her insistence.

"It is of no consequence," he assured her. "A man has more blood than you would think—enough to fill three basins that size."

Madeleine lifted his shirt from the pegged wall and with his dagger cut a strip of cloth from its tail. Of all their clothing, only it was reasonably free of mud and weed chaff. At his remark she made a scowling expression. "I doubt a horse has that much blood."

As for horses, he said, he could not swear but told her that in Lombardy he had seen men strung up by their heels and their throats slit in order that every drop of their blood could be drained into jars.

"Criminals?" Madeleine asked, binding his thigh and securing the ends of the cloth.

He shrugged his thick shoulders. "In the eyes of the Prince di Scalla. There were those who said he was in league with Satan and used the blood to cast spells. His servants said he mixed it with small amounts of poison and drank it so that if his enemies poisoned him, he would not be affected."

"Did they poison him?" she asked, for Wulf had told her that the Prince had once been his lord and that he had been murdered. But she had not learned how the deed was accomplished.

"No," he said, inspecting the bandage. "They stabbed him while he sat in his bath." He smiled up at her suddenly, remarking "I should not tell you such tales." The thought occurred to him that he would never have repeated such a grisly incident to a woman, particularly one to whom he intended to make love. But Madeleine was no ordinary woman. Over the months, he had told her things he had never repeated to another living soul, man or woman.

He watched her cross the room, wrapped haphazardly in her cloak. She lifted the trap door. As she did a blast of icy air raised a rash of gooseflesh on her arms and the cloak slid from her shoulder exposing a small pale breast. "Why?" she called, grasping the cape with one hand and covering herself. "Because I am a woman?" Below, the mill pond was still and black as doom. She tipped the basin and let the door slam shut with a bang.

Wrapped in the unraveling, not quite completed, blanket he had stripped from the loom, Wulf limped to the miller's bed, eased himself down, and stretched out full length. There was room for him, but his feet hung over. He altered his position, flexing his knees.

Madeleine came huddled in her cape and crawled in beside him. The rope sling bed jiggled under their combined weight. "Being a woman is dull," she said. Her tone was so sober, he could not keep from softly laughing. She regarded him with a dark look. "It is true. It annoys me to be treated like a woman."

"Yes," he agreed. "You are a puzzle. I will never understand you; you are different from any woman I have ever known."

Her oval face, at once so gravely earnest, dimpled

into a smile. "Oh?" she cooed, arching her dark brows. "In what way am I different?" She giggled, fending off his hands beneath the cloak, and swore she would not give in to him until he should give her an answer which pleased her. She was teasing him and herself as well, for the hollow between her legs fairly ached for want of him.

He mauled her over, gently. "You are more beautiful," he smiled, playing the game, handling her as he pleased while she protested with giggles.

"Even though the artist from Arles gave me a nose as long as a turnip?"

"Yes," he laughed. "In spite of that." In the shadow of the loft, his eyes appeared dark as deep water and his warm flesh smelled faintly of rosemary.

"And?" she prompted, moving against him, feeling his erection slide against her thigh.

"Is that not enough?" He grinned and dipped his head to plant a trail of wet kisses across her breasts and suck at her upturned nipples.

"No," she sighed, playfully catching a handful of his coarse-cropped hair between her fingers. "Tell me more," she demanded with a tug.

"Your lips are like strawberries," he told her, his voice muffled by her flesh. "Your eyes are bright as summer sunshine. You have bewitched me." His large hand dropped between her legs, ruffling the springy curls and tickling her.

At his touch, she laid her hand on his and moved against him. "That is what has bewitched you," she teased, thrusting her hips forward and forcing his finger deep inside her.

He gave a soft laugh. He could hardly deny it, for his erection swayed imposingly between them, feeling thick as a log. "I am more high-minded than you might think," he said in his own defense, moving atop her.

Instinctively she raised her legs and wrapped them

355

'round him.

Still, he made no move to take her but reached to cup her small breasts and run his fingertips lightly over the erect, bud-like nipples. He looked her full in the eyes, confessing, "Today at the stream, when I thought I would die, it was your face I held in my thoughts." He would have said more, but she closed her hand over his shaft, brushing its swollen, sensitive head against the lips of her mons.

His eloquence, indeed his sense of time and place, evaporated in the heat of passion. He closed his hand over hers to guide himself and entered her, thrusting gently at first, rhythmically. But so strong was the need in them, and so long denied, that their desire exploded into climax almost at once.

They lay together still joined, made helpless by the sudden violence of their release, suddenly weary, as the exhaustion of the previous days returned to drag at their muscles with a dull heaviness.

He brushed his lips over her throat, her cheek, advising, "It will be wet where you are lying." He separated himself from her, drawing her into the curve of his body and pulling the blanket over them.

In the moments before they fell asleep, they talked in soft murmurs, words of love. They did not speak of the morrow, or of Nevers.

Madeleine awoke chilled to her soul and alone. She bolted up, startled, until she saw him sitting on the floor before the fire.

She wrapped herself in the blanket and crossed to the hearth. "Why did you leave the bed?" she asked, stifling a yawn.

He raised his eyes, looking as if he had been called back from a great distance, and said simply, "The fire had died to ash." His gaze focused on the pale oval of her face, warm in the firelight, and he smiled at her—

a vague, haunting smile.

"I was cold without you," she said, crouching down as guilelessly as a peasant's child might, and sat against him wrapped in the woolen blanket.

He took her under his arm. The feel of her soft pliant body beneath the blanket sent a sudden rush of erotic thoughts pulsing through his mind. He turned his eyes toward the hearth and the flames leaping in the blackness.

Madeleine yawned once more and looking up at him asked, "What do you see in the fire?"

"The last of the miller's benches," he replied in his blunt, bland way, though he was smiling at her, and said, "In truth, I did not see the fire."

"What, then?" she posed, snuggling deeper.

"Yesterday, tomorrow, all the days after." He fixed his eyes again on the flames. "A way, perhaps, that we might yet live out our lives together."

She sat up swiftly, clasping his hand. "You must not stay in Nevers. I could not bear for you to be so near and know that I—"

He did not let her finish. "Then go north with me."

Her dark eyes darted to his. She pursed her lips to speak, but before she could utter a word, he pressed a finger to her lips. And suspecting she had not entirely forgiven him for the past, or because of his own guilt, he said, "I was not free to choose my own path then. But after tomorrow, I am bound to no man. I may claim the title of knight, even though all I hold is Rügen. And if you choose to go north with me, there is no sin in that. Your marriage to du Boulay is not yet consummated and no man has a more valid claim than I."

For a moment she was speechless, held captive by the resolute blue eyes. To go with him was what she wanted above all else. But her sleep-addled brain darted off in tangents, and when she spoke, her words blurted involuntarily from her lips. "After tomorrow the marriage will be consummated. You will no longer be my guard; we would have no opportunity. It is useless to speak of—"

He tilted her face to his and kissed her lightly, and, with his lips a hair's breadth from hers, whispered, "Listen at least to what I have to say."

Madeleine looked away, smothering her anguish with a deep sigh, tempted to remind him that he had let the opportunity for leaving slip through his fingers like smoke. But she did not. Instead, she moved to share the blanket with him and allowed herself to be drawn inside his legs, secure with a large knee on either side and her back snug against him. She listened as he explained how they might leave Nevers—he a free man and she not yet a wife to the Duke of Burgundy.

It was all so reasonable. Even de Luchaire and the ordeal he had forced upon her could be turned to their advantage. How better to explain her exhaustion and the swoon that would enable Wulf to carry her to her chamber, thereby learning its location, and how he might again reach it later that night.

With the wedding banquet in progress, for such affairs often lasted for days, the entire château would be in a festive mood. It would matter not that the ailing bride was bedridden in her chamber where naught but a serving woman would be left to attend her—and at the gates, drunken guards.

Madeleine could be silent no longer. "Yes," she interrupted with a frown. "All that is well and good, but if Burgundy refuses to set his seal to the parchment?"

"That he cannot do. The bishop's seal is there already, and if he is to claim you, he must set his seal beside it." He gave her shoulders a reassuring squeeze. "It is but a bothersome formality for Burgundy, and of no consequence: a liegeman's freedom."

In the drowsy warmth of the fire they talked and fell silent, only to speak again. There was no doubt in Madeleine's mind, nor in her heart. He would do just as he said, succeed or die in the attempt.

Giddy with the emotion of the moment, she nearly told him of the child growing inside her, for she was certain it was so. But the moment passed and she thought better of her candor and kept her silence.

She listened to his words, her feelings wavering between fear and boundless joy. She fixed her gaze upon his features, unable to dispel the thought that he appeared somehow different.

It was the firelight, she decided, noting the way it blazed up in his eyes, hardened the line of his jaw, and played across his lips. Or was it? He looked older, confident, and yes, she thought, unable to repress a smile—dangerous.

After a time, Madeleine gave a musical little laugh. Wulf looked at her curiously and she laughed again. "I am so starved," she said in a merry mirthful voice. "I was thinking that I must swoon before I am offered food, otherwise you will not be able to lift me."

Neither had taken more than an apple and a few swigs of wine since the day before. It seemed much longer.

He laughed, admitting he, too, was hungry. "The cat was wise to hide." He said it only half in jest as he stroked her beneath the blanket, though truthfully, the vague discomfort he felt was not for want of food.

Madeleine looked up and smiled, aware of his erection, for it nudged against her back. "I would not eat a cat," she stated flatly.

"No?" he murmured, pressing his lips to her hair.

"No," she repeated. "They must surely taste like mice."

"I would not know," he confessed. "I have never eaten a mouse." His tone was calculated to amuse, his hands otherwise occupied.

"No," she laughed, wriggling at his touch. "Nor

359

have I." It was impossible for her to remain still, for his hand worked between her legs. She was as eager as he—slick with desire where the gentle movement of his finger, back and forth, left her aching to be filled.

He held her imprisoned between his knees a moment longer, then shrugged the woolly cloth from his shoulders and lowered his head to nuzzle her throat, coaxing, "Spread the blanket for us."

She sent him a coy darting glance. "I will be cold," she giggled.

He reached behind and gathering the blanket, dropped it before her. "There is a remedy for that," he promised.

She smiled and moved on all fours, fumbling with the ragged blanket. The soft deep pitch of his voice sent a shiver of delight racing along her spine. The first time they had made love in such a way, it had shocked Madeleine's sensibilities—to be covered like a mare in heat. But the excitement and pleasure of the act whet her appetite for more and when she later proposed it, his good-natured mockery made her blush.

In the firelight, her slight form was pale as a lily. He reached after her to cup a small breast and rising to his knees, he leaned forward, kissing the nape of her neck and trailing his lips down the ridge of her spine, thinking of nothing other than the wild throbbing in his groin.

Braced on her arms, Madeleine planted her knees wide in breathless anticipation and offered her smooth white rump.

The fire hissed and crackled in the blackness of the hearth and the blanket bunched beneath them was forgotten.

Wulf anchored his large hands in the hollows of her hips. His every thought, the very fiber of his being, now devoted to curbing his desire. His erection bucked, bumping against her. She moaned softly, and when she quickly reached between her legs to grasp his shaft and launch it inside her, he nearly spilled his seed over her hand.

Only the miller's cat saw them naked in the firelight and heard the soft pleasurable sounds of their coupling. Later, when they deserted the dying fire for the rope sling bed, the cat crept from its hiding place and padded past their sleeping forms. On silent feet it went into the stable and, through a gap between the boards, slipped into the snowy night to hunt.

Chapter Twenty-Three

Snuggled deep in the miller's bed, they woke slowly, cherishing for a few moments longer the moist warmth of flesh against flesh. The room, indeed the whole world, seemed pillowed in silence and they guessed snow had fallen during the night.

They led their horses out into the still morning. Every sound was muffled by the blanket of snow. The dark waters of the mill pond moved sluggishly over the wicket, and below, a thin skim of ice etched the shoreline of the stream.

As they rode, the blaze of winter sunlight coaxed icicles from the snowy branches to dazzle their eyes. In the meadow, clumps of drab brown weeds made a stark pattern where the wind had capriciously swept away the snow and heaped it against the sides of trees, filling the ditches and blanketing the slopes with a cushion of blinding whiteness.

At midday they halted to rest their horses at a crossroads beside a small stone shrine. The snow-covered country paths before them were unmarked by prints, save for those of small creatures.

Madeleine's eyes were drawn to the rustic shrine and to her surprise saw it was a shring to St. Jean. It was a very ordinary shrine and yet its existence at that moment and in that place was somehow remarkable.

After a moment, Madeleine asked, "What day is this?"

Wulf released the mare's hoof, which he had been inspecting, and brushed the snow from himself, replying, "The ninth day of December." He had kept a careful tally of the days since their departure from the château and recalled the date that had been set between the bishop and the Duke of Burgundy. "It is two days past."

"He has sent no one to search for me," Madeleine mused. Standing in the trampled snow her feet, in the thin slippers, were without feeling.

"At least they have not found us," Wulf agreed. "They would search the course of the road, not here."

He stepped to one side of the shrine to relieve himself. Madeleine followed, also feeling the need. He smiled down at her squatted in the snow, mentioning it was not unusual for wagons and pack horses to be a day or two late of their destination. "The weather has been harsh."

He completed the ritual, adjusting himself inside the leather hosen. His thoughts turned again to the paths, determining they must follow the route which led south and west for surely it would lead to the Roman road and Nevers.

He raisèd his eyes to the distant meadows, fields, and woods, certain there was no danger. Guiles de Luchaire and even the Cardinal's guards would not dare to trespass onto the Duke of Burgundy's lands. The little tavern keeper had been all too clear as to who had levied the exorbitant toll at Pont Payant, and whose lands lay beyond the fork of the Loire.

They rode for long hours with the winter sunlight warm on their shoulders and the cold breeze stinging their faces.

At first the sound was no more than a distant growl carried on the thin cold air—the wind, perhaps. But with every stride of their horses, the sound grew to a rumble and was soon distinguishable as the trundle of traffic and garble of many voices. Cresting a hill, they sighted Nevers, stark against an amethyst sky. Across the sun-bright winter landscape of snow broken by patches of brown and gray lay the Roman road, its course thronged with a moving line of humanity and all manner of conveyances. As they drew nearer, they saw what appeared to be the populace of Nevers in full flight—a caravan of misery that stretched into the distance as far as the eye could see. Approaching the crush of traffic, they saw burghers and their families borne along in litters, while others jolted by in carts or astride palfreys. Peasants, too, trudged past, staggering under the weight of their meager belongings and driving livestock before them.

The traffic moved in one direction, away from Nevers. There was no place upon the road's course for two bound toward the city's gate. Skirting a snow-filled ditch that ran parallel to the road's edge, they plodded onward. Madeleine cast uneasy glances at the exodus as she rode, thinking it was surely the pestilence that had sent them fleeing in panic. This thought was at once confirmed by the sight of several humped forms in the deep snow of the ditch—corpses, for the snow had shifted to expose a frozen arm with blackened flesh.

Pack horses and carts, merchants and councilmen jostled upon the road amid peasants who drove herds of swine and cattle.

Neither Wulf nor Madeleine saw the wild-eyed young peasant amid the crush of cattle and carts until he leapt before them, waving his arms over his head and wailing, "Go back! Go back! There be pestilence in Nevers!"

They had guessed as much, but would have no opportunity to learn more. Wulf caught a glimpse of scarlet from the corner of his eye. He turned in his saddle and in the glaring sunlight made out a cluster of red-combed helmets—eight, perhaps as many as ten, skirting the road and flood of refugees and making straight toward them. At a farther distance, he sighted another group of riders: Guiles de Luchaire and his villeins? He could not be certain.

Madeleine had also seen them and her face, which a moment before had been calm, resolute, was now frozen in an expression of terror. A numbing fear seized her heart, the fear that Guiles de Luchaire might yet succeed in carrying out his avowed revenge. A wave of nausea swept over her and all before her eyes spun dizzily. Suddenly the passing throng upon the road and the ground beneath her horse seemed to move in opposite directions. Colors blurred and flowed and only dimly did she see Wulf turn his horse from the roadside.

He called to her, but his voice sounded strange and far away. The flaxen mane of her chestnut mare lifted with a jerk, and she felt the mare shift under her and lunge after the stallion.

The wide-open span of the ditch that Wulf's bay had avoided loomed before Madeleine. She sawed at the reins, but too late to turn the mare aside. She felt the mare gather herself to jump, but instead, came down heavily on her forelegs in the deep snow of the ditch. Madeleine was thrown forward with a jolt. She saved herself by grabbing a handful of flaxen mane and hanging on for dear life. For then, as if it were but a single fluid movement, the mare's hindquarters struck down and the chestnut hurtled upward in a spume of snow, clambering over the frozen bank. With level ground beneath her, the mare tucked back her ears and lengthened her stride, straining to catch the bay.

Wulf kept to the berm, clear of the road, avoiding the snarl of carts, cattle, and refugees. At the stone gate to Nevers, they had no choice but to rein in their horses and plunge into the conflagration of panic-stricken residents and frantically driven beasts.

Inside the city they sent their horses down the cobbled streets at a gallop. The donjon of the ducal château towered above the disorder of close, dark streets and abutting rooftops.

Few remained in the snowy streets: the dead and small bands of looters. The winter sun blinked between the close-set houses, splitting the darkened streets with blazing shafts of light and purple shadows. Household furnishings lay heaped and stacked in the snow: the possessions of a lifetime dragged from kitchens and solars by men and women loath to leave them behind, only to discover that the items were too weighty or cumbersome.

In the market place, snow had etched and piled against the empty booths and the hooves of their horses clashed against the frozen earth. Wulf curbed the bay's pace and, drawing even with Madeleine, pointed toward the ramparts of the château's outer walls. Madeleine followed, the mare close behind the bay.

They urged their horses through the narrow, winding streets and alleyways, skidding and clattering over the icy cobbled stones and terraced steps.

Behind them, the desolate streets echoed with the crash of hoofbeats and the harsh shouts of their pursuers. It seemed the guardsmen had split their force, for the sounds, baffled by the close-set houses, came from several directions.

At the château's north wall, they crossed a drawbridge. The massive portcullis of the outer court stood open, as did the grills of a smaller court. Wulf drew in the bay, thinking to secure the grille, but could not from horseback and kicked his heels into the bay's flanks, following Madeleine into the inner court. The grille at its entrance was differently fashioned and he was able to drop the bar without dismounting. The coming together of bar and grille shattered the cold air like a hammer blow.

In the large yard before the citadel, Madeleine

pulled at the mare's reins and slid from her back. The innermost hall of the Château de Nevers was flanked by strong towers and fortifications. Guardrooms, stables, servants' quarters, and dwellings of court officials and churchmen bounded the yard, but nowhere did she see a servant, a porter, another living soul. The eerie solitude of trampled snow and empty doorways sent pinpricks of fear racing along her spine.

She pounded against the hall's doors with numbed hands, but neither her determined assault nor her cries were answered.

As Wulf dismounted, she threw him a desperate look from over her shoulder. "Why do they not answer?" she called breathlessly. And with a catch of terror in her voice, shouted, "Why will they not admit us?" She ran frantically to peer in a window, but it was set above the level of her eyes and she cried out in frustration, banging at the greenish glass with both hands and shouting.

Wulf tested his weight against the doors, determining they were indeed barred. He took several backward steps and raised his eyes to scan the towers; all was still. The rumble of hooves swiveled his attention to the inner court. They had forced the grille, or found a way around it.

He grabbed Madeleine by the arm and, towing her along, sprinted toward a long gallery set between the tower and the hall.

The guardsmen thundered into the yard, milling in the slush. Several sighted the fleeing pair; a cry went up and they dismounted, giving chase.

The narrow door, the last of four Wulf had bruised his shoulder against, gave way at the touch of his hand. He stumbled inside, thrusting Madeleine into the blackness beyond, and drew his sword. Coming in from the radiance of the sunlit snow to the dim passageway had turned them both half-blind. Madeleine groped to steady herself against the wall.

A moment later, the door burst open with a crash and splintering of wood. The first man through the door, Wulf killed. He claimed the dead man's leather buckler, and for a brief time held them at bay beneath the door arch.

In the close confines of the passageway, they were forced to fight him one at a time. He wounded another, all but hacking through his forearm, and disabled a third with a slash to his legs. At first, he held them, hacking away stubbornly, but he was tiring. He had no idea how many they numbered— too many. In time they would wear him down and he realized with a growing sense of desperation that once they forced him from the passageway they would overwhelm him, come at him from all sides and cut him down.

Madeleine ran blindly along the passageway, pounding on doors, thrusting them open and shouting into empty rooms, frantic and sick with despair, fearing Roland du Boulay had fled Nevers. Nothing would be as they planned. There would be no seal set upon the parchment and neither of them would ever be free.

In the hollow passageway, the sound of the battle was deafening. Surely, Madeleine thought, someone must hear the clang and clamor and know it for what it was. Where were Burgundy's men at arms, his servants? Even if he had fled there would be a steward or servants left behind, someone. She halted, sobbing breathlessly, defeated. The vicious ringing batter of steel against steel drew ever nearer as Wulf was beaten back.

She raised her eyes and saw the dark cavern of a door arch. She ran toward it murmuring a prayer, seeing the passageway ended in yet another passage and not a blank wall as she had feared.

Miraculously, for it seemed a miracle to her, a light like a glowing red eye wavered at one end of the passage. They were not alone.

She hung beneath the door arch for only a racing heartbeat, then flung herself toward the light.

Wulf heard her shouts, but to turn would have been a suicide for the guardsman before him pressed forward with a series of hammering blows which battered the leather buckler against his arm and shook him to the marrow.

He heard Madeleine's scream. He knew only that she was somewhere behind him in the darkness. With his last reserves of strength he lashed out, slashing a furious counter attack, taking the guardsman down with the point of his sword brought swiftly across the curve of his throat below the jaw and above the mail collar. Blood spurted and the guardsman fell heavily to the stones with a hoarse bubbling scream.

Where the passageways intersected, a cold draft touched Wulf's sweating face and the waft of air that drew swiftly past was filled with the sick sweet stench of decay.

He shook the battered leather shield loose from his arm; he would have no further use for it. Nothing could shield him against so many; better to have both his arms free, to take as many down with him as he could. He slung the buckler into the midst of the guardsmen advancing over the body of their dead comrade, then turned and ran.

Madeleine's silhouette lurched before his eyes. He dashed toward her braced and silent form, catching her up and crushing her to him and sweeping her along into the hall.

Wulf was little prepared for the apparition of death before him or the look of mindless terror in Madeleine's eyes. The hall was like a mortuary, no, more a hell devised by some fiendish twisted mind, populated with mocking blackened corpses and reeking to heaven of the vileness of their dying. Amid the guttering candles and low-burning lamps the dead lay where they had fallen, discolored and with gaping mouths.

Upon the dais, braziers like fiery eyes glowed before the ruins of the banquet table and from the narrow slotted windows the dying light of day cast pale bars across the sprawl of corpses. They lay everywhere, some face down upon the table in long-dried pools of vomit; others were beneath, sprawled upon the rich Eastern carpets which were soiled and stained with viscous blossoms of blood and body fluids. The noisome stench all but gagged him and Madeleine.

A heavy blow upon the brass-sheathed doors roused Wulf to vigilance. A cry leapt from Madeleine's parted lips. She clutched at his arm, her eyes streaming tears.

A stout bar blocked the door, but a second heavier blow followed and with it the sound of splintering wood and the groan of metal.

From the direction of the passage, the jangle of mail and armor and the heavy tread of boots spun Wulf on his heels. He thrust Madeleine behind him and raised his sword to meet the guardsmen.

But those who charged beneath the door arch checked and stumbled, their features convulsed with horror. And those who followed collided into them with dropping jaws and staring eyes. They wavered at the door arch, making sounds like wounded dogs, loath to enter King Death's hall. Frightened witless by the hellish scene before them, they fell back and fled.

From the door, a third blow jarred the hall like a clap of thunder, buckled the doors, and with a rasping groan flung them wide.

Wulf's gaze fixed upon the open doors and the formidable figure of Guiles de Luchaire, armed for battle and flanked by his villeins.

With a high defiant yell, Guiles de Luchaire charged into the hall. None followed him. They quavered, as the guardsmen had, struck dumb by what their eyes beheld, their faces masks of fear. They took to their heels and ran.

Wulf surged forward to meet him. The reach of his rangy Saxon arm was longer, he was younger and taller. But what Guiles de Luchaire lacked in height and youth was well made up for by his ferocity. He was a broad powerful man, older by ten years, but ten years of hard experience. He came at Wulf confidently in a steady, battering onslaught.

In the first moments, Wulf met the punishing blows, scarcely shifting his balance and losing little ground, for wherever the cold steel of de Luchaire's hacking blade crashed in, Wulf's sword was there to meet it and turn it aside.

The air vibrated with the clash and clang of their swords. Madeleine, mute with helpless terror, scrambled from the path of the violent struggle. She stumbled backward, catching her heel in the hem of her skirts and falling onto the dais among the dead, sprawling face to face with the hideously discolored and contorted features of a dead woman. With a shriek of horror, Madeleine sprang to her feet, cracking her shoulder against the banquet table and dislodging the arm of a dead man. The lifeless arm brushed her hand. She drew back with a gasp, only to singe her sleeve in the molten heat of a glowing brazier.

Slowly but steadily, de Luchaire edged Wulf backward, feinting with his shield, slashing in with his blade.

Without the leather buckler Wulf had so foolishly caste aside, he was at a dangerous disadvantage. Again and again he was forced back, then with great effort hacked his way forward until at last he was driven back so sharply that he blundered onto the out-flung limbs of a corpse. The flesh gave beneath his boots, throwing him off balance. He staggered backward, then recovered himself, but not quickly enough. de Luchaire's blade bit into his shoulder and had it not been for the broad metal clasp of Wulf's cloak, which deflected the blade's slashing strike downward, it would have surely been a death blow.

Wulf cried out in pain, a harsh yelp, and went down on one knee. De Luchaire loomed above him, poised to strike. But with one foot still beneath him, Wulf lunged away, swinging his sword in a lop-sided arc as he gained his feet. The swath of his blade, though it fell short, sliced into the meaty calf of de Luchaire's leg. He squealed with pain and reeled to one side, his advance momentarily halted.

Wulf slashed in for the kill, but his blade was met by de Luchaire's shield thrust into his face. The heavy metal disc struck Wulf's jaw a glancing blow, then clattered away.

With both hands gripping the hilt of his sword, de Luchaire charged forward like a madman, hacking away, intent on driving the Saxon to the wall.

The savageness of the offensive forced Wulf to the dais. An ever-widening stain of blood soaked the breast of his leather jerkin. He countered and blocked, but de Luchaire's blows came in a steady, battering assault until he had beaten Wulf to his knees.

Madeleine gazed on with huge desperate eyes, braced and rigid from head to toe. The brazier before her smoked and fumed until it seemed the fire was in her very lungs.

She screamed—perhaps she only thought she had. He would kill Wulf, there before her eyes. The jut of de Luchaire's brutish jaw, his hulking shoulders, filled her vision. With a tearing cry she reached out, seized the brazier for an agonized instant, then sent it toppling from the dais.

The falling brazier struck de Luchaire's shoulders, showering him with glowing coals. He shrieked with surprise and reeled backward, smoke pouring from his blue lake cloak.

She had defeated him. He would burn if he did not strip off the cloak, but in those precious seconds the Saxon would strike a killing blow.

De Luchaire turned, oblivious to Wulf, who staggered to his feet, and to his own smouldering cloak. He swayed toward the dais, raging curses, his face dark and clenched with fury.

Madeleine gasped and stumbled backward into the banquet table, clutching her burned fingers to her breast. She saw de Luchaire's naked blade flash above her head.

Wulf lunged forward, swinging his sword with both hands. As the blade cleaved the smoky air, de Luchaire sagged to one side, reeled drunkenly, and collapsed onto the smouldering carpet, dragging his sword after him.

For an instant, Madeleine stared in petrified silence. She had seen Guiles de Luchaire falter; truthfully, it seemed the light had gone from his eyes. His jaw dropped as if to cry out, but only a thin retching sound rose from his throat as he fell. She blinked and sprang from the dais into Wulf's arms, not quite daring to believe they had survived.

Wulf stared at the crumpled form in silent bewilderment. A thickening pall of smoke hung just above the floor. He nudged de Luchaire's shoulder with his boot, rolling him over.

"Is he dead?" Madeleine sobbed, afraid to look, fearing he might rise. From the outer edge of her vision she saw little tongues of flame spark and leap from the burning carpets.

"I did not bring him down," Wulf said as much to himself as to Madeleine, who ventured a fearful glance. Only then did they see the trickle of blood seeping from his nose and lips and the blue-tinged swelling on his throat below his ear. "Plague." Wulf said the word in a tone barely audible above the crackling voice of the fire. King Death had claimed him.

Madeleine turned her eyes away; relief flooded into her veins only to be replaced a moment later by the numbing realization that even though they had survived the hand of death, without the seal upon the parchment, freedom was still beyond their reach. She turned to Wulf, blinded by her tears and sobbing a torrent of words. But in that instant, what she glimpsed upon the dais stilled her voice.

There among the nameless dead was the face that graced the gold-framed miniature: the lank hair and the humped nose lying squashed against the banquet table, the lips twisted and blackened in death, and devoid of the shining armor but without a doubt, Roland du Boulay, Duke of Burgundy.

Flames fed by the draft from the open doors raced along the hall's wooden beams and licked at the base of the dais. Sparks from the burning rugs floated on the thickening pall of smoke, igniting the heavy tapestries which lined the walls. The fire sighed and groaned like a smith's bellows, greedily consuming the rich embroidery whose vivid colors blazed for an instant, then blackened and peeled away in great writhing chunks.

The words babbled from Madeleine's lips, all but lost to her tears and fit of coughing. Frantically, she thrust away his bloody hand that urged her toward the open doors. "No!" she screamed, pointing to the dais. "He is there! The seal is surely on his hand; we can be free!"

Wulf made no reply. It was too late. The hall was encased in flames, the timbers of the walls and ceiling groaned and cracked and spurted flames. Yet, he let her tow him back.

At the dais, Wulf braced himself against the table, slid his sword among the ruins of the banquet and fumbled for the parchment, smoothing out its folds as best he could. A bright red flower of his blood had soaked the upper half.

With her burned fingers forgotten, Madeleine grasped a guttering quarrier and tipped a pool of wax upon the parchment.

Wulf reached across the table, clutched the clammy stiffened hand, and set the seal into the wax.

Rolling smoke stung and blinded their eyes and flashing bursts of flame raced along the tapestry above the dais. The rippling motion of the heavy cloth caught Wulf's eye. He glanced up just as a huge section quivered, then slid away in a slow glittering avalanche. He grabbed Madeleine and with his other hand the sword, stumbling backward.

Madeleine saw only the parchment. She screamed and twisted free, darting back to seize the paper, knowing she must have it. Though her child might be born a bastard, it would be at least a free man's bastard.

She heard his shouts. She did not understand the words—a Saxon oath, no doubt. She leapt upon the dais, snatched the paper from the flames, and clutched it to her.

In an instant, his arms were 'round her, leading her through the suffocating smoke. The heat of the fire, its snapping, crackling voice, followed at their heels. They half-ran, half-stumbled into the snowy yard, choking on their first breaths of clear cold air.

In the trampled slush of the courtyard, she held out the parchment. It was bloodied and singed, but little worse for it; enough remained. In a voice broken by coughing, she offered it to him. "It is your freedom."

He hugged her to him. "Yours as well." The cold air stung his throat, choking him. He croaked, "The hand that set this seal will not reach after you."

She clung to his arms, ignoring the pain of her burned fingers. "We will go north?"

He nodded, unable to speak for coughing. He saw Loki and the mare had wandered across the yard and were nosing in the snow for something to browse.

With a cry of alarm, Madeleine noticed the dark russet stain on his chest where the blood had soaked through and stiffened. "You are sorely hurt; let me look."

"There is no time," he said. He caught her probing hands and, seeing she had burned her fingers, scooped a handful of snow from the rampart wall and pressed it in her hands.

She wrenched her hands from his. "We should stanch the blood," she insisted, shaking the stinging ice from her hands.

He coughed and spit, then walked toward the horses.

She called his name and ran after him, catching his arm. "You will not die?" she cried.

"No," he told her. "It is not deep." He caught the mare's reins and for a moment leaned his head against the horse's withers, exhausted. His trembling legs threatened to buckle under him. He felt giddy and suddenly weak. Blood had soaked his shirt beneath the leather jerkin. He felt its queer, slippery warmth against his skin. He felt sick.

Madeleine pressed close to him, her dark eyes rounded with panic. He looked at her and smiled. "I am not going to die," he told her, and prayed he would not heave up his empty stomach.

Madeleine turned away, then turned back, her eyes brimming tears, unable to keep her secret another moment. She must tell him, she thought. He must know. "I am with child," she said, and plunging on, with words that came in breathless gasps, confessed, "At first, I could not tell you because I thought you would be lost to me forever. And last night, I dared not, for fear you would say I must remain in Nevers for my sake and the child's."

He looked at her, for a moment dumb with amazement, not quiet believing he had put a child in her. "I did not realize," he mumbled, only that and nothing more.

Madeleine stared at him oddly, waiting for some deeper response, not daring to blink or breathe. After a moment, she could no longer bear the uncertainty of his silence and said, "Do not say it is too dangerous

376

for me to travel north!"

He smiled and met her eyes. How strange and wondrous was the secure feeling of possession: to know she would never be taken from him and to know also that for all his days, this woman would be certain to remind him of what he was obliged to do.

"I have come this far without grief," she cried, her dark eyes flashing with emotion. "Do not say—"

"No," he interrupted. "I was only thinking it will likely be spring before we reach Rügen; your belly will be out before you and there will be no doubt you are my wife." He was powerless to halt the smile which spread across his face to idiotic proportions, or so it seemed to him. He gave a soft laugh, reached out a hand to cup her face, and kissed her lightly. "I will love you always," he murmured, and drew her near so he might boost her onto the mare's back.

Behind them, the fire had spread to the towers, smoke belched from the slotted windows, and the interior of the hall blazed with a hellish glow.

They turned their horses from the yard, free as the north wind that met them with a flurry of snow. The world beyond the long shadows of the gates was theirs to share . . . God willing.

Epilogue

Sister Kamilla traced the sign of the cross upon her forehead and, rising slowly, made her way through the chapel. The scent of beeswax hung in the still air and the guttering candlelight stirred by her passage cast a rippling amber sheen upon the intricately carved stations of the cross.

She stood a moment at the chapel door, dazed and blinking in the brilliant April sunshine. The humid air was sweet with the musk of grass and rain, and sunlight spanked off puddles standing on the garden path.

A plain-faced girl, a tender-voiced novice, had come to her during devotions and whispered, "Visitors await you in the garden." She said only that and nothing more. It was not unusual; many came, pilgrims to view the miraculous statue of Saint Lucia. So widespread was the statue's fame that the Bishop of Lübeck himself had come to pray for peace among the princes.

Sister Kamilla stepped from the portico and, raising her skirts, carefully picked her way among the puddles. She went toward the garden arch, the sunshine warm upon her face. A row of apple trees, heavy with bloom, bordered the garden wall, and the sweetly scented air was abuzz with the sound of bees.

At the stonework arch, a scene of tranquil beauty

met her eyes. Seated on a bench beneath a brace of apple boughs she saw a young mother, serene as a madonna in the speckled sunlight, with a yearling babe at her breast.

Beside her sat an old woman in peasant garb. Her blunted hair, not unlike a juniper shagged with snow, escaped in great tufts from beneath her richly embroidered kerchief. The face was tanned and wrinkled as an old boot, but little changed from their last meeting years before. Erna, the midwife; the sight of her was volatile as touchwood, kindling memories long died to ash, bittersweet, that sent her heart to racing.

Only when she stepped from the shadow of the arch did she see the young man—rather only his back, for he was turned away, his attention momentarily captured by some happening beyond the garden wall. Involuntarily, her eyes seized upon the back of his head; the wheat-colored hair, darker where it was cropped close to his skull, and it, so like another's she had fondly held. Her sharply in-drawn breath, a little gasp, betrayed her presence to all. She stood there quite unprepared, breathless, in the humid spring afternoon, heavy with the perfume of apple blossoms and bright with the song of birds.

The young man turned suddenly at the sound of her voice and the face before her was like an apparition, a ghost in the glancing sunlight: the face of one too well recalled and too long mourned.

Her arms and legs lost their certainty. She clutched wildly for the support of the stonework arch, overwhelmed by the stinging sharpness of her memories. In an instant the young man was beside her and she was buoyed up on his arms, her eyes blinded by tears.

"Erna," she said in a voice struck with wonder and reached to clasp the old woman's offered hand. "Erna, so you have brought my son to me."

"Ja, maitresse, and his son as well." To Erna she

would always be the old lord's daughter: the tall, pale child who had lived in the shadow of her brothers.

The young man guided her toward the bench where the plump young mother nursed her babe. But she laid a hand on his, pleading, "No, not yet," and turning to examine his face through her tears, said, "How often I have longed to touch your face. At times I thought I only dreamed, but the years, the long years . . ."

"I am real, Mother. Flesh and blood of yours, and I have come to take you home."

"There is a place for you, madame," Madeleine said, "in our hearts and in our hall," and added hopefully, "I would be much comforted by your companionship." The babe kneaded at her breast and made a suckling sound. Madeleine quickly shifted him in her arms, for if the nipple slipped from his mouth, she knew he would surely squall.

Sister Kamilla looked from one face to another, wondering how she might put into words what she must say. "This is my home, my life is here with God, though my heart rejoices at the sight of you and I pray you will come again. If God wills it, I will see my grandson grow to be a man." With a hand to steady her, she sat beside her son's wife and held the babe's tiny hand in hers. After a moment she raised her eyes to her son, inquiring, "You are called Wulfric?"

"Wulf," he replied.

Sister Kamilla turned her eyes on the old woman, gently chiding her. "Oh Erna, you could never be trusted to remember. No," she said, refusing to hear the old woman's excuse. "There is no harm. By any name he has grown tall and strong." She raised her eyes to Wulf once more. "What do you call this grandson of mine?"

"Hasso," Wulf responded, uncertain at the last moment and fearing it would displease her.

But the smile remained no less fond than before.

"That is good," she said evenly. "To forgive is the way of our Blessed Saviour, the way I have chosen, and I have long ago forgiven my father."

While the sundial marked the hours, Wulf told her all: the fate of her father and brothers and how he had returned to claim Rügen.

She listened, moved to tears and smiles, and for a precious time she cradled her grandson in her arms. "Such a fine mother you are," she told Madeleine, "for he is a rosy, perfect babe." She cuddled him, breathing in the sweetness of little creatures newly made and mother's milk. With love she gazed upon the soft brown curls, the cherub face and bright blue eyes.

They bid farewell at the abbey gate and, in the cool spring evening, made their way again to Rügen. The sun was low and the sharply cast shadows of the budding trees lay diagonally across the country lane, purple shade and pure golden light and all in between lost to the mist-colored background of undergrowth and dead bracken.

Wulf glanced to Madeleine, nodding in her saddle; she looked very young and sleepy. He smiled to himself, deeply satisfied, thinking he was surely blessed by God. He had his love, to love for always, and he held Rügen. The world had turned but brought no end to grief. Still the pestilence reared its ugly head and with it death and lawlessness.

With each turn and rise, the woods became familiar and in the distance, Rügen's stone keep rose above the cool blue evening mist. Before them the woods closed upon the road once more. The last rays of sunlight caught the edges of the distant tree trunks and lit them in a sharp line, igniting the lane with a blaze of golden tints, coloring all beyond warmly dark. Wulf did not fear for their safety here. It was his own lands he crossed and he was lord, though even that was not without a price. There were walls to be mended, decisions to be made, and, if unwisely, the fault would rest with him alone. There was the quarrel among the princes, and he, as liege lord, was bound to serve Fredrick's cause if reason failed. On his own lands, there was talk of witchcraft, of sacrifices, and other nonsense. Yet it was there and would not go away, and he must settle it—rout it out, or put an end to the talk once and for all.

He reined in the bay and drew near to Madeleine's mare. With a jerk of her flaxen mane, the mare threw up her head and Madeleine woke with a start. "I was not asleep," she mumbled groggily, then realized, "Oh, we are nearly home." Her eyes clouded with concern and she glanced suddenly to the cart, for the babe, born with such difficulty, was never far from her thoughts. All was well. Erna's head lolled with the motion of the cart; the babe, beside her in a basket, was fast asleep and the driver stared into the distance, lost in his own thoughts.

"Did you have a good rest?" Wulf asked.

She looked at him quickly with sparkling eyes. He was smiling and had been watching her. "Yes," she confessed, and, with a soft laugh, held out her hand to his. How wondrous it was to be at peace in her heart, to be secure, and to be loved.

Author's Note

In all fiction there is some element of truth. Such was the case with CAPTIVE TO HIS KISS. Set in tumultuous mid-fourteenth century France, the story touches upon the disastrous defeat of the French at Crécy, the black plague, and the religious and political fomentation of the times.

Crécy was among the many battles, truces, and treaties which marked the intermittent course of the conflict that would later be known as the Hundred Years War. At its root was English intervention in France and an English king who connived to rule both countries.

The black death (1348), which spread unchecked across Europe and eventually to England, Scotland, and Ireland as well as north to Scandinavia and Russia, took for its awful toll fully one-third of the total population. In places the mortality was nearly complete.

Indeed, King Death in the guise of *pasteurella pestis* is also credited by some historians as bringing an end to the medieval age. It was without doubt a factor in the political and social unrest of the late fourteenth century.

As to the fate of the historical figures, the beleaguered King Philip VI of France died in 1351. The plague, the great equalizer, claimed noble, peasant, and clergy with indifference, and so it was that Philip's eldest son John (John II) succeeded him on the throne, much to the displeasure of many French nobles.

John's first wife, Bona of Luxembourg, died in 1349. He took a second wife in 1350, choosing Jeanne, daughter of the Count of Auvergne.

The ever-cautious Pope Clement VI died in 1352. He was one of seven popes (1305-1378) who ruled the Holy Church from Avignon during the period often referred to as the French or Babylonian Captivity.

The fictional account and characters were drawn from a mélange of folklore and writngs of the medieval period. Life in medieval times, like life in any age, was darkened by the shadow of death, buoyed up by faith, filled with love and laughter, touched by great tenderness and unspeakable cruelty. And so, the threads of fancy are easily entwined in the fabric of history—a design, I pray, that has entertained you.